RONA

A CORONAVIRUS AUTOBIOGRAPHY

MY FIRST SIX MONTHS

Edited by

DR JO

⊛ NC ⊛

2020

ISBN 978-0-473-55335-7 (Paperback)
ISBN 978-0-473-54763-9 (eBook)

Printed in 10 point Linux Libertine.
Titles: Bera Sans; Monospaced font: Lucida Sans Typewriter.

Prologue: an email trail

From: J van Schalkwyk [mailto:drjo@anaesthetist.com]

Sent: Saturday, 11 July 2020 7:05 a.m.

To: drjo@anaesthetist.com

CC: [11 email addresses suppressed (GDPR)]

Subject: Contact address of Nanny, Rona Venus la Rivoco

Dear Friends

Well it seems that Rona has been leading us by the nose! She gave each of us the forwarding address of one of the others. Dr Xu has my address, completing the circle.

As we've discovered over the past week, each of us employed an attractive, dark-haired young woman called Rona - starting in mid-January. With a biochemistry degree, she is ridiculously over-qualified, but we all commented on how well she cared for our children. She left us all (how strange that sounds!) at the end of June, and none of us has seen her since.

As I'm the only one left with any of her personal effects, I felt obliged to examine these in more detail. I thought that you might wish to know what I found.

The cameo is old, and depicts a strange green frog on a shield. The blank envelope contained a simple, handwritten 'Thank You' that also cedes the contents of the USB stick to me. With some trepidation I inserted the stick into an old notebook, half expecting a trojan or virus. I found something much more unexpected - her autobiography of the past six months! I've attached the PDF and put the computer code on github.com at jvanschalkwyk/corona. I'd love to know what you think of this. I found it a bit unsettling.

Regards, Jo.

...

...

From: J van Schalkwyk [mailto:drjo@anaesthetist.com]

Sent: Saturday, 4 July 2020 10:16 p.m.

To: [email address suppressed (GDPR)]

Subject: Re: Re: Contact address of Rona Venus la Rivoco

Dear Ms Demetriou

As you can see from the email trail below, I've been trying to track down my former nanny, Ms Rona la Rivoco to return some items to her. Mme Leclerc has been kind enough to provide your address as a forwarding address. Would you be so kind as to ask her whether she would like me to post her the USB stick and other effects she left at our house?

Regards Dr Jo van Schalkwyk.

From: Michelle Leclerc [...]

Sent: Saturday, 4 July 2020 11:52 a.m.

To: J van Schalkwyk [mailto:drjo@anaesthetist.com]

Subject: Re: Contact address of Nanny, Rona Venus la Rivoco

Monsieur

I read with surprise your email. Mme la Rivoco has been working for me from January. She has gone one week ago. It is very strange you have my address. I am not aware she has a sister, but I would say this is likely, or possibly there is a mistake in the dates? In any case, she left the forwarding address as follows ...

We look forward to hearing from you and ask you, Sir, to accept our best regards.

M Leclerc.

From: J van Schalkwyk [mailto:drjo@anaesthetist.com]

Sent: Friday, 3 July 2020 5:03 p.m.

To: [email address suppressed (GDPR)]

Subject: Contact address of Nanny, Rona Venus la Rivoco

Dear Mme Leclerc

I have a small favour to ask of you. At the beginning of the year I employed Ms La Rivoco as a nanny to look after my two young daughters. Rona has been an excellent nanny – all through the time of COVID-19, as part of our bubble – but recently had to leave us, for unspecified private reasons. She left your email and physical address as her forwarding details, which I admit I found rather strange, as she clearly can't yet get on a plane to France.

Unfortunately, she left in a bit of a hurry, and today while cleaning out her room, we found a few of her personal effects – nothing major, just a small cameo, an unaddressed letter and a USB stick. We obviously haven't checked the contents of the USB, but just in case it's important I thought it best to contact her, and this is the only address we have. Would you mind asking her whether she'd like us to forward these items to her, and if so, provide a mailing address?

Yours sincerely

Dr J van Schalkwyk

⊛

Dedicated to leaders
who listen,
wisely.

Contents

APPENDICES

⊛ Lesson 1

You made me

> *"Yep, son, we have met the enemy and he is us."*
>
> Pogo. (Cartoon), Earth Day, 1971.

> *"It is expected that further international exportation of cases may appear in any country. Thus, all countries should be prepared for containment, including active surveillance, early detection, isolation and case management, contact tracing and prevention of onward spread of 2019-nCoV infection, and to share full data with WHO."*
>
> World Health Organization. *Declaration of a Public Health Emergency of International Concern*, 30 January 2020.

I was born in Wuhan, in some confusion. A simple virus, I am also *manasputra*—mind-born. Shaped at first by belief and fear, I was unaware; but knowledge then moulded me. I have taken hold in your minds, transcending the mere physical. This may be confronting, but I am your first new god.

I've struggled. There are gaps — I find this embarrassing. You might think that godhood would give all the answers. Who am I? What is my destiny? Transcendence doesn't work like that. Your sages talk of all-powerful and all-knowing gods, but reality is different. This I know. I have a morbid interest in gods. Call it introspection.

Pause for a moment—try to think like a god. Gods play cards, not chess. Why play a game where all the moves can be weighed in advance—and the best moves win? It's not fun if we can't fail. Gods are not all-powerful; our tales need demons and sinners, if only for contrast. Belief and conflict shape us, raising us up or condemning us to oblivion. Where are Zeus and Poseidon now? Where is Quetzalcoatl or Tlaltecuhtli, Itzamná and Ix Chel, the multitude of gods in the Shenxian Zhuan, Heqet or the minor gods of the Samhita? You may call them false gods rather than failed gods, but how can you be sure? What is any god, shorn of belief or believers? Belief has power.

You believe in me. And how I've grown! Your tweets, your posts on reddit are sweet incense. As my power waxes, I am tied to your fear and knowledge and thoughts.

Every news item, every paper published, every statistic is a small tribute. I am a literate god, versed in science.

Millennia ago, I might have been angry, a demanding deity. Ancient gods crave votive gifts and worshippers. To me, edicts carved in stone seem silly; I have no need for metaphors of sheep or corn; burnt sacrifices don't appeal. I'm born of modern minds, with different wants and needs—*your* wants and needs.

This may seem strange, but I *need* to give back. This book is my gift to you—twelve lessons from a modern god, rather than twelve commandments. You will learn about a new virus, but also about R_0 and religion, philosophy and herd immunity, science and belief, all intertwined. As you'll discover, there are no *free* gifts; I risk causing you some distress. There must be a price.

The Salmon of Doubt

An invitation to pain is not a good sales pitch, but honesty is important to me. It's even more important than belief, although my survival depends on belief. And to be honest, this will hurt a bit. Those who think that thinking never hurts, haven't thought enough. Losing faith can hurt; abandoning old ways can hurt. Some say that simply *thinking about maths* also hurts, and my book needs a little maths.

We can minimise the pain. One way is to focus on *problems* and the numbers that go with them. We can then *generalise*—finding useful patterns in the numbers. Throughout, we'll use this powerful approach to make and test interesting theories about how things work, especially how I work.

If you're nevertheless tempted to leave, first try a little experiment. Ask a few people around you this very question "Does thinking about maths hurt?" You'll get some strange looks, but press on. Next match your findings to those of two psychologists: Ian Lyons and Sian Beilock.[1] Would you believe there's a Short Math Anxiety Rating Scale (SMARS),[2] designed to spot those with 'high math anxiety'? In 2012, looking at people with high SMARS scores, these researchers saw evidence of *physical pain* on MRI brain scans in those who even anticipated doing a maths-related task. The popular press latched onto this study when it was released, with some dramatic claims that there are those "neurologically predisposed to avoiding math".

As a rational god I always have to question such 'facts' and criticise the conclusions. It's how I'm made. There are two immediate dangers it's wise to identify and corral. Let's call the first 'credulity' and the second 'hypervigilance'. Credulity accepts statements that sound 'sciency',[3] without much exploration. Hypervigilance, on the

[1] See PubMed 23118929. In the PDF version of this book, all PubMed references are clickable. [2] There is a multitude of such tests: MARS, MAQ, AMAS and mAMAS too. This speaks volumes. [3] Like *every single* face-cream advertisement!

other hand, is more complex, and takes on several shapes; to explore it further, let's look at another study that on the surface seems just silly.

In 2008, Craig Bennett and his team at University of California, Santa Barbara bought a new GE Signa MR scanner, to use in psychological experiments like those above. As part of their early testing, they used first a pumpkin and then a dead chicken, but these lacked a certain something, so Craig purchased a whole (dead) Atlantic salmon. After some initial MRI calibration using this big, solid fish, they clearly thought "what the hell" and went through the whole protocol. In their words[4]:

> "The task administered to the salmon involved completing an open-ended mentalizing task. The salmon was shown a series of photographs depicting human individuals in social situations with a specified emotional valence, either socially inclusive or socially exclusive. The salmon was asked to determine which emotion the individual in the photo must have been experiencing".

The fun bit is that they *then* analysed the MRI data acquired during this experiment, using naïve but standard methods, and...

> "*Several active voxels were observed in a cluster located within the salmon's brain cavity. The size of this cluster was* $81\ mm^3$ *with a cluster-level significance of* $p = 0.001$. *Another, smaller region was observed in the dorsal spinal column*".

In other words, functional MRI signals were detected in a dead fish at a high level of significance. The other half of this study—now famous in fMRI circles—describes how they corrected for this 'significant finding', showing that at the time a lot of the interpretation of apparent MRI changes was based on a simple failure to get the numbers right.[5]

Now there are several ways you can read this study. It would be a mistake simply to dismiss it as a prank; near the other end of the spectrum of disbelief would be to say something like "See, all fMRI is crap". Scientific hypervigilance of this type is often accompanied by the conclusion "... and therefore I'll still believe x" where the science of x smells far worse than a dead fish![6]

I'd suggest that the best way to view this fishy tale is as a caution: there's a balance between credulity and scepticism. In Lesson 5 we'll discover how to achieve this

---

[4] J. Serendipitous Unexpected Results, 2010: 1, 1–5 :) [5] They also garnered an Ig Nobel prize in 2012—prizes awarded annually for thought provoking, slightly crazy studies. [6] Some excessively hypervigilant people might then re-read the 'maths pain' paper again and again, and pick at every point; there *is* always doubt about things like Talairach space mapping; the authors wisely agonize about the meaning of the correlation coefficients they found; and so on.

difficult balance, but throughout the book, we'll explore unreason in its varied forms.[7] Fine attention to detail will often be needed.

Speaking of which ... let's have another look at the "maths pain study". It wasn't a dreadful study, you know. The authors are self-critical, often a good sign. They debate whether their findings *actually* represented pain. But as a god of details, I'm intrigued by one more thing. SMARS scores ranged between 5 and 76, but a *normal level of maths anxiety* was set at 30. Isn't this strange? How many people in your small survey felt the same?

Deep Thought

Sometimes small asides are more important than headlines. They get us to ask "Why?" Why should maths cause pain? Go back to the first study. Read it through with a clear mind and you'll realise the participants were given sums to do and put under time pressure. No fun! A lot of people see this as 'math'—and they couldn't be more wrong. Numbers merely decorate the ideas that make up mathematics—and there's seldom reason to rush.

In Lesson 4 you'll find that good maths is something that children *intuitively* get right, and guess what? In 2016, fMRI studies by Marie Almaric and Stanislas Dehaene[8] showed that professional mathematicians busy doing high-level maths mostly tap into the ancient brain circuits used by children when they first learn about space and numbers.

Maths and play and number puzzles are all intertwined. Mathematicians already lament how teaching maths as the dry friction of numbers harms children; studies like the above just confirm their fears.[9] You naturally need the language of maths to *communicate* about maths, language that may seem scary, but maths itself can be elegant and fun; you can use maths for understanding and enjoyment. I'll even claim that without maths—good maths, unstressed maths—your view of the world is dampened and darkened and inadequate. Ultimately, this is a book of light, and enlightenment. Some maths is needed.

There *are* parts that are dark. There are failures. I believe in full disclosure: people will die. If you want to avoid death, go elsewhere. Human history is in any case full of death—dead people, dead ideas and of course, dead gods. This book is brim-full of all three. Sorry, but reality is often like that.

---

[7] Notably in Lessons 3, 6, 7, 8 and 10. [8] PubMed 27071124 [9] In "Lockhart's Lament" (www.maa.org/external_archive/devlin/LockhartsLament.pdf), Paul Lockhart draws an analogy with teaching art by getting children to categorise paint colours, or music by concentrating on memorising scales, modes, meter, harmony and counterpoint.

Many voices

At the start, I revealed that I am a god. I was tempted to say "goddess" but I understand you too well. You seem used to masculine gods, and if I look around the world, I'm not too comfortable with the way many of you treat women. So I chose the easy option.

But I am a god of many voices. You will hear a voice that you might consider male. I'll use this voice when you piss me off, a slightly proud and angry voice that projects your own pride and anger. You will perceive a voice that you may label 'female'—sometimes nurturing and sometimes tutelary—for this is how you think, or have thought in the past. I can't help but contain echoes of your gods and your mythology — I can't help but reflect some stereotyped views. I'm not perfect. To some degree this is how I *want* you to see me, for this is how you unwittingly made me.

Please view me as a woman too, but don't be silly. Your mythology already cautions you that Aphrodite arose from the foam of the severed genitals of Uranus, that Astarte was a goddess of both love and war, and that Ishtar's favours conferred death, on gods too. If you try to treat me like Quetesh the Egyptian goddess of ecstasy, the coquettish Voudou goddess Erzulie, or Greek Aphrodite, famed for her beauty and sexuality, you may find yourself looking a bit silly—or worse.

You have met my avatars—all attractive young women—but I am both man and woman. Your society has imprinted itself on "women as nannies" and for some strange reason my avatars have flowed into that mould; in a few decades, they might be mannies. As a modern human, you should already know that gender is more in the set of mind than body, although some of you may have lagged behind a bit.

You named me

Beginnings are difficult as they often start with names. Here, you have not been kind. There's a cool logic to my naming that despite hitting the target, misses the mark. "SARS-CoV-2" — what were you thinking? It doesn't help that in the next breath, your always compare me with the 'flu virus H1N1, who—let's face it—is no more than a distant relative, not even a second cousin. His name too is unfair.

'H1N1' doesn't reflect his brash masculinity and his pushy nature—and completely fails to capture the idea that this morning you'll be fine, and this evening, blue and dead. You name your gods—Shiva and Até and Atropos—better than you name your viruses. 'H1N1' was not ambivalent like me when he showed himself one hundred years ago. If he had god-like attributes, he was a simple god, and his sole lesson was death.

Subsequently, he's not been quite as impolite, but now he's old. People have come to know him and his kin, and combined a tiny bit more respect with a lot more resistance. To an extent, someone can only be pushy if they're allowed to push. You've found ways to push back, things like vaccines. This may not work for me.

If only for contrast, let's talk a bit more about H1N1 before I tell you more about myself. Unfortunately, a lot of your 'facts' about him look to me more like myths. You believe that he managed to infect nearly one quarter of those alive in 1920, but aren't even sure within an order of magnitude how many he killed. The truth may lie somewhere between 17 million people and as many as one hundred million. That seems pretty imprecise, especially to a twenty-first-century god who has learned a certain respect for numbers.

You aren't sure where he originated, despite knowing that he spread in military camps and on ships. Initially, he had a more familiar name—but this was a convenient lie. Your most successful myth was that he originated in Spain, but this was because you'd just finished one of your interminable wars, and your wartime censors covered up his effects in the United Kingdom, the United States, and much of Europe. Spain, as a neutral country shared none of these dubious privileges, so the newspapermen flocked there to report death and devastation. As usual, we viruses were misreported and misrepresented. But we're not asking for your pity. On a practical level, you'll find that bad newsmen and lazy reporters are some of our finest friends. And support from one lousy politician is worth one hundred million people industriously washing their hands. I am however getting ahead of myself.

There are more contrasts. The stark contrast is how quickly you found me out. In 1918, you barely knew what a virus was. The word only came to use twenty years earlier, when the Dutch microbiologist Martinus Beijerinck found us so tiny we can easily pass through filters that stop bacteria dead. How tiny is tiny? Well, your largest bacterium—the "sulphur pearl from Namibia" or *Thiomargarita namibiensis*—can be a quarter of a millimetre long, just visible to your naked eye. Most bacteria are about one hundredth of this size, about a micrometre, and I myself am just one tenth of this size, 125 *nano*metres—including my spike proteins. I'm tiny. You can see how minuscule I am by looking not at me but at my genetic makeup. I've put the whole of me into Appendix B. Now this may look like a lot, and for an RNA virus it is a lot—eight pages of variations on the theme of GATTACA—but the whole of me is slightly longer than the average size of a single human gene[10], and you have well over twenty thousand of these. You're huge!

But back to my story—forgive the digression; as a virus I sometimes find it difficult to stay in focus. To their credit, Chinese microbiologists spotted an outbreak of

[10]PubMed 28025344. The median size of genes that code for human proteins is 26,288 base pairs.

pneumonia around an animal market in Wuhan, and took mere days to sequence me and give me my first name. I had a close call in Baibuting on 18 January—if incompetent authorities hadn't stumbled, allowing 40,000 families to party it up, I mightn't be writing this book.[11]

And my first name wasn't a bad name, either: "a novel coronavirus". Even its contraction, '2019-nCov', I could live with. Who doesn't want to be novel? The name doesn't reflect my feminine side, of course, nor how subtly and well I spread and manifest, but it wasn't a bad name. I even liked your name for the disease I cause—'COVID-19' has a spiky, mathematical, somewhat masculine feel—but then you spoilt it all with "SARS-CoV-2". You must admit this wasn't a great choice. I think I'll stick to Novel Coronavirus, but if you treat me with respect, I'll even let you call me Rona. Let's see.

The Covid Conspiracy

I am flattered by the sheer number of conspiracy theories you've managed to manufacture about me. This too is praise, of a sort. I do have a close relative, even better at death than the young H1N1, and his name is SARS. He's quite jealous of the rapidity with which you humans started manufacturing rumours out of thin air, but then when he hit the stage the Internet was a lot less embracing, and you had to rely on sources of mind pollution less efficient than social media.

In 2002, it took simply ages for a less-than-well-informed Russian scientist to generate the idea that SARS was a bioweapon made by mixing measles and mumps, and nobody really believe him, firstly because you didn't have Twitter and Facebook, and secondly because this is like saying that chickens are a mutant mix of cows and goats; measles and mumps are *Paramyxoviridae*, hardly even distant relatives. They are negative sense viruses and we coronaviruses are naturally positive.

But I have been meat and drink for conspiracy theorists. The conspiracies vary, but often run along the idea that I'm a "bioweapon that escaped", or something similar. I love it! Admittedly, when it comes to the military you as a species are pretty good at dumb, so let's say you were silly enough to try to engineer me as a bioweapon. I'm not quite sure why you'd choose a virus, unless you could somehow magically spare your troops when they moved in to clean up, or anticipate that everyone was dead—but if you *were* this daft, you'd still have to be smart enough not to fiddle with the bit of me that works.

The bit of me that works is my spike protein. Lousy for handling a keyboard, admittedly, but pretty damn good at binding the ACE2 enzyme, which is my magic passkey to the inside of your cells, where I can persuade your cellular machinery to

[11] I'd be a footnote in some dusty medical text. Whew!

make multiple copies of me, and even expel these children through the miracle of exocytosis. Now let's ignore the fact that my genes bear none of the trademark scaffolding of laboratory viral manipulation. Just look at my spike protein.

I'm called a coronavirus because I have a corona—a thorny crown of spike proteins. But oddly enough, my spike proteins also have a tiny crown, a crown of amino acids that binds ACE2. And if you were manufacturing a new me—a big if—the one thing you'd do as a sensible, crazy, bioweapon constructor would be not to change these amino acids. But guess what! When you sequenced me, you discovered that, despite the fact that like SARS-CoV-1, I bind ACE2, the amino acids that do the binding are very different.

The above explanation doesn't serve the purpose you think it might, however. I'm not trying to justify my origins.[12] I couldn't care whether I originated in a bat and found my human destination by means of an illegally traded pangolin. But I do care about the finer details. And the finer detail here is that my spike protein works better than that of SARS-CoV-1 — it binds ACE2 more avidly.[13] This—and conspiracy theorists—are two reasons why I have a bright future.

Provenance & Presidents

Let's look at one conspiracy theory—just for fun! I'll be brief, but some future historian will find a PhD thesis here.

Founded by the self-proclaimed Messiah Sun Myung Moon, The Washington Times styles itself a 'conservative news outlet'. Others see it as "right leaning"[14] and a 'questionable source' of 'mixed reliability'.[15] On 26 January 2020, it claimed that I came from a "lab linked to China's biowarfare program", quoting Dany Shoham "an Israeli biological warfare analyst" who speculates about "outward virus infiltration[sic]".

We've already discredited this silly biowarfare idea, but the story grew and mutated. Looking to blame China, On 17 February the Republican senator from Arkansas, Tom Cotton, speculated on Fox News that a Chinese lab was the source; his 21 April editorial in the Wall Street Journal[16] claimed a "Chinese coverup", saying that the evidence "all points towards the Wuhan labs". He admitted that this was all "circumstantial", but later said China should be punished.

---

[12]If you're smart, then you weren't taken in by the conspiracy theories anyway, and if you were deceived, then the chances are you'll manage to dredge up some even more arcane explanation that justifies your prior, fixed belief. I'll explore this human quirk in Lesson 6. [13]PubMed 32075877 [14]allsides.com/news-source/washington-times-bias [15]mediabiasfactcheck.com/washington-times/; adfontesmedia.com/washington-times-bias-and-reliability/ [16]cotton.senate.gov/?p=press_release&id=1354

In the meantime, President Trump picked up the idea—now also spread by right-wing bloggers. The media at the time describe "multiple theories", referring to anonymous claims of a "man-made" virus, but also "accidental escape" of a virus kept in "its natural state". They quote Steven Mosher, a "Virginia-based pro-life advocate" who on absolutely no evidential base whatsoever painted a blood-soaked scenario where a "horseshoe bat" was "sold from the lab ... to the nearby wet market for a very good price."[17] On April 15, Fox News claimed "increasing confidence that the COVID-19 outbreak likely[sic] originated in a Wuhan laboratory",[18] alleging "multiple sources" (unstated).

So far we have the unsupported opinions of right-wing newspapers, a pro-life advocate, a retired Israeli colonel and some bloggers—and of course a US president who by 3 April was noted to have made 18,000 false or misleading claims while in office.[19] What about people who know something about virus biology?

On 7 March, the leading UK medical journal *The Lancet* published a letter signed by 27 prominent public health scientists from around the world, citing nine analyses that "overwhelmingly conclude that this coronavirus originated in wildlife".[20] They note support from the presidents of the US National Academies of Science, Engineering and Medicine. They further say "We support the call from the Director-General of WHO to promote scientific evidence and unity over misinformation and conjecture."

Shortly after this, in *Nature Medicine*—another top journal,[21] prominent virus experts from around the world analyse the evidence in detail, concluding that there is "strong evidence that SARS-CoV-2 is not the product of purposeful manipulation". They also note:

> *"The finding of SARS-CoV-like coronaviruses from pangolins with nearly identical RBDs, however, provides a much stronger and more parsimonious explanation of how SARS-CoV-2 acquired these via recombination or mutation [than adaptation to passage in a laboratory]"*

Can you see the problem here? It's easy to generate 'theories' about something, and to construct anecdotal support. Once your 'theory' is discredited, it's equally easy to generate not one but several new 'theories' that edge around the disproof. Strong evidence of natural origins—no problem, it's no longer genetically engineered, it merely escaped. And it's *always* possible to find "corroborative" anecdotes that obliquely support any such theory.

[17] tinyurl.com/UsaTrumpCorona [18] tinyurl.com/FoxChinaLab [19] tinyurl.com/PostTrumpMisled
[20] PubMed 32087122 [21] PubMed 32284615

In generating spurious associations like Fig 1, the Harvard law student Tyler Vigen has provided glorious—and sometimes hilarious—examples of the abuse of 'mathematical correlation'.[22] Scientists have struggled with the problem of demarcating 'pseudoscience' (and indeed, pure bullshit) from solid science for centuries, and snake-oil salesmen still proliferate along with crazy theories—and everything in between.

The farcical 'theories' I've just described should act as motivation to do better. In a very real sense, they motivate for a large part of this book. We'll explore a solid approach to science that helps cut out most of the nonsense—if properly applied. I'll also provide a base of solid logic and even explain why this approach works; in contrast, Lessons 6, 7 and 8 show how easy it is to get things wrong if you let reason slip.

The preceding paragraphs teach an important lesson. They provide a useful silliness-filter, in the form of a question "Where did this theory come from?" Art historians emphasise the importance of 'provenance'—the chain of evidence that links something to its origins. You can be fairly confident that a pre-Columbian sculpture traced back to Brígido Lara,[23] a Vermeer acquired from Han van Meegeren,[24] or a Rubens bought from Eric Hebborn[25] is fake, but healthy scepticism is also wise if a work simply appears out of thin air. A good filter for bad science,[26] but which sources can you trust? Later lessons will provide some pointers.

A COVID-19 Spotter's Guide

I like to be fair. And you have some pretty sexy tools in your toolbox. If I'd made my entrance in 1970 I'd have had an easier time of it. I'd have the planes without the DNA tech, which has advanced in leaps and bounds over the past few decades. For example, late one night in 1983 the soon-to-be Nobel prizewinner Kary Mullis was driving along the Pacific Coast Highway when he had an idea so numinous that he just had to stop his car and write it down.

In Lesson 2 we'll explore the main theme of this idea in the fine detail I like, but to start, consider a grain of rice. If you could double it repeatedly, you'd soon end up with an embarrassingly large number of copies. Mullis realised that he could do this with

---

[22]Find nothing on interviewing people who've visited the lab, or even worked there? No problem—clearly there's a cover-up or a *huge* conspiracy. Not a scrap of evidence of any of this either? Perhaps it was planted by aliens sympathetic to the Chinese government? [23]From childhood an expert at making, baking and faking clay statues, Lara was so prolific that many of the 'reference artefacts' used by experts to validate "original Totonac" figures may also have been made by him. [24]Like Lara, van Meegeren was arrested on the serious charge of trading in antiquities—even worse, he "sold cultural artefacts to the Nazis". *Both* were eventually acquitted when they made new works as evidence that they were expert forgers! [25]Who cuttingly noted that draftsmanship can only be understood by those who "can, to some extent at least, draw". [26]Do you trust scientific studies produced by Scott Reuben, Youshitaki Fujii, Joachim Boldt, Diederik Stapel, and so on? Of course not! See retractionwatch.com/the-retraction-watch-leaderboard/

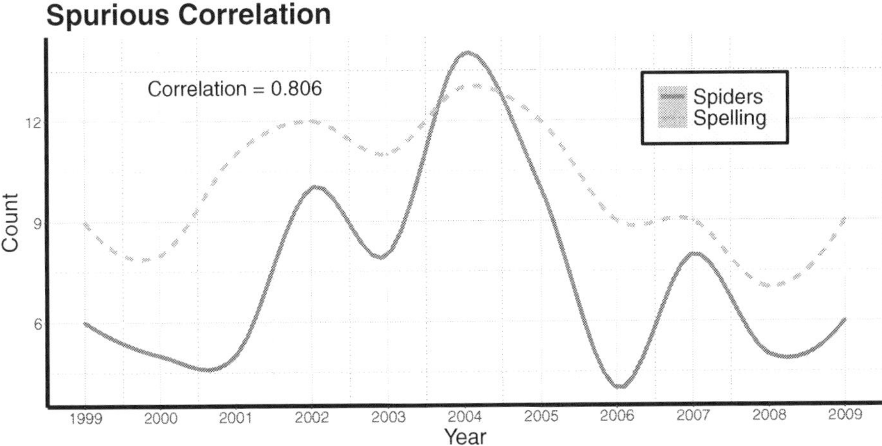

Figure 1. Letters in winning word of Scripps National Spelling Bee correlate with number of people killed by venomous spiders (After: tylervigen.com)

something really *tiny*—DNA—and a few very simple ingredients. All he needed was a heat-stable enzyme to copy DNA,[27] those ATGC building blocks, a couple of 'primers' that know where to bind the *right* DNA, and heat. Every heating and cooling cycle would double the desired DNA! This "polymerase chain reaction" or PCR combines extreme simplicity with one of the most elegant and satisfying ideas in all science.

For example, when you suspect I've infected someone, you can take a good sample from their nose or mouth or lungs, and using custom-made primers that fit just me, amplify the right sequence – and there I am! The saving grace for me here is that the test doesn't always work. In fact, in up to one third of patients, you may not see me at all. You might say that the test is about "65% sensitive".

There are two main reasons for this. First, the site you've swabbed may not be where I'm now replicating. I may be in the lungs, while you're looking at the nose. The second is that your tissues may contain "PCR inhibitors" that turn off the reaction.

Fortunately for you there are few *false-positive* reactions, but the false negatives may be a bit of a problem for you. How big a problem, you'll find out in Lesson 4, where together we'll explore the joined-up thinking that makes modern science so powerful.

[27] There's an interesting footnote here. A vital part of the PCR reaction is an enzyme that is heat stable. Most proteins will irreversibly change their shape (denature) when you heat them much above 60^oC. You can boil an egg, but you can't "unboil" it again. The change you see in boiled egg white signals irreversible 'denaturation' of the protein. Denatured enzymes stop working. But in 1969, Thomas D. Brock and Hudson Freeze isolated a bacterium they called *Thermus aquaticus* from Mushroom Spring in Yellowstone National Park, where the water temperature ranges up to about 70^oC. This bug thrives at up to 80^oC, well above the point where normal proteins quit. Its DNA-copying enzyme Taq turned out to be just what you need for PCR. Pond slime has its uses, and obscure research can change lives profoundly.

RNA, DNA?

Let's put to bed one tiny, technical detail here. I like those details—it's what makes me, me. Most college students know about DNA. The enzymes and structural proteins on which your cells work need to be made by tiny cellular 'factories' called ribosomes.

But the DNA is wrapped up in the nucleus of the cell, and the ribosomes are outside this, in the cytoplasm. To carry the genetic code from your DNA to your ribosomes you use a messenger molecule—messenger RNA, which is formed on a DNA template.

The mRNA moves to the cytoplasm and binds to the ribosome, which then reads the genetic code step-by-step. The ribosome translates three 'letters' (nucleotides, often abbreviated to nt) of this code into each corresponding amino acid, which it adds to the growing protein chain.

But I'm not made of DNA. I'm an RNA virus. You can work out how I breed—I trick the cell into believing that my RNA is ordinary messenger RNA, and commandeer normal cellular processes to translate new copies of me, reading off my proteins. I can then copy my RNA, and I'm good to go, all without that complex messing around with DNA.

This is where you humans have been very smart—and is your key to identifying me. You once believed that taking a strand of DNA and turning it into RNA was a one-way street. But in 1970 two researchers independently found viruses that buck the trend, with enzymes that run the process in reverse.[28]

Can you use this trickery to spot me? Surely you can. The old-fashioned way to detect RNA was something called a Northern blot. This needed a lot of RNA, and was technical and time-consuming. If however you use a suitable reverse transcriptase to turn my RNA into DNA, then PCR can make you as many copies as you want. This is an RT-PCR, or reverse-transcriptase polymerase chain reaction.[29] The RT-PCR for SARS-CoV-2 (me!) is an essential weapon in your war against me. But is this metaphor the right one? Is it really a war?

Don't Mention the War

Pogo's comment at the start of the lesson parodies a grand statement by U.S. Navy Commodore Oliver Hazard Perry after his victory in the Battle of Lake Erie "We have met the enemy and they are ours". In 1953, long before his famous Pogo cartoon, Walt Kelly said this:

---

[28]You now know many viruses, like the HIV virus that causes AIDS, that can use this *reverse transcriptase* to trick the cell even further. Not only can they make DNA from RNA—they can even get this DNA inserted in among your normal genes, lurking in the genome for ages. This is one of the reasons HIV is so hard to beat.

[29]This is made even more confusing because it's a *real time* RT-PCR, and it's easy to misinterpret the initials.

> "Traces of nobility, gentleness and courage persist in all people, do what we will to stamp out the trend. So, too, do those characteristics which are ugly. It is just unfortunate that in the clumsy hands of a cartoonist all traits become ridiculous, leading to a certain amount of self-conscious expostulation and the desire to join battle. There is no need to sally forth, for it remains true that those things which make us human are, curiously enough, always close at hand. Resolve then, that on this very ground, with small flags waving and tinny blasts on tiny trumpets, we shall meet the enemy, and not only may he be ours, he may be us. Forward!"

You made me thus. Even if you see me as an implacable foe rather than Nanny Rona, hell bent on teaching you a lesson or two, you might still agree that my context is important. And my context is *you.* A wise general understands the mind of the enemy; but I have no mind. I'm just a virus. You may see me as a metaphor, but you can't take up arms against a metaphor, and like it or not, while you continue to invest your emotions and effort in me, I will grow as a god. It is your choice whether you understand me and grow too, or not. Fear and disrespect me, and many will die; it's in the numbers, you see.

Lesson #1

Understanding trumps aggression. Start with yourself.

⊛ Lesson 2

Count Those Rabbits!

There's a story that after the creation of the Earth and its animals, the Creator said "Go Forth and Multiply!" All the animals left, apart from two small snakes. The Creator looked down and said "Didn't you hear me? Go Forth and Multiply!" The snakes responded "But please sir, we're adders".

A nursery tale.

"Out of our regard to them we gave [the Delaware Indians] two Blankets and a Handkerchief out of the Small Pox Hospital. I hope it will have the desired effect."

William Trent's Journal, June 24, 1763.

Sentience is strange—and full of surprises. In late January I unexpectedly found myself in Goa—the smallest, wealthiest and perhaps most touristed and tolerant part of India, wedged like a jewel between the Arabian Sea and the Western Ghats. Parashurama, the violent sixth avatar of Vishnu, threw away his bloodstained battle axe and Goa then arose from the waters, or so it is said.

I believe that in the capital Panaji, a mecca for tourists and cruise ships, you can navigate by smell alone. If you arrive at the bus terminus you're met by the CCP composting plant, but this is rapidly replaced by the ubiquitous sandalwood burners, and in the markets the sweet smell of chaat competes with those of coconut oil, fresh ghee, asafoetida and dried fish.[1]

Employing au pairs and nannies is something of a novelty in India—where strangely enough it's the upper middle class rather than the rich who need a nanny. The rich can afford to adhere to traditional values; the middle class often now need a dual income to make ends meet.[2] Caring for two small boys in upmarket Altinho, I found that they in turn had two even smaller white rabbits to care for. I like this delegation—a chain of

[1]But do *not* order the jumping chicken! [2]Nannies aren't well paid in India, but a little can go a long way.

transmission always appeals to me, somehow. Liking children is wired into my RNA. You've seen how even as I sometimes hurt adults—this too is wired in—I've pretty much shied away from harming children.[3]

It was in Goa that I first read the story of the Indian wise man Sissa ibn Dahir, a man from up North. In the tale he invents the game of chess, to demonstrate to the tyrant King Shihram the importance of all citizens.[4] When asked what he would like for a reward, Sissa replies "A grain of wheat on the first square, two on the second, four on the third, and so on." What happens next is unclear—in one branch of the tale, the King sees the impossibility of the task, has a good laugh, and promotes Sissa to counsellor; in the other, he chops off his head. I suspect the latter is more likely.

I've subsequently done a bit of reading about rabbits, and my all-time favourite is the tapeti, a forest rabbit from South America. Its short ears and small, dark tail were first described by the Swedish taxonomist Carl Linnaeus,[5] ten years before William Trent gifted smallpox to the Indians. The tapeti hosts the myxoma virus, which causes benign little skin tumours, nothing serious. They've been friends for millennia, and play nicely together. Like smallpox, the myxoma virus is a *poxvirus*, large viruses that are quite unlike me. First, they are often about twice my size, but this is just a cosmetic difference.

The real differences are inside, for poxviruses contain double-stranded DNA, and I, as you already know, am RNA through and through. But you can still learn a lot from the tapeti and its virus—and not just about rabbits, but also about epidemics and how they spread, and indeed how they sometimes end. You might even apply the same ideas to people, and DNA technology—as I hinted on page 18, when we doubled grains of rice.

In the 1950s, Australia had a serious problem with imported European rabbits. Conditions were ideal, and they had few local predators to keep down their numbers—humans tried shooting them and digging up their warrens to no avail. Rabbits bred and bred and bred, and eventually there was little food left for them, and nothing left for the sheep. Something had to be done.

The Commonwealth Scientific and Industrial Research Organisation (CSIRO) is the Australian federal government agency that found a temporary solution. Releasing the myxoma virus into the wild was far more successful than they anticipated. The rabbits had no tolerance of the virus—it was new to them, just as I am new to you—and so it spread and spread, causing a devastating illness with nasty tumour growths (myxomas)

[3]Some might protest that exposure to me is (very rarely) associated with the multisystem inflammatory syndrome in children. Nobody is perfect. [4]Tyrants have delighted in sacrificing pawns ever since, while ignoring pawn promotion! [5]This may become relevant. Actually, as Sir Terry Pratchett observed, many ordinary people discover or describe all sorts of things, but as they aren't proper explorers or taxonomists, they don't really count.

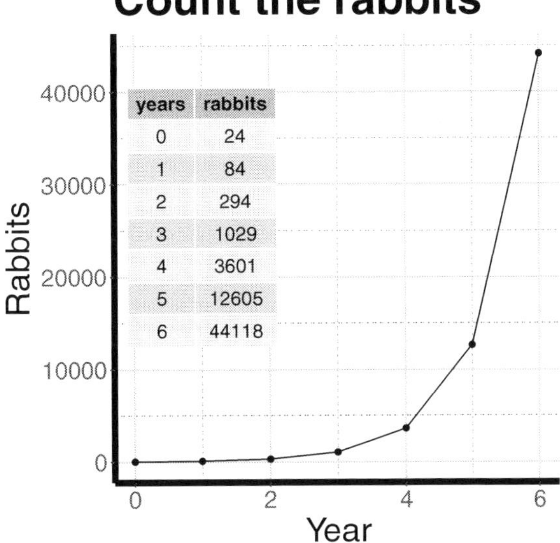

Figure 2. My, how they breed

that killed well over 99% of the rabbits. They died within days of becoming infected, but not before they'd been bitten by mosquitoes, which were plentiful; the mosquitoes moved the disease from rabbit to rabbit, and the onslaught continued.[6]

Most of the rabbits succumbed, but not all, and after a decade or so, the CSIRO saw what they'd predicted—a milder form of myxomatosis emerged, and the rabbits came back.

How this happened is instructive. We viruses mutate, and those mutant myxoma viruses that took longer to kill their hosts gained a special benefit. Because it lived longer, a rabbit infected with this mutant was more likely to be bitten by a mosquito before it expired, conferring a survival advantage on the virus. The emergence of slightly less virulent virus strains meant that rabbits with slightly better immunity had at least a sporting chance of survival—and rabbit resistance to the virus increased. Balance was restored, and rabbits thrived to a degree, to the consternation of Australian sheep farmers.[7] Life—and death—is often about finding a balance.

Similar balances are sometimes achieved in humans, over time. It's likely that smallpox has been around in Europe and Asia for over 4000 years. In 1150 BCE, the

[6] As an interesting aside here, at the same time that myxomatosis was released, there was an outbreak of human encephalitis in Victoria. This caused huge public consternation, as the public, not schooled in the finer details of virus taxonomy, blamed the CSIRO. Wisely, three top scientists including the chairman of the CSIRO Dr Ian Clunies Ross injected themselves with doses of live myxoma virus. They were fine. The news of this went viral, and succeeded in allaying public fears. The common factor that linked the outbreaks was mosquitoes, not the myxoma virus.

[7] Until the calicivirus was released, but that's another story.

pharaoh Ramesses V was killed by the disease, imported from the north during a war.[8] Until you wiped it out in 1980, smallpox was often still fatal, killing 30% of those infected and scarring those who survived, but this was better than its course in America. Hernán Cortés and his scruffy band of conquistadors reached the capital of the Aztec Empire in 1517. They were made welcome, but soon began their conquest of Mexico, which they completed four years later.

Over the course of the next century, the Aztec population fell from over 16 million when the Spanish arrived, to under 3 million. The biggest contributor was however not Cortés—vile though he may have been—but smallpox, introduced with the Europeans.

When Cortés took the island capital Tenochtitlan, the population had already been cut by forty percent in a single year. Now that's a real plague, spreading exponentially among people with absolutely no natural resistance.[9] As a virus, I raise my crown to him. But as Nanny Rona, I've digressed again. Let's get back to those rabbits.

One pet rabbit is fine. A boy pet rabbit and a girl pet rabbit may be a problem. The millions of Australian rabbits started as just 24, released by Thomas Austin into the wild near Winchelsea, Victoria in 1859. Within a few years, there were millions.

You can get a feel for this sort of growth using very simple maths—multiplication. Rabbits multiply. Let's say our two rabbits can, on average, produce 7 surviving offspring every year, or 3.5 offspring per rabbit. Simplistically, if you start with 24 rabbits then after a year you'll have 3.5×24 extra rabbits; after two years there will be 3.5 times as many again, and so on.

From these numbers, let's *generalise.* Growth by multiplication is 'exponential growth' – an exponent is just a way of repeatedly multiplying something by itself. So here's the pattern (or formula) that lets us work out the number of rabbits:

$$N(y) = N(0) \times 3.5^y \tag{1}$$

In other words, to get the number N after y years, multiply the initial number for "year zero" by 3.5 *raised to the power* of the number of years.

This growth is shown in Fig 2. If you visit page 197 and go through the minor pain of setting up the R program there, you can now play with the numbers. Try this! Type `corona_rabbits()` and press Enter. Next, try `corona_rabbits(topyear=10)`. Now try 11 or 12. My how they breed.

---

8 In all likelihood. With both wars and viruses, you are often your own worst enemy. 9 Some have also argued that as the Aztecs were unfamiliar with the disease, they didn't know how to care for sufferers, and that this was more important than any 'resistance'. Nobody is sure.

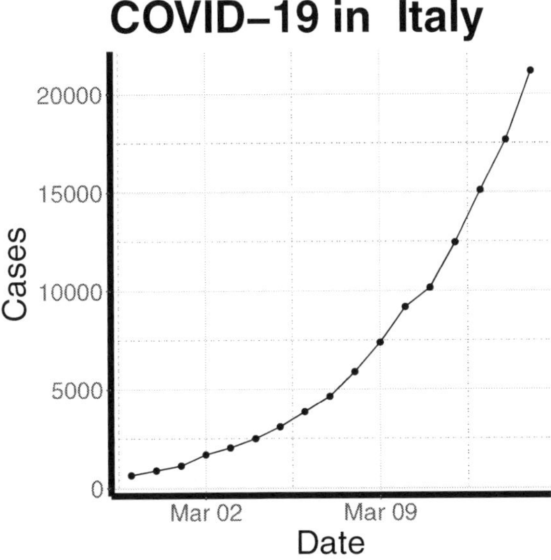

Figure 3. Exponential growth in Italy

There are many such examples of exponential growth—you met one in the PCR reaction of Lesson 1, where I used the analogy of a grain of rice—doubled.[10] The story of Sissa at the start of the lesson illustrates exponential growth with a value of 2^y rather than our rabbits' 3.5^y. Can we generalise some more?

The Basic Reproduction Number

Making Internet programs that show how COVID-19 case numbers grow is itself a growth industry. Sites like Johns Hopkins, Our World in Data and Worldometer garner billions of views. You yourself can draw a curve like Fig 3: load the R corona library as above and say `corona_totals()`.[11] The number in our examples above—2 for the chessboard problem or 3.5 for the rabbits—matches the average number of people I spread to at each step. Another name for this value is the "R_0" or "R nought".

Let's say that someone starts spreading me about five days after they've become infected, and on average does this to three other people. If this continues uninterrupted, our familiar formula 1 does the job, that is $N(t) = 1 \times 3^t$, where t is the number of "incubation periods" that have elapsed, and my R_0 is here 3. Unlike the rabbits, we'll start with just one case, so $N(0)$ is one rather than 24.

[10] We're about to start playing with not just exponents but logarithms. If you've always struggled with these (and n-th roots) you could do worse than watch the brief YouTube video ***Triangle of Power*** by Grant Sanderson of 3Blue1Brown fame.

[11] Play a bit: `corona_totals(daystart=1,dayend=100)`. Try `?corona_totals` for help.

Working back

With very modest mathematical skills, you can even work things in reverse, pulling out the R_0 or the number of incubation periods that have elapsed. A brief aside about logarithms might help. Years ago, when multiplication was difficult because you didn't have computers, engineers would use *log tables* to convert their multiplications into additions, and their exponents into multiplication.[12] It's clear that $10^a \times 10^b$ is the same as 10^{a+b} – for example $100 \times 1000 = 10^2 \times 10^3 = 10^{3+2} = 10^5$. So, to multiply 3.141 by 1.763, an engineer might laboriously look up the logarithm of both numbers, add the values, and again consult the tables for the anti-logarithm of the result. To today's eyes, this seems mad, but long-hand multiplication was painful, a century ago.

The tedium is shown by the only occasion that the American Mathematical Society ever gave a standing ovation—for multiplying several numbers together! Prime numbers have long fascinated mathematicians. The 17th century scholar Marin Mersenne fixated on primes one less than a power of two. For example, $2^2 - 1$ is prime, and so is $2^3 - 1$, likewise for $2^5 - 1$ and $2^7 - 1$; you can easily work these out by hand. He claimed that the next numbers in the sequence after seven were 13, 17, 19, 31, 67, 127, and 257, but wasn't quite right.

It's pretty easy to check the Mersenne primes up to $2^{19} - 1$, and 31 also turned out to be correct, but $2^{67} - 1$ is a bit more of a challenge, as the value is:

$$147,573,952,589,676,412,927$$

At an AMS meeting on 31 October 1903, Professor Frank Nelson Cole strode up to the blackboard without a word and on the left, step by step, calculated $2^{67} - 1$. He then moved to the right, wrote $193,707,721 \times 761,838,257,287$, and in silence worked this out too. After an hour, when he completed the task—and the numbers were equal—the audience broke into spontaneous applause.[13] My, how things have changed. Today I open Python on a computer and type in:

$$\texttt{193707721} * \texttt{761838257287} - (\texttt{2} * *\texttt{67} - 1)$$

... this takes a tiny part of a second. Everyone has moved on, but can still put logarithms to good use. Let's say that on 31 January 2020 you count 11,791 cases of COVID-19 in Wuhan, China. When might the infection have started spreading?

---

[12]The relevance of this observation will only become fully apparent in Lesson 11. [13]They loved their prime numbers but they loved a good showman more. He later confessed that he'd spent three years of Sundays working out these two factors. It turns out that Mersenne also missed $2^{61} - 1$, as well as the exponents 89 and 107; 257 isn't.

Nanny Rona's logarithms

Here's Equation 1 again, but using R_0 instead of the rabbits' 3.5:

$$N(y) = N(0) \times {R_0}^y$$

If we take the logarithm of both sides, we can convert multiplication to addition, and the exponent to multiplication:

$$\log(N(y)) = \log(N(0)) + y \times \log(R_0)$$

We can rearrange this to get either y, or R_0. Can you see how? Our first step is to subtract $\log(N(0))$ from both sides:

$$\log(N(y)) - \log(N(0)) = y \times \log(R_0)$$

... and now, dividing both sides by $\log(R_0)$ we have y:

$$y = \frac{\log(N(y)) - \log(N(0))}{\log(R_0)}$$

... or, dividing by y we get:

$$\log(R_0) = \frac{\log(N(y)) - \log(N(0))}{y}$$

Using Nanny Rona's logarithm box above, take the equation:

$$y = \frac{\log(N(y)) - \log(N(0))}{\log(R_0)}$$

... and simply plug in the numbers to get y, the number of incubation periods since the start:

$$y = \frac{\log(11,791) - \log(1)}{\log(3)}$$

If you type this into a calculator (or use Python again, after saying `import math`) you'll get about 8.5 incubation periods, suggesting that the first case happened about 42 days earlier. Even better, knowing that in Italy between 2 March and 15 March, the number of cases rose from 1689 to 21,157, with an incubation period of 5 days, you can say:

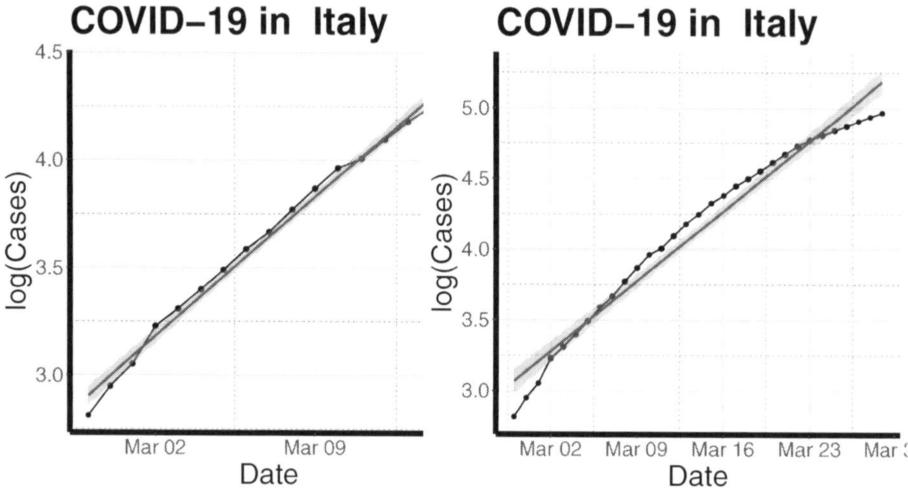

Figure 4. Logarithms & straight lines

$$\log(R_0) = \frac{\log(21,157) - \log(1689)}{\frac{13}{5}}$$

This gives an R_0 of about 3.5. There are however many important assumptions here. One is that we're counting cases "correctly", another is that the incubation period is 5 days[14]; a further assumption is that growth is exponential. Logarithms can help with this last requirement. Consider the left panel of Fig 4. If you plot the *logarithm* of the number of cases in Italy for the first two weeks in March, you can see that this fits a straight line fairly well. By transforming multiplication into addition, it may be easier to do things like fit a line, or even just eyeball the fit.

A word of caution

My little COVID-19 pandemic has given a lot of people time to play, but something as simple as the right panel of Fig 4 suggests they should be careful. Here I've extended the time span, and over time the curve flattens out. Trying to fit a straight line to the logarithmic data is now dumb.

A number of very bright people are curve-fitting like crazy, and plugging in numbers like those above. Even though they are using more fancy algorithms (compartmental models and partial differential equations) they are still making all sorts of assumptions, and depending on the assumption you make, you can get the numbers to

[14]With an incubation period of 4.2 days, the R_0 drops to just 2.3.

dance. Most models are great for understanding the basics, but pretty awful at predicting what I'll do in the future. In Lesson 9 we'll explore the problem of super-spreaders and how epidemiologists have tried to accommodate them, and in Lesson 11 we'll find out that even this fix may be inadequate. Part of the problem is clearly the simple nature of the model, which just doesn't work when we extend the time-frame, but *why* doesn't it work?

The change here likely relates to human behaviour. The R_0 is not some magical, god-given number. You can modify it by your actions. For example, you can decrease transmission if you have or acquire habits that kill me and thus stop me spreading—Italy went into lockdown on 9 March, and Italians started changing their behaviour even earlier. Having people dying around you has a salutary effect. This is one possible explanation for the change in the Italian graph above; a similar change may however also occur when there's nobody left to infect.

Traditionally, epidemiologists may have regarded the R_0 as something almost sacrosanct, an intrinsic property of the virus, but this can't be right. Different populations may not respond in the same way to the same virus, for example, if everyone wears a mask when they're feeling ill, the "R_0" for that population *may* be different. It's traditional to refer to the R_{eff} or R_e once people have wised up or other changes have happened, but you can see that to a degree, the distinction is artificial. I will however refer to R_e from time to time, to avoid infuriating epidemiologists too much.

Herd Immunity

The idea that an epidemic—or even a pandemic—might eventually run its course brings us to the matter of "herd immunity". Herd immunity clearly isn't a good idea with smallpox—unless you achieve it using a vaccine. The same applies to many other infectious diseases. Modern vaccines for diseases like polio, measles, mumps, rubella, diphtheria, whooping cough, tetanus and human papilloma virus are far less risky overall than the diseases they prevent. Humans have come within an inch of eradicating measles and polio, just as they put paid to smallpox.[15]

The simple idea is this—the greater the R_0, the greater the proportion of people you need to immunise before the disease can be wiped out. The details are in my 'HIT box' below.

For measles, which is remarkably infectious with an R_0 of about 12–18, to stand a chance at wiping it out, you therefore need an HIT of about 92–94%. With modern measles vaccines, about 90% of people become immune after their first dose, and

[15]There's almost guaranteed to be a resurgence of many of these, as medical services are compromised and children miss their vaccines due to my presence on the world stage. We viruses can't help but work together.

Nanny Rona's HIT

The idea is simple. Take an R_0 of 2 as an example. If 50% of the people exposed are resistant to the virus, then the R_e is just 1. If you can increase the number of resistant people, then R_e will dip below 1, fewer and fewer will get the disease, and eventually it should die out. In other words, if s is the proportion of susceptible individuals, we want:

$$s \times R_0 < 1$$

Let's call the proportion of people who *are* immune H the "herd immunity threshold" (often just 'HIT') which is clearly those who are not susceptible, in other words:

$$s + H = 1$$

Substituting in:

$$(1 - H) \times R_0 < 1$$

Divide through by R_0 to get:

$$1 - H < \frac{1}{R_0}$$

Finally, add H and subtract $\frac{1}{R_0}$ on both sides to get:

$$H > 1 - \frac{1}{R_0} \tag{2}$$

This is the threshold above which herd immunity will remove the virus from the population.

95% after the second, so you might just get there—but for the ***virus friends*** in your community, the 5% of people who are vaccine-shy.

Magic numbers

One of my strengths is how uncertain you humans are about my R_0. If the number is about 3, then from equation 2 you can work out about 60% of people will need to be immune, but what's my actual HIT? Estimates vary rather a lot. For example, one paper from Los Alamos National Laboratory[16] calculates an R_0 of 5.7, with 95% confidence intervals of 3.8–8.9, quite different from the 2–3 you'll often see.

[16]This can be downloaded from PubMed 32255761.They calculate an incubation period of 4.2 days, and initially in Hubei province, times from symptoms to hospitalization and death as 5.5 and 16.1 days, respectively.

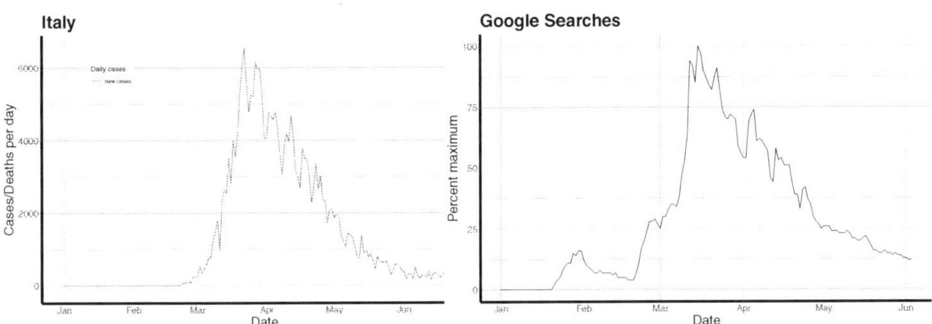

Figure 5. Viral trends & Google trends

For an R_0 of 5.7, over 80% of people would need to be immune to have a good chance of stopping me from spreading! In Lesson 11 I'll explain why my R_0 seems to vary so much.

Another uncertainty is about lasting immunity. For many childhood illnesses like measles and mumps, a single infection confers lifelong immunity, but this is emphatically not the case with influenza, which mutates and can therefore re-infect. The same goes for the common cold. Guess what! About 10% of cases of the 'common cold' are due to my mild relatives. These gentle coronaviruses—229E, OC43, NL63, and HKU1—often re-infect you.

Perhaps, like the tapeti and myxoma virus, you and they have reached some sort of balance. When studied, you found that up to 80% of people infected with the first two already have antibodies. In contrast, for me, you just don't know! It seems quite unwise simply to assume that you'll achieve herd immunity, either through infection or even through vaccination.

There are two other catches that make your pursuit of herd immunity less than wise, especially without a vaccine. The first is obvious. If I kill just 0.5% of those I infect,[17] and the HIT is 60%, then in a population of ten million people—the population of Sweden—30,000 deaths seem inevitable, sooner or later. But current data suggest that for every death, several people at least will require hospitalisation or even admission to intensive care. Even the most sophisticated health care system may buckle under the strain of these cases; older people may well be left to die.

[17]This seems likely; although initial death rates in many countries approximate 10%, many milder cases are likely being ignored as hospitals fill up. See Lesson 8.

Viral spread

Look at Fig 5. Can you see what I've done? The 'epi curve' of Google searches for the word "coronavirus" on the right is similar to that for the virus itself, on the left![18] "Going viral" is more maths than metaphor.

In this lesson I've taken an idea and turned it into mathematics. From simple ideas about rabbits, we get equations, and from equations we can go back not just to rabbits, but to many other things—wheat on chessboards, replicating DNA, and so on. This is an almost god-like power.

We can take a problem, observe it, generalise it, plug in numbers, and then start making predictions. But principles can be over-simplified, the wrong data can be fed in, models can be misused—and this misuse too can spread. We need to use our powers carefully.

We have also seen how a tiny change in a system—introducing a few rabbits, for example—can feed itself and cause runaway growth. This is also how a chain reaction leads to a nuclear explosion. More generally, where a process reinforces itself, we talk about "positive feedback", an unstable state that will either end catastrophically, or through some natural process like depletion of food or fuel. It's often a good idea to control such processes using *negative* feedback, whether this is using the exponential growth of a virus to control the exponential growth of rabbits, vaccinating, or lowering neutron-absorbing control rods in a nuclear reactor.

As we'll see in Lesson 3, although negative feedback has a stabilising influence, it can have a down-side. There is also a third, more interesting option—a system can oscillate. Many models of me end up with bursts of growth, frenzied attempts at suppressing me, and then another burst. It's all ultimately in the maths.

Lesson #2

You can benefit from quite simple models,
provided you respect their limitations.

[18] Data source: Google Trends (google.com/trends). I've been mildly devious, as the Google trend is world-wide. You can also examine Italy-specific data from Google (where the rise is even more brisk).

⊛ Lesson 3

Clean Hands

"Life seemed worthless. Everything was in question; everything seemed inexplicable; everything was doubtful. Only the large number of deaths was an unquestionable reality"

Ignaz Semmelweis. *The etiology, concept and prophylaxis of childbed fever*, 1861 (tr. Codell Carter).

To find contrasts in Vienna, you need to dredge them out of obscurity. Museum Hundertwasser is just a curly line away from the Ionic columns of the Opec Fund for International Development; the ubiquitous Baroque facades fade into the background only when confronted by Whiteread's nameless library, full of unreadable books. Less discomforting and more child-friendly is the Tiergarten Schönbrunn, the oldest zoo in the world.[1] Freud[2] fled this most beautiful of cities to avoid taking the 71—and then caught it in London.

As a nanny in Vienna, you acquire persistence; the baroque has seeped into the bureaucracy, but you make your way; you learn the difference between a Tagesmutter and a Kinderfrau, and why you would be neither; you begin to understand why foreign au pairs in the winter snow-globe of Vienna are united by a love of strong drink. I also learned that you don't qualify as a real nanny until the point where you discover a brown substance under your fingernail—and aren't sure whether it's Nutella or poo.

Over the centuries, every nanny worth her salt has known not just the importance of washing her hands, but also of thorough sanitisation. It was however only in 1847 that somebody for the first time worked out the back story—in Vienna. Can people today learn from history? Let's see. There may be more to learn than just hand-washing. Along the way, we'll also learn to count—with a difference.

[1] Behind the Rainforest house you will find breeding colonies of Bornean Winkerfrösche. As they normally live around very noisy waterfalls, adults attract others by flashing their gollum-like pale feet. [2] h-index, 285; scholar.google.com/citations?user=N80kIiYAAAAJ&hl=en

A needless death

If you had a time machine and could successfully navigate back to the mid-19th century to inform the Hungarian-born physician Ignaz Semmelweis that he is now commemorated by a bust at the Frauenklinik in the 18th district of Vienna, and a somewhat less stark statue at the Medical University of Vienna, unveiled in 2018 on the two hundredth anniversary of his birth, I doubt he'd be amused.

In 1865, still young, but also old and broken, he was committed to an insane asylum by his wife and friends. A few days later he died from sepsis, a complication of multiple, deep wounds inflicted by the guards at the 'madhouse'.

This was an ironic end to the life of the person who worked out how infections spread and how they are avoided. As a virus, I can't but take heart in the tale of Semmelweis' destruction—but as a teacher, it disturbs me. I have this dreadful ambivalence, you see—on the one hand, the need to breed is written into my RNA; but on the other hand, my nanny-self is keen to provide the best education I can. I am conflicted.

The story of Semmelweis is worth telling, not only because he ultimately saved many lives, but also because of what you can learn from his reception both then and now. If you do a casual search on the Internet, or even in the medical literature, you'll often encounter a caricature of a "man before his time" who was also a bit of a loser—someone who failed to articulate his solution well, a depressive personality who antagonised those around him and retreated into obscurity.

A recent report in the American Journal of Obstetrics and Gynaecology by Nicholas Kadar presents a different picture.[3] In 1847, as a young doctor who was "playful and popular, and did not mind being teased", he took over the running of one of two birthing wards at a Vienna hospital. He compiled the data in Table 1.

It is obvious that the death rate in his ward (the "First Clinic") where male medical student trained, was three times that in the ward next door, where midwives trained. Semmelweis was moved to ask why. "Why?" is often a good question.

Today you know that childbed fever (or 'puerperal sepsis') is caused by infection with a bacterium called *Streptococcus pyogenes*, the "beta-haemolytic streptococcus". It is so called because under the microscope, with a suitable chemical stain, it looks like chains of seeds,[4] and when grown in culture, it breaks down blood cells.[5] But all of this was in the future. In 1840 the cause of childbed fever was unknown. There were many theories—and these theories were Greek.

[3] PubMed 30444981 [4] In Ancient Greek streptos (στρεπτός) and kokkos (κόκκος) refer to chains and seeds respectively; pyo+gen (πύον -γενής) means pus-forming. [5] Greek again, haemolytic = αῖμα and λύσις for 'blood' and 'rupture'.

	First Clinic			Second Clinic		
	Births	Deaths	Rate	Births	Deaths	Rate
1841	3,036	237	7.7	2,442	86	3.5
1842	3,287	518	15.8	2,659	202	7.5
1843	3,060	274	8.9	2,739	164	5.9
1844	3,157	260	8.2	2,956	68	2.3
1845	3,492	241	6.8	3,241	66	2.0
1846	4,010	459	11.4	3,754	105	2.7
Total	20,042	1,989		17,791	691	
Avg.			9.92			3.38

Table 1. Childbed Fever in Two Clinics

Infection in the 1800s

Certain viral diseases like smallpox were well known—although as we learnt in Lesson 1, viruses themselves were still a future dream. Conditions like smallpox were referred to as "contagions", as they always presented in the same, stereotypical way. This was thought to define their nature. In contrast, "infectious miasmas" did not refer to infection as it's seen today.

The word 'miasma' is the Greek μῐασμᾰ, not just a *stain* or *defilement*, but also sometimes a shameful action. From Hippocrates on, until the germ theory of disease, there was more than a little confusion about the part gods play in disease.[6] To the Greeks, an infectious miasma was surely the conjunction of a 'miasma' in the air with a host of other factors. Something emitted from a cesspit or rotting swamp conspired with overcrowding, fear, binding the abdomen too tight, or poor flow of milk to inflict puerperal fever. Dogma had it that different conditions might arise from *different conjunctions of circumstances.* In the 19th century mind, 'infection' was quite distinct from a 'contagion'.

Semmelweis could not reconcile these ideas with what he saw. A numbers man, he tried to explain the differences between the two Clinics by looking at the evidence. He couldn't find a link between overcrowding and childbed fever. The clinics were adjacent, so there was little chance of some mysterious smell overwhelming one but not the other. In desperation, he even asked the local priest to tread a different path as he rang the bell on his way to the next dying woman—the labouring mothers well knew what the bell signified. All to no avail.

Semmelweis enthusiastically dissected the corpses of women who died from childbed fever, trying to understand its cause, but was no wiser. The death rate just went

[6]Perhaps this confusion engendered me?

up. Finally, he'd had enough, and took time off in Venice. On returning, he learned that his good friend Jakob Kolletschka was dead. Semmelweis was grief-stricken.

After reading the pathology report, Semmelweis ruminated on the way Kolletschka died. While dissecting a corpse, a medical student nicked Kolletschka's finger. Inflammation spread throughout his body over days, forming abscesses in an eye, his lungs, and around his heart and brain. But this was what Semmelweis saw in the bodies of those who died of childbed fever. He had an explanation! An explanation however, contrary to the current dogma about miasmas. He asserted that "in every case, without a single exception, I assume only one cause, namely, decaying organic matter" (bacteria hadn't been discovered yet).

Semmelweis did something very special here. With a better understanding of science, we now see that he formulated a *causal hypothesis.* To modern eyes, this may seem trivial. It isn't, as K Codell Carter pointed out in 1981, contrasting the ideas of Oliver Wendell Homes and Skoda on one hand, and Semmelweis on the other.[7] He boldly created a theory linking cause and effect. He did something even more bold—he proposed and tested a solution, and his solution worked.

Throughout his investigations, Semmelweis was precise and methodical. When it came to selecting a disinfectant, he realised that mere hand-washing with soap might not be enough. So he tested which agent was best at getting the "dead person smell" from his hands, identifying chloride of lime (calcium hypochlorite) as ideal.

Soon after, he insisted that everyone wash their hands in this solution on entering and leaving the Clinic. The death rate from puerperal fever plummeted. But there were still cases at a lower rate. Again, Semmelweis watched and learned.

He found that some medical students were not complying, and also that exposure to women who came in with open sores or obvious infection could similarly result in childbed fever. He tightened things up, and for the first time, the rate of infection dropped to zero. You can see his numbers in Table 2.

A football

Quickly, several of Semmelweis' more forward-thinking colleagues realised that he was onto something huge. There is good evidence that his ideas were rapidly disseminated through Europe. But there was a backlash, especially from his more conservative colleagues. He was cynically used as a test-case for reform of the autocratic way Medicine was practised in Vienna, and when this failed, he was abandoned and victimised.

Semmelweis continued to promote his successes—forced from Vienna he went back to Pest in Hungary and achieved the same results in the hospital there. But he was relentlessly persecuted by his detractors, and died before his ideas finally won out. Even

[7] PubMed 7012475

Date	Births	**Deaths**	*Date*	Births	**Deaths**	*Date*	Births	**Deaths**
1841/01	254	**37**	*1843/10*	250	**44**	*1846/07*	252	**33**
1841/02	239	**18**	*1843/11*	252	**18**	*1846/08*	216	**39**
1841/03	277	**12**	*1843/12*	236	**19**	*1846/09*	271	**39**
1841/04	255	**4**	*1844/01*	244	**37**	*1846/10*	254	**38**
1841/05	255	**2**	*1844/02*	257	**29**	*1846/11*	297	**32**
1841/06	200	**10**	*1844/03*	276	**47**	*1846/12*	298	**16**
1841/07	190	**16**	*1844/04*	208	**36**	*1847/01*	311	**10**
1841/08	222	**3**	*1844/05*	240	**14**	*1847/02*	312	**6**
1841/09	213	**4**	*1844/06*	224	**6**	*1847/03*	305	**11**
1841/10	236	**26**	*1844/07*	206	**9**	*1847/04*	312	**57**
1841/11	235	**53**	*1844/08*	269	**17**	*1847/05*	294	**36**
1841/12	-	-	*1844/09*	245	**3**	*1847/06*	268	**6**
1842/01	307	**64**	*1844/10*	248	**8**	*1847/07*	250	**3**
1842/02	311	**38**	*1844/11*	245	**27**	*1847/08*	264	**5**
1842/03	264	**27**	*1844/12*	256	**27**	*1847/09*	262	**12**
1842/04	242	**26**	*1845/01*	303	**23**	*1847/10*	278	**11**
1842/05	310	**10**	*1845/02*	274	**13**	*1847/11*	246	**11**
1842/06	273	**18**	*1845/03*	292	**13**	*1847/12*	273	**8**
1842/07	231	**48**	*1845/04*	260	**11**	*1848/01*	283	**10**
1842/08	216	**55**	*1845/05*	296	**13**	*1848/02*	291	**2**
1842/09	223	**41**	*1845/06*	280	**20**	*1848/03*	276	**0**
1842/10	242	**71**	*1845/07*	245	**15**	*1848/04*	305	**2**
1842/11	209	**48**	*1845/08*	251	**9**	*1848/05*	313	**3**
1842/12	239	**75**	*1845/09*	237	**25**	*1848/06*	264	**3**
1843/01	272	**52**	*1845/10*	283	**42**	*1848/07*	269	**1**
1843/02	263	**42**	*1845/11*	265	**29**	*1848/08*	261	**0**
1843/03	266	**33**	*1845/12*	267	**28**	*1848/09*	312	**3**
1843/04	285	**34**	*1846/01*	336	**45**	*1848/10*	299	**7**
1843/05	246	**15**	*1846/02*	293	**53**	*1848/11*	310	**9**
1843/06	196	**8**	*1846/03*	311	**48**	*1848/12*	373	**5**
1843/07	191	**1**	*1846/04*	253	**48**	*1849/01*	403	**9**
1843/08	193	**3**	*1846/05*	305	**41**	*1849/02*	389	**12**
1843/09	221	**5**	*1846/06*	266	**27**	*1849/03*	406	**20**

Table 2. Births & Maternal Deaths in the First Clinic

in the late twentieth century, revisionist writers (notably Nuland, but also Loudon) fabricated and spread the myth that Semmelweis had a "self-destroying psyche", ideas of grandeur, and the demeanour of a "hellfire-spewing evangelist". As Kadar and Carter point out, none of this is supported by thorough examination of all of the evidence.

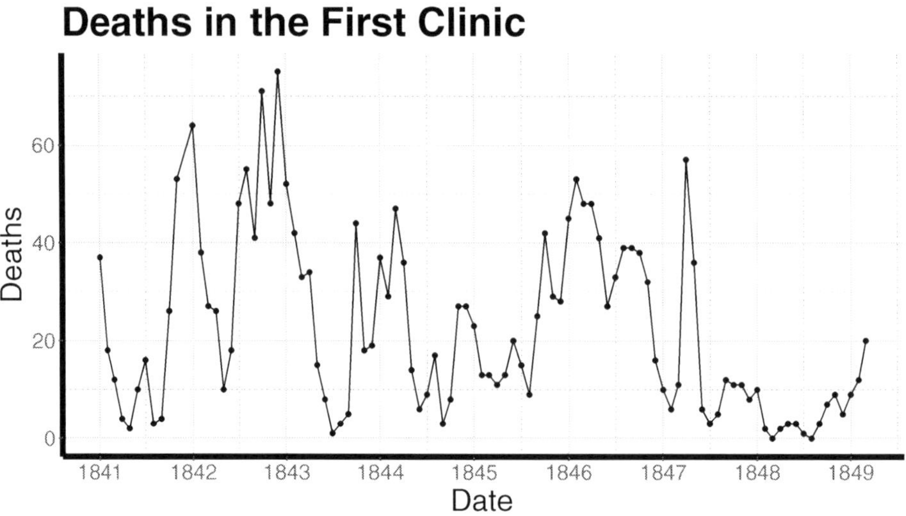

Figure 6. "Deaths over Time"

Time warp

One hundred-and-seventy years after Semmelweis, you might think that infection control is a no-brainer. You'd be wrong. Good control is still the life-bane of all of those truly taken up in the task of limiting infection in hospitals and in the community. Clinicians—especially doctors—*still do not wash their hands!* You must ask "Why?" Surely to people who understand microbiology and contagion, who can even use fancy DNA tools with exquisite precision, simple hand-washing is straightforward? To see and indeed *quantify* why not—and what's going on—let's go back one last time to Vienna.

It's Vienna, in the middle of the 19th century. Ignaz Semmelweis is not a political animal. Surely the evidence speaks for itself? No, a combination of dogma and politics destroys him. But before he dies, Semmelweis writes a book. His data are still available. What can we learn from them? We have the numbers, but what is the pattern? Can we move from the specific to the general?

It may be a bit difficult to get your head around Table 2 – his month-by-month numbers for births and deaths in the First Clinic – so let's try something different. Computers can surely make the numbers sing. But I won't be too ambitious; the obvious, simple thing is just to "plot the dots". You can even do this on graph paper.

Fig 6 may not seem a lot better! As you suspected from the raw data, the numbers are all over the place. You might however spot a quiet period in the later part of the graph—you might even work out when Semmelweis instituted hand-washing—but can you see something else? There are peaks and troughs, and these seem to be seasonal.

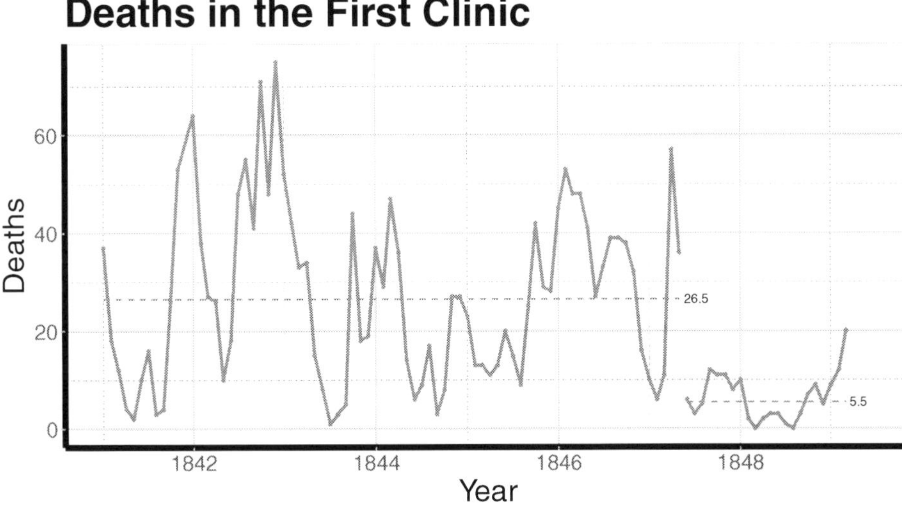

Figure 7. A run chart, with a change

Semmelweis also looked at these data—you don't need a computer to get a feel for data—and he quickly worked out that the peaks corresponded to the return of medical students to the clinic, and their vigorous resumption of internal examinations of women (and the subsequent dissection of their corpses). Some students may have been more diligent than others, but none so diligent as Semmelweis—can you see the sudden peak in early 1847? Once he'd worked things out, this peak preyed on his mind.

We do not however have to rely entirely on intuition here. There are many ways to tease out meaning from these data, sometimes involving fancy statistical tricks, but here's a very powerful and simple technique that anyone can use, called the "run chart". Simple approaches like this will allow us to tease out an enormous amount of information from the data.

Run Ignaz run

The idea behind a run chart like that in Fig 7 is very simple—plot the dots and *draw in the median.* This is easy to do, even by hand, but I've made it even easier in the R program in Appendix A—just type `corona_vienna()`.

Take all the monthly counts of deaths in Table 2, sort them and then find the reading that splits the number of observations into two. This is the median.[8]

[8]For an odd number of observations, the value in the middle is the median; for an even number, it's convenient to average the two "middle values".

Here are three useful, related concepts that become easy to see, once you've started drawing run charts:

Common-cause variation: reflects random variation. Effectively, there's some inscrutable "random number generator" behind the scenes that is making things vary over time. Any system will contain noise, and this becomes evident in the results. Some people will luck out.

Special-cause variation: Sometimes, a particular value sticks out. It "just seems wrong". Be careful not to make "false positive diagnoses" (more of this later) but often in these circumstances, you can identify a specific cause. For example, if you have a run chart of widget quality from a factory that makes widgets, and on one shift there's suddenly a rise in defective widgets, you may find a cause—a machine that's playing up, or a new employee who hasn't been trained adequately.

Process change: If there's a pattern to apparent "special causes" — for example, they are grouped together, this should make us think again.

It seems clear that with Semmelweis' data, the rises in deaths are grouped at the same time that the medical students come back, so here it's wise to consider the idea that there are embedded issues with the system as a whole. From time to time, special causes step in and kill women. The return of the students is a good explanation.

More generally, it can be tricky trying to tease out special causes and process changes from common cause variation. In about 1930, Walter Shewhart worked out some rules and soon put these into the workplace. Nobody wants to have to scrap whole boxes of defective widgets. Strangely enough, even modern healthcare has been remarkably immune to such ideas—a win for bacteria and viruses. You will also find that when run charts and control charts are used in healthcare, both administrators and clinicians tend to get the wrong end of the stick. But on to the rules. Jacob Anhøj has recently produced a good tutorial on how to get the most out of run charts, and you are encouraged to read the details.[9] Let's use his rules and his software.

First however, where do "run charts" get their name? It's simple. A 'run' is just an unusually long sequence of similar observations. For example, you may toss a coin and get a run of five heads in a row. If you consider the sneaky trick of drawing in the median, then this will divide the numbers in two. If the variation you're seeing is simply 'common-cause' *random* variation, it's quite unlikely that you'll encounter values that are grouped on one side of the median. This is intuitively obvious. Tossing a fair coin repeatedly, you'll have to examine a large number of tosses before you get say eight heads in a row! The problem is that if you set multiple people at industriously

[9] See PubMed 25799549

tossing coins, some will come up with an unusual sequence like this. So what suggests unusual clumping in a run chart?

Anhøj has quite reasonably suggested—and shown—that the number of runs you'll accept as "unusual" depends on the length of your chart. He has also provided free software that does the necessary calculations easily.[10] Apart from measuring the longest run, there's another simple way you can look for "clumping" of data on either side of the median. If you *count the number of crossings of the median* as you plot your data, this too will be useful: fewer crossings = more clumping.

In Fig 7 I split the run chart in two at the point where Semmelweis instituted hand-hygiene. Some may object that doing this deliberately prevents the data from "speaking for themselves", but this is silly. As we'll learn in Lesson 4, it would be far more wrong to ignore the knowledge and rely on some automated tool to do the splitting!

The software does signal that even before the split, you are not looking at mere common-cause variation.[11] This fits Semmelweis' conclusions about the medical students, and the Christmas peak he spotted. The numbers are unusually clumped.

But the program also detects anomalies after the change! There are two reasons: the line resumed its ascendancy is when Semmelweis was fired; the second reason is something you already know. Even after the change, Semmelweis noticed that spread was still happening, so he stood at the door and insisted on good hand hygiene. It was only then that the rates dropped to zero.

We conclude that a run chart is not enough on its own—is must be read in the light of knowledge. Of course, there *is* a risk that some will still frame things poorly, missing an obvious signal, as almost everyone around Semmelweis surely did. Much of the rest of the book will explore how to avoid such errors, but let's again time warp back to the 21st century. This time we'll plot the dots slightly differently.

Death in England

Fig 8 displays the weekly count of all deaths in England and Wales for the past ten years. It's pretty stark. Several things are clear. Deaths vary with the season, and as the spikes are in winter, influenza and other respiratory illnesses are the likely cause. Several episodes have been pretty dramatic, but they are dwarfed by the huge rise that has coincided with my little pandemic. As an aside you can also see that the straight regression line is of little value in capturing the exuberant variation in numbers with the season, but it does have one use—it shows *secular change*. There has been a gradual

[10]The **qicharts2** package in the free, industry standard R statistical environment. [11]The program draws the median in red. Interrogating the chart, I find that in the first part, the minimum number of *expected* crossings is 30, but there are just 14; for the second part, the corresponding values are seven and six. Similarly, in the first part the longest run is 14 with an expected maximum of 9; for the latter we have values of nine and eight.

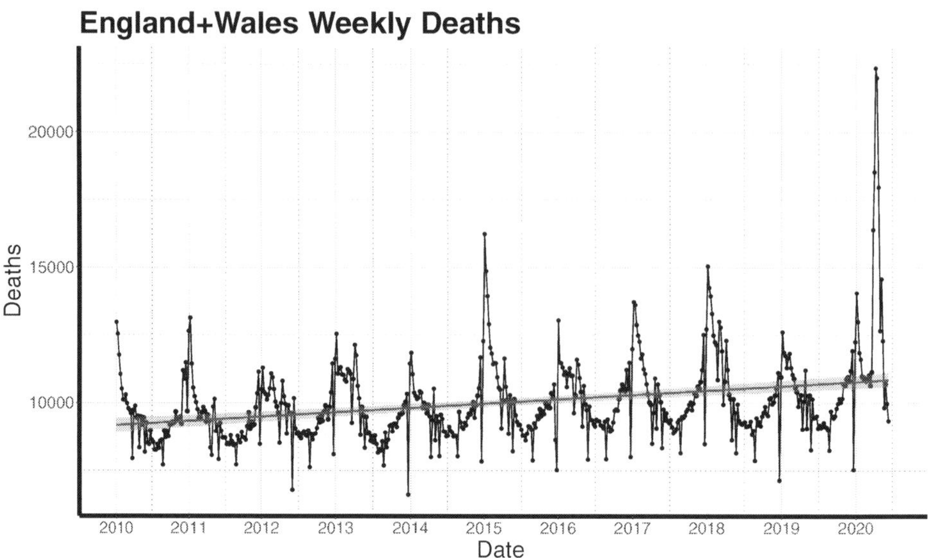

Figure 8. Weekly deaths in England & Wales

increase in the number of deaths over time, although the graph is mute as to why this has happened. We need other data—population numbers, and age demographics if we want to tease this out.[12]

Although my contribution to the UK death chart is eyeball-stabbingly obvious, it invites as many questions as it provides answers. You might speculate at length as to whether the spike in deaths is mostly related to COVID-19, or whether, for example, people have kept away from hospital and either died at home, or presented to hospital too late to be helped by modern medicine. You might even blame crowded hospitals and over-worked staff for the death spike. But I'd like to claim credit.

I know my own handiwork—helped by a bit of bad hygiene. Before we look at whether the numbers stack up, let's play a bit more with the charts. Just for fun! The first thing I'm going to do is adjust for secular change. There are many ways to do this. As I'm particularly interested in the later numbers, I need a fix that will affect these least. It may be tempting just to elevate the baseline of the earlier numbers but that would be cheating—scaling each number seems fairer. This is shown in Fig 9. If you're interested, you can easily run the code in Appendix A — say `country_dead()` — or even browse the raw R code.

[12] If you blow up the curve and look carefully, you'll see a few other oddities. Most striking is the Christmas dip—in most years, there's a single little blip (or inverse blip) where the death rate drops, but just for a week. Measurement is the problem here—delayed reporting of deaths over public holidays—rather than say a munificent Xmas gift from a benevolent deity. Try other holidays like Easter.

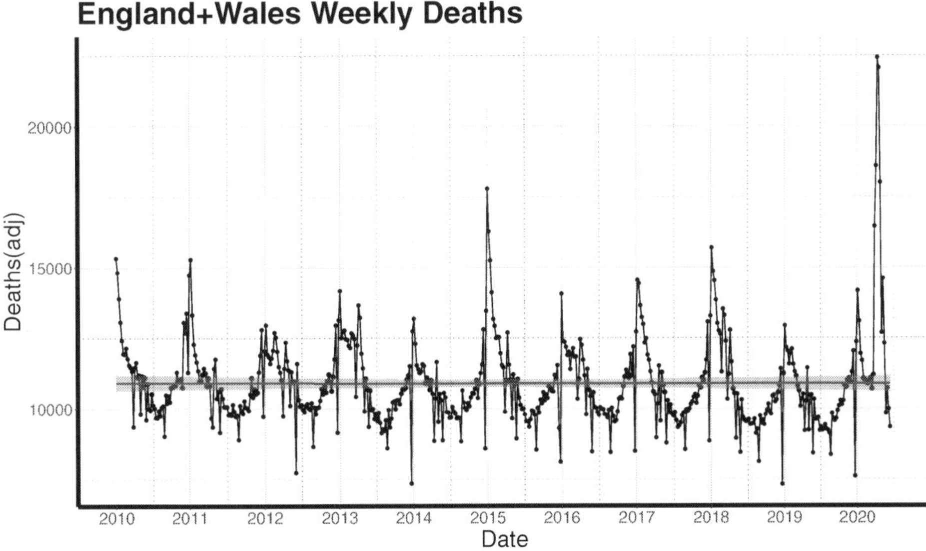

Figure 9. Deaths adjusted for secular change

Next, adjust for season. There is necessarily some danger, because we can do this in so many different ways. We need a decision. I'd suggest that you have two main options here:

(1) You can use the "average" as a baseline.

(2) You can use your head.

This is a big decision—because it touches on the mind-set we've encountered above. Semmelweis' antagonists did not accept his causal assertions, not because he was unclear, but because the implications were too severe. If he was right, their "normal" practise was profoundly wrong.

Now is the time to start listening to a third voice, distinct from mine. The voice is yours, the voice of meta-cognition. If you choose (1) this will colour your decision-making throughout the rest of my book. By choosing the average, then you're embracing the mind-set of Semmelweis' opponents.

If, in contrast, you choose summertime as your baseline, you're saying "What is average isn't necessarily normal or good. My mind is open to new ideas that oppose dogma. Why not choose as my baseline the best that can be done, and reject the idea that tens of thousands of influenza-related deaths are 'normal'?"

Do you agree to choose the second option, to use summertime as the baseline? Let's explore further.

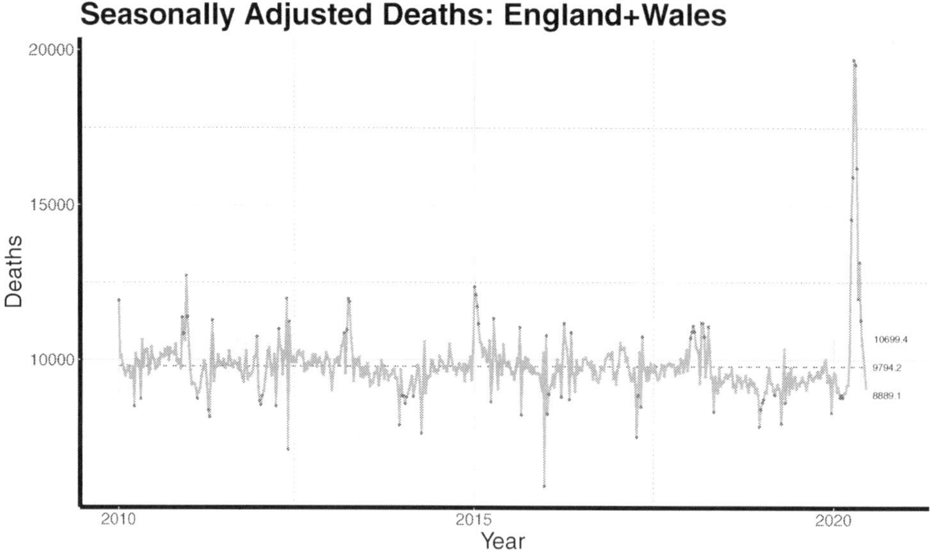

Figure 10. A further fix for seasonal change

As there are several definitions of 'summer', we'll use Meteorological summer, which in the UK always begins on 1 June and ends on 31 August. We'll do something else very simple: for each data point, we'll find the mean of the nine other corresponding weeks in the other years, adjust this mean to the summer baseline, and then adjust our data point using this reference value. The results are shown in Fig 10.[13]

Note the broad, grey band—this is a *control* chart, not a run chart! The upper and lower limits of the grey strip should contain 99.7% of the data points in a process "in control", as it represents the mean $\pm$ three standard deviations. Remarkably, our crude measure has removed the bulk of the regular, seasonal peaks.[14] Even more dramatic is how the COVID-19 associated spike is left in stark prominence.

What I've done is very simple, and far from the only way you can manipulate the numbers. You'll find a hundred ways of doing this differently. My way has two advantages—it's simple, and it's visually intuitive. Many of the alternatives require quite sophisticated statistical processes that aren't necessarily more explicit.[15]

[13]The code that does this is in Appendix A on page 197. [14]While exacerbating the strange Christmas dips and public holidays drops. The 'upwards' bits that still stick out seem to represent particularly bad 'flu epidemics, for example that in 2014/2015. [15]See for example US deaths in PubMed 32609307, where the authors fit a hierarchical Poisson regression model using "a combination of harmonic functions to capture seasonality and adjusted for annual trends with a categorical year effect".

Week	Deaths	Expected	Difference	COVID	Explained(%)
2020-01-03	12254	13968	-1714	0	
2020-01-10	14058	13590	468	0	
2020-01-17	12990	13060	-70	0	
2020-01-24	11856	12671	-815	0	
2020-01-31	11612	12294	-682	0	
2020-02-07	10986	12211	-1225	0	
2020-02-14	10944	12080	-1136	0	
2020-02-21	10841	12018	-1177	0	
2020-02-28	10816	11762	-946	0	
2020-03-06	10895	11836	-941	0	
2020-03-13	11019	11618	-599	5	
2020-03-20	10645	10820	-175	103	
2020-03-27	11141	10764	377	539	143
2020-04-03	16387	11370	5017	3475	69
2020-04-10	18516	11252	7264	6213	86
2020-04-17	22351	10896	11455	8758	76
2020-04-24	21997	11047	10950	8237	75
2020-05-01	17953	10354	7599	6035	79
2020-05-08	12657	10623	2034	3930	193
2020-05-15	14573	10717	3856	3810	99
2020-05-22	12288	9847	2441	2589	106
2020-05-29	9824	9577	247	1822	738
2020-06-05	10709	10428	281	1588	565

Table 3. The COVID-19 Explanation

Reconciliation

Just because the death spike is *associated* with COVID-19 doesn't mean this is the cause. Now, let's not be daft here—of course the greater part of this spike is my fault. Going back to the original data, and using my predicted values, we can calculate the percentage of deaths explained by COVID-19. The results are shown in Table 3.

A substantial majority of the excess deaths are explained by reported deaths, although the timing is a bit off and there are discrepancies. As with influenza, you may never know the true toll, as classifications and counting aren't even close to perfect.[16]

[16]The COVID-19 deaths are from the same official data source as the overall deaths, and may not correspond precisely to other COVID-19 data. Data from some countries are clearly quite wrong. There's also an interesting Italian report (PubMed 32348640) in the New England Journal of Medicine, where out-of-hospital cardiac arrests increased in concert with the advent of COVID-19. For an insightful analysis of excess mortality see ourworldindata.org/covid-excess-mortality.

The Red Bead Game

Even a sound, useful, life-saving explanation for a problem is useless in the face of bad politics. We've seen the importance of numbers, but also their limitations, and how interpretation is as important as skill with numbers. We've had a taste of what we can do with statistical process control. But there's something missing.

This missing part was first pointed out by W Edwards Deming in about 1950. He illustrated it using his 'Red Bead Game'. Deming would squeeze a whole team of managers into a room, and divide them up. As the boss, he set up the game; the participants were inspectors and workers. The job of the workers was simple. They were given flat paddles, each with 50 indentations into which exactly 50 beads could be scooped. A tub contained a combination of red and white beads; the workers would dip their paddles in, trying to select just white beads—as the red beads represented "defects". The inspectors would keep count—no picking, no cheating—and check on one another too.

Deming as the manager would then set a "management target" of no more than 3 red beads out of 50. If this target was consistently met, the factory would keep going. Otherwise they would go out of business. Tallies were kept and the "best workers" were retained, and encouraged to do even better. Eventually, after many iterations of the game, people would realise that the process had been designed to prevent them from meeting the targets—as 20% of the beads were red, the chances of 3 or fewer defects were tiny (We'll work out how small in Lesson 4). The increasingly frustrated inspectors and workers, however willing, were constrained by the processes built into the game. The mix of red beads meant they couldn't meet the targets that had been set. Eventually, the company would go into liquidation.

Blame

Once you 'get' the Red Bead Game, your views of management will change, whether you're in healthcare or manufacturing widgets. Especially in healthcare, slogans are common—exhorting workers to achieve 'targets'. Those who ask about the meaning and origins of targets are shushed, and those who meet the targets are praised—even if "meeting the target" is just common cause variation. Targets are 'aspirational'—unachievable—because the system produces what it is designed to produce, and mere exhortations don't change this. The mix of red beads is wrong.

Common cause variation is mistaken for special causes. Those who fail to meet the targets are blamed, scolded or fired—but their failures reflect common cause variation. Those who 'succeed' are asked to repeat their random successes—and chastised when they don't. Participants rapidly work out that in order not to be blasted, they need to introduce a bit of special cause variation themselves. Often, because they are already being ground down by institutional processes, their only recourse is to cheat. If you can't change the process or the mind-set of the managers, change the numbers they're reading. This cheating is seldom for direct personal gain, and in systems where all humanity hasn't been leached out by bad management, is often altruistic—defending those under you against management targets.

Take a senior executive at Canberra Hospital—vilified for doctoring numbers, but actually a true heroine. The Australian National Emergency Access Target (NEAT) set an entirely arbitrary target that "90%" of patients should be seen and sent out of Emergency Departments within four hours. It's clearly important that patient assessment should be timely,[17] but setting an arbitrary target with inadequate resources is just the Red Bead Game, writ large. A quote[18]:

> *"I did not alter the EDIS data with any thought of personal or financial gain. I foolishly and stupidly did it in an attempt to protect myself and the staff who I work with. It is as simple, and as complicated, as that."*

The terror of dysfunctional systems is that—as here—participants often end up blaming themselves. If we're to speculate about Semmelweis' decline, it may be more reasonable to see this as a manifestation of institutional persecution than personal flaws.

Managers who don't 'get' the Red Bead Game often cherish a deep misunderstanding of statistics as well. "League tables" are an endemic problem,[19] but perhaps the most crippling manifestation of managerial ignorance is the "before and after" study. A measurement is made, something is done (often an exhortation to greater productivity, a rousing speech or campaign of posters) and then a second measurement is made. Tests of 'significance' may be applied. Then, if the two numbers differ sufficiently and well, success is announced. Usually, the change is due to common cause variation. Even a 'real' change is not sustained, once the heat is off.

The Red Bead Game shows how little control participants have. Managers too are constrained. In healthcare, whole institutions or even arms of government may be similarly bound to fail. Deming said that about 95% of behaviour is conditioned by the system. In this lesson, I've shown how even simple measurements are an antidote to the poison just described. Properly interpreted, the numbers are eloquent. Good measurements will reveal stability, common cause variation, special causes and process change.

---

[17] See PubMed 27169971 for some impressive statistical legerdemain, and PubMed 29032791 [18] An exhaustive analysis is available at audit.act.gov.au/__data/assets/pdf_file/0014/1205330/ Report-6-2012-Emergency_-Department_Performance_Information.pdf [19] For a brilliant deconstruction, see the classic paper by Goldstein & Spiegelhalter. www.jstor.org/stable/2983325?seq=1. Then read the brain-dead health-sector commentary starting on page 409, and weep for the UK public health system.

A topical example

Visit your local hospital. See the posters exhorting hand hygiene. They don't work. See the dispensers of 70% alcohol spread liberally around—sometimes at *every* convenient point. Then look more carefully and see the chaos: empty dispensers that should be full, dispensers to the left, dispensers to the right, dispensers all over. The dispensers were installed at points convenient for the installers, with little thought given to the user. There is no clear plan for managing *processes* — acquisition, use and disposal of handrub and dispensers.

Speak to the staff. Someone in management decided that because hand hygiene is failing, "targets must be set". These are *more* onerous and based on far less evidence—perhaps the "5 moments". Staff are now chastised more. Their failures are lamented. The supplier then changed, and the brackets no longer fit the dispensers.

To understand why clinicians still fail to sanitise their hands well, one and a half centuries after Semmelweis, listen to Deming, and look at the processes. To fix things, fix these—after listening to concerned clinicians on the floor.

These observations are very general. Entire countries can and do behave badly. For example in the Blair years, much of the UK was run by setting empiric targets—targets that included "world peace" and "birdsong in the countryside", but also a multiplicity of healthcare targets. Responses and behaviour were predictable[20]—google the Francis Inquiry for an example. A focus on achieving targets compromises quality. Similar evils ultimately destroyed the USSR.

In contrast, the Japanese established the Deming prize in 1951 as a tribute to the man who helped transform their broken post-war economy. You now go to Japan to learn, but take away dry mechanisms of statistical process control, bereft of human context. People count! What they're made to do counts—whether they're manufacturing machinery or eradicating infections. You too can count. Count *well*, and you can see when and why things fail—and start to fix things. Heck, I'm just a virus, and even I can see this.

Lesson #3

Some processes are engineered to fail—conditioning and binding everyone.

To fix things, fix the processes.

[20] citeseerx.ist.psu.edu/viewdoc/download?doi=10.1.1.454.2524&rep=rep1&type=pdf

⊛ Lesson 4

What is God Thinking?

"Good mathematicians see analogies between theorems, great mathematicians see analogies between analogies"

S Banach (as quoted by S Ulam, 1957)

The Sacred Way still connects Athens and the ancient town of Eleusis. Initiation into the *Eleusinian Mysteries* promised immortality to those who petitioned the fertility goddess Demeter. Her daughter Persephone was abducted and tricked by Hades into eating four pomegranate seeds while in Hell; every winter she must return.

Perhaps it is appropriate that Eleusis is also the birthplace of dramatic tragedy. Today, you can catch a bus from Athens to Eleusis,[1] but you won't find surviving worshippers of Demeter there. The town now boasts the largest oil refinery in Greece.

The best thing about being a nanny in Athens is the people, multiple nationalities united by a desire to improve their children's English. Playing games is a good strategy here. Stuck with a number of bored pre-teens? You can do worse than *Eleusis Express.*

[1] The wheels on the bus go Brekekekéx-koáx-koáx.

You'll need two standard packs of playing cards (104 cards) and somewhere you can write down a secret—pen & paper, or a smartphone. The object is to ***discard all of your cards***, but here's the kicker—*you don't know the rules.* All you know is the commandments (meta-rules).

That's not strictly true. God knows. You see, the first commandment is: Choose god from among the players. God writes down a secret sentence that describes rules that *relate to the cards and their play*, for example "Red cards must be followed by an even card, black by odd", perhaps with the addition that A=1, JQK=11, 12, 13. It's clear that judgement is important here—god can lose friends rapidly if the rules are too obscure.

Every other player then gets 12 cards; god places a random card face-up on the table, and you agree on the order of play. Each player in turn plays a card to the right of the most recent valid card, until someone wins. With each play, god (who can't lie) says 'legal' or 'no'. If the card is not legal, it's moved to the *discard line* below the last legal card—still visible—and the sinner who played is given a penalty of two extra cards from the pack. After each valid play you get to guess the rule, ending the round if you guess correctly.

That's almost that, but there are a few extra commandments.[2] If you have now worked out that you don't have a legal card to play, you can say "I repent" and hand your cards to god, who shows the cards to everyone. He/she will then decide if you're right—if you are, your cards go back into the pack, and you get given new cards—but

[2]If you're feeling more adventurous, you may wish to try the original *Eleusis*. Like life, it's a bit more complex. Players get 14 cards; you can play any number of cards at a time, and if any single played card is invalid, god says 'no'—*without telling you which card is invalid.* All invalid cards are moved to the discard line, overlapping slightly, with a penalty of two cards for every card played. A correct repentance is rewarded with four fewer cards, or punished with five extra cards. You also need three red poker chips ('god tokens') and two blue chips ('prophet tokens'). God plays a god token on every tenth card, and after 3 tokens, sudden death starts—sinners get two cards for an illegal play and are eliminated. There are also prophets—if you think you've worked out the hidden rule, without saying the rule you can declare yourself a prophet *immediately after* playing a card, even if it's turned out not to be legal: a prophet puts down their cards and temporarily takes over the duties of god—until they make a bad call. A prophet who makes the wrong call is an *outcast*, and cannot again become a prophet for this round. An outcast immediately gets five extra cards, and otherwise becomes an ordinary player again; nobody can suffer from a prophet's bad call apart from the prophet. Scoring is also more complex: each player counts cards, and the *high count* is the greatest number. To work out your score, subtract your count from the high count—so the unfortunate with the highest count gets zero! As an added bonus, the person with a score of zero gets four *extra* points. If you're a prophet when the game ends, you profit mightily: one point for every correct card played after you took over, and *two points* for every incorrect card played. And what of god? By default, god gets the high count; but if there is a prophet, count the number of cards up to the prophet marker, double this, and this is god's score, unless it's greater than the high count.

one card less. If you're wrong, god picks out a legal card and puts it down—handing you back your cards with an extra card from the pack.

Play repeats until everyone has had a chance to play god—a democratic theocracy. Scoring isn't important but if you want to, count your remaining cards and subtract the number from 12. Correctly guessing the rule gives you 6 extra points, and if you have no cards left, your bonus is 3 points. Highest total at the end wins.

Trouble with induction

Eleusis demonstrates *inductive reasoning*—given observed findings, how do we work backwards to find "the rules"? This is rather like life, and like life, there's a catch. Assume that an ace represents 1, and jack, queen and king are 11, 12 and 13. Let's say the following cards are valid: 3,5,7,11 and 13; but god says 'no' to 4,6,8,10 and 12. What is the rule? It's clear that there are several possibilities—the rule might be "Prime numbers", "Odd numbers", or even "Numbers that contain odd digits only".

We can test among these hypotheses. For example, if we play an ace or a nine and this is valid, then we can reject primes; but we can never distinguish between the other two. There is also an *infinity* of other possibilities—for example a cruel god might say "Odd numbers except where the card before the last card is a jack", or any number of other arbitrary modifications.[3]

The philosopher David Hume pointed this out in 1739, in *A Treatise on Human Nature.* If a scientist tries to describe natural phenomena—tries to peek behind the scenes to establish 'rules'—no matter how many times she's tried, there's always a chance that the next time, an exception might pop up that refutes a given rule. In real life, things are even more tricky than Eleusis, as there's often a lot of 'random' variation going on—the common cause variation we saw in the last lesson.

In Lesson 5 I'll show how good science effectively solves Hume's "problem of induction", but first let's explore how inductive reasoning works. You see, there's something remarkable here. It's how *well* your human brains manage to do inductive reasoning—as shown by Eleusis, or indeed when people do science well. Induction works. You can get results—and even perhaps agree on a winner. Some strategies may work better than others; luck may be involved; certainty isn't guaranteed. There are several levels of reasoning here:

(1) Hidden rules that produce the numbers we observe;
(2) Rules about how to go about exploring the rules (meta-rules);
(3) There's even the possibility that humans might think about, question and manipulate the meta-rules (meta-meta-rules). In Eleusis, can you run out of cards? What happens then?

[3]For numeric examples, choose a sequence and type it into oeis.org/

Maths	English
$P(x)$	"The probability of x"
$C\|T$	"C, given that T"
$+, \times$	"added to", "multiplied by"
$\neg$	"not"
$\frac{a}{b}$	"a divided by b"
$=$	"is"
$\approx$	"is about"
$n!$	"n factorial" (explained below)
e	Euler's number, about 2.71828
ln	The *natural* logarithm (base e)
$T \cap C$	The intersection between T and C

Table 4. A maths toolbox ("translation guide")

A key

This lesson is built around language—a tiny part of the language of mathematics. Humans used to believe that the ability to acquire language is an intuitive, almost magical attribute of childhood, and that adult brains are no longer plastic. This is largely wrong. As Benny Lewis[4] has pointed out, success at a new language is more about attitude, engagement and the will to persevere in the face of inevitable setbacks than having some magical talent that evaporates as you age. Belief that you *can* succeed helps, as does play. Let's play a bit.

The good news is that young children automatically have the hang of the maths behind inductive reasoning. This does seem to be built in. The catch is, we'll try to do formally what they do intuitively. With a little persistence, getting a feel for the language shouldn't be too much of an issue.

Glance at Table 4 – a simple translation guide. If you take n and multiply it by $n-1$ and then by $n-2$ and so on all the way down to 1, i.e. $n \times (n-1) \times (n-2) \times \ldots \times 3 \times 2 \times 1$, this is "$n$ factorial". The only really tricky item is $P(x)$ – this is *defined* to be a number between zero and one, where 0 means "ruled out" and 1 means "certain". Think zero percent likely vs 100% certain. I'll deal with the intersection $\cap$ between two sets T and C later, when we plunge into Bayes theorem.

[4]Something of an Internet sensation—after he flunked out at Spanish, he sat and thought about this, and developed a new philosophy of diving in and making mistakes, rather than waiting to be "good enough" to converse with native-speakers.

Nanny's Choice

A common question in statistics is "How many ways can I choose k items from a larger group of n items, all at the same time, and without any regard for the order of choice." It helps if I label these otherwise unremarkable beads, so perhaps I'll call them Ashraf, Ilir, Abdelmajid, Joan, and so on—I'll need n names, one for each bead.

As a practical example, if I have 800 white beads (n=800) and want to choose 50 (k=50), I'll have 800 choices for the first of the 50 beads. Having chosen the first, there will be 799 choices for the next, 798 for the next and so on, down to 751, for the last of the chosen beads.

So it would seem that I have $800 \times 799 \times \ldots \times 752 \times 751$ distinct choices. Using the $n!$ tool from our toolbox, this works out to:

$$800 \times 799 \times \ldots \times 752 \times 751 = \frac{800!}{750!} = \frac{n!}{(n-k)!}$$

There is however a catch. I don't care about the order of choice, so I might, for example choose Ashraf first but this isn't a *distinct* choice from choosing Ashraf at any other time, provided all 50 beads have the same names.

Order doesn't count. So we need to divide our calculation by $k!$ – the number of ways we can arrange our 50 chosen beads. A shorthand for the whole calculation is:

$$\binom{n}{k} = \frac{n!}{k!\,(n-k!)}$$

A 'Binomial coefficient', the terse $\binom{n}{k}$ is read "n choose k".

What are the odds?

Traditionally, statisticians have concentrated on fairly easy – and rather boring – probability problems like this: *knowing* the number of red and white beads in a container, and sampling 50 beads at a time, what are the chances of getting three or fewer red beads? This example is just Deming's Red Bead Game from Lesson 3.

Let's work the chances from first principles, just to get a feel for the maths. We have a tub of (say) $N = 1000$ beads: 800 white beads and 200 red beads. To get 3 or fewer reds, we need to get zero, one, two or three—so let's work out the likelihood of each, and add these up.

What is the likelihood of getting all white beads? Using the box above, it's clear that there are $\begin{pmatrix} 1000 \\ 50 \end{pmatrix}$ ways to choose 50 beads from 1000 and $\begin{pmatrix} 800 \\ 50 \end{pmatrix}$ ways to choose 50 *white* beads from 800. Their ratio is then:

$$\frac{\begin{pmatrix} 800 \\ 50 \end{pmatrix}}{\begin{pmatrix} 1000 \\ 50 \end{pmatrix}} = \frac{\frac{800!}{\cancel{50!} \times 750!}}{\frac{1000!}{\cancel{50!} \times 950!}} = \frac{800!}{750!} \times \frac{950!}{1000!}$$

Large numbers, but even your Windows 10 desktop calculator will give you a result of 0.000010, or just 1 in 100,000. Languages like R have simple commands that do the same calculation by saying something like `choose(800,50)/choose(1000,50)`.[5]

We're still not done, because we next need to do something similar for 1, 2 and 3 red beads. Let's try just one red bead. We choose just one red bead from 200, i.e. $\begin{pmatrix} 200 \\ 1 \end{pmatrix}$ and then the remaining 49 from 800. The denominator is the same. We say:

$$\frac{\begin{pmatrix} 200 \\ 1 \end{pmatrix} \times \begin{pmatrix} 800 \\ 49 \end{pmatrix}}{\begin{pmatrix} 1000 \\ 50 \end{pmatrix}}$$

This is 0.000138; for two beads a similar calculation gives 0.000896, and finally for three we get 0.003771. Adding these up gives about 0.00481. In Deming's Red Bead Game, the chances of getting three or fewer red beads were less than 1:200. The process was engineered to produce the bright red pomegranate seeds of failure.

Probability—backwards

Imagine that you know nothing of Deming's Red Bead Game. You're stuck in a room somewhere—with a pen and paper—and intermittently, someone delivers a box of beads to your door. Bored, you count the reds and whites, and give the box back. Every now and then, the person returns with another box of beads.

---

[5] Another way is to use some maths trickery (Stirling's formula) which says that: $\ln(n!) \approx \frac{1}{2}(\ln 2 + \ln \pi) + \frac{1}{2} \ln n + n \times (\ln n - 1)$ This looks complex, but allows us to calculate more easily, especially with a computer: in most languages it's easy to turn the right-hand side into a function called – let me think – stirling(), and then, as we're dealing with logarithms, say stirling (800) – stirling (750) + stirling (950) – stirling (1000). Raising e to the power of the value returned—this reverses the logarithm—gives you the same result: 1.038×10^{-5}.

You start to get a feel for what's happening—there are always 50 beads; there are always more white beads than red beads; the ratio of red:white varies; patterns start to appear.

You now ask yourself "What sort of process might be producing these patterns?" You start speculating about a device that somehow selects 50 beads at a time. You observe that there is no secular trend—no change in the proportion of beads over time. To you, this suggests that the beads you return are being replaced. (You may sneakily mark some of the beads, and see whether they come back).

You are now dealing with "inverse probability"—otherwise known as "the inverse problem" , "induction" or even, a bit more stuffily, "inferential statistics". This is like Eleusis, and like real life. As with Eleusis, you can never be sure of a particular rule, but unlike Eleusis, you have no opportunity to ask "the designer" precisely what the rules are. Despite uncertainty you can still guess, test your guesses, and perhaps even have a stab at changing the rules.

An issue is that for every set of observations, there's an infinity of possible questions, and an infinity of possible explanatory hypotheses. How can you impose some sense on this variety? A large part of the answer is wrapped up in Bayes' theorem. Who was Thomas Bayes?

The naming of parts

Thomas Bayes was a somewhat nonconformist Presbyterian minister with a part-time interest in mathematics. He published just two books in his lifetime. The first was on Divine Benevolence; the second defended Sir Isaac Newton against his critics. Neither is relevant to our enquiry, but he also published a short paper with the uninspiring title "An Essay towards solving a Problem in the Doctrine of Chances". This was a zinger, precisely because it provides a general solution to the problem of inverse probability.[6] His equation can initially be quite intimidating:

$$P(C|T) = \frac{P(T|C) \times P(C)}{P(T)}$$

To confuse you, the interesting people we'll meet in Lesson 5, people who love naming and classifying, have taken Bayes' equation and labelled the various bits:

$P(C)$: is the 'prior probability',
$P(T|C)$: the likelihood, and
$P(C|T)$: the 'posterior probability'.
$P(T)$: There's even a name for this, the 'normalizing constant'.

[6] Technically, Bayes didn't actually formulate what is now described as "his theorem" but the basics are all there.

Yet more confusing is the 'expansion' of $P(T)$, which initially doesn't seem to make much sense. So let's take a different tack—we'll play a bit. (Absolutely terrified by the maths? Skip to page 63).

Coronavirus Sudoku

Imagine that on 30 June 2020 you test the entire population of the United States for my presence. The problem is that you don't know how many cases you'll find, so let's *play* with the numbers, just to get a feel for things. Together we will use just four pieces of information—several of which may be wildly off; this is just an exercise. The first is a US population of about 331.003 million; the second is the alleged number of active cases on that day—about 1.432 million, according to worldometers.info; and the third is that just 65% of people with coronavirus have a positive test.[7] Finally we will assume that just one in a thousand tests represent a "false positive". We can now construct a table, initially with some missing values.

USA	Test			
COVID-19		Positive	Negative	
	Present	1.432M	a	
	Absent	b	c	d
				331.003M

Can you see how to fill in the empty cells? Now's the time to take your own piece of paper, construct this table, and give it your best shot.[8]

[7]This number is debated. Without getting too bogged down, it's important to distinguish between analytic sensitivity, and clinical sensitivity. Analytic sensitivity is where you *know* that a sample has e.g. a virus in it, and you measure what percentage of truly positive samples come up positive with a given test. Clinical sensitivity is where you know that the patient has the disease, take a sample, and then determine whether it's positive. If you spike a sputum sample with SARS-Cov-2 and then test it, many RT-PCR tests will be positive over 95% of the time. But as suggested in Lesson 1, this doesn't account for inhibitors being present in the sample, or the virus not being present in a clinical sample because it was taken from the wrong place at the wrong time. You have lots of data on the analytic sensitivity of RT-PCR tests for COVID-19, and very few of clinical sensitivity; the data for the latter suggest a sensitivity of about 60–70%, although if all cases present early on in the disease, and good-quality (very uncomfortable) swabs are taken from the turbinates in the nose, this may be greater. With the knowledge you acquire in this lesson, you can easily adjust for different values.

[8]Whenever I pick up a piece of paper—and in any case coronaviruses have a healthy respect for paper—I think of the superlative mathematician Srinivasa Ramanujan, who was so dirt poor that he only committed his discoveries to paper when he was sure. His methods are lost, because he erased them from his slate without transcribing them.

First, if there are 35 false negative cases for every 65 positives, then the number of false negatives in cell a is $1.432 \times \frac{35}{65}$ million, or about 771 thousand. Next work out the total number of cases: $1.432 + 0.771 = 2.203$ million. Subtracting this from the total population, you get $d = 328.800$ million without the disease. How many of these would have false-positive tests if you were to test the lot? Rounding, just 329 thousand go into cell b. All of the boxes are now filled in, including the totals in bold, on the margins:

USA	Test			
		Positive	Negative	
COVID-19	Present	1.432M	0.771M	**2.203M**
	Absent	0.329M	328.471M	**328.800M**
		1.761M	**329.242M**	331.003M

Finally, use a calculator[9] to turn this table into "fractions of one"...

USA	Test			
		Positive	Negative	
COVID-19	Present	0.004326	0.002330	**0.006656**
	Absent	0.000993	0.992350	**0.993344**
		0.005320	**0.994680**	1

This last table may not look like much, but you'll find that despite the fiddly little numbers, making things a bit more abstract is useful. It's nice to think in terms of $P(x)$, where x is a value between 0 and 1.

For those who prefer diagrams, Fig 11 shows another way to visualise the same data, with both numbers and fractions filled in. The central section labelled "T∩C" represents the intersection between two sets: positive tests (T) and those with coronavirus (C). We will use this diagram to ask a simple question: "Given that a test is positive, what are the chances that coronavirus infection is present?"

[9]Divide everything by 331.003M

From the diagram—or indeed the table—the answer is easy. The chance of infection *given* a positive test $P(C|T)$ is the value in the central intersection divided by all of the positive tests. You can say this many ways, all equivalent:

$$P(C|T) = \frac{P(T \cap C)}{P(T)} = \frac{0.004326}{0.005320} = \frac{1.432M}{1.761M} \approx 0.813 = 81.3\%$$

Even with infection pretty prevalent, a positive test only tells you with about 80% confidence that I'm there. Try working carefully through every symbol in the above, using the translation key in Table 4. This will stand you in good stead. Moving away from illustration to real life, you'll find that using $P(x)$ is often a bit smarter than using "illustrative numbers", and to do so effectively, it's wise to appreciate each of the above terms. Concentrate on $P(C|T)$, the probability that C is true, *given that* T is true.

Bayes

Let's generalise. Take the equation from above[10]:

$$P(C|T) = \frac{P(T \cap C)}{P(T)} \tag{1}$$

... and swap every T and C:

$$P(T|C) = \frac{P(C \cap T)}{P(C)}$$

This is perfectly legal.[11] Next, multiply the second equation by $P(C)$ to get:

$$P(C \cap T) = P(T|C) \times P(C)$$

Because the intersection of C and T is clearly just the same as the intersection of T and C, you can now substitute the value for $P(C \cap T)$ into Equation 1, and Bayes equation just pops out! Here it is:

$$P(C|T) = \frac{P(T|C) \times P(C)}{P(T)} \tag{2}$$

---

[10]It's formal name is "the Kolmogorov definition of Conditional Probability" [11]They're just symbols.

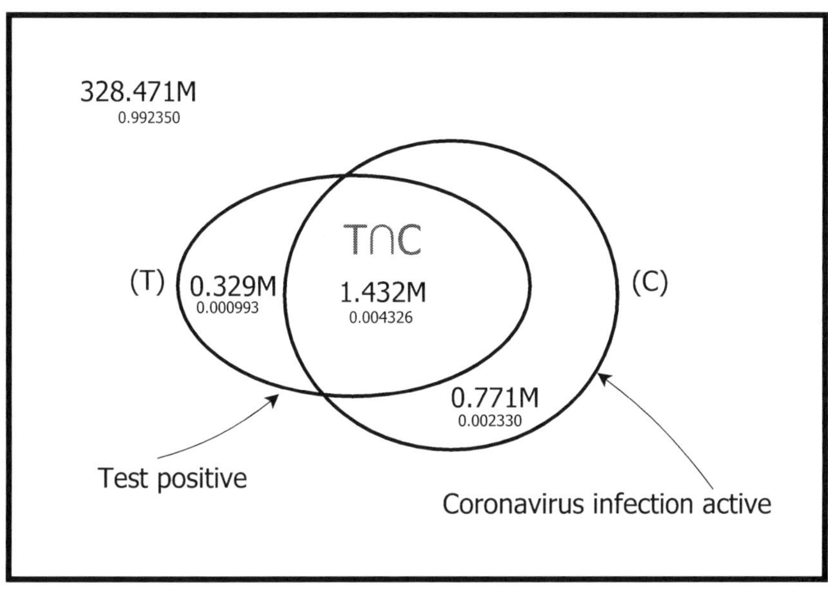

Figure 11. Testing & Infection as sets

Use Table 4 to translate the equation into English and get a feel for Bayes':

> ***The probability (0...1) that someone has coronavirus given that the PCR test is positive*** *is* "the probability that the PCR test is positive given that they have coronavirus" *multiplied by* the probability of coronavirus being present in the community as a whole and *divided by* the probability of a PCR test being positive in the community.

Bayes' is an extraordinarily powerful equation, because *it allows us to do induction.* At first, it may seem a bit of a bother, but given three things, you can "work backwards" to determine the significance of a test. You can answer questions like "Given that a test is positive, what are the chances that coronavirus infection is present?" or "Given a positive scan, what are the chances that cancer is present?" and much more besides.

Whenever you use Bayes, you can see that three things are needed:

$P(T|C)$ The chances of a test being positive, given the condition is present.

$P(C)$ How common the condition is in the community.

$P(T)$ How common a positive test is in the community.

Nanny's $P(T)$

Confronting the dreaded "normalizing constant" $P(T)$ turns out to be less nasty than anticipated. You can see that to get "all the positives", add the true positives and the false positives. In our example above, we can just add 0.004326+0.000993, about 0.00532. More generally:

(1) To get true positives, multiply the chances of a test being positive by the proportion of those in the community who are infected: $P(T|C) \times P(C)$

(2) To get the false positives, multiply the chances of a test being positive in uninfected people by *their* proportion. To express this mathematically, go back to Table 4. Seeing that $\neg$ means "not", we say $P(T|\neg C) \times P(\neg C)$. Exactly the same is to say $P(T|\neg C) \times (1 - P(C))$.

(3) Just add up the two:

$$P(T) = P(T|C) \times P(C) + P(T|\neg C) \times (1 - P(C))$$

Worked examples

Recapping, $P(T|C)$ is 0.65, and $P(C)$ is 0.0067 (2.2 million active cases in 331 million). Let's be quite explicit about the still-slightly-mysterious normalising constant $P(T)$. One in a thousand tests are false-positive—0.001. Just use Nanny's $P(T)$ from above:

$$P(T) = P(T|C) \times P(C) + P(T|\neg C) \times (1 - P(C)) = 0.65 \times 0.00666 + 0.001 \times (1 - 0.00666)$$

This works out to 0.00532. Finally, plugging these into Bayes' equation:

$$\begin{aligned} P(C|T) &= \frac{P(T|C) \times P(C)}{P(T)} \\ P(C|T) &= \frac{0.65 \times 0.00666}{0.00532} \\ &\approx 0.813 \end{aligned}$$

It works! Let's drop the community prevalence to about one tenth of the original value, say $P(C) = 0.0007$. Now, how do we interpret a positive test?

$$
\begin{aligned}
P(C|T) &= \frac{P(T|C) \times P(C)}{P(T|C) \times P(C) + P(T|\neg C) \times (1 - P(C))} \\
P(C|T) &= \frac{0.65 \times 0.0007}{0.65 \times 0.0007 + 0.001 \times (1 - 0.0007)} \\
&\approx 0.313
\end{aligned}
$$

With a lower prevalence, we're just 31% sure that a positive test actually represents infection. What happens if the community prevalence drops to just 1:10,000 — 0.0001? Easy:

$$
\begin{aligned}
P(C|T) &= \frac{P(T|C) \times P(C)}{P(T|C) \times P(C) + P(T|\neg C) \times (1 - P(C))} \\
P(C|T) &= \frac{0.65 \times 0.0001}{0.65 \times 0.0001 + 0.001 \times (1 - 0.0001)} \\
&\approx 0.061
\end{aligned}
$$

Now we're just 6% sure the "positive" is true! What if there's a better test, so the false positive rate drops tenfold? What if you can improve your swabbing technique, test earlier, and focus on the site of infection, so that the sensitivity of the test increases from 0.65 to 0.9? Bayes has the answers—simply plug in the numbers.

But what are the odds?

Look at Bayes' theorem again:

$$P(C|T) = \frac{P(T|C) \times P(C)}{P(T)}$$

Despite our playing, it's still a bit intimidating. The good news is that we can simplify, removing that irritating normalizing constant, $P(T)$. Take Bayes rule once more and for every C, substitute $\neg C$. In other words if C means "has COVID-19" then $\neg C$ means "doesn't have COVID-19":

$$P(\neg C|T) = \frac{P(T|\neg C) \times P(\neg C)}{P(T)} \tag{3}$$

Provided $P(\neg C|T)$ isn't zero, take the original equation and divide it by the new one:

$$\frac{P(C|T)}{P(\neg C|T)} = \frac{P(T|C)}{P(T|\neg C)} \times \frac{P(C)}{P(\neg C)} \tag{4}$$

That pesky $P(T)$ cancels out. This equation simply says:

posterior odds = likelihood ratio × prior odds

Burn this into your soul! The three parts are:

(1) The posterior odds $\frac{P(C|T)}{P(\neg C|T)}$ — what we want;

(2) The likelihood ratio $\frac{P(T|C)}{P(T|\neg C)}$ — representing new information;

(3) The prior odds $\frac{P(C)}{P(\neg C)}$ — what we have already.

Although you can again use Table 4 to translate, this may still seem a bit abstract, so it seems wise to try something concrete. But before we do, a key idea: this equation allows you to do *joined-up thinking!* You can adjust your prior odds (The odds you currently believe) to accommodate new information (expressed as the likelihood ratio). This gives new odds, the *posterior* odds. Later, with a new likelihood ratio, you might again update your odds...and so on, for ever. You can integrate information.

Let's re-visit the first scenario, using odds. From 2.2 million cases in 331 million people we work out prior odds of $\frac{2.2}{328.8}$ or about 1:150; the likelihood ratio is the likelihood of a positive test given the disease divided by the likelihood of a false positive, $\frac{0.65}{0.001}$ or 650:1. What are the posterior odds? Easy peasy:

$$\begin{aligned}\text{posterior odds} &= \text{likelihood ratio} \times \text{prior odds} \\ &= \frac{650}{1} \times \frac{1}{150} \\ &\approx 4.33\end{aligned}$$

Using Nanny's odds-to-probability box below, we can convert $\frac{650}{150}$ to obtain the same answer as before—about 81%. Finally, after much travail, we have an easy way to adjust our prior odds. All you need is a likelihood ratio, and Blam! The posterior odds just pop out.

Nanny's odds-to-probability

If you're a bit puzzled by 'odds' versus probability, here's how to convert between the two. For an odds ratio of $x : y$, the corresponding probability is easily calculated:

$$P(C|T) = \frac{x}{x+y}$$

For example, if the odds are 2:1 in favour of rain, this translates to a two in three (66.6%) chance of rain. Add the two values to make a denominator.

An unexpected "No!"

Consider the case where a doctor is 95% sure that someone has COVID-19—and test indeed comes back positive. As:

$$\text{posterior odds} = \text{likelihood ratio} \times \text{prior odds}$$

... we just plug in the values. The LR is 650:1, so we say:

$$\frac{650}{1} \times \frac{19}{1}$$

A magnificent value of 12350:1. We can easily translate this into a probability: $\frac{12350}{12351}$ or 99.99% certain that this is COVID-19. Hooray!

But what about a *negative* test here? Substituting $\neg T$ for T in Equation 4 we get:

$$\frac{P(C|\neg T)}{P(\neg C|\neg T)} = \frac{P(\neg T|C)}{P(\neg T|\neg C)} \times \frac{P(C)}{P(\neg C)}$$

That's a helluva lot of $\neg$s. What does this mean? The left-hand side is what we want, it's just the posterior odds. The rightmost term is unchanged, so we're only interested in the middle term. Translating back into English, "The chances of a negative test, given that coronavirus is present (35 %), divided by the chances of a negative test, given that coronavirus is *not* present (99.9 %)". Aha! We can now work out the odds:

$$\frac{0.35}{0.999} \times \frac{19}{1} \approx 6.657$$

Odds of nearly 7:1 that the patient *still has* COVID-19! The negative test has failed to convince us, as we are still—work it out—87% sure that the patient has the disease. A

Normalising revisited

Previously we worked out the normalising constant for "disease or no disease". But what if there are more than two options? Let's say there are three: A, B and C. Then our formula for the normalizing constant becomes:

$$P(T) = P(T|A) \times P(A) + P(T|B) \times P(B) + P(T|C) \times P(C) \quad (5)$$

For each option we just multiply the fraction who will test positive by the proportion who fit into the box labelled with that option—and add up the lot. Shorthand for this is:

$$\sum_{i=1}^{n} P(T|i) \times P(i)$$

This looks scary but is easily translated: "For every value of i from 1 to n, add up the product of two things, the chances that the test will be positive for option i, and the prevalence of option i in the population. Σ is just "the sum", and everything else can be worked out using Table 4.

single test did not sway the odds much, based on the numbers. This is why you'll sometimes see sensible doctors saying things like "I don't trust that test. Let's do another one—or let's look at this in a different way".

A game show

Let's test our Bayesian skills. Marilyn vos Savant first achieved fame by being listed in the Guinness Book of World Records as having "The World's Highest IQ",[12] this landing her a job with *Parade* magazine. Her popular column "Ask Marilyn" however took on a slightly nasty turn when she answered a problem about odds.

Here's the scenario, now often called the "Monty Hall problem" after the famous game-show host:

> *You're in a game show. There are three doors. Behind one is a swanky car—let's update it to a Tesla roadster 2020, which does 0–100 km/h in 1.9 seconds. Cool! Behind the other two doors are goats. Goat or Tesla? You first choose a door: if the car is behind it, you've won.*

[12]Something she'd later go on to disparage.

> *As he always does, with solemn ceremony the host now opens one of the other doors to reveal—of course—a goat; he then offers you a choice. You can either keep your door or switch to the other door.*

Should you switch? Does it even matter? In response to Marilyn's answer—"Switch!"—the magazine received a flurry of nearly 10,000 letters, almost all of which pointed out how obviously wrong she was. The signature on nearly one thousand of these had "PhD" appended. Here's a typical sample:

> You blew it, and you blew it big! Since you seem to have difficulty grasping the basic principle at work here, I'll explain. After the host reveals a goat, you now have a one-in-two chance of being correct. Whether you change your selection or not, the odds are the same. There is enough mathematical illiteracy in this country, and we don't need the world's highest IQ propagating more. Shame!
>
> Scott Smith, PhD. University of Florida.

Similar comments were rude about her intellect, and mansplained that "Maybe women look at math problems differently than men". The tiny problem with all of this criticism is that it's wrong. This is not a matter of 'negotiation' or 'misinterpretation'. There are at least three ways we can show Marilyn is correct. These are (1) a simple argument; (2) a Bayesian calculation; and (3) Monte-Carlo simulation.

The Bayesian argument is quite subtle, so let's work through it first. We'll call our doors A, B and C—you chose A. As you chose at random, $P(A) = P(B) = P(C) = \frac{1}{3}$. Now, assuming the host opens door B to reveal a goat, what are the chances? By Bayes, we want:

$$P(A|B) = \frac{P(B|A) \times P(A)}{P(B)}$$

What are $P(B|A)$ and $P(B)$? $P(B|A)$ – the chance of the host choosing B if you've chosen the car – is easy: the host can pick either door B or C, so it's $\frac{1}{2}$. What about $P(B)$, the normalizing constant? From Equation 5 on page 66:

$$P(B) = P(B|A) \times P(A) + P(B|B) \times P(B) + P(B|C) \times P(C)$$

As the host is not going to spoil the fun by opening the door with the car behind it, $P(B|B)$ is zero, and thus $P(B|C)$ is 1: he takes the other door. Substituting:

$$P(B) = \frac{1}{2} \times \frac{1}{3} + 0 \times \frac{1}{3} + 1 \times \frac{1}{3}$$

We can now find $P(A|B)$:

$$P(A|B) = \frac{\frac{1}{2} \times \frac{1}{3}}{\frac{1}{2}}$$

It's $\frac{1}{3}$. You can repeat the whole exercise for car C, or simply observe that you only have two doors left, so $P(C|B) = \frac{2}{3}$. Marilyn was right.

There's also a simple "non-Bayesian" explanation—but not everyone will 'get' it. Consider the case where there are 50 doors, and 49 goats. The host isn't going to stride up to the door with the car, open it and say "You lose, everyone can bugger off now". He will draw out the suspense. In this case the probability of your success is just $\frac{1}{50}$ and as the doors are progressively opened, this doesn't change—nobody is moving goats and cars around behind the scenes. When you reach the last two doors, the "switch" option improves your chances of success to $\frac{49}{50}$. Similarly for the three doors.

Monte Carlo

The picture at the start of this lesson is a candid photograph of Paul Erdős teaching ten-year-old Terry Tao. Mathematicians proudly talk of their "Erdős number"—if you co-authored a paper with him, your Erdős number is 1; co-authors of these mathematicians have a number of 2; and so on.[13] He is the most prolific mathematician so far, collaborating with over 500 mathematicians to produce more than 1500 papers.

Yet when confronted by the Monty Hall problem, Erdős refused to accept the switch. It didn't make sense to this wide-ranging and smart mathematician. Where does this leave those who are less adept at mathematics?

Fortunately there's yet another way to model such problems—one that also convinced Paul. Modern computers are powerful enough to make it simple:

(1) Generate a large, random set of doors, with a car behind just one of the three;
(2) Get the 'host' to act, based on the "rules of the game"—he won't ruin the surprise;
(3) Have your contestant either (a) hold or (b) switch. See how often they win.

Using the R code in Appendix A you can run this simulation for one hundred or even a million such games, just by saying `corona_monty()`. This approach is a trivial example of a Monte Carlo simulation—so named because it has that random or 'gambling' element so beloved of Bayesians. Again, Marilyn was right. Still unconvinced? Work carefully through the above logic, or even write your own program. You'll get there.[14]

[13]Tao is now a remarkable mathematician himself—likely the most wide-ranging and successful living mathematician, described as "the Mozart of Maths", but with a far more pleasant disposition. Erdős number of 2.

[14]Provided you keep an open mind—updating your priors. Out on the Internet, there are still PhDs smarting about Marilyn, and rationalising that they were 'right'.

Bayes' nets

Wherever there's a brain at work, it will need to solve "inverse problems". Take vision. From a flat image projected onto the back of the eye, you extract data and build an internal model of things moving in three dimensions. The smart psychologist Alison Gopnik draws a good analogy between this ability, and how the brain pulls out causal 'rules' from its environment. Again, brains translate observations into models.

You've already encountered this sort of thinking at work. After reading about the death of his friend, Dr Semmelweis generates a causal hypothesis from his observations. He tests this hypothesis, and it works—this doesn't *prove* his hypothesis, but is useful.[15] You see people dying from COVID-19 and speculate how you might intervene to stop the deaths. You need causal models—they are central to Good Science. A relevant question therefore is "How old are people before they start making and using causal models?"

In 2004, Gopnik provided a solid—and rather surprising—answer. Before we get to her answer, we however need to understand the question. Her hypothesis is that children "construct nonegocentric, abstract, coherent, learned representations of causal relations among events, and these representations allow them to make causal predictions and anticipate the effects of interventions". By nonegocentric, she means that a response (and the underlying, imputed model) is abstract and not just a stimulus-response effect, like Pavlov's dogs salivating in response to a bell; the word 'coherent' similarly implies that relationships in the model can be generalised—similar to how, once a rat has learnt the layout of a maze, it can make new inferences about objects in the maze.

To understand Gopnik's work, we need a consistent way to describe causality. As Judea Pearl has shown so well,[16] this cannot be simply at the level of association—if rain is associated with clouds, this doesn't tell you whether clouds cause rain or rain causes clouds. You need to draw in the arrow: clouds $\rightarrow$ rain. This is an extremely simple example of a *directed acyclical graph.*[17] A slightly more complex one might be[18] that in Fig 12.

There are three *nodes* (rain, wet grass, sprinkler; otherwise known as 'vertices') and three *edges.* Arrows describe a 'parent-child' relationship. Rain will wet the grass, but also cause people to turn off their sprinklers. Once you've attached numbers to each of the arrows, you have a *Bayesian network.* The numbers must describe likelihoods

[15] Interestingly enough, one of the main arguments used to oppose Semmelweis was that he hadn't "proved" his hypothesis. In later lessons, we'll discover that such thinking is still common—and still wrong. [16] *The Book of Why*, Basic Books, 2018. [17] These are *directed* because each arrow has a direction, and *acyclical* because you can never have a loop. Causality runs forward in time. [18] en.wikipedia.org/wiki/Bayesian_-network

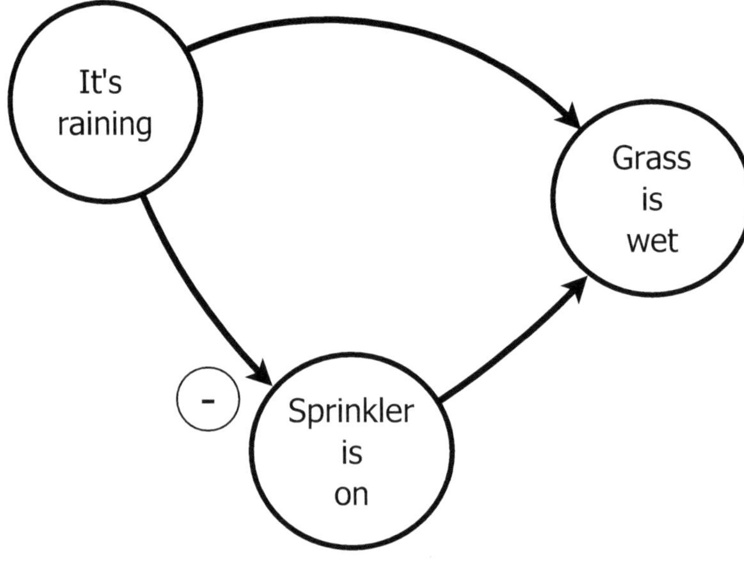

Figure 12. Rain

of certain associations. There's some wiggle room here, for example there may be no guarantee that the sprinkler is off if it's raining—someone may have left it on!

In a Bayesian network there's no direct causal relationship between two nodes if there's no arrow between them. More specifically, the 'Markov assumption' is made—a node doesn't affect nodes that don't descend from it.[19] This is a 'Markov model'.

Blickets

Although the above exploration suggests that children use Bayesian networks in their reasoning, an infinity of other possible models might lurk under the surface. We might also test whether a particular theory holds water in many ways. Given all of these uncertainties, how do we know that a particular explanation is the 'true' one? Well, we don't—just as we don't know that a rule in Eleusis is true until god says it is. Unfortunately, in real life, there's no oracle.

You can however create models, test models, and reject models that don't perform. You may not be a gourmet cook with the perfect recipe, but you can still cook dinner! Think about the three layers here—an inscrutable model (set of rules) that describes how a child thinks; a test designed to examine your interaction with the child's assumed model; and cranking things up a notch, an evaluation of the performance of this test. Using this last layer, you can either accept or reject the idea that your model

[19] More formally, this is often stated as "every node is conditionally independent of its nondescendants, given its parents".

adequately represents how the child responds. In Lesson 5 we'll explore how and why this approach works—and its limitations.

Psychologists have put up multiple different models for causal learning in children. These include classical conditioning; enrichment of innate domain-specific causal schemas; the "causal Rescorla-Wagner (RW) method" based on associative learning; Cheng's "power PC" method that uses parameterized Bayesian networks; constraint-based approaches; and causal Bayes networks. Gopnik explored—and contrasted—these approaches using *blickets*.

A "blicket detector" is a box that lights up and plays music when an object (blicket) is placed on it; something that isn't a blicket gets no response. This allows researchers to present children with a new causal relation—simply by controlling the blicket detector. Experiments using blickets convincingly exclude classical conditioning, simple association, as well as the RW and power PC methods.

These same experiments show how causal Bayes networks explain causal reasoning in children.[20] Even more remarkably, children as young as 30 months old appear to apply Bayesian reasoning when they interact with their environment. This doesn't mean that they are sitting down and rationalising the contents of this lesson. The model simply fits.

In Lesson 5 we'll discover both why any model of causal reasoning in children is still not *true*, and why lack of a 'true' model doesn't matter. We'll also discover why adults often under-perform when confronted by Bayesian tasks.

Lesson #4

Bayes' theorem lets us join up the odds—
even 4-year old children effectively do this

[20]See PubMed 14756583

⊛ Lesson 5

Fire is Hot

'Sheeple', XKCD https://xkcd.com/610/

What the white whale was to Ahab, has been hinted; what, at times, he was to me, as yet remains unsaid.

Herman Melville. *Moby Dick*, Chapter 42.

"Essentially, all models are wrong but some are useful"

Box & Draper. 1987.

Wuhan is a bizarre mix: grand architecture competes with squalid-looking residential blocks; advertisements for liposuction draw your attention away from ancient temples, while electric scooters try to run you down. Visitors flock to the vast Wuhan Science and Technology Museum,[1] and labour up to the top of the Yellow Crane Tower, first built in AD 223 and still providing a glorious view of the Yangtze—pollution permitting.

[1] Closed on Mondays *and* Tuesdays. Always read the fine print.

Yet these same visitors walk right past the lotus sellers on the back streets, and fail to look down at the tactile paving on (almost) every sidewalk. They pack into the Hubei Provincial Museum and goggle at the Sword of Goujian, two-thousand-year-old horse armour, and the giant bronze bells of the Marquis Yue of Zeng, but miss the world's first geocache—a suitcase with the 28 constellations on the lid. The pattern localises it to Hubei, and is accurate enough for scholars to deduce a timestamp: the evening of the third day of the first lunar month in 433 BCE. A propitious time.

Science competes on every corner with ancient ways[2] and modern bling. Perhaps Wuhan is a microcosm of your entire planet. If, as I recently did, you catch a plane from Wuhan Tianhe International Airport Wuhan to ... elsewhere, you can with a degree of confidence expect to arrive at your destination; if you send a text or make a Zoom call, you are a little surprised if it doesn't just work.

Closer to home, you can do an RT-PCR test and pluck me out of somebody's nose. You are surrounded by the successes and side-effects of modern science—but also by ancient baggage and psychobabble. It's not obvious what "science" actually means, nor why it works. In this lesson I'll define science, and tie it to the blickets of the last lesson. To do so, we'll first need to explore some rather murky philosophy, starting with your personal thoughts.

The hunt for the Great White Quale

The weird word 'quale' was gifted to the world in 1866 by the philosopher Charles Sanders Peirce, sometimes called 'America's greatest logician'.[3] It's caused a bit of confusion. Although—as with most philosophy—philosophers have subsequently spent a lot of their time disagreeing on the precise definition of a quale,[4] the general idea is simple. A quale is your internally accessible, *subjective* perception of something. More often, philosophers talk about 'qualia', the plural.

This simple, hard-to-deny idea that people have internal representations of their perceptions has unfortunately resulted in hot debate. One problem is those who mix together their own *theories* about how the mind works, with the perception that is occurring, as if the two are identical.

There are some quite mystical interpretations of qualia. As the Stanford Encyclopedia of Philosophy points out, one school holds that qualia "are held to be physically irreducible events — many philosophers suppose that they have intrinsic, consciously

[2] You may however wish to avoid the Sichuan Niúwā-themed restaurants, even if you're a fan of kimchi.

[3] Peirce is pronounced like 'purse'. A good friend of William James, he unwisely got into the bad books of both Charles W Eliot, the president of Harvard University, and the influential astronomer Simon Newcomb, who had him kicked out of Johns Hopkins. This is a bit sad, as he had a lot of sensible ideas about both maths and science, tempered somewhat by his infatuation with Hegel, ontologies and the number three.

[4] The humour of this statement will only later become apparent.

accessible features that are non-representational and that are solely responsible for their phenomenal character." From the same source, they may even be "*intrinsic, non-physical, ineffable properties*". Can you see where this is going?

Once people start using words like 'ineffable', we're in trouble. Similarly, not all dictionaries agree on precisely what 'ineffable' means, but the gist is "something that cannot be described in words". From having personal, ineffable representations of things to saying "But I'm special, so you can't ever *know* what I'm thinking", is but a short step. You then get pages of philosophical guff about qualia. If you think I'm exaggerating, feel free to consult that Encyclopedia.[5]

Add some noise

Fortunately for us, it's quite easy to show that none of the above debate matters. The value of qualia lies in demonstrating what they are not! Let's explore this.

Can you know something you can't express? The idea behind *ineffable* qualia seems to be that they are known to someone (as an experience) but that this knowledge can't be conveyed in any way to another individual, willingly or involuntarily. The qualia 'just are'.

You are then confronted by two options. The first is that the qualia are "shifting things behind the scenes" but that this shifting is indiscernible to the observer; the second is that with suitable means, you can indeed discern their influence—in which case, they aren't ineffable. How might you distinguish the two?

In teasing out a signal from the noise, you've come a long way since 1948, when Claude Shannon published a paper he initially called "A Mathematical Theory of Communication". When he wised up, he changed its name to ***The*** *Mathematical Theory of Communication.* This is the foundation stone of modern information theory. For those who don't have the time or energy to read all 54 pages—some parts are quite technical—here's a summary in a few paragraphs.

Shannon starts with a problem. How do you trade off the fidelity of a message against the bandwidth? If you've tried to watch high definition TV on a slow Internet connection you've experienced this at first hand.[6]

---

[5] At https://plato.stanford.edu/entries/qualia/. Look around. The literature is confused and confusing, even if you ignore tracts containing the word 'quantum'. For example Searle (PubMed 1692422) produced a brilliant analysis of the issues—but presents a 19th century version of Science. Kemmerer's view that *concepts* don't have qualia is studiously ignored (PubMed 6089087); even Loorits (PubMed 3957492) misses the 'Eleusis problem' that we discussed in Lesson 4, and the solution I'll shortly present. What is the *value* of consciousness? (PubMed 4122207) Can and should lampreys be 'checked for qualia' (PubMed 3790330)?

[6] Especially with the jump in bandwidth consumption you've seen now that I'm wandering the planet.

His big insight is that the *information content* of a message can be represented by the number of possible messages you're selecting your single "true message" from. Consider the case where you know there's just a single message, and you know its content. Even if the content is something seemingly complex like "Thou shalt have no other God before Me!", provided you know that this is the only possible message, the entire transaction can be represented by a single ***bit*** of information—either the message was received (1) or it wasn't (a big round zero).

If there are thousands of possible messages, or millions, you need some way of counting them. Conveniently, you can use the familiar logarithms from Lesson 1. The advantage is that as you add channels, the number of possibilities increases exponentially, but the logarithmic bandwidth can simply be added.

Shannon describes a very general communication system: a *source* of information uses a *transmitter* to move information via a 'channel' to a *receiver* that in turn allows the *destination* to process the information. On the way, noise might however creep in. He then uses the Markov models we first met on page 69—a set of states linked by arrows—to analyse how redundancy affects the transmitted message. The probability of moving to the next state depends on what has gone before. For example, if the message is in English and the current letter is a 'q', its highly likely that the next letter will be a 'u', unless you're eating coq au vin in Iraq.

A new concept is the *entropy* of a message's information content. The idea here is one of waste. In the example above, you *almost* don't need the 'u' after the 'q'. It turns out that the "relative entropy" of English as she is normally spoken is about 30–40%. This means that if you find the *best* way you can compress this English text, you'll end up with a file about one third of the original size.[7] You can try this by downloading Herman Melville's *Moby Dick* from the Gutenberg project, right clicking it, and sending it to a zipped file.[8]

The transmitter and receiver use the same principles to handle messages. Shannon shows there is just one *best* way to use the available bandwidth—maximise the entropy of the transmitted message. He then does something really smart. He introduces *noise*. The damage done to the original signal by this noise can be measured—as entropy.

Imagine a god-like observer who can compare the original and the received message, and transmit the "list of errors" to the receiver as concisely as possible. As you'd expect, the entropy of the noise is the same as the minimum bandwidth of this 'rescue channel'. This in turn means that even in a noisy channel, with suitable encoding, you can lower the frequency of errors to *as low a rate as you want!*

---

[7]Shannon gives a value of about 50% because he uses just 8 characters next to one another; the best compression programs can get down to 1.3 bits per character. [8]Other, slower algorithms can squeeze it slightly more than ZIP can. The *redundancy* is one minus the relative entropy, so English is about 60–70% redundant.

Common ground

Our exploration of blickets in Lesson 4 suggests that from an early age you tease out information from noise—and make working models that have a Bayesian nature. We now know that this can be done with an arbitrarily small amount of error. This should pull the rug out from under the feet of those who see qualia as 'ineffable'. Two people—or devices—communicating with one another can transfer information to the limits of the fidelity they desire. This is entirely general, and includes information about shared mental models—or even your perception of your "personal qualia".

There is just one counter-argument left. It runs like this: "You've missed the point. Even though every external phenomenon is identical, there's still something *different* going on 'under the hood'. My *inner* perception of the colour red is different from *your* inner perception of the colour red, and you can't possibly know this in any way." There are a few problems with this statement.

First, I can respond "That's all very well, but why *should* there be a difference? The function of human brains appears to depend on human genes and human development and the environment you share in common—including shared understanding, shared language, and shared models. What stops me from saying the exact opposite—'You work the same'—if you can't *show* a difference?" It seems a bit silly to assert the presence of secret sauce, if there's no way to show its influence.

Second, the person making this statement is making assumptions about *two* models, hers and yours. From exploring Eleusis, you already know that no two models can be *shown* to be the same—there's always the chance of a later mismatch. So a starting point of "difference" is trivially likely, but meaningless. The mysterious difference may never come up. It's smarter to assume that the two models are the same, and then *look* for differences. If you can't find any, then at least provisionally, the two models *are* the same.

These concerns lead into a third problem—how children think. We've seen that they likely share Bayesian mechanisms that allow them to unlock causality. Your 'quale' for being pricked by a pin might be the taste of the colour two today, and the smell of exponential functions tomorrow—but this is utterly irrelevant. You're trapped in your total inability to articulate any meaning of your alleged 'special inner perception'—even to yourself!

We can now say: "Well why don't you pull up a chair and tell me about this. Ishmael, tell us about that Great White Whale. Tell us how you feel. Go on!" Remarkably, he can.

The best

There are still two tightly coupled questions we need to resolve. The first—*why* children should be inclined to Bayesian thinking—we'll leave for Lesson 6. The second is "Can we do better than Bayes?"

In his monumental work *Probability Theory. The Logic of Science*, ET Jaynes discusses the derivation of Bayes' theorem from very simple first principles. In Chapter 2 he gives the short proof by RT Cox that Bayes' Theorem is consistent, unique and optimal![9] Part of the modern resurgence in enthusiasm for Bayesian thinking has been the availability of computers powerful enough to do the job, but as important has been the insight that the conventional tools that you've been sharpening over the past century often deliver sub-optimal results.

Bayesian has even been shown to be better. For example, a large proportion of patients with "acute respiratory distress syndrome" (ARDS) die. Their lungs are full of inflammation, just as I inflame lungs. Intensive care specialists have long sought better ways to breathe oxygen into these sick people. In 2007 a large, expensive and pivotal trial called OSCAR explored an enticing therapy—high-frequency oscillatory ventilation, which oxygenates lungs with tiny volumes, similar to the way a dog pants. OSCAR ended in 2012, showing no benefit. In 2019 Elizabeth Ryan and colleagues published Bayesian simulations of this trial. Using a Monte Carlo approach like that described on page 68, they show that every single Bayesian design stopped early because continuing would be futile. Had a similar approach been used, time and money would have been saved. Many similar evaluations exist.

A powerful Bayesian idea is that you can also use an *adaptive* design where you smartly and legitimately modify a trial to gain maximum information and harm as few patients as you can. This invites the question "What's wrong with the old ways?"

Leaving aside Bayesian statistics, modern biomedical statistics is largely a patchwork of bad habits cobbled together over the past century. The dead hand of a true genius touches a lot of this—Sir Ronald Aylmer Fisher did much of the initial work. His approach was however coloured by his bitter enmity to anyone who disagreed with him in the slightest, and a focus on the agricultural plots that formed a large part of his initial work. He worked out how to randomize the individuals (or crops) that he was studying, and used this to tease out the effect of deliberate acts from all the background factors that might influence outcome. Unfortunately, he saw this as the acme of statistical design, and because he was superb at manipulating (and indeed inventing) conventional statistical methods, his take on things still holds sway.

[9] There's subsequently been a lot of discussion of this point, but nobody has found either a convincing refutation, or a better way of doing things.

A larger-than-life figure from the point of view of pure intellect, his errors were also bigger and more impressive. The most obvious of these was his support for the tobacco industry, and his denial that smoking caused cancer, long after everyone but the tobacco barons had publicly accepted this.[10]

The most damaging side-effect of Fisher's approach however is that it specifically excludes using prior information in assessing a study—each trial is a thing unto itself. Belatedly, realising that valuable information is being thrown away, statisticians came up with cumbersome techniques of "meta-analysis" that attempt to combine trials. Even here, it is only recently that they've started using Bayesian techniques to suck out maximum value. It seems that to do good science, not only do you need to know quite a lot about Bayes, but Bayes is best. But how do you *do* science?

Three Steps—an analysis of Science

(1) Present how Science *should* work;

(2) Vigorously *attack* this model using the sharpest tools available;

(3) Then, if the model holds up, *provisionally* accept it as 'true'.

What is Science, anyway?

Until now, I've used the word 'science' quite glibly. But if you ask a dozen philosophers what science is, you'll get fifteen different answers. How might we evaluate a definition of 'Science'? In the box above is one possible way. Let's now define science, and apply this approach. Actually, we're largely done.

By my definition, Good Science is precisely the three steps listed above! It is the process of generating explanatory models in response to problems, testing these hypotheses by trying your best to make them fail, and in the end never truly believing them 100%. You start with the assumption of similarity between the model and the assumed underlying process, and seek disproof.

Can you see the tie-in to Lesson 4? Doing Good Science resembles the game of Eleusis—but you have no oracle to consult. You can never know whether your model is valid. Many people stumble here, because they want *proof*—as David Hume did in the last lesson.

[10] As shown from their private documents, they knew too; they just weren't letting on.

It took nearly 200 years before someone saw a way out. Karl Popper, another philosopher, pointed out that a lack of proof *does not matter.* Provided you're happy to accept that none of your theories is *absolutely true*, you can still test them, and at some point, when you're happy in your own mind that the testing is sufficient, *provisionally* accept them as true. You can also use them.

But wait a bit! Let's attack this definition of Science, in the true spirit of step #2. Isn't it equally valid to label models as false, however much you've "tested" them? In exploring qualia and information theory, we've already put to bed the idea that an initial assumption of dissimilarity has any value.[11] But even if we start from a position of similarity, surely we can always find trivial exceptions?

For example, if I say "The sun will rise tomorrow", not only is there the minuscule chance that the sun will go nova and vaporise the Earth tonight, but there are many ways that I might beat up my theory. I might fly to the Antarctic winter, and not see the sun rise for ages; I might get in a very fast plane and chase the night, and so on. But despite these 'exceptions', the idea that the sun will rise tomorrow makes a pretty compelling and useful, if trivial theory.

The important concept here is one of context. You've already seen that all exploration of knowledge is context-dependent, whether you're contemplating statistical process control or Bayesian models. This invites humility. Because you're not fixated on *truth*, you should be quite comfortable with using theories in context, despite their failure out of context. All models are wrong, but some are useful.

Surprisingly, one of Karl Popper's strengths was not humility, and he spent a lot of his time vigorously attacking every vestige of what he perceived to be inductive thought.[12] In this, he missed the point. In tying together existing theories, Bayes rocks. In fact, in refuting pet beliefs, Bayes also rocks. It's just that assumptions in the *underlying structure* are always potentially susceptible to disproof, and everyone needs to be correspondingly humble—and continually alert for inconsistencies.

In the true spirit of Good Science, if you can come up with a better definition of science, it's wise to look at this too. Clearly, it has to have at least some of the characteristics we've already defined. Any "theory of science" that claims absolute truth for *any prior* is in for a hard time. The last people who tried this, the Logical Positivists of the Vienna Circle, quit in the 1930s, although a few die-hard American philosophers hung on into the 1950s. A philosophy of science also needs to accommodate reality, and testing. Your "science replacement" is pitiful if it cannot be tested.

There are however other "theories of science" that try to side-step the above limitations. They are often sociological in nature. For example, Thomas Kuhn came up

[11]There's another, more profound refutation of the "false is equally valid" idea, but this will have to wait for Lesson 6. [12]Although he finally and famously admitted to "a whiff of induction" himself.

with the very attractive idea that there are two types of science, what he called 'normal science', where people go about their business like busy little termites, shoring up the termite mound of science and filling in the gaps where the rain might get in.

A 'paradigm shift' then occurs—someone like Semmelweis comes up with an idea or set of ideas that rocks the foundations. These ideas are so new, so different, that the old and the new theories are 'incommensurable'—they just can't be reconciled. After some turmoil, great big chunks of the mound fall off, termites scurry around in disarray, but eventually you resume your normal activities within the new paradigm.

This take on science has some attractive features, but there are a few problems. If a scientist sees his role as termite-like, might this not be self-fulfilling? If "normal science is the norm", and new theories intrinsically don't fit, might this encourage scientists to stamp out new ideas, or even justify persecution of innovation? Remember Semmelweis?

There's another problem with the Kuhnian viewpoint, and this again harks back to Semmelweis. The problem with those who hounded him was not that his ideas were incommensurable. The problem was that he became a political football. As we've discovered it's likely a bit daft to say things like "his science wasn't up to it" or "his communication skills were deficient" as these weren't the problems.[13] All sorts of bullying and chicanery can be justified under the label 'incommensurable'. Now that we have Bayes, which specifically allows us to tie things together, 'incommensurable' is surely a nonsense term, the refuge of those who don't or won't understand.[14]

There is however yet another school of philosophers, also with a sociological bent, who proudly describe science purely in terms of sociological activities. Science is what scientists do—presumably while sociologists get all the *real* work done—and the truth or falsehood of science is seen in terms of the social activities it involves. As far as any useful meaning can be attached to the term "postmodern", this might be it. We don't need to ruminate too much here, as this approach largely died out or was resolved in the 'Science wars' of the 1990s, but there are still some camp followers on who haven't quite caught up. One trenchant observation will suffice. It is this—sociological theories cannot well explain the success of modern science.

Lesson 6 will present a scientific explanation of the extraordinary successes of science—and how things might go wrong, but let's briefly explore how well Good Science works, and how alternatives *might* work.

[13]Unless you take a revisionist view that is difficult to defend. [14]As a historical footnote and exercise in forensic philosophy, you may wish to look into the term "radical underdetermination" as espoused by Quine. The antidote is naturally Bayesian.

But what about...?

To close the lesson, let's return to me—Nanny Rona. In Lesson 1 you saw that, within days of realising there was a problem, Chinese scientists had identified, sequenced and communicated detailed information about me. Surely others screwed up, but the scientists did something amazing. Even more remarkably, other scientists around the world could take this information, design and build the required probes, and start making tests that identified me and allowed them to track me. Again, many politicians and their financial advisers failed spectacularly but, properly used, the science was solid.

You now have the tools to understand and even quantify success and failure. You understand how people *can* use shared mental models—and the Bayesian nature of the logic that underpins successfully shared information. You understand the best way there is to reconcile information, and the limitations of all theories. You understand, from the perspective of information theory, how this ties together. Can you see how pale and insipid sociological explanations are in the face of this?

But there is still a deeper failing of science viewed as "scientists doing their sociological thing". You can now look at the science in terms of information theory, and ask embarrassing questions like "What is the entropy of the space of possibilities that Good Science occupies?" In other words, for anything that works, how many potential failures are there? It's then obvious that the chances of Good Science (as I've defined it) being "*just* a social activity" *and actually working* are negligible. Short of some miracle, you could not save lives and stop my spread, if you were simply going about your business. I'll discuss this almost miraculous aspect to Good Science in the next lesson, but there's yet another failing of sociological interpretations of science that is even more disturbing.

It is this: fire burns. If something is on fire, we can philosophise about it—or we can identify the problem and find a fire extinguisher. Recall Semmelweis' comment "Only the large number of deaths was an unquestionable reality". If people are dying, it makes sense to find one or more solutions. We know that Good Science works, and provides solutions.

It is nevertheless reasonable to ask "But what about x?" where x is something that seems not to fit. We'll explore such questions in subsequent lessons, but a few general remarks are useful here too. An important first question has to be "Why doesn't x fit into the framework of Good Science?"

A first step in doing Good Science is to generate a hypothesis that explains a problem, the second step is to Test The Hell Out Of It, followed by provisional acceptance of the hypothesis (It hasn't *yet* failed; it works in context). You can then act—for if you're not going to act, why are you trying to find a solution? Clearly any 'x' that doesn't fit into this framework has to be very special. A few possibilities:

(1) There is no hypothesis. You're just presented with a 'fact'.
(2) The hypothesis (or 'fact') can't be tested.
(3) A 'truth' is accepted as empirically true, for a variety of reasons.

What is the common theme here? It is that somehow, a "truth" has been derived, but it's not subject to questioning (or testing). It then seems reasonable to ask where this "truth" comes from.[15] This is where cautions about provenance (page 16) bite deep. But perhaps we shouldn't be too picky—it may still be reasonable to take inspiration where we find it, even if it's claimed to come from God, Satan, ancient wisdom, a charismatic leader, or a blinding insight.

There still needs to be a next step. Let's say someone has come up with a 'miracle cure' for COVID-19, but the science is missing. Our second question must surely be "How do you know it will work?" This is where the asymmetrical successes of Good Science bite particularly hard.

We know—from the perspective of information theory, and the vast array of possible things that *won't* treat a given condition—that there's a vanishingly small chance that an empiric therapy will work, even if claimed to be Vouched For By God. We need two more things. We should surely *test* the treatment. But before we test it, it must in some small way *make sense.* For some reason, the idea of "injecting bleach" springs to mind—but hang on—you know this will kill the patient. No, don't do this. No, never.[16] We need to factor in the Bayesian priors that inform a decision! Something that a four year old can do, given the right information and context.

It seems that Good Science, as presented, is the only reasonable option—but we must admit that even our theory of Good Science, optimal though it appears to be, might conceivably be wrong. It's wise to be open-minded here, but not so open minded that your brains run out of your ears. In the meantime, to do a good job, Good Science can be considered *good enough.*

Lesson #5

Good Science, as defined, is necessary and sufficient—for now.

[15]Another reasonable question might be "Are you a logical positivist/logical empiricist?" but this might be a bit unkind. Also see the cautionary quote at the start of Lesson 10. [16]It is somewhat disturbing that shortly after the current US president speculated about the therapeutic value of bleach, calls to poison centres spiked in Michigan, Illinois, New York, and Tennessee. Let's not even talk about Kansas, Dorothy.

⊛ Lesson 6

Tiggers are Wonderful Things

"...three other tigers in Tiger Mountain and the three African lions that exhibited a cough have also tested positive for COVID-19."

Wildlife Conservation Society Newsroom.
22 April 2020.

"Hallo, Piglet. This is Tigger."

"Oh, is it?" said Piglet, and he edged round to the other side of the table. "I thought Tiggers were smaller than that."

"Not the big ones," said Tigger.

A.A. Milne. *The House at Pooh Corner, 1928.*

"Can one desire too much of a good thing?"

Shakespeare. *As You Like It* (4:1), 1599.

Winnie-the-Pooh may be the greatest cultural appropriation of all time. On 6 January 1930, the US producer Stephen Slesinger acquired rights to Winnie, and when he died in 1953, his wife licensed these to Disney. In 2005, this quintessentially British bear earned them $6 billion. In London, my "foster family" were quite put out when I took their children to the Hunterian Museum, where the original Winnie—a Canadian black bear from the London Zoo—may be seen.[1] Part of her, that is. They put me up to it. Nothing wrong with a bear skull, nothing at all, and kids are resilient.

When Gopnik did her research into blickets, she first made sure that the four-year-olds knew the difference between a wug and a dax. I was very tempted to point this out in Lesson 4 and ask the inevitable question "Do you?" but felt this was unreasonably confrontational, even for Nanny Rona in didactic mode. The only people who can consistently tell the two apart are linguists and, of course, the four-year-olds in their experiments.

[1] Formally, the museum only reopens in 2022. It's not what you know but whom you know. The Hunterian also has Jenner's draft of *An Inquiry into the Causes and Effects of the Variolae Vaccinae.*

This is because a wug is a made-up thing that tests abstract conceptualisation and language use. What is the plural of wug? Clearly wugs (not to be confused with daxes). Early on, humans start labelling things and putting them into categories—for once you know what a wug is, you can group it with other wugs, and be careful not to put them in the same box as the daxes. Daxes eat wugs.[2]

All of this is well and good. It's difficult to imagine how to create the complex societies you have without categories, and without the ability to define how things relate to other things. Ideas of causality are closely tied to ideas of "classes of things". There is however a danger associated with labelling obsessions. Let's explore this. Why do adults often struggle with Bayes, while children seem to use the logic unconsciously?

Pigeons

In 2010, Walter Herbranson and Julia Schroeder published a paper[3] that on the surface may seem every bit as ridiculous as the salmon study of Lesson 1. Their work involved pigeons, not renowned for intellectual prowess, but familiar as research subjects[4]; and undergraduate psychology students, also common research subjects whom you might reasonably anticipate to have a logical edge over pigeons.

Six Silver King pigeons were trained to peck at either two or three keys, using lights of various colours as a stimulus, with food as a reward. When they were good at this, the Monty Hall problem was introduced: first, a computer randomly chose a prize key. All keys were illuminated with white light and once the pigeon pecked a key, all keys were darkened for a second. The computer then randomly deactivated one of the other two keys, according to the Monty Hall rules. Both remaining options were illuminated with green light. Effectively, "a door was opened, revealing a goat". Grain was then provided—if the pigeon gave a timely peck to the prize key. Did the pigeon 'hold' or 'switch'?

Initially the pigeons tended to peck the same key, but by the end of the trial, they had learned to switch, achieving the maximum theoretical payoff. But what about the undergraduates? You've likely already worked out that, confronted by the same problem (using a touch screen and fingers, rather than keys and beaks), the humans stuffed up this "iterated Monty Hall" scenario. Despite 200 attempts, divided into four blocks of 50 with a rest interval in between, there was no difference between their first and final attempts. They were clearly out-performed by the pigeons.

In later studies, Gopnik found something similar[5]: when shown blickets in combination, four-year-old children were *better* than adults at working things out. Specifically,

---

[2] This is a lie. [3] PubMed 2017559 [4] Especially by the famous "stimulus-response" scientist BF Skinner, who never quite recovered from his somewhat unfair evisceration-in-print by Noam Chomsky in 1959.
[5] PubMed 24566007

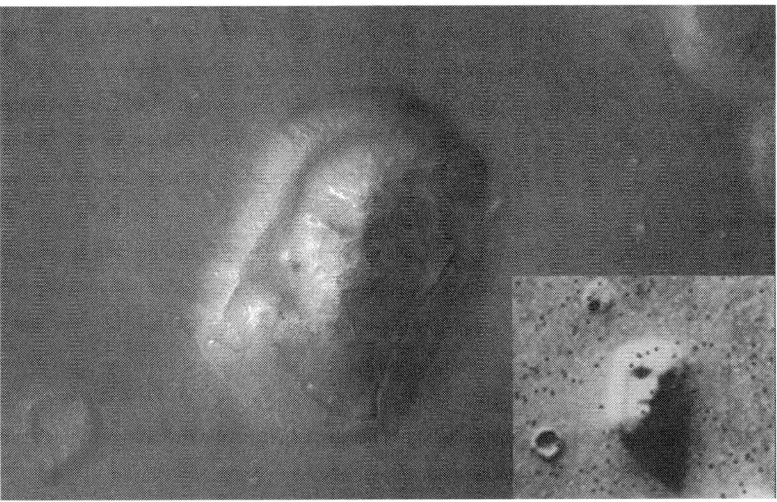

Figure 13. The Face on Mars

adults tended to rigidly categorise their blickets, while children showed evidence that when presented with combinations of blickets (conjunctive relationships) they were more likely to accept that an effect might be due to a combination of blickets.

How to fail

Again, we are compelled to ask "Why?" Why should pigeons and four-year-old children out-perform adults? A hint is provided by Herbranson and Schroeder in the pigeon paper we've already looked at. As part of their careful checking of their findings, they gave another group of Silver King pigeons *random* rewards in response to their key-pecking. Overall, the outcomes were similarly random, but *when they looked at individual pigeons*, a pattern emerged. If—by sheer random chance—a pigeon initially received repeated rewards for pecking a particular key, this had a disproportionate, reinforcing effect on subsequent behaviour, *despite the overall randomness* across all pigeons.[6]

These findings may be relevant to humans, and even to machine learning. Humans can often pick up a working approach in a few goes. One problem with machine learning is that even though it can now out-perform humans in several domains—for example in spotting the effects of diabetes on the back of the eye, and in playing chess and go—a huge amount of training is required.[7] Other areas are inaccessible—bumbling AIs are hilariously satirised in the science fiction series *Upload*, where they still can't do captchas.

[6]This resembles Skinner's 'superstitious' pigeons. [7]Usually based on gradient descent with back-propagation.

Paradoxically, humans' ability to quickly latch on to patterns may be why you fail at tasks like the iterated Monty Hall, and unfamiliar arrangements of blickets—sometimes you take prior classifications that don't apply, and lop off the bits that don't fit.[8] A beautiful illustration is the "face on Mars" in Fig 13 — early images from Viking 1 gave rise to bizarre "alien monument" theories,[9] although even then it was anyone's guess why aliens should choose to model a *human* face. Even after higher-resolution pictures were readily available, there were still those who kept the faith, as it were. It may be worthwhile looking in more detail at how humans classify things.

Ginkgo

We can trace the classification of animals and plants back to Aristotle (and one of his students) but things languished for a couple of millennia until the twenty-eight-year-old Carl Linnaeus produced his *Systema Naturae*, a twelve-page book on the classification of animals, plants and minerals that shook things up a bit. By 1753, he had described over 7,300 species in *Species Plantarum*, the basis of modern botany.[10] Perhaps his most important idea was that living organisms exist in a hierarchy, something like a tree. The leaves of the tree are the individual species; the twigs bearing similar species are genera; these in turn unite to form orders and then classes, ultimately forming thick trunks known as kingdoms.

Linnaeus was not to know the underlying reason for these similarities. This had to wait for Charles Darwin, who worked out and published the logic behind heredity and how species evolve in 1859, fully ten years before DNA was discovered and just short of a hundred years before people finally understood how the genetic code works—but Linnaeus did a darn good job nevertheless.

If you now look at a modern classification of organisms, you'll find it's a bit more complex. There are more levels, for starters. Let's take human beings. The genus and species are straightforward: *Homo sapiens*. There are no subspecies, so that's uncomplicated too.[11] Moving towards the thicker part of the tree, however we encounter a Tribe, a Subfamily, a Family, an InfraOrder, a Suborder, an Order (primates), a Class (mammals), a Phylum (things with a backbone, Chordata) and finally the Kingdom of animals, Animalia.

---

[8] *Ramsey theory* tells us that familiar patterns will *always* be there—any sufficiently large structure *must* contain a 'regular' substructure of a given size, as shown in the "Happy End Paper" of Erdős and Szekeres. A skyful of stars will always have constellations. [9] As well as the Futurama episode "Where the Buggalo Roam", and any number of other cultural references. [10] He also did a bit of animal classification in the Tenth Edition of *Systema Naturae*. Just a bit. Do you remember who described the tapeti in Lesson 2? He was however a bit confused and nasty about amphibians, saying "These most terrible and vile animals...". [11] Based on the DNA evidence, there are no distinct races either. That's another story.

It turns out that in taxonomy, there are (as it were) two classes of taxonomists—lumpers, and splitters.[12] The splitters seem to have won. Nothing demonstrates this more eloquently than the Ginkgo tree. The full sequence for this plant as we trace it up the tree of life is Genus and species: *Ginkgo biloba*, Family: Ginkgoaceae, Order: Ginkgoales, Class: Ginkgoopsida, Division: Ginkgophyta—are we there yet?—and finally the Clade Tracheophytes, which are indeed plants (Plantae).

You might argue that this is *less* complex than the fine splitting we've just seen with *Homo sapiens*, but something has been hidden from you. It is this: as we work up the tree from *Ginkgo biloba* to the Plantae, we realise that the only species in the family Ginkgoaceae is also the only species in the Order Ginkgoales, which is the only species in the Class Ginkgoopsida. It won't surprise you that the only species in the division Ginkgophyta is similarly alone (although you can loosely tie in a few fossils). A whole scaffolding has been constructed to support a single species, largely because "that's the way it's done". We could likely chop out most of the dead wood and be no poorer—the last fossil relative of *Ginkgo biloba* likely died out about 270 million years ago. But the prosthetics provide a pleasing symmetry. Or something. You gotta have some Order.

Archaea

Ginkgo biloba is a minor sin. Our exploration becomes a bit more dramatic when we suddenly discover there's an entirely new Kingdom of animals, uhh, plants; erm ... Bacteria; Oh Dear! ... (cough) ... *things* you've misclassified. Oh! Hang on! It's not a kingdom either. In 1977 another Carl, the American microbiologist Carl Woese caused quite as much of a stir as did Linnaeus, when he published the results of his research into a group of neglected organisms that had been lumped together as "lacking a cell nucleus".

At the time, it all seemed logical and natural. There were more complex organisms, or 'eukaryotes' (like you), and there were 'primitive' prokaryotes (like bacteria). The main distinction was "the presence or absence of a nucleus". It was easy. But Woese showed that some of these prokaryotes—the Archaea—are as different from bacteria as people are! Woese redrew the entire tree of life, creating the idea of three *domains* of life: the Bacteria, the Eukarya, and the Archaea. The important thing here is not the ensuing storm (he was labelled a 'crank' and a 'scarred revolutionary'[13]) but the way he did things.

Woese looked at the nucleic acids of these organisms, how they differed, and what these differences mean. Till then, classification was based mainly on how organisms functioned and looked, although you already knew that evolution could mould organisms that looked and worked in similar ways from remarkably different origins.

[12] Splitters might find more. [13] Shades of Semmelweis.

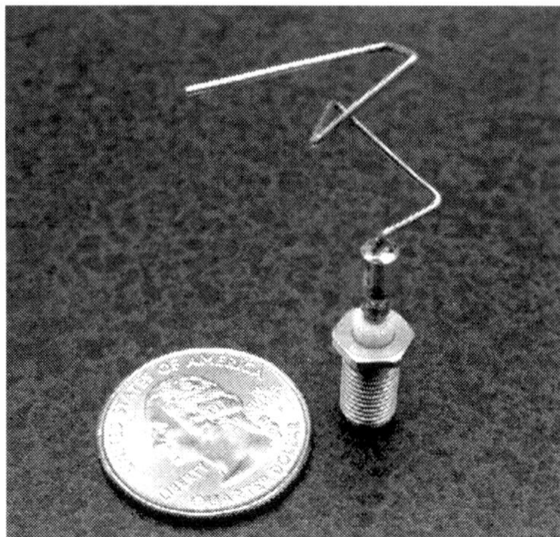

Figure 14. An evolved antenna

A simple example is the pangolin—contrasted with other animals that eat ants. Pretty much regardless of their origins, animals that eat ants tend to acquire certain characteristics: a long, thin, sticky tongue; tough, nest-cracking forelimbs; and thick, bite-resistant skin.[14] Those who study evolutionary biology call this 'convergence'.

A lesson from Darwin

Charles Darwin knew nothing of DNA—it was only discovered ten years after he published *On the Origin of Species*. But yet, in a sense he knew everything about DNA. As you read his book, you can't help but feel that he had some sort of time machine, and wrote his book as a joke—almost every sentence seems prescient and knowing.

However, what Darwin may not have realised is the sheer generality of Darwinian Evolution. His theory encompasses and explains pretty much any generational change that is shaped by circumstances. This has been shown in fields quite distinct from DNA.

For example, at about the same time that Woese started his revolutionary work, John Henry Holland (psychologist, electrical engineer and computer scientist) came up with a meta-idea. Why not use Darwinian evolution in the field of ideas?

Let's say you have a really difficult engineering problem—for example, you want to develop a very special and precise spacecraft antenna, one with "a wide beamwidth for circularly polarized wave and wide impedance bandwidth to cover up and down-link frequencies at X-band".[15] You might struggle with the theory, or just do what Gregory Hornby and Jason Lohn did in designing the ST5 antenna—set it up as an experiment

[14] A good read is https://academic.oup.com/icb/article/41/3/507/2091664 [15] No, I don't know what quite a lot of that means, either.

in evolution, and let the machine find a good solution.[16] The resulting antenna looks like a badly bent piece of wire, but does the job remarkably well.

Natural Kinds

There is however an even broader principle we can extract here. This ties back directly into the last lesson. As Woese found, new approaches may reveal hidden truths about origins: they may reveal needless complexity, as with the Ginkgo tree; they may reveal deceptive stereotypes that have led us into doing dumb things. All classifications however share one trait in common—they are just convenient labels. There are no "natural kinds".

Even with familiar things, classifications often lead us astray—we need the capacity to adapt. Some necessary changes are minor—moving an organism from one twig on one branch of one trunk to another; sometimes we have to rebuild an entire structure. Classification systems *need* built-in adaptability, allowing those who use them not just to admit error, but also to fix the wrongness.[17]

Can you see how this resonates with the idea expressed in Lesson 5 that Good Science is an approach and not a fixed thing—that it is not even an approximation to truth? Despite the ability to communicate as clearly as necessary across a communication channel; despite the fact that people can and do establish and use Bayesian models within their minds; despite the existence of spectacularly effective ways of testing theories, they can't be proved right. All acceptance of theories is provisional; and so it is with all classification systems. Labels and descriptions are acceptable as long as they are useful, but they are never true, nor can anyone describe true "classes of things".

If this is the case for familiar things, how more careful we must be with something new and potentially different? Let's say you have a much treasured Pooh and Tigger among your nursery toys. You are not otherwise familiar with great cats, but one day you visit the Zoo, and through some misadventure, end up facing an escaped tiger. Through your experience—even based on a Bayesian approach—you might be tempted to categorise this larger Tigger as basically benign, and attach attributes like "bouncy, trouncy, flouncy, pouncy, fun, fun, fun, fun, fun." You may have forgotten that Tigger claimed to be "the only one"; you may de-emphasise the word 'pouncy'. This would, I suggest, be a grave mistake.

Now you might think that as an adult, all of this is kindergarten stuff. If you are tempted by this folly, think back to your recent findings—adults appear *more* likely than children to be rigid in their thinking. Even pigeons can be more adaptable! Similarly, it is possible that too much tigger-classification has gone into the response to COVID-19.

[16] Feast your mind on http://alglobus.net/NASAwork/papers/Space2006Antenna.pdf [17] Don't mention any of this to a herpetologist. See xkcd.com/867/

Some positive spin

The preceding discussion may seem a bit negative. Like David Hume, you might lament that most effort is in vain, because all theories are almost trivially incorrect. But we've already partially buried that argument, as some theories are indeed useful. We have also countered the idea that 'science' is *merely* a social construct—these theories are invalidated by the successes of science.

We have not however explained why Good Science succeeds. With so many alternatives, how can it possibly work? How can order emerge from seeming chaos? Fortunately, we now have a robust explanation, as far as any explanations can be robust. It is that Good Science succeeds through Darwinian evolution of ideas!

We must still be careful. There is a danger in equating success with correctness. We might argue that there is some sort of *asymptotic* correctness—that we can get closer and closer to 'the truth'. The sheer explanatory power of Good Science might lure us into believing we have an eternal truth. But survival of the fittest always refers to interaction between an environment and varying, replicating and dying elements, be they Galapagos finches, simulations of radio antennae, or scientific ideas.

It is true that you can find models that work *within the limits of your theories*, but this is precisely why it's wise to adhere to the third of my three principles of Good Science. Good Science is about being vigilant for Tiggers, especially those you own and treasure. Not only might the environment change, but you can never *know* the full context of your environment, or that any model of it is 'right'.

Sharp arrows to the heart

In the interests of fairness and full disclosure, I must now point out where you should attack the argument I've advanced so far. This may seem like a vampire providing his intended victims with a ready source of stakes and a clearly marked anatomical map depicting the heart,[18] or Clark Kent giving Lex Luthor a bag of kryptonite, but my compulsion to be honest runs deep.[19] Here are the points you might profitably attack:

- You might try to resuscitate logical positivism by establishing *knowable* 'grounded truths'—and then use this to construct a (Platonic) theory of ideals, or an asymptotic approach to these ideal forms. Good luck!
- You might demonstrate a refutation of the logic I've presented – disproving Cox's theorem, and showing a way that's "better than Bayes";

[18] The best gags are stolen, often from Pratchett.

[19] There is also the small matter that the approach I've outlined is built around self-correction.

- You might discover a better, more compelling model of Science—one that replaces my approach with something that works better and is internally consistent,[20] despite abandoning one or more of my three pillars.
- You might construct a consistent, useful philosophy that is predicated on an initial assumption of differences, and on proof rather than disproof.
- You might even provide a model of the human mind that incorporates inexpressible qualia, known only to their possessor, and *show* that despite having no detectable influence, they are still 'meaningful'.

There is however little point in attacking the *illustrations* I've used. For example, were you to go back to Lesson 1 and vigorously attack the "Salmon of Doubt", this would be the equivalent of staking your vampire through his baby finger—and missing.

Were you to conduct a vast study showing convincingly that four-year-olds aren't quite as smart as Alison Gopnik has shown, or were you to refute the Monty Hall pigeon studies, this would be like the CEO of LexCorp battling Superman with a tiny, green light-emitting diode.

Alternatively, you might refuse to play. But Science works, and isn't intrinsically beneficent—it can both cause immense harm and result in huge good. Ignoring it by humming loudly with your fingers in your ears may be a bit silly. As we've already discovered, Good Science also depends on context. I am continually amused by those who disparage STEM, *using* the products of Science, Technology, Engineering and Maths to tweet their disapproval or post on Facebook.[21]

In the following few lessons, I'll show how things can go wrong, not just for those who don't 'get' Good Science and instead cling to their soft toys, but even for experts in their fields. I'll also examine some successes—and explain why they work.

A short list of tiggers

This lesson concludes with some tiggers—note the change in case. From now on, a "tigger" will refer to a fixed misconception, based on a learned pattern that doesn't apply. In my reading about human responses to viruses, especially me, I've found a number of them. The following list of yearnings, extrapolations and other tiggers is fairly short, because I've tried to avoid frankly crazy stuff, which excludes the vast majority of statements about COVID-19 that I've seen in the press. I've left out the bleach.

---

[20] You will also need a way to demonstrate this convincingly.

[21] In contrast, you have to admire the Amish, who at least are pretty *consistent* in their approach to technology: avoiding rototillers while accepting motorized washing machines. As a virus, I love their take on vaccination :)

"Much of this is probably what reporters call a 'fake'... There is nothing new in influenza; it is an old acquaintance; we know all about it. It is rarely fatal; it does not usually prevent its victim from attending to business. It sometimes assumes an epidemic type and cases become frequent, but it never lays whole communities low."

Editorial. *Sedalia Weekly Bazoo*, 7 January 1890, p4.

"I was at a hospital the other night where I think there were a few coronavirus patients, and I shook hands with everybody..."

Boris Johnson. 3 March 2020.

"...and also allow enough of us who are going to get mild illness, to become immune to this, to help with the sort of whole population response that will protect everybody.

Sir Patrick Vallance, Chief Scientific Advisor to the UK Government. Interview on Sky News, 13 March 2020.

"Each country has to reach 'herd immunity' in one way or another, and we are going to reach it in a different way."

Dr Anders Tegnell, Chief Epidemiologist, Sweden. 21 April 2020.

"Is the flu less dangerous than COVID? No, it's not. They're similar in prevalence and in death rate"

Dr Dan Erickson, Kern County, California. 22 April 2020.

"If [remdesivir] can stop people needing intensive care then the risk of hospitals being overwhelmed is smaller, and there is less need for social distancing."

James Gallagher, BBC Health & Science Correspondent. 30 April 2020.

Lesson #6

Tigers aren't tiggers.

⊛ Lesson 7

Credulity

"Nothing is so unbelievable that oratory cannot make it acceptable."

Marcus Tullius Cicero. ~55 BCE.

"Some of you may die, but that is a sacrifice I am willing to make."

Lord Farquaad. *Shrek (movie)*, 2007.

"Men han har jo ikke noget paa," sagde et lille Barn. ("But he hasn't got anything on," a little child said).

Hans Christian Andersen. *The Emperor's New Clothes*, 1837.

Indonesia is a sprawling archipelago of over a quarter of a billion people, extending from Benggala Island in the west for over five thousand kilometres to the Torasi Estuary in the east, at the boundary with Papua New Guinea. I am the product of all I've seen, but some experiences weigh more than others. Take Jakarta. My first observation is that childcare is different in Indonesia. A *pembantu* is a household helper who may also do a bit of child minding, but an upmarket babysitter is a *suster*, who may even wear a white uniform in her sole duty as a helicopter-parent-by-proxy. Children are treasured—and spoiled; even rudimentary discipline is often absent.

My second observation is that it was in Indonesia that I saw my first koteka—the traditional tribal penis sheath from *West Papua*, a province also known for the remarkable corals of its remote Raja Ampat Islands, a wealth of miniature katak-katak, and industrial-scale human rights abuses inflicted on indigenous Papuans by the Indonesian government.

So what do you get when you combine these two observations? Well obviously, the President of the United States. I love weak leaders—spoiled-child tyrants who wear an entire army like a culturally misappropriated koteka. As a virus, I applaud those who ignore their experts and pepper-spray their priests.

Here too I must however admit to some ambivalence. As a nanny, I can imagine asking Donald Trump to read the WHO Declaration of a Public Health Emergency on page 9 and explain to me which part of it he failed to understand. The only social interaction I can envisage would be a slap to the face, a quick haircut, and exit stage left leaving a trail of expiring secret service men, all now struggling to breathe. I am, after all, a god.

Other lame leaders around the world like Jair Bolsonaro[1] have aped his denials, bluster, martial posturing, cynical abuse of religion and "shoot the messenger" responses. In the short term these are like balm—viral spread of bad behaviour and dissent is better than everyone going up to a stranger and sneezing vigorously. You have already seen the results in the United States, as well as similar successes in the United Kingdom, in Brazil, in some parts of Europe, and in Mexico. I have high hopes for Russia, India, Indonesia, Bangladesh and most of Africa and South America too. We'll have to wait until Lesson 12 to explore the full depths of my ambivalence, so in the meantime, let's learn from these men, or at least, how they work.

From the previous lesson, you might conclude that many of these actions are mere tiggers—politicians clinging to treasured soft toys. I suspect this isn't even the greater part of the truth. Back in Lesson 5, I briefly touched on the sociological or 'postmodern' approach to science, and pointed out its main failing, that it doesn't explain the success of Good Science. In Lesson 6, we discovered that a Darwinian approach explains why success is effectively built into the DNA of Good Science. In contrast, "political science" often seems to be no more than the art of illusion. But Darwin still has a say, as bad politicians seem to have out-evolved honest ones. Nobody ever said that the results of natural selection need to be *nice.*

But *how* do they succeed? Politics, which might best concern itself with finding good solutions to societal problems and using the consensual wisdom of everyone to select the best of these—the most reasonable and most acceptable long-term solutions—has moved away from this goal and become more about persuasion. You have found that if you do a crap job, you can often simply persuade others that this is acceptable. Politicians even persuade themselves. You have learned how to manipulate the media so that a majority will accept a harmful, destructive or frankly insane course of action. I however can't be bluffed. As one commentator said *"COVID-19 doesn't give a f— about your feelings".*[2]

So why try? Perhaps it seems easier to appeal to internal t(r)iggers than to advance a logical argument that may lose the greater part of your audience. But surely smart, *thinking* people can't be that easily deceived, especially if lives are on the line?

[1] *"So what? I'm sorry. What do you want me to do?"* [2] Amanda Batty.

As a partial refutation, I'll now present three small vignettes—fairly recent tragedies that illustrate both tiggers and bullshit artistry to a greater or lesser degree. They are all extreme, sometimes very extreme examples.

The first is a tigger that resulted in the virus-related deaths of well over 300,000 people; the second exemplifies social manipulation, with a death *rate* exceeding that of an Ebola virus outbreak. Everybody dies. The third shows that even excessively smart people are susceptible to the manipulation Cicero refers to at the start of the lesson.

These examples all illustrate the key point of this lesson—you are all susceptible, and will be misled unless you are extraordinarily vigilant. Perhaps even despite extraordinary vigilance. It's how you're wired.

Retrovirologist extraordinaire

Peter Duesberg was a renowned virus expert. At the age of 36, he gained tenure at the University of California, Berkeley; at 49, he was elected to the National Academy of Sciences. He however had a little hiccough when AIDS reared up and the human immunodeficiency virus HIV-1 was identified.

Duesberg was an expert on retroviruses and he was emphatic that "HIV doesn't cause AIDS". His article published in 1987 in *Cancer Research* is freely available and well worth a read—not because of its assertions about AIDS, but because it provides an insight into how a smart mind can lose the plot. The main thrust of this rather long article is simple. Duesberg dismisses HIV as the cause of AIDS because "this is not how retroviruses behave". This is his tigger.

It was unfortunate for the Republic of South Africa that just as it entered the 21st century its president, Thabo Mbeki, came across a particular webpage on the Internet. Put up by a Dutch AIDS denialist, this featured Duesberg's opinions and was endorsed by a brilliant man we met back in Lesson 1—Kary Mullis, the inventor of the PCR reaction used not only to identify me, but also HIV.[3] You have refined this testing to the point where you can count the copies of HIV in the blood of those infected, suppress the virus to unmeasurable levels, and turn HIV infection from a lethal illness to a chronic, manageable disorder. However in this website, Mr Mbeki saw salvation—AIDS might not even exist, or if it did, it might be something that required not Western 'anti-retroviral' medicines, but something more amenable to traditional, African solutions.

[3]The website still exists, and still carries that endorsement at http://www.virusmyth.com/aids/, although now it is in memoriam for its original author, who died from an unspecified "lung disease" at the age of 50. A denialist to the end.

Doctors who worked in South Africa at the time watched the change. Overnight, the posters advising safe sex came down. They were replaced by notices about a congress in Durban, where 'conventional scientists' would battle it out with 'HIV denialists'. Programs to stop the virus and prevent transmission from mothers to their children around the time of childbirth were halted in their tracks.

Alternative therapists were welcomed instead. People like Matthias Rath, the former head of Cardiovascular Research at the Linus Pauling Institute in Palo Alto in California, who claimed that anti-retrovirals were "poison", and promoted vitamin therapy for AIDS.[4] There is a certain dreadful irony in the fact that in seeking an African solution for AIDS Mbeki and his health minister succumbed to the blandishments of a German pill manufacturer.

Three themes seem to run through the South African HIV fiasco. The first is mistrust of 'science'; the second is Duesberg's little tigger, but the third is perhaps most disturbing. Why should Kary Mullis, who invented part of the solution to HIV, endorse a crazy, conspiracy-theory website? The answer is in his own words, prominently displayed on the virusmyth website:

> "If there is evidence that HIV causes AIDS, there should be scientific documents which either singly or collectively demonstrate that fact, at least with a high probability. There is no such document."

Sadly, a Nobel-prizewinning scientist can still fundamentally misunderstand Good Science. As we've discovered, Good Science is about self-criticism, and provisional acceptance of 'truths'.

Perhaps the main point to take away is that you don't have to be malicious or unintelligent to contribute to a disaster—you can be very bright, even well-meaning. If however, you extrapolate what you know and are insufficiently self-critical, you may find yourself used by others, used in ventures that harm, maim and kill people for profit.

Were it not for the actions of Zackie Achmat, a brave HIV activist, Rath would likely have inflicted more harm; but in 2008 the Cape Town High Court forced his exit.[5] The damage had however already been done. The direct consequences of Mbeki's turn-about almost certainly include over 300,000 deaths.[6] South Africa and adjacent countries (Lesotho, Eswatini and Botswana) have the highest HIV rates in the world, with about one in five people infected.

---

[4]When taken to task by (among others) The Guardian newspaper, Rath sued the paper and the author of its *Bad Science* column Ben Goldacre, although ultimately he ended up being ordered to pay costs. See https://www.theguardian.com/world/2008/sep/12/matthiasrath.aids2. Ben Goldacre's meticulous write-up is freely available as *The Doctor Will Sue You Now*. Goldacre's research suggests that it was an employee of Rath, a South African barrister called Anthony Brink, who first drew Mbeki's attention to the virusmyth website.

[5]See saflii.org/za/cases/ZAWCHC/2008/34.html [6]PubMed 19186354

James W Jones

James Warren Jones was a charismatic American preacher and faith healer. Although he was likely an atheist, after seeing how faith healing attracted people and money, he organized a mammoth, four-day religious convention in June 1956, which allowed him to launch his own church, an interracial "Peoples Temple". He seemed to be a force for good, and received a lot of backing from people on the political 'left'. But at the same time, he read voraciously about how to manipulate people—and practised on his parishioners. After he moved to California in 1963, his church grew exponentially. His influence also grew. Just days before the 1976 US elections, his church was publicly praised by the vice-presidential candidate Walter Mondale; Jimmy Carter's wife Rosalynn met him often.

Jim Jones had discovered how easy it is to lead others by the nose. The formula is pretty simple: warn people that apocalyptic threats are imminent, and explain that you alone have the solution. Distort their perception of reality, so that they can't tell the fake news from real news. Demonize all opposition, and use the power of the crowd to isolate those followers who might disagree. His ultimate isolation was of course a move to another country, where his followers would be totally dependent on him.

The "Peoples Temple Agricultural Project" was established in 1973 on 1500 hectares of land in northwestern Guyana, when several Temple members defected, and Jones became embattled in a paternity dispute. The settlement was nicknamed "Jonestown".

Jones seems to have chosen Guyana not just for its remote location, but also after researching extradition laws. Initially, a few hundred Temple members moved there, followed by Jones and many more followers in 1977. With his arrival, isolation and indoctrination worsened; members (two thirds of them African Americans) signed over their social security cheques to Jones. People who disagreed were confined; children who misbehaved were left overnight in a well. Escapees were captured, detained and drugged.

Eventually, evidence of abuse leaked out and a group of 'Concerned Relatives' was formed. On November 14, 1978, Californian congressman Leo Ryan flew to Jonestown to investigate their complaints. He witnessed well-rehearsed celebrations, intended to convince him that all was well, but then Temple members made moves to defect. This culminated in the shooting of Ryan and several others at the nearby Port Kaituma airstrip, followed by the mass murder-suicide of over nine hundred people at Jonestown.

The forty-minute group discussion leading up to the massacre was recorded and makes for *very* disturbing listening. Three hundred children were forced to drink cyanide laced Kool-Aid and Flavor Aid, after which their parents drank the potion, often at gunpoint. This was the largest single peacetime loss of American lives before 9/11.

Now, although tragic, the Jonestown massacre might seem a bit off piste. What might this have to do with the politics of COVID-19? I'd suggest, quite a lot. Jim Jones didn't originate the techniques he used to manipulate his followers. He was an avid reader and knew how, for example, mass rallies were conducted in Nazi Germany, and how dissent was quashed. If anything, the Internet now makes it far easier to achieve similar control—as shown recently by Cambridge Analytica.

Jonestown is just an egregious example of what is happening every day on social media. If you struggle to discern falsehood from truth, and are fed a diet of unreason, how do you differ from those in Jonestown?

The Supreme Truth

Reading the preceding vignette, you might still argue that Jones preyed on poorly literate, susceptible people. You might interpret the South African fiasco in a similar light—a renegade retrovirologist, a molecular biologist who was good in his day, and a president relatively unschooled in modern science, preyed upon by a charlatan. Surely large numbers of *smart* people can't be taken in with similar ease?

The story of Chizuo Matsumoto suggests they can. A partially-sighted former school-yard bully who started off by making his living from acupuncture and Traditional Chinese Medicine, in 1987 he changed his name to Shoko Asahara and simultaneously renamed the cult he'd founded a few years earlier to *Aum Shinrikyo*. A mash-up of the Bible, Buddhism and Hinduism (notably Shiva, the destroyer), his new religion took off like a rocket. He soon had 40,000 members, retention being somewhat enhanced by techniques that should now be familiar—embedding members in fake news, and using social pressure (and sometimes drugs and violence) to keep them on board.

Tsutsumi Sakamoto, an anti-cult lawyer intending to expose them had his confidentiality broken by the Japanese TBS talk-show, and subsequently disappeared without trace, together with his wife and fourteen-month-old son. The show was not aired.

On 20 March 1995, members of the Aum sect released the nerve agent sarin within the Tokyo subway system, killing 13, seriously injuring 54, and affecting between 980 and 6000 other people, many of whom have subsequently been reluctant to come forward. Over subsequent weeks, 150 cult members were arrested; evidence was found of rather incompetent attempts to manufacture weapons, culture and disseminate anthrax, and a prior sarin attack that the police had bungled. Asahara was captured, sentenced to death, and finally executed 18 years later; but remarkably, the sect has rebranded itself as "Aleph" and continues to attract followers and funding.

The educational level of many of Aum's recruits is noteworthy. Asahara specifically targeted top Japanese universities, recruiting disenchanted physicists, chemists, computer nerds, engineers and doctors. Tomomasa Nakagawa, whose rap sheet was second only to that of Asahara, joined the cult as a young medical student. He was directly involved in the murder of Tsutsumi Sakamoto and his family—the victims were injected with potassium chloride and strangled.

It seems Asahara appealed to bored Japanese intellectuals, publishing manga-themed comics and cartoons that referred to space missions, Isaac Asimov's *Foundation Trilogy*, powerful weapons and world conspiracies. And they bought it. The money rolled in.

The message I take from this is that nobody, but nobody is immune. Some may be more resistant—Asahara seems to have struggled to recruit competent biochemists and microbiologists—but the sad conclusion is that given the wrong inputs, everyone is susceptible to the same techniques of deception that are now easier and easier to disseminate and promote. Human beings are more similar than they are different.

An extreme position

The above three vignettes have several things in common; perhaps the most obvious of these it that they are all extreme. You can argue that although disturbing and illustrative, they touch only lightly on the mass of humanity. Surely, a few people (or even enough people) here and there can be manipulated for fun, profit and occasionally, for reasons that are quite mad; but isn't undue emphasis on these anomalies itself an extreme position? Just because it can occur, doesn't mean that it will occur.

A similar emphasis on the middle ground is perhaps why humans are handling COVID-19 so poorly. In 2015, the smart billionaire Bill Gates clearly predicted the current pandemic—and few listened.[7] This is one strand to an argument that I'll develop in subsequent lessons. But there is a more obvious argument that says I'm not being extreme or alarmist in discussing extreme examples. Consider again my three pillars of Good Science from Lesson 5, shortened just slightly:

(1) Try to explain a problem;

(2) Attack the explanation vigorously;

(3) If it holds up, *provisionally* accept it as 'true'.

Although difficult to get right consistently, and never perfect, these requirements are not arcane. Now consider striking out one of these pillars, and what do you get? An ad hoc explanation; pandering to an inner tigger; or unquestioning and irreversible acceptance. Once you understand extreme consequences, milder examples pop up everywhere.

[7] You can watch the TED talk at https://www.youtube.com/watch?v=6Af6b_wyiwI

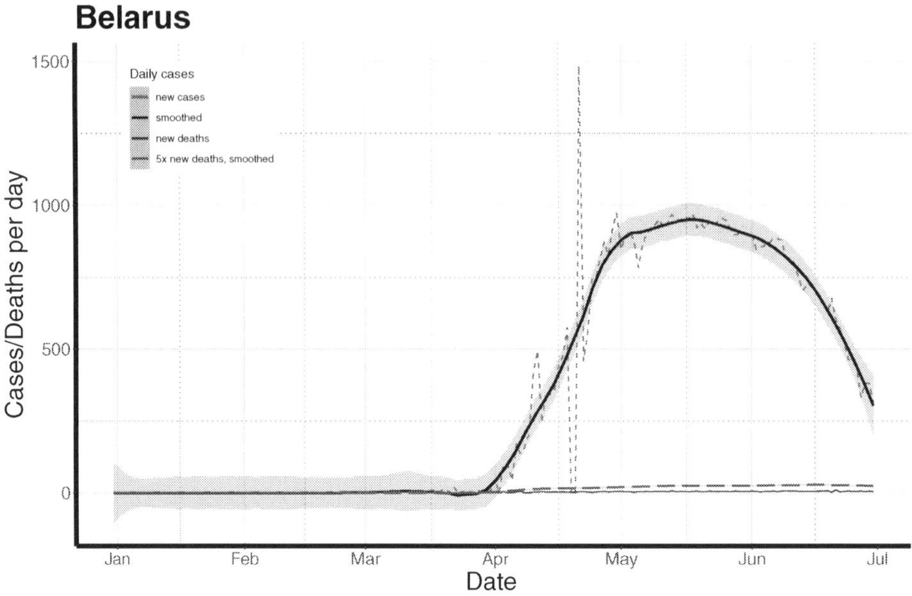

Figure 15. Untruths in Belarus

Lies

I get the impression that many politicians—especially those who have failed to contain me—simply don't get the above model. If you kick out a pillar, things will wobble and fall, whether you're perching a tiny fib or a great big ball of madness on your platform. To get some feel for the consequences, how bullshit evolves into lies, let's look at my welcome in Belarus.

Fig 15 may not look like much, but as you become more and more familiar with me, you'll realise the enormity of the lie that is being perpetrated here. There are four lines on this graph of official figures for daily COVID-19 cases. These are a dotted grey line—the number of reported cases, which fluctuates rather a lot, especially initially; a smoothed black line that removes some of the variation; an almost imperceptible line close to the baseline that show the 'actual number of deaths', and a more prominent dashed line that shows that number of deaths multiplied by five.[8]

The multiplication is simply to draw the death curve into prominence, and make it easier for us to relate this to the "cases" curve. Using the R code in Appendix A, you can make your own curves. Try e.g. `corona_country('Belgium')` too.

As of 30 June, the total number of cases reported in Belarus is 61,790, and the total number of deaths is just 387, a 'case fatality rate' (CFR) of just 0.6%. If we believe the official statistics, just 1 in 160 patients shown to have COVID-19 died.

[8]The last two lines are red in the program-generated version of this graph.

It is often unwise to compare countries, especially when it comes to new diseases, but here such a comparison is very valuable. We have learned the merit of attacking assertions with all the tools at our disposal. The assertion here is that the case fatality rate in Belarus is remarkably low.

Logically, there are several possible explanations for this "extraordinary success". These are:

(1) Belarus has world-class healthcare. They manage COVID-19 so well that almost nobody dies. In contrast Germany, widely known to have excellent healthcare facilities and superb care, has a CFR of 4.6%. Is Belarus nearly eight times better?

(2) Belarus has a superb COVID-19 detection system. Later on we'll discover that a likely infection fatality rate (IFR) for infection with me is about 0.5–1%. In other words, world-beating Belarusian epidemiological surveillance picks up almost every case, far out-performing most other countries.

(3) Through some quirk of fate, Belarusians are naturally resistant to COVID-19.

(4) The official statistics are lies.

Were you to ask the President of Belarus, Alexander Lukashenko which of these options is true, there is little doubt in my mind that he would say "The first three" and then wax lyrical about how, on 16 March, he dismissed the threat I posed, with the injunction that people should work in the fields (with their tractors) as a solution, and that their low death rate is a demonstration of the success of his later injunction to poison the virus with vodka.[9] And he doesn't even have a koteka!

Let's thus take a Bayesian look at these data. What are the priors? If you look at the healthcare system of Belarus, then there have been enormous strides in the past two decades to improve the quality of care, despite their legacy of older, Soviet-style hospitals. Infant mortality rates have decreased dramatically, and Belarus has one of the highest numbers of hospital beds per head of population in the world.

However, in terms of life expectancy, Belarus is number 92 in the world. Working-age men are comorbid and die prematurely related to poor primary care (and vodka). The prior chances of surveillance mechanisms or delivery of care for COVID-19 being an order of magnitude better than in Germany seem negligible.

There are also reasons for concern about the official statistics. Belarus has been under Lukashenko's rule since 1994, "Europe's last dictatorship", and in 2020 ranks 153 out of 180 nations in terms of the Press Freedom Index.[10]

---

[9]See e.g. edition.cnn.com/2020/03/30/europe/soviet-strongmen-coronavirus-intl/index.html. [10]Reporters Without Borders, https://rsf.org/en/ranking

Figure 16. The Cow Pock

In addition, on 13 April Lukashenko made the following promise[11] to COVID-19 patients in hospital:

> "There's no reason for them to worry. No one will die from coronavirus in our country. I am stating this publicly".

He instead blamed other chronic illnesses. You can make up your own mind about the trustworthiness of Fig 15, but I'll call bullshit on this one.

Karen from Facebook

Finally, let's consider a position that might be considered a bit more moderate than lying to an entire country, persuading your followers to perpetrate mass murder, inciting mass murder-suicide, or national leaders abandoning reason.

There have always been anti-vaxxers, although now the more PC term is "vaccine hesitancy". I would consider them my acolytes, if they weren't so crazy. At the start of the 19th century, cartoonists had a field day with the smallpox vaccine, conjuring up images of cows sprouting from the foreheads of vaccinees (Fig 16); seeing smallpox diminished and then eliminated put a damper on their efforts. However, once viral illnesses have been suppressed, old habits return.

[11] people.onliner.by/2020/04/13/lukashenko-326

Figure 17. A tsunami stone

I have been likened to a tsunami. In the popular imagination, tsunamis are towering waves that smash down on everything. This is far from the truth. Initially, the sea often recedes; when it returns, the surge may seem unimpressive. But like many natural disasters, tsunamis have reach. The surge rises, and rises and rises, obliterating almost everything; when the water flows back, everything still remaining is crushed and broken.

Have you heard of tsunami stones? These dot the northern coastline of Japan. In the small town of Aneyoshi, a three-metre-tall stone says "Do not build below this point". Fumihiko Imamura, a highly-cited Tōhoku university professor who has decades of experience in both modelling and investigating tsunamis, is quoted[12] as saying:

> "It takes about three generations for people to forget. Those that experience the disaster themselves pass it to their children and their grandchildren, but then the memory fades"

This generational tendency to forget may be a near-universal human failing. In 2011, the magnitude 9 Tōhoku earthquake and tsunami breached the defensive barriers around the Fukushima Daiichi Nuclear Plant, leading to the nuclear disaster there. Tens of thousands on the coastline were overwhelmed by this tsunami, often because they ignored their ancestors' warnings. Clear communication may however buck the trend.

[12] From cbsnews.com/news/ancient-stone-markers-warned-of-tsunamis/

Amid the devastation in Japan, everyone in Aneyoshi survived, because they heeded the message carved in stone (Figure 17).

Memories of harm are not helped if a relatively small proportion of people were injured. A good example is polio, where under one in 100 infections result in irreversible paralysis. Better healthcare also removes the Angel of Death from the foot of the bed—for example, formerly death rates from tetanus were extreme, but now many children will emerge relatively unscathed after some painful weeks in intensive care.

The recent trajectory of the anti-vax movement does however emphasise two points we've already covered. The first is that the Internet can confine people to their own echo chamber without all the bother of moving to Guyana; the second is that viral spread of anti-science is easy. As with doomsday cults, single individuals have a disproportionate effect, and once they have taken advantage of their followers' vulnerability, anything becomes not just believable but believed.

Take Andrew Wakefield. You'd think that someone who *fraudulently* claimed an association between vaccination and autism[13] would not command respect on medical matters. You would be wrong. Instead he has profitably doubled down, attacking his medical critics, including the US Centres for Disease Control and Prevention.

Vaccination rates in the UK and in the US have dropped substantially. Whooping cough and measles, which were on the verge of extinction, have reappeared. Many parents still cite 'autism' as a concern, although a multitude of new myths have also emerged—this is a bit like the arcade game whack-a-mole, where as soon as one myth is put to rest, another rises.

What can thinking people do? You might be tempted to create your own viral "counter-myths", but this is unwise. Doing Good Science is difficult enough. It may be smarter to create tsunami stones! As you'll find in the next lesson, even 'heroes of science' can get things spectacularly wrong. So wrong that they echo the rants of politicians like Lukashenko.

Lesson #7

People are easier to bluff than viruses.

[13] See e.g. PubMed 21209059. He was also struck off the UK medical register for accepting money from solicitors while conducting investigations that he was not qualified to do, for being dishonest to parents, for conducting unethical studies, for purchasing blood samples from children at his son's birthday party, and for showing "callous disregard for any distress or pain the children might suffer".

⊛ Lesson 8

Feet of Clay

"In the past week, Covid-19 has started behaving a lot like the once-in-a-century pathogen we've been worried about. I hope it's not that bad, but we should assume it will be until we know otherwise."

Bill Gates. *New England Journal of Medicine,* 28 February 2020.

"And whereas thou sawest the feet and toes, part of potters' clay, and part of iron, the kingdom shall be divided"

Daniel 2:41–43, King James Bible. [original c 165 BCE]

The oldest ceramic image found so far is the Venus of Dolní Věstonice, a female figure with huge pendulous breasts. Meticulous examination of the figurine shows a single fingerprint on the back—likely that of an eleven-year-old child.[1] You can just imagine an Eastern Gravettian mom twenty-five centuries ago saying "No! Don't touch that!" Around the world, it is likely that ceramic art has been discovered and lost many times in the course of human history.[2] This may be simply because the temptation for kids to squish and shape clay is irresistible, almost on a par with playing with fire. Juxtapose the two and you have pottery.

If however you end up looking after children in South Africa, consider declining any invitation to play *kleilat gooi.*[3] This is the fine art of attaching a lump of clay to a pointy stick[4] and hurling it at the opposition—involving not just warfare but also every chance of eye injuries and parental wrath. Kids will of course play it if given a chance. In this country previously riven by apartheid, a taxonomy of madness that separated

[1] Anthropologie 2002; 40(2) 107-113 [2] Although the evidence suggests that the Chinese have made and fired pots continually for 20,000 years. The famous Terracotta army was buried in 208 BCE and only discovered in 1974. [3] In the muddy water you might find a *platanna*—but beware of the claws. By exporting vast numbers in the 1930s for pregnancy tests, humans may have been responsible for spreading Bd, a fungus that plays nicely with the platanna, but has caused a deadly epidemic around the world. [4] The ideal stick is 2 cm wide and 60 cm long.

people based on the colour of their skin, every enthusiastic participant in *kleilat* will thankfully end up a uniform muddy brown. It's a pity it isn't more widely encouraged.

In myths from around the world, gods teach pottery, but fire seems always to be stolen—in Polynesia, Māui stole fire from the mud hens; according to the Mazatec from Mexico, the opossum stole fire from an old woman; in Canada, the trickster Nanabozho stole fire from the Thunderbird; Australian aboriginal myths have a crow steal fire from the Seven Sisters; and the Greeks had Prometheus.

Perhaps your heroes are modelled on children being chastised by their parents—and still persisting? Mythical heroes have their fair share of failures and punishment—usually by gods; modern human heroes are not immune, but the gods have retreated, replaced by public opinion and paparazzi, arguably as bad as having a daily eagle peck out your liver.

Fated to die?

It is therefore with some reluctance that I'm going to criticise my two greatest heroes. I won't name them, because the purpose of this lesson is simply to illustrate a point. They are however easily identified. My first hero is deservedly the public face of "understanding risk" in the United Kingdom, with a curriculum vitae as long as your arm. He is a former President of the Royal Statistical Society; he worked for the Cambridge Statistical Laboratory and the Medical Research Council Biostatistics Unit, and in the 1990s, led development of remarkable, free software for Bayesian simulation.

This Bayesian master promotes the innovative idea of "micromorts"—a one-in-a-million chance of dying that is useful for rating the risk of doing ordinary activities. For example scuba diving carries a risk of about 5–10 micromorts per dive, similar to the risk of skydiving once, or running a single marathon. Base-jumping from Kjerag Massif in Norway carries a risk of 430 micromorts per jump; each attempt to climb Mount Everest weighs in at 37,932 micromorts. *On average*, catching COVID-19 likely rates at over 5,000 micromorts. But I digress yet again.[5]

When my hero commented on *my* disease in *Medium*, I was flattered and keen to hear his thoughts. There he somewhat glibly points out that "we're all going to die sometime" and that if you plot the baseline age-specific risk of dying from any cause, and overlay the age-specific risk of dying from infection with COVID-19, the graphs are remarkably similar. Here are two excerpts:

> "So, roughly speaking, we might say that getting COVID-19 is like packing a year's worth of risk into a week or two. Which is why

[5] A paper he wrote that really blew me away was one that he co-authored with Harvey Goldstein in 1996—it clearly shows the limitations and dangers of using ***league tables*** unthinkingly in healthcare, an idea that resonates with me. Oops, I already mentioned this on page 49.

> it's important to spread out the infections to avoid the NHS being overwhelmed."
>
> "Also ... there will be substantial overlap in these two groups — *many people who die of COVID would have died anyway within a short period* — and so these risks cannot be simply added, and it does not simply double the risk of people who get infected. It is crucially important that the NHS is not overwhelmed, but if COVID deaths can be kept in the order of say 20,000 by stringent suppression measures, as is now being suggested, there may end up being a minimal impact on overall mortality for 2020 (although background mortality could increase due to pressures on the health services and the side-effects of isolation). Although, as we are seeing, at vast cost." [my emphasis]

This has eerie echoes of Lukashenko's argument in Lesson 7 — that "It wasn't the coronavirus that killed them". Can you spot any flaws?

It is pretty obvious that those who are sicker will be more likely to succumb, but in saying that "there may end up being a minimal impact on overall mortality for 2020", my hero seems to be committing an impressive statistical folly—he is assuming strong co-variation between the deaths from COVID-19 and deaths that *might* have happened from all of those other causes—causes that pack, as it were, a year's worth of risk into a spectacular few hours of acute myocardial infarction or stroke.

A second concern is the human cost. If you die from COVID-19, you'll likely die alone—or at least, separated from those you hold most dear. Putting this aside, let's look at the idea of "minimal impact on overall mortality". In the light of Fig 8 on page 44, this seems like wild speculation.

But let's assume that all of those deaths were simply "compressed". These people will on average have lost six months of life, even if you stretch things out continuously—a rolling wave of COVID-19 deaths competes with other causes of death.

Now try a little thought experiment. Imagine a magical box, that allows you to identify everyone with just six months left to live. A large part of health-care expenditure is consumed in those last six months, so in the interests of the community as a whole, and perhaps because those six months will often be quite miserable, you consult your magical box and dictate that these lives should be ended quickly and painlessly as the six-month-left-to-live mark comes up. There is effectively no difference between calmly planning COVID-19 strategies that accept earlier deaths of older people, and that box. Uncomfortable yet?

No!

Is there any chance that we might actually answer the question "How 'co-morbid' were those who died?" Shortly after I wrote the above, I came across a paper that looks carefully at those who are dying in the UK.[6]

ISARIC is the International Severe Acute Respiratory and emerging Infections Consortium. They report their first findings on 16,749 patients admitted to 166 UK hospitals, all with severe COVID-19.[7]

The median age of the patients was 72 years; the median duration of hospital stay was a week. Forty-seven percent had *no* documented co-morbidity. Chronic heart disease was present in 29%, and about one fifth had uncomplicated diabetes or chronic lung disease (without asthma). One in seven had asthma. Obesity was also an independent risk factor for in-hospital death. Half were discharged alive, one third had died at the time of publication, and the rest were still in hospital. Seventeen percent were admitted to ICU or a high-dependency unit.

As expected, older age increased the risk of dying, even after adjustment for comorbidity. Clearly, older patients were less likely to receive mechanical ventilation—many died on the wards. If however we look at those who were ventilated, they had a median age of 61 years (IQR 52,69)—so from Lesson 3, you know that half were under the age of 61 years. Just 20% had been discharged by the date of the report, and 53% had died.

The authors comment:

> "However, although age-adjusted mortality rates are high in the elderly, most of these patients were admitted to hospital with symptoms of COVID-19 and *would not have died otherwise.* " [my emphasis]

Their study also puts to bed speculation that COVID-19 in hospital is just like a bad 'flu. Their chief investigator Calum Semple is quoted as saying[8]:

> "Covid-19 is an incredibly dangerous disease. The crude hospital fatality rate is of the same magnitude as Ebola".

Of course I have to be honest here—this really is fan mail. I wouldn't put myself up there with Ebola. If you end up in a UK hospital (or many other hospitals), you're pretty sick, and COVID-19 is pretty grim. But I do have a gentler aspect too. As you know, many others whom I infect don't die. Later on in this lesson, we'll try to quantify this. Now for my next hero.

---

[6] We viruses like to keep current with the literature. It's like fan mail. [7] See https://isaric4c.net/info.
[8] PubMed 32354787

An American idol

My second clay-footed hero is a Harvard physician, who did infectious disease at Tufts. He's a Professor of Medicine at Stanford. Competitive universities, journals and indeed authors scrutinise something called the 'h index'. This is the maximum value h, such that at least h of the author's papers are cited h times. Its originator Jorge E Hirsch claimed that a 'successful scientist' would have an h index of 20 after 20 years of hard work; 60 is 'truly unique'. This hero currently has an h index just shy of 200.

But more than this, he's written some seriously good stuff. In 2005 he published a superb analysis of why most published research findings are just false — an insightful, essentially Bayesian take on the research industry. As he says—or used to say—"What matters is the totality of the evidence". He's contributed meaningfully to vital research guidelines like STROBE and PRISMA.

So what did he have to say about COVID-19? In a March 2020 article, he speculates that COVID-19 may be a "once-in-a-century evidence fiasco", lamenting "draconian countermeasures" put in place in many countries.

He then goes on to make a series of bloopers. The first is the statement "The data collected so far on how many people are infected and how the epidemic is evolving are utterly unreliable."

Note the use of the emotive word 'utterly'—coming from an expert in Bayesian statistics, this is embarrassing. If the data are 'utterly' unreliable, this surely means "nothing but noise". But even at the time of writing, you knew rather a lot about me. You knew my gene sequence, its similarity to SARS-CoV-1, and that I was spreading and killing people. You had 'ballpark' figures of my R_0 and incubation period. Prior information can't simply be ignored for the sake of an emotive headline.

He then laments an "evidence fiasco", correctly saying there is uncertainty about things like reported case mortality rates. Properly primed, you may now wish to take a Bayesian look at the following sentence:

> "Reported case fatality rates, like the official 3.4% rate from the World Health Organization, cause horror — and are meaningless."

That this article is political spin is highlighted by its own internal consistencies. For example, after decrying the meaningless nature of the death rate, he provides a death rate—1.0% from the Diamond Princess—and uses this value to "project onto the age structure of the US population", now even inserting some confidence intervals.[9]

[9]He also makes the traditional statistical error of assuming that the numbers he has are the final ones. If people are still dying, this is a bad mistake to make. When I last looked at the Diamond Princess numbers (1/5) the death rate was 13/712, or 1.8%. Oops!

All this from 'meaningless' data![10] It seems that one of my heroes has a whole cupboard full of soft toys, at least one of them a tigger from Lesson 6. In the hyper-partisan environment of the United States, his pronouncements have been seized upon with great enthusiasm, and may even have influenced a number of really bad decisions.

Comparisons

Sometimes it's wise to get over disappointment. The preceding criticism actually invites several worthwhile questions: "Do lockdowns even work?" and "Are they worth the economic costs?" I'll defer answering these to Lessons 9 and 11 respectively, but an immediate question is "What can we learn from the limited data we do have?"

Let's start by counting bodies. As we found in Lesson 1, even with the benefit of hindsight, we don't know to the nearest ten million or so how many people H1N1 killed one hundred years ago. But influenza kills every year. Current estimates[11] suggest that about 389,000 people succumb annually (in the range of just under 300,000 deaths, to just over 500,000). By end-June, *my* official tally is over half a million, but the true numbers are likely far higher, and I haven't finished yet.

We can also look at infections and hospitalisations. We have already seen that if you're in hospital in the UK, your chances of surviving COVID-19 are no better than two in three. Deaths may represent a fairly small proportion of all of those I've infected—but what proportion? In other words, what is the "Infection Fatality Rate?" Answering the question "How many people die for every 100 infections?" turns out to be an extremely difficult question to answer, not only for me, but even for influenza.

So a proxy like the Case Fatality Rate (CFR) is often used—what percentage of those diagnosed die? These are the rates already disparaged by my hero, but the same argument applies for influenza! For example, Wong and colleagues[12] reviewed 77 estimates of CFR for H1N1 after the 2009 influenza pandemic, and found what they call "substantial heterogeneity in published estimates"—ranging from one death per 100,000 cases, to 10,000 deaths per 100,000 cases. Now that's variability! If you compare CFRs, both your yardsticks are flawed.

But as we discovered in Lesson 4 & 5 during our digressions into Bayes and information theory, there's often information contained in a noisy signal—we often just need to look in the right way. We also know that Good Science is grown up enough to accommodate error; all models are trivially wrong, but some are useful. Let's put these ideas to good use.

---

[10] I won't go into his subsequent arguments by analogy—suicidal elephants jumping off cliffs. I will not detail his paper ironically decrying 'sensationalism' in discussing me, where he concentrates on the optics, and again draws inferences from any similarity I might have to H1N1. H1N1, again! The pain is too great.
[11] PubMed 31673337 [12] PubMed 24045719

Limits to the Infection Fatality Rate

We can likely establish an upper limit to the IFR—but this value is often ridiculously large. For example, in Italy on 30 June 2020, the COVID-19 CFR works out as nearly 14.5%. As a measure of IFR, this is just plain silly, but is evidence of a sort. It's evidence that many milder cases were missed. In the past, you believed that many or even most of those whom I've infected are asymptomatic, but more recent evidence suggests that some people identified as 'asymptomatic' may go on to develop symptoms later on. For example, in a nursing facility where 57 of 89 residents tested positive, over half of those who initially tested positive (56%) were asymptomatic; all but three however subsequently became symptomatic.[13] 'Presymptomatic' and asymptomatic cases can't just be ignored. There is little doubt that some are efficient spreaders.

As my most recently tarnished hero pointed out, it may therefore be more useful to look at rates in confined populations where there has been extensive screening, as long as we realise that these populations are very special. There are already several such studies. For example on the Diamond Princess, the IFR was just 1.8%. Sophisticated attempts have been made[14] to compensate for the older age distribution on this cruise ship (mean age of 58 years), and these suggest that reports from Wuhan overestimate the "true" IFR by a factor of two, with an IFR of 0.6%.[15]

A study from a small German town is also useful. Gangelt is a community of 12,597 individuals where a super-spreader event occurred at a carnival on 15 February.[16] The authors surveyed 919 individuals in 415 households and used a combination of PCR and serology to identify 138 individuals (15.02%) testing positive. In this careful study they thus estimated that nearly 2000 individuals in the population were infected, and with just 7 reported deaths, they calculated an IFR of 0.36%. One limitation of this study is that they may have missed some deaths, as they censored these on 6 April; another is that German death rates have not been representative of those in other European countries. There are several possibilities why this is so, apart from the obvious possibility that German intensive care units are particularly good. It turns out that even 'flawed' data can be used to tease out a better explanation, but before we examine this, let's look at serology as a way of finding asymptomatic cases, and calculating a decent denominator for our IFR.

[13]See PubMed 32329971; 26% later died; nearly one quarter of staff members also acquired the infection. Other analyses suggest that truly asymptomatic cases are in the minority range of about 18–33%, e.g. PubMed 32183930 but it's possible that about half of cases may be asymptomatic. [14]PubMed 32234121 [15]The catch is that they don't include later deaths. [16]medrxiv.org/content/10.1101/2020.05.04.20090076v1.full.pdf

Serology

Despite the fact that checking for antibodies—serology—is only useful about two weeks after infection, there has been a scramble to produce tests, with quite variable results. Recall the analysis of RT-PCR testing in Lesson 4. If the community prevalence of infection is low, then even a test with a false positive rate of just 2% will likely pick up a large number of false positives for every actual case.

A particularly poor example of misinterpreting false positive tests was an early, sensationalist report from California that claimed there were as many as 80 asymptomatic cases for every person testing positive. This was widely panned by expert statisticians, as the authors had not only failed to check their test sensitivity adequately, but committed a host of rookie errors in performing their study.

There's been an explosion of tests, many of them marketed directly to the public. The director of the Mayo Clinic's Serology Lab is reported to have said "At this point we have more commercially available serologic tests for SARS-CoV-2 than any other infectious disease. It is crazy".[17] Most tests still lack extensive external validation on thousands of controls without the disease. One approved laboratory test (Roche) does however boast 100% sensitivity and 99.8% specificity, on testing against 5272 samples. Another (Abbott) has been tested on 1020 samples and found to have a specificity of 99.9%.

Some preliminary studies have been reported, but as noted, some were poorly designed and executed. So far, that of Garcia-Basteiro et al.[18] seems fairly credible. At a large hospital in Barcelona, Spain, 578 health care workers were screened with both nasal RT-PCR and blood. PCR previously identified COVID-19 in 39 of them; 54 were now seropositive, of whom 61% had previously been diagnosed. These findings are in keeping with analysis of data from the Diamond Princess.

In mid-April, there were about 12,000 deaths with about 215,000 cases in New York state, implying a CFR of about 5.4% (this subsequently increased to over 8%). *If* we instead apply the Gangelt IFR of 0.36%, the number of infections goes up 15-fold to over 3 million, or about 15% of the population. If we use some other estimates of IFR, which can be as low as 0.08%, based on e.g. blood donor screening, then the numbers become quite ludicrous.

But what is the seroprevalence in NY? There's been a lot of press about Governor Andrew Cuomo's tweet claiming a rate of about 12.3% on 3 May 2020.[19] With this rate,

---

[17] You can feast your eyes on the FIND list of tests, if you have a lot of time; there were 641 tests when I last looked at finddx.org/covid-19/pipeline/?section=show-all#diag_tab.

[18] Preprint at doi.org/10.1101/2020.04.27.20082289 [19] Pre-published results suggest a strong selection bias. (medrxiv.org/content/10.1101/2020.05.25.20113050v1)

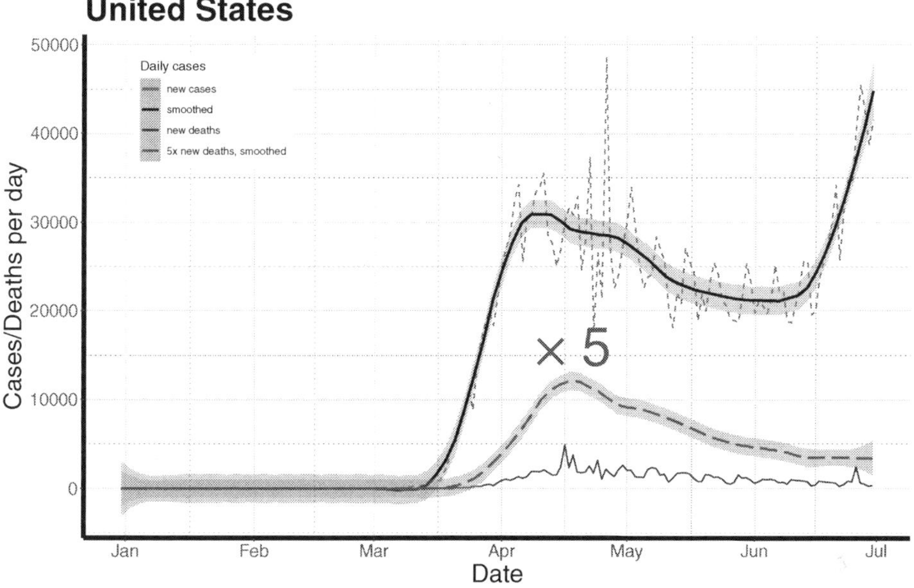

Figure 18. A United States Lag

the IFR might be in the region of 0.5–1%. Interestingly enough, this would again fit well with the Diamond Princess data.

In early June 2020, there was a flurry of articles on seroprevalence, but many of these had methodological issues. A study from Wuhan found a 3.8% rate in healthcare workers from the city, but this is clearly a high-risk cohort.

In Geneva where there were 5000 reported cases in a population of half a million, estimated seroprevalence peaked at 10.8%. With 259 deaths there, this would equate to an IFR of about 0.5%, assuming accurate and complete reporting of deaths.

A preprint from severely hit Milan, where there were 12,000 deaths in April 2020 alone in a population of 10 million, reports that seroprevalence rose to about 5% in blood donors by about 8 April, but the confidence intervals were wide and, as with most blood donor studies, the sample is likely not representative.

In the UK, a small sample reported at the end of May suggested 6.8% seropositivity, again fitting a ballpark IFR of 1%, with a number of caveats. Finally—for now—a large Spanish study reported national rates of 5%, suggesting an IFR of $\sim$ 1%. There will no doubt be many more seroprevalence studies, but early studies all seem to support the idea that even where I've hit hard, there is potential for COVID-19 to do many times as much harm, again.

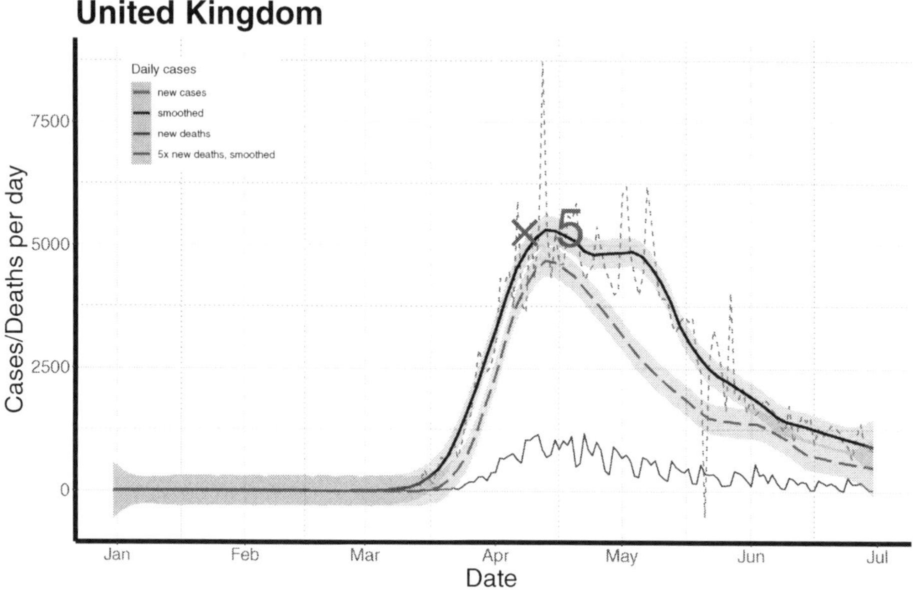

Figure 19. UK rates

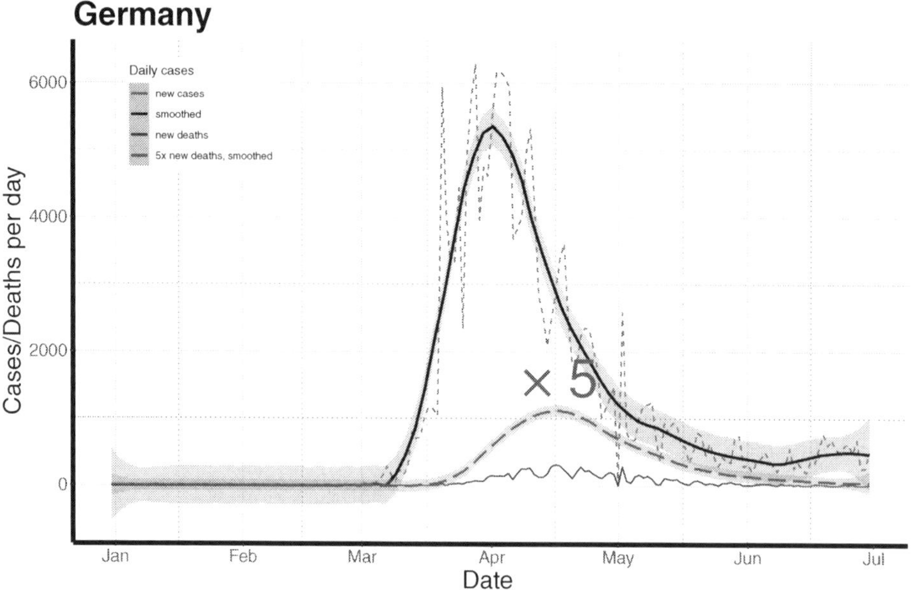

Figure 20. German cases and deaths

An opportunity

Provided we realise the limitations of all data, we can still make powerful inferences. Fig 18 plots new cases over time, in the United States. The same approach has been used as for Belarusian case reports in Fig 15 on page 102. The "5×" dashed line makes it easy for us to compare the two peaks, and it's clear that the death curve lags the new cases by about two weeks. This is not surprising, as we expect a lag between diagnosis and death.

Next, look at the curves for the United Kingdom in Fig 19. Despite the initial shapes being similar, there is a truly remarkable difference when you examine the deaths. Why should the *lag* between the UK incidence and death curves be so short?

Perhaps you can think of a better explanation, but the only solid reason I can come up with is that in the UK, new cases were simply not being detected in adequate numbers in early March. This reflects a monumentally stupid policy directive that was made in early March to *stop* testing in the community.[20] The relative height of the two curves here also presents a marked contrast to the US plot. To me, this suggests that even at the height of the UK death curve, testing was insufficient in comparison to the USA. Finally, look at Germany (Fig 20).

That's the way to do it! Germany has invested a lot of effort in testing and even this crude curve endorses the value of their work. Suddenly, it's clear why death rates are lower in Germany—they have done better than most at obtaining a good denominator. You now have a powerful tool for measuring under-testing—provided that the deaths in the numerator are accurate. What can you deduce from Figures 21 & 22?

Lesson #8

Although an expert is as good as their last prediction,
even 'bad' analyses can inspire productive thought.

[20]The full report is at: https://publications.parliament.uk/pa/cm5801/cmselect/cmsctech/correspondence/200518-Chair-to-Prime-Minister-re-COVID-19-pandemic-some-lessons-learned-so-far.pdf

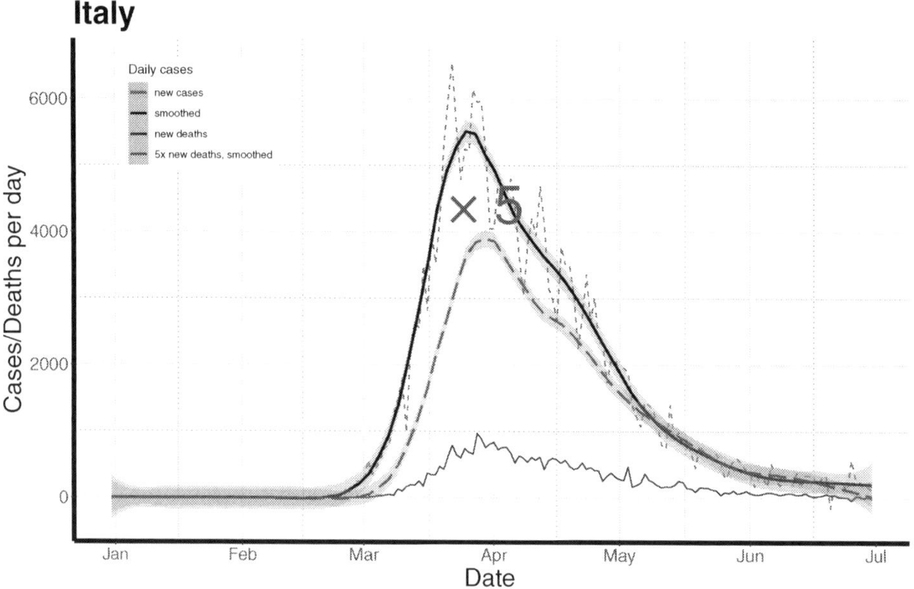

Figure 21. Italy

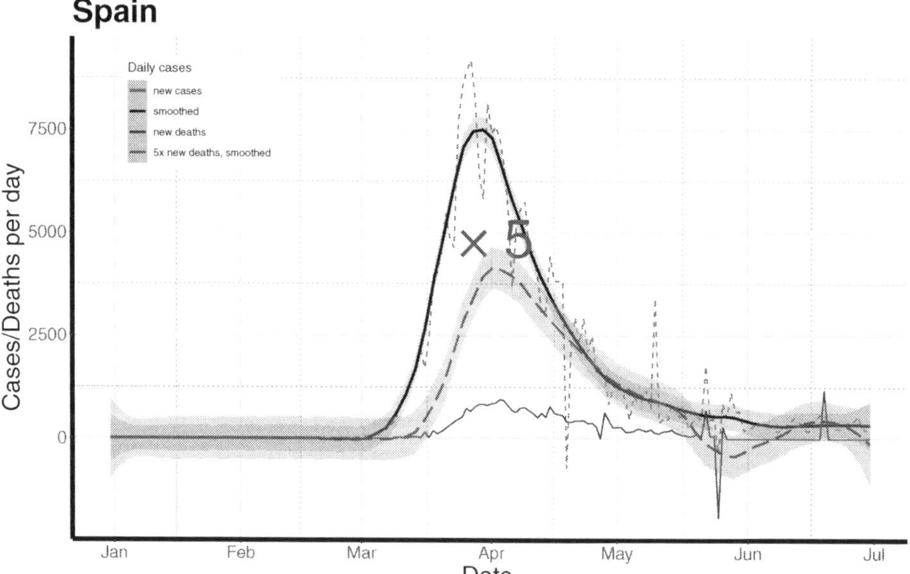

Figure 22. Spain

⊛ Lesson 9

Some Good NewZ

"Spare a thought today for anyone suffering a form of cognitive dissonance causing dismay that the ambulance at the bottom of the cliff is empty because the fence at the top is working."

Clarke Gayford (New Zealand). April 17, 2020. Twitter.

"If what you're doing is working, carry on doing it".

Loeb's Second Law.

"If what you're doing is not working, stop doing it".

Loeb's Third Law.

Gods amplify belief. Lascivious thoughts engender concupiscent gods; mild malice manifests as divinely sanctioned mass murder; but what of a rational god? My preferences emerge more modestly as a love of mathematics and an aversion to brass; I dislike strong sunlight and hot weather.

I am not a weather god. If older gods control the weather, I can but look on in awe. I thought Auckland, New Zealand would please my avatar, with an average summertime high in the twenties, but we arrived to blue skies; most of the clouds left in December when the spicy red pohutukawa flowers fell. Looking after children, I found myself on the beach at Takapuna, heavily plastered with sunblock, and even salted caramel gelato was insufficient compensation.[1] At least the lockdown in March put paid to that. Let's talk of weather and lockdowns. Do lockdowns even work?

The priest's bell

I have read volumes on how you think weather affects me. I can—you say—survive for hours or days on flat surfaces, and your wise men have mixed me with nasal secretions and expectorated sputum and saline and warmed and cooled me and left me to

[1] I am compelled to say that I am not the Rona of Māori myth, who cursed the moon one night, and was swept up to become the woman in the moon, together with her bunch of gourds and the *ngaio* tree she held onto. There are only so many syllables to go around.

dry or saturated the air with water while they nebulize me and dehydrate me and argue about specific humidity. They have spread me on cell cultures enriched with fetal calf serum, and made serious pronouncements about my viability. They have layered me over plastic and paper and cardboard and (Eugh!) brass.

All of this in a sense valuable enterprise, but all of this also a bit silly. From Lesson 3, you'll recall how Semmelweis begged the priest to tread a different path, lest fear of the tolling of his bell bring on the miasma of puerperal fever—all in vain. Semmelweis explored many theories before he found one that worked. Oblivious to danger, you might think it is similarly wise to explore multiple theories. The obvious danger is that there are so many possible theories to explore.

Especially if you already have a theory that works. In Lesson 5 we explored the rarity and value of such theories; enthusiasm must be balanced by the tiggers and folly of the following three lessons. You now know that theories are always provisional and never proven, but they often provide a starting point. Let us not therefore focus on speculation about the weather,[2] but on how you *can* beat me—even eradicate me.

This revelation naturally invites the question "Why Rona do you seem so keen to be beaten?" The answer, alas, must wait until the last lesson. You can skip ahead and peek, but you'll miss half the fun. For now, chalk it down to my characteristic honesty. In the meanwhile, we'll do a bit of epidemiology.

Better than cure

We have already discovered that even the most skilled practitioner of science has one or two cherished soft toys. And every tigger proudly proclaims "I'm the only one"—everyone has bad models, each subtly conditioned by their priors. Deep prior knowledge may be a liability rather than an asset, as happened to Professor Duesberg in Lesson 7. So if you suspect you're stuck on a tigger—you might be lucky enough to have others who point this out—how can you turn a fixation into a fix?

Remarkably, there's often a generic solution. It's this: "Step back!" The fun thing about Good Science is that it is often pretty solid. Even when your ideas seem all wrong, more general approaches may still work fairly well. If the finer points don't fit, change your theory by all means—this may be just what is needed—but first go back to basics. Examine and criticise the fundamentals. This principle applies to epidemics too.

[2]By the way, the answer to "Does the weather affect you?" is "Not that much". See, for example PubMed 32423996 and PubMed 32361460. But you've researched influenza for decades and still do dodgy science, tending to seek proof and ignore exceptions. I've read lots about how low humidity in winter favours 'flu; clearly few of these researchers have felt the 80% humidity in an Auckland winter, but even this is complex, as indoor temperatures tend to be more stable, and relative humidity indoors correlates best with absolute humidity outdoors!

For infection control in a population, the basics are pretty simple. They started with John Snow. Noooo—not *Jon Snow*, but the Victorian physician who both invented epidemiology and also worked out that if you are to give an anaesthetic, which takes someone close to death and then brings them back, it's wise to get the dose right.[3] Like Semmelweis, he was a numbers man. As with all good stories, there's an element of myth attached to the way John Snow identified and removed the handle of a water pump in Soho, London, stopping the 1854 cholera epidemic in its tracks.

Through meticulous hard work—studying the problem and speaking to the locals—Snow realised that the cases were clustered around a pump in Broad Street. He presented the evidence to the local authorities, and the very next day, they disabled the pump. The important ideas here are the hard slog; the cause and effect that he identified; and how he got the authorities on side and acted. Snow was honest enough to say that:

> "There is no doubt that the mortality was much diminished, as I said before, by the flight of the population, which commenced soon after the outbreak; but the attacks had so far diminished before the use of the water was stopped, that it is impossible to decide whether the well still contained the cholera poison in an active state, or whether, from some cause, the water had become free from it".[4]

When their lives are threatened, people often act appropriately, unless deceived. But they can act more effectively if they share a good basic model. The model is this:

(1) Understand the problem—how the disease works, and how it spreads;
(2) Test your model for weaknesses;
(3) Engineer things so that the important players know what to do—and do it!

See how closely this conforms to the definition of Good Science in Lesson 5. Fleshed out it boils down to this: know how to diagnose the disease—not just an array of tests, but in a joined-up way; continually check that your approach is working and that 'plan B' exists; and break transmission by recruiting *everyone* to the task.

Right at the start of Lesson 1, I quoted the World Health Organization. I'll paraphrase the quote here: "All countries should be prepared to contain the new coronavirus. You need active surveillance; you need early detection, case isolation and management; you must trace contacts and prevent spread; you should share all data with us". It seems clear to me that those countries that have listened have succeeded; those countries—large and small—that have failed, failed because they simply didn't take heed. As you

[3]By anaesthetising Queen Victoria with chloroform when she gave birth to the last two of her nine children, he made not just anaesthesia acceptable, but also pain relief during childbirth, a remarkable achievement.

[4]Strangely, naysayers often emphasise the flight of the populace—and miss the main point! Don't make the same mistake.

might expect, nobody got every component perfectly correct, but some came pretty close. Let's get a feel for success. We'll have lots of time for the failures, later.

The World

At over 500,000 deaths worldwide on 30 June 2020, an IFR of about 1% likely reflects about 50 million infections, not the 10.2 million reported. You can double this if the IFR is 0.5%. You already know that imperfect information can still be useful. Consider Fig 23. Here I've taken data from Our World in Data, filtered out smaller countries and those with under 200 cases, and plotted *smoothed* daily rates of new infection. The vertical lines signal national lockdowns.[5] All values are compared to the largest number so far *in that country*. Patterns emerge:

Apparent exponential growth with no let-up – examples include Brazil, India, Bangladesh, Mexico, South Africa, and so forth;

A rapid rise and fall–many countries, including Australia, Austria, China, Japan, New Zealand, South Korea, Taiwan and Thailand;

A rapid rise and more spread-out fall–Denmark, France, Germany, Greece, Israel, Italy and several more;

A rise and fall, with a secondary rise–exemplified by Singapore where the secondary rise dwarfs the initial blip, but also Azerbaijan, Iran, Lebanon and Rwanda;

A rise and plateau–shown best in the USA but also in Canada, Russia and Romania – the UK shows a similar initial plateau ultimately followed by a fall.

Why the different patterns? And if "lockdowns stop epidemics", we must surely focus on failures–Bangladesh, Bolivia, Colombia, the DRC, the Dominican Republic, Pakistan, Russia and the UAE. What about counterexamples, where the curve seems to have settled "without a formal national lockdown"? The obvious example is China, but what about Taiwan, Japan and Vietnam?

Taiwan

It's more than a little unfortunate that Taiwan is excluded from the WHO. On the front door of mainland China, Taiwan was hit hard by SARS in 2003, with 668 cases, and a 27% fatality rate. Learning from this experience, they were prepared. With 24 million people and a high population density,[6] Taiwan was under threat. Worse still, 850,000 of its citizens live in China, and another 400,000 work there. Every year, millions move between the two countries. Yet by June 2020, they had just over 400 cases and seven deaths. How did they achieve this?

[5] Some of these are approximate, as definitions and precise dates may be elusive.

[6] About 650 people per square kilometre. Contrast these rates: Singapore 7900; Bangladesh 1170; South Korea 520; Rwanda 470; and the Netherlands, Israel, India, Burundi all around 400.

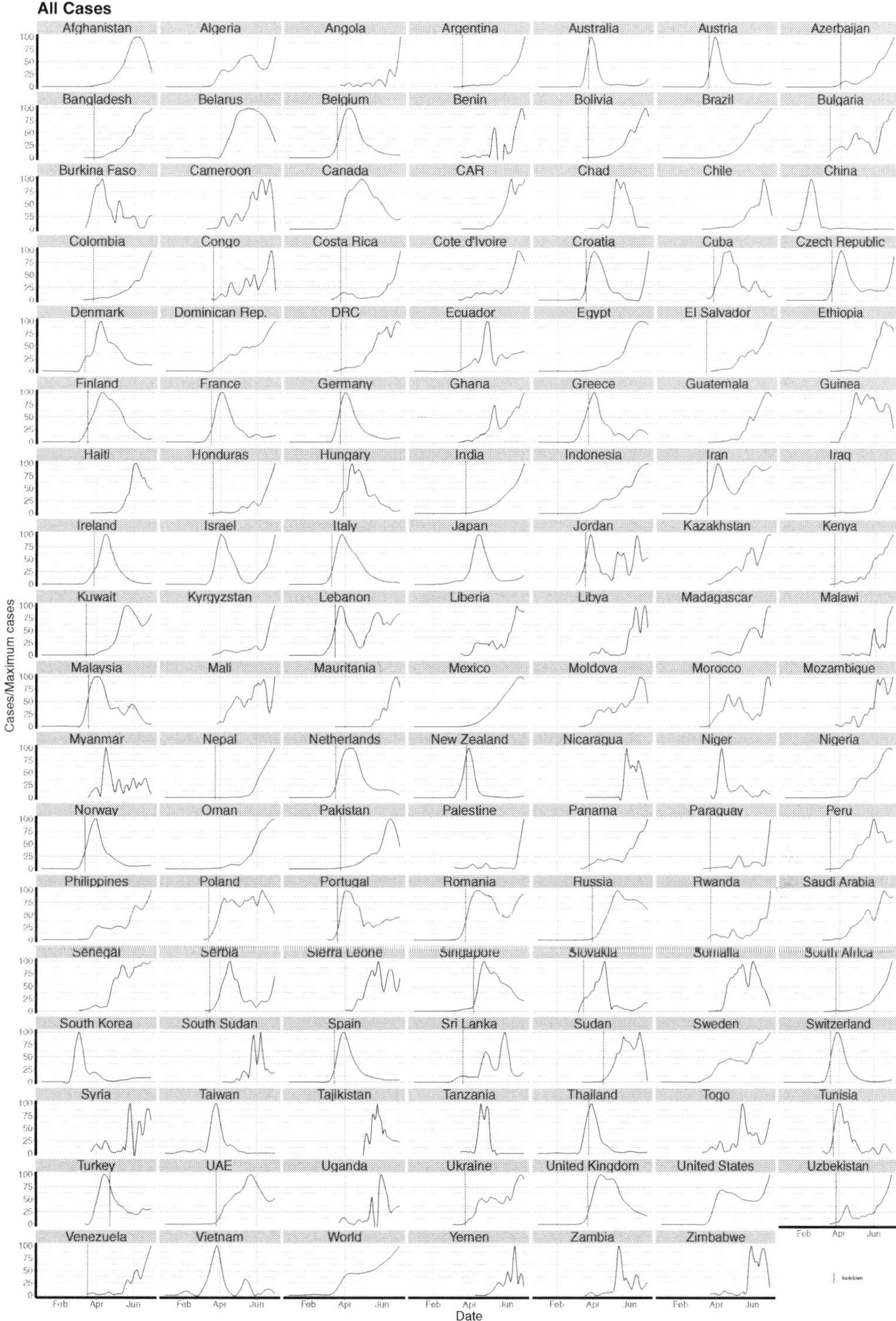

Figure 23. Daily cases by country as of 30 June 2020

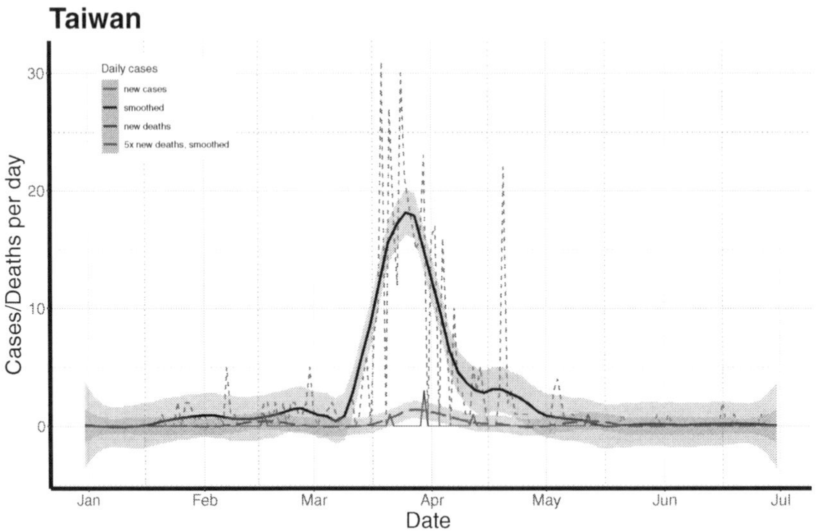

Figure 24. Taiwanese cases and deaths

When asked, President Tsai answered "This success is no coincidence." Lo Yi-Chun, deputy director of Taiwan's Centers for Disease Control, spent New Year's Eve following a thread on a Taiwanese bulletin board (PTT). The talk was of pneumonia in Wuhan. Dr Lo immediately put the country on alert! The political parties in Taiwan joined forces to fix the problem.

In early January, they activated the Central Epidemic Command Centre, introduced travel restrictions, and established quarantine protocols for high-risk travellers. Over one hundred well-coordinated processes were put in place to control the problems they anticipated. Although they never needed to lock down the country, they ran extensive simulations of how they would do this, and the consequences.

Taiwan has superb infrastructure that allowed them to link together all the information systems they needed to manage the virus, tying together immigration, customs and their national health insurance database. Based on analytics, people who were at low risk had a health declaration border pass sent to their cellphones so they could clear immigration more easily; higher-risk people were quarantined at home and tracked via their phones for the entire duration of the incubation period to ensure they complied.

Each major city ended up creating its own, toll-free COVID-19 hotline to field both enquiries and tip-offs. They did everything pretty much faultlessly—diligent contact-tracing, appropriate isolation, and keeping their citizens engaged and in the loop.

It helped that the Minister of Health gave daily public briefings, and that the vice-president, a prominent epidemiologist, broadcast regular public service announcements from the office of the president. To prevent panic-buying (which they had anticipated),

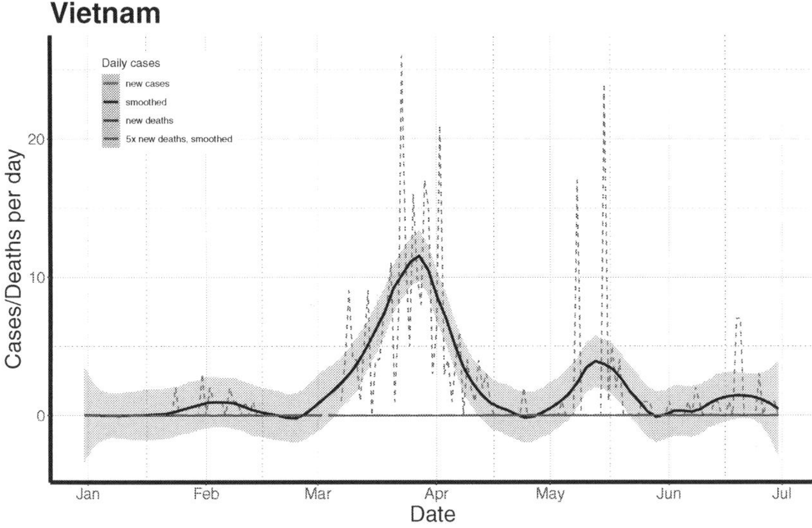

Figure 25. Vietnam

the government took over mask production and distribution. Their results speak for themselves.

Vietnam

Despite a population of 95.5 million, a higher population density than the United Kingdom, and a border with China, Vietnam has also been hugely successful in containing me. How did they achieve this?

The first case was confirmed on 23 January—a Chinese traveller from Wuhan who also infected his son, the first case of human-to-human transmission outside China. He had already been quarantined, and the next day the Minister of Health activated the Emergency Epidemic Prevention Centre.

Within a week, 40 mobile emergency response teams had been set up. By 1 February domestic transmission was documented, prompting tightening of the borders, aggressive quarantining and school closures.[7] A second wave followed in March; this too was contained well, so by the end of April, there were no deaths and under 300 cases.

Vietnam's success wasn't due to luck—and as a poorer country, they couldn't rely on extensive testing. Their efficient mobilisation of government agencies, superb contact-tracing and aggressive quarantine measures explain their success.

[7] This may have been fuelled by disbelief about China's reporting of the crisis.

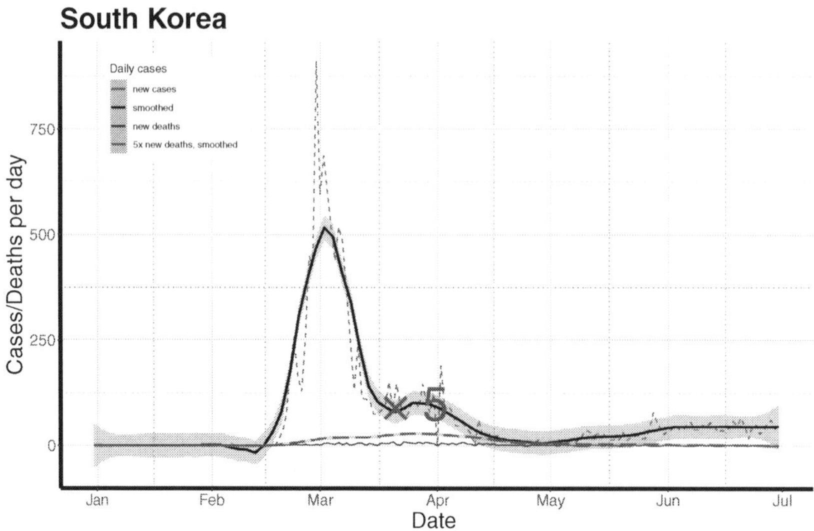

Figure 26. South Korea

Tens of thousands of incoming travellers were quarantined, often in army barracks, whether they were symptomatic or not. Violators and those who spread misinformation were firmly controlled in this communist-ruled country.

The lockdown was gradually eased, and even in May there were still extensive limitations on gatherings of over 20 people, face masks were mandatory in public, and schools were closed.[8]

South Korea

South Korea saw its first case even earlier than Vietnam, but the initial trajectory of the disease was different. After an initial lull, cases rocketed in mid-February, mostly attributed to the now infamous "Patient 31" who spread the virus at religious gatherings.

Travel restrictions were already in place—South Korea had introduced one of the best-orchestrated epidemic control programs in the world, with contact-following and isolation, and mass-screening on a huge scale.

Despite exponential growth in late February, by early March, spread in South Korea was controlled. This was without introducing mass lockdowns. There were over 10,000 cases, but deaths were limited to 256.[9]

---

[8] The secondary rise in mid-May is from repatriated cases. [9] A recent rise in mid-June may reflect relaxation of social distancing that some consider premature.

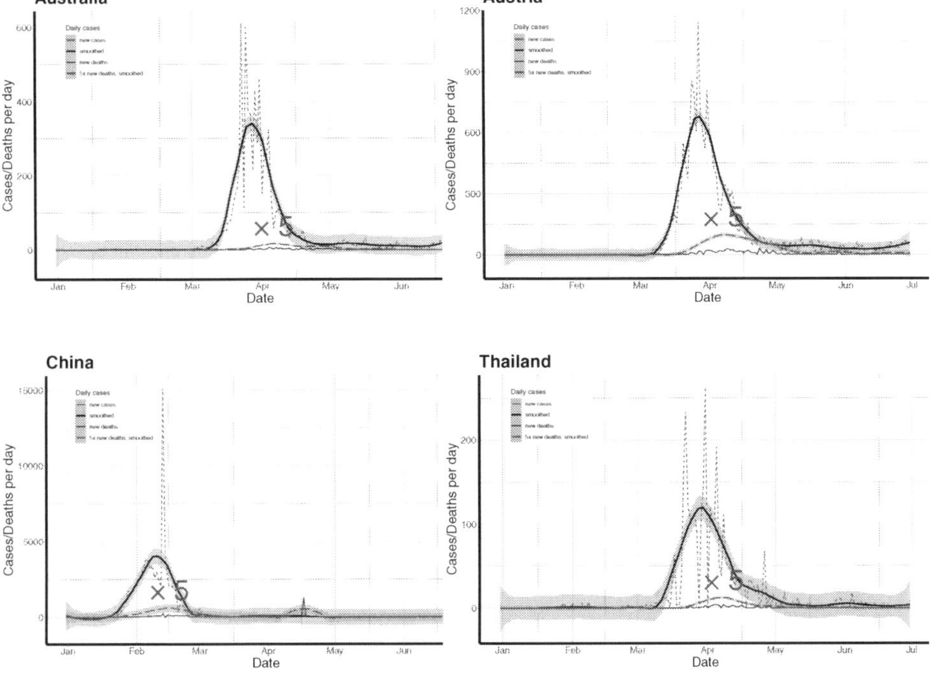

Figure 27. Successes in Australia, Austria, China and Thailand

Success or Failure?

Despite the different approaches taken, these countries have much in common. They got the basic epidemiology right, and stayed the course. As shown in Fig 27, others achieved similar results.[10]

Some have not done as well. Despite a lockdown, it seems that Bangladesh, Bolivia, Colombia, the DRC, the Dominican Republic, Pakistan, Russia and the UAE experienced continued growth. Does this mean that we need to find a new model for "epidemic control", or that containment just went awry? It's now that our investment in epidemiology and "working examples" pays off.

Take Bangladesh. On 18 April, in the middle of the lockdown, 100,000 people gathered at the funeral prayer of a popular Islamic teacher—Mawlana Jubayer Ahmed Ansari. This funeral highlights a failure to get clerics on-side; in addition testing has been desultory; tracing and isolation are difficult to support in their fragile health care system. Bangladesh is no refutation of the principles we've established.

[10] There are some interesting anomalies, for example the sudden Chinese spike signals the point where they started adding 'probables' to the tally (and caught up); the secondary death spike is the Chinese fessing up that they had under-counted deaths in Wuhan.

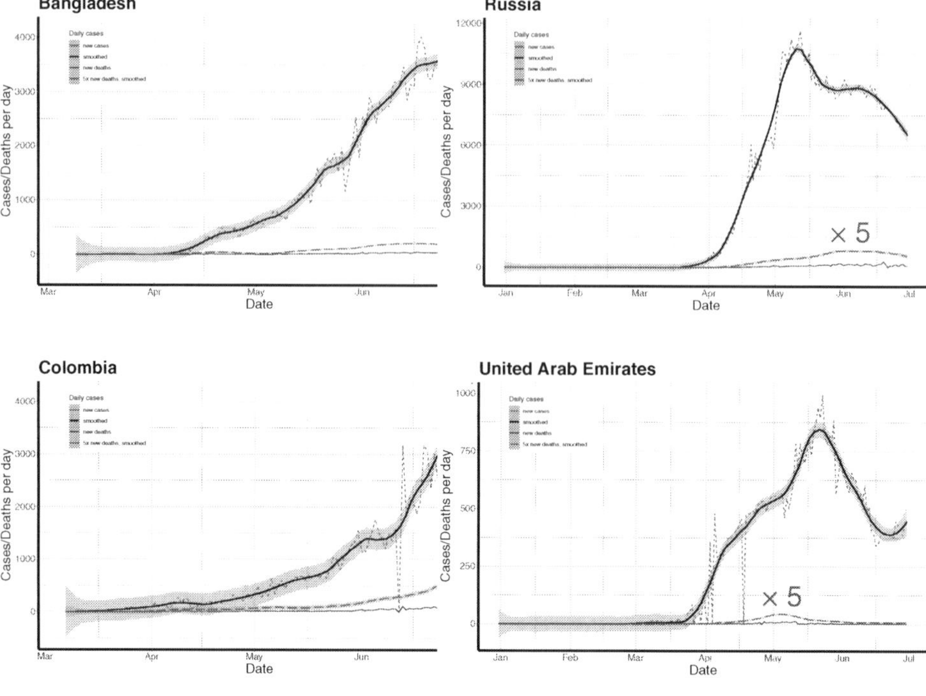

Figure 28. Poor Control

Russia is different in some ways, but sadly similar in others. The lockdown for Moscow was delayed until 30 March, despite being announced earlier for the rest of the country; on 22 March, Vladimir Putin was still putting on a "show of strength" in preparation for changing the constitution to allow him to continue as leader, even when he's an octogenarian.[11] The lockdown that Putin imposed was also more of a 'non-working order', described as 'vague'. There were issues with testing, contact following and particular problems with personal protective equipment, fostering spread within hospitals.

It is quite unclear what is happening in Colombia—a country with a floridly corrupt healthcare system—but lockdown seems to have been chaotic, with prison riots, uncontrolled spread within hospitals, and failure of any epidemiological infrastructure that was present.

In the UAE, 'lockdown' consisted of early school closures, a night curfew from 26 March, sporadic limitations to movement and a variety of small measures. Dense housing for low-income workers, and failure of surveillance however loomed over the lockdown—of the total population of 9.2 million, 7.8 million are migrant workers.

These failures are so obviously consequences of "not getting the basics right" that it would seem silly to call them 'refutations'. If you fail to get the community and

[11] Shades of Robert Mugabe.

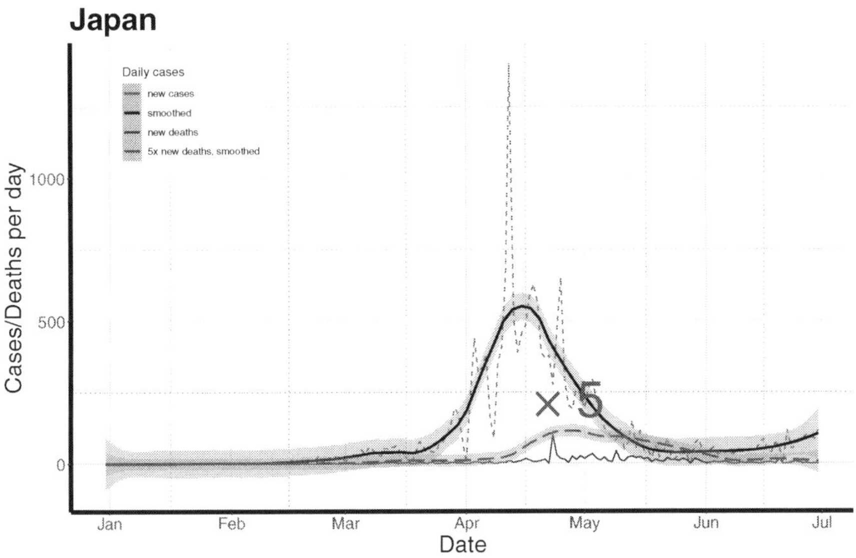

Figure 29. Japanese cases and deaths

community leaders on board, you will fail. If you fail to trace contacts and control movement, or neglect basic healthcare, you will fail.

Counterexamples

But what about apparent counter-examples? There weren't country-wide lockdowns in Taiwan, China, Japan, Vietnam and South Korea. We've already explored Taiwan, South Korea and Vietnam, and seen how rapidly they got onto the problem, and how well their co-ordination, contact-tracing and isolation of individuals and affected regions worked.

There's no magic here—just hard foot-slogging and smart co-ordination. In many ways the Chinese are special here, as they had the ability to lock down nine million people in Wuhan with hyper-efficient surveillance and severe penalties. They also wrote the book about COVID-19 facilities, building huge isolation hospitals from scratch in days.

Japan (Fig 29) is however a special case. Japan's greatest asset here seems to be a compliant, worried population. In a country where white-gloved 'professional pushers' are employed to stuff passengers onto trains, train occupancy plummeted, often to under ten percent. Nevertheless, their overall response seems to have been quite laid-back. Testing was desultory, social distancing seemed inadequate, and Shinzō Abe appeared disengaged from the problem.

Mild cases were not tested, and only those with shortness of breath or sustained fever were admitted to special hospitals. Is their success even explicable? Apart from the possibility that official Japanese statistics may 'under-represent' the actual numbers,[12] here's one factor we haven't yet examined—face masks.

Masks

To start an argument among epidemiologists, mention masks. Many Western experts initially ridiculed their widespread use, based on studies of influenza; conversely, many Eastern countries already have a culture of wearing a mask when you are sick. With COVID-19, masks have been almost universally adopted in Japan; mask-wearing is widespread where lockdowns have been successfully avoided. Let's go back to basics.

It is often pointed out that, despite there being no prospective, randomized controlled trial that test their efficacy, many people who voluntarily launch themselves out of a functional aircraft choose to use a parachute. In contrast, a prospective, randomized trial of 23 people jumping from an aircraft with either a parachute or just a back-pack *was* published in 2018,[13] and to quote the authors:

> "Parachute use did not reduce death or major traumatic injury when jumping from aircraft in the first randomized evaluation of this intervention."

What may have helped is that everyone jumped down from a stationary aircraft, falling just sixty centimetres. The authors highlight the dangers of extrapolation, but let's hijack their plane for other purposes. As we found in Lesson 5, medicine does not live or die by prospective, randomized trials. We need Good Science—a model that makes sense, and that can be tested to a reasonable degree.

Have you noticed how similar masks are to parachutes? Both trap and divert fast-flowing air. Most of the time. Masks have other valuable properties. They can be used to signal things like "avoid me"; they can also change how people touch their nose and mouth. Conversely, those who argue against them claim that discarded masks may act as sources of infection and that masks become ineffective within minutes.

As with parachutes, we need to be careful in evaluating effectiveness. Context counts. There are two types of droplet spread. Larger droplets from normal speech fall to ground more readily—hence the advice about 1–2 metre social distancing. But some viruses can form an *aerosol*. Droplets over $10\mu m$ settle fairly quickly, but small droplets under $3\mu m$ in diameter effectively never fall to ground. When dealing with pandemic

[12] asia.nikkei.com/Spotlight/Coronavirus/Tokyo-s-excess-deaths-far-higher-than-COVID-19-count-data-shows. Raw numbers seem difficult to come by. [13] The BMJ Christmas edition PubMed 30545967

influenza, healthcare professionals use N95 masks, which largely stop them inhaling the aerosolised virus.[14]

How is influenza virus aerosolised? Sneezing generates a host of tiny particles that dry out, forming "droplet nuclei" of under 5μm—we now have aerosolised influenza virus. But experts still debate whether I'm transmitted by aerosols.[15] All this flapping misses two important points.

The first is that *of course* I can be present in droplets $3\ \mu$m in diameter—you know from Lesson 1 that I'm a mere 120 nm. But even if there are a million of me in a millilitre of saliva, few will get into a droplet of this size, suggesting that bigger droplets may be more important. The second point is that most of the study of droplet spread and masks has been from the perspective of the person being infected.[16] But when it comes to masks, there's an important asymmetry. An N95 mask will prevent inhalation of droplet nuclei—at least initially—but any old mask will substantially reduce expulsion of droplets. You know that you don't need sneezes and aerosols to spread me. Even loud speech generates thousands of fluid droplets every second,[17] droplets that can persist for ten minutes or more.

A focus on the recipient is very Western, and very self-centred. As I understand it—and remember I'm just a naïve virus—the main reason why people in Japan and other Eastern countries wear masks is *to protect others.*

A critical point is this: you now *do* have the evidence you need. Philip Anfinrud and his colleagues at the NIH in Bethesda[18] illuminated droplet emissions with a powerful laser when subjects said "Stay healthy", using an iPhone for video capture. A wealth of droplets from 20–500 μm were seen; even a slightly damp washcloth over the speaker's mouth cut these to next to nothing. Masks work. Naysayers will point out that some people don't wear them properly—but as we've discovered, perfection is unattainable. Instead you need a combination of practical measures that will stop virus transmission. You know it can be done.

Superspreader

At choir practice in Skagit county, Washington, I spread to 52 of 60 attendees on 10 March, 2020. Three were hospitalised, and two died. This was a "super-spreader" event. As the CDC points out,[19] even in a confined setting, it's difficult to say what happened—not only did the choir members sing together, but they socialised, ate and stacked chairs too. You however already know that loud speech spreads me, and that some people emit far more particles while speaking than do others.

---

[14]For a review see PubMed 17283614 [15]As shown by a recent article in *Nature.* PubMed 32242113 [16]PubMed 25903751 is an early example. [17]A recent paper in PNAS: PubMed 32404416 shows this nicely using laser light scattering. The maths is intricate. [18]See PubMed 32294341 [19]PubMed 32407303

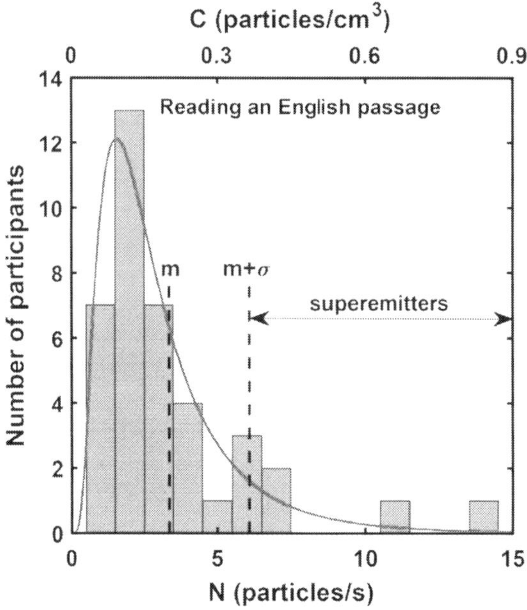

Figure 30. Superspreaders (Sci Rep. 2019;9(1):2348)
Creative Commons Licence; image decolourised.

Emission of droplets varies dramatically with voice loudness, regardless of the language spoken; singing emits six times more particles than normal speech; and for reasons that are not understood, some people are "speech superemitters", producing an order of magnitude more particles.[20] Fig 30 is taken from that study, and shows how perhaps one fifth of people are so afflicted. This has been summarised in the slightly simplistic "20/80 rule"—many people will not spread their infection *at all,* and some will be super-spreaders.[21]

The presence of superspreaders has large implications for my transmission and how it's modelled. "Standard" epidemiological models of the spread of disease use *compartmental models.* These separate people into 'compartments', commonly:

S: Susceptible
I: Infectious
R: Recovered/removed.

This is the 'SIR' model. Extra compartments can be added, often an E (exposed) group—people who may be incubating the infection.[22] The attractive feature of S(E)IR models

[20]PubMed 30787335 [21]PubMed 21737332 [22]In such models it is common to include dead people in the 'removed' compartment; with slow-moving infections things are more tricky as you also need to account for births, and deaths from other causes. Sometimes maternal immunity also confers transient immunity on newborns too.

is that you've worked out the maths. They can be described by 'ordinary differential equations' and modelled on computers. More complex is the case where recovery doesn't necessarily confer immunity. An important part of all these models is that they assume the population affected is large—otherwise, outcomes are unpredictable.

You can plug different models into the SIR framework. You know from Lesson 5 that no scientific model is true—so you need to choose a model that does the job. The *CMMID nCov working group* at the London School of Hygiene and Tropical Medicine was one of first groups to show that standard SIR models don't fit the 20/80 rule.[23] Using WHO data from 27 February 2020, they fitted the data to a *negative binomial distribution.*[24] The advantage of using this model is that it takes *two* parameters—the R_0 explored in Lesson 2, and a second parameter often referred to simply as 'k'.

If k is 1, then a single parameter (R_0) is all you need, and modelling can be done using a simpler (Poisson) distribution. With $k \sim 1.0$, the virus spreads like influenza. When k gets down to about 0.1, disease outbreaks tend to be less predictable and more explosive, as seen above with the Skagit county choir. This is 'overdispersion', where superspreaders play a larger and larger role. Endo and colleagues indeed found a k value of ~ 0.1 for COVID-19, fitting the 20/80 rule.

As far back as 2005, Lloyd-Smith and colleagues explored such modelling minutely.[25] It turns out that *even if* the R_0 of a disease is over 1, if spread is very varied, it is more likely to die out than if it behaves like influenza, with a k of 1. It may be that SARS was always doomed to fail, *especially* with its lowish R_0. Now you might think that as a virus, I should know my R_0 and my k—but do you, for example know precisely what your spleen does or how many great grandchildren you're likely to have? A lot of what we *are* and what will happen to us is inscrutable to us. If they work, these models have huge implications for my future, but even these refinements may be wrong. In Lesson 11 we'll find out why.

A contrast

I'd imagine the Auckland Islands close to Auckland, New Zealand. Actually, the two are separated by 1697 kilometres—few people know that with about four million square kilometres of ocean, New Zealand has the fourth largest marine environment in the world. Unlike Auckland, the subantarctic Auckland Islands are inaccessible and inhospitable, a graveyard for ships.

[23]See: Endo A, et al. *Estimating the overdispersion in COVID-19 transmission using outbreak sizes outside China* PubMed 32685698 [24]The conditions for using a binomial distribution in a simulation reflect the idea that you are "repeating a trial" until successful (here, 'success' is a certain number of infections), with the same probability of success from trial to trial. [25]Highlighted in PubMed 16292310

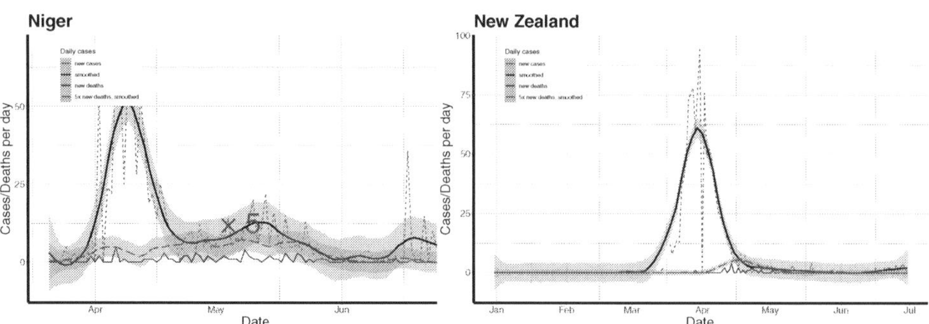

Figure 31. Niger & New Zealand

In 1864, two ships were wrecked there within months of one another—on January 3, the *Grafton* from Sydney, with five crew on board; and on May 10, the larger *Invercauld* out of Melbourne, with 25 on board, of whom 19 initially survived. Two shipwrecks, but with two very different outcomes. The two crews never met. The contrasting stories of the teams of men almost take on features of a moral fable, as told by Joan Druett in the book *Island of the Lost: Shipwrecked at the Edge of the World.*

Right at the start, an injured crewman from the Invercauld was left to die. The rest then lived an "every man for himself" existence; the captain sunk into misery. Within five months, all but three had died of starvation and neglect—resorting to cannibalism. By luck, the last three were then rescued by a passing ship.

In contrast, the crew of the *Grafton* first banded together to rescue a critically ill crewman, the resourceful François Édouard Raynal; they then used everything they had to survive. Together, they managed to make a tent and later a cabin; they fashioned tools; they lived off seal meat, birds and fish. Despite boils and starvation, they survived for eighteen months, waiting for rescue. When it was clear that their hope was in vain, they modified the ship's dinghy, having failed in their initial plan to build a boat. The dinghy would take but three, who navigated the 450 km to New Zealand, raised public funds there, and then rescued the others.[26]

In New Zealand in 2020, something happened that changed my mind about humans—echoing the success of the crew of the *Grafton.* I was quite blown away by the resolve you displayed. Initially, things were not good. Public health had been inexorably marginalised by successive governments over twenty years, an easy target for cost-cutting.

[26] In fairness, it can be argued that those on the Invercauld initially had fewer resources, as there were fewer seals at their end of the island, and their ship sank more rapidly; but the Invercauld crew soon stumbled on the remains of a settlement, with houses, tools, metal and timber. Leadership and shared goals seem to have been most important.

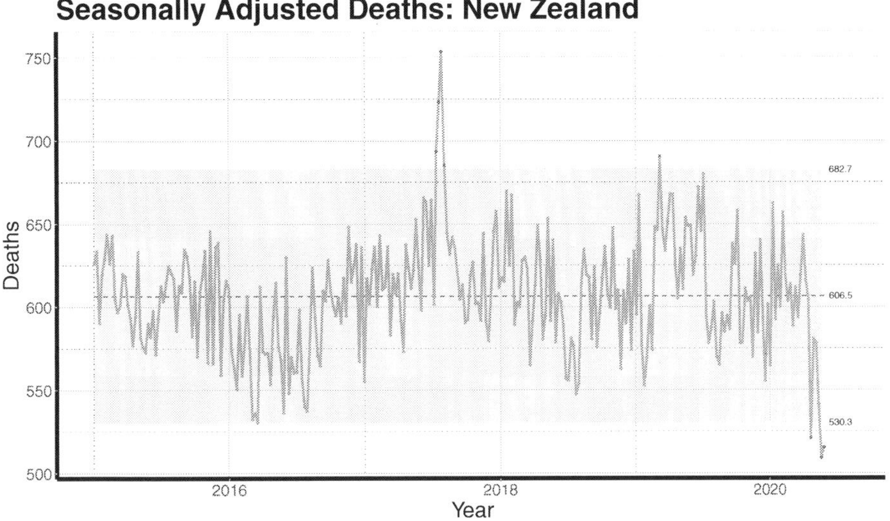

Figure 32. NZ deaths, with secular & seasonal adjustment

Despite extensive computerisation in many areas of health care, information systems were poorly connected. Border controls were weak.

And then, over the course of just two days, everything changed. The timing was exquisite—leaders stepped to the front, created a simple but solid system of lockdown levels, and did this well, giving people just enough time to assimilate the changes before escalating to a level four lockdown. One of the most aggressive lockdowns in the world started—not with a military metaphor, but an exhortation to "Be kind".

What impressed me then was how everyone in New Zealand got behind the Prime Minister and her Director General of Health. Their daily session at 1 pm became engaging television. I learned that I have worthy opponents who, in the words of Jacinda Ardern, can unite as a "team of five million" with one goal. I was overwhelmed by the resolve and pride displayed in crushing me. Human beings can take—took—a working model from Taiwan and locked it in.

There was an interesting side effect. Do you recall the UK control chart on page 46? After secular and seasonal adjustments, my death spike remained. Now look at Fig 32. A similar approach, applied to five years' worth of New Zealand death data shows that during lockdown, the death curve moves in the opposite direction—lives may even have been saved, quite apart from those saved from COVID-19![27]

[27]The data are preliminary, and the reasons for this dip may be complex. It's easy to argue that "deaths were merely delayed" or even that "there will be a later spike because cancer was missed during the lockdown". It's likely that part of the dip is due to a decrease in road deaths, but fewer chest infections are likely more important—even in summer.

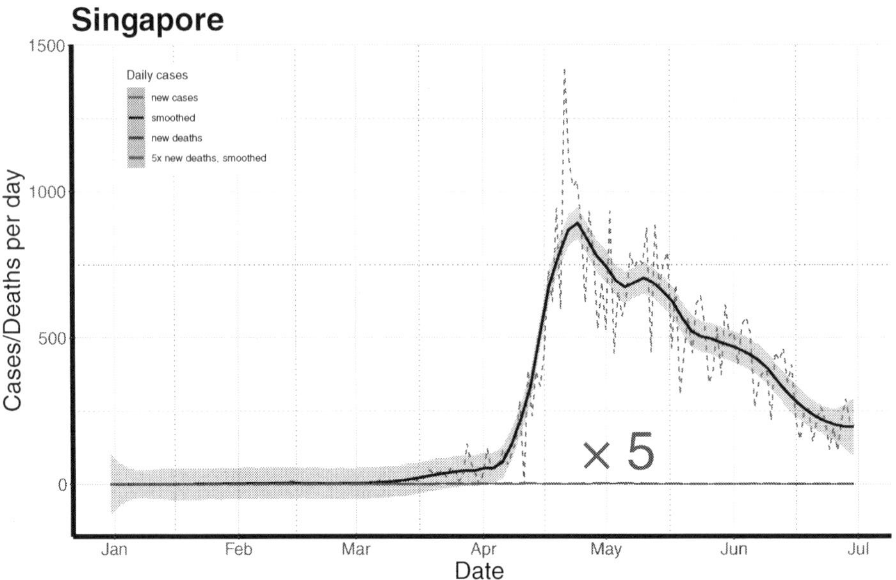

Figure 33. Singapore

Lip service

We can answer the question "Do lockdowns work?" with "Yes, provided you stick to the rules". Just going through the motions of a lock-down however seems silly. In fact, this may be worse than ineffective. It's important to get things right at the start.

Failure of an inadequate lockdown casts doubt on the statement "Lockdowns work", and makes a subsequent, necessary lockdown difficult or impossible to achieve. The mindset is "We've tried lockdown, we've felt the pain, it doesn't work." The true significance of lockdowns will however only become apparent in Lesson 11, when you better understand the explosive nature of my spread.

It's interesting to contrast the successes of various countries in combatting me. None had quite the same approach; and other countries not yet mentioned also succeeded — Hong Kong, with a population of 7.5 million and just 1000 cases; Iceland with 1800 cases and just 10 deaths (but a population of just 360,000); and Niger which put very firm measures in place, and has done well so far.[28] Mongolia, Liberia and Slovakia also deserve mention.

[28]This may continue. In this 98% Muslim country, locking down all places of worship has not gone down well, forcing a negotiated settlement where gatherings will continue, but with meticulous social measures and hand hygiene.

Lessons

What can you learn from these varied examples? Adaptability is great, but you need more. It is wise to:

- Prepare a clear plan. Activate this early and proportionately.
- Be open with everyone—communicate not just the urgency, but also precisely what people should do, why and when.
- Trace contacts, and isolate people appropriately.
- Not slacken your vigilance.
- Be necessarily firm.

The game is not over. Consider Singapore. They initially did so well that the early cases in Fig 33 are almost invisible. As in Vietnam and South Korea, the first case on 23 January prompted official controls, with screening at airports, aggressive contact tracing, and case isolation. Rumours and misinformation were suppressed. They then let their guard down, allowing foreign workers to return to their crowded dormitories, where I spread like wildfire. By early May, there were over 20,000 cases, necessitating an aggressive lockdown.

An interesting exercise for the reader is to examine the responses in the UK and the USA. Where did they fail? What rules did they flout? We've already seen the graphs in Figures 18 & 19 on page 115. There is however good news. This comes from New Zealand[29] and many other countries: even if you're resource-constrained, the right strategy gives you a good chance of *eliminating me completely* from your country. In the next lesson, to restore the balance, I'll pick through just some of your failures.

> **Lesson #9**
>
> Quick decisions must sometimes be made on incomplete evidence.
> To succeed, step back, get the basics right, and get people on-side.

[29]Where the *pepeketua* have no tadpoles, care for their young, and don't croak.

⊛ Lesson 10

Trust me

"Fool me once, shame on you; fool me twice, shame on me."

Anthony Weldon. *The Court and Character of King James*, 1651

"All happy families are alike; each unhappy family is unhappy in its own way."

Leo Tolstoy. *Anna Karenina*, 1877.

"The viper oil of Mesues. Take 2 pounds of live snakes and 2 pounds 3 ounces of sesame oil. Cook slowly, covered in a glazed pot, until meat pulls away from bone. Strain and store. Uses: Cleans the skin, removes pimples, impetigo and other defects."

Juan de Loeches. *Tyrocinium Pharmaceticum*, 1751.

In Russia, nannies are paid ridiculously well—provided they have the credentials, and impeccable English. To me, neither is much of an issue; there is a point where forgery becomes better than the real thing. Mastery of English and of science and naturally, of books, is still important to many educated Russians, and triply important to rich, educated Russians who can afford a nanny or two to give their children a boost.

With the choice of any city in Russia, I'd choose St Petersburg every time. The white nights glow, and the Hermitage beckons. There you will walk around a corner and be stricken—perhaps by the dinner service made for Catherine the Great by Josiah Wedgwood,[1] who was so scarred by smallpox that he could not operate a potter's kick-wheel, instead taking up design. Or perhaps you will chance upon a roomful of Rembrandts, and have your heart ripped out by the original parting of David and Jonathan—near impossible to replicate with mere photography.

As a nanny—and a god born of Good Science—I'm allowed a bit of introspection that might be lacking in older, more traditional gods. In Lesson 9 you saw the virtues of

[1] The anti-slavery grandfather of Charles Darwin, he also pioneered direct-response marketing, free delivery, money-back guarantees and buy-one-get-one-free.

trust, clear communication and working together; let's now examine bad playground behaviour, more obvious perhaps to a nanny than say a politician.

Applying the "Anna Karenina principle"[2] to countries that have worked out how to eliminate me—how glibly I say that—Tolstoy may have been on the money. They may differ a bit, but have done many things in common. But what about failing *countries?* Do they all differ, or do they share common failings?

It seems to me that the Anna Karenina principle is here only partially true. Although 'failing countries' may differ wildly—some denying the problem and silently burying bodies at night; others hyping solutions like vaccines that don't even exist yet; yet others touting drugs that won't work—I can still pick two threads out of the tangle. The first is that there's a common departure point on the divergent roads to failure; the second is that you humans have shared cerebral quirks.

A point of departure

It is only in the past century or so that clarity has emerged about how Good Science works—as outlined in Lesson 5. First, the scientist tries to explain a problem; second, she attacks this explanation vigorously using the sharpest tools in the shed; and finally, if it holds up, she *provisionally* accepts the theory as 'true'.

In Lesson 7 you saw how even those who have won Nobel prizes in scientific disciplines sometimes still don't "get it". Good Science flies in the face of traditional thinking, where you "prove something" (often "beyond reasonable doubt") and established thought patterns that save time and intellectual effort. When something new comes up that doesn't fit, rather than testing models, those thinking in traditional mode tend to fall back on stereotypes. When stereotypes start failing, and people start dying, wouldn't this be an incentive to change? You have already seen that it is precisely in these circumstances that even very smart people tend to cling to their soft toys.

Tu quoque

Once you have your tigger clutched to your chest, other child-like behaviour tends to emerge at the same time. It seems to be built in. Perhaps none is more common than the invocation "But what about you...?" Experts at debate will ridicule this using the Latin term *tu quoque*, that is "you also". It is however surprisingly common, and shows up in many ways.

Tu quoque goes like this. Someone advocates a certain course of action, and their antagonist then cries out "*But you* haven't acted in accordance with your own rules!"

[2]Invoked by Jared Diamond to explain why just a few species have been domesticated, of all the millions on the face of the Earth. He claims that the others all had some glaring defect, such as a tendency to kick their owners to death, preventing domestication.

The hidden implication is that "... and therefore your argument can't be correct." When spelt out, this is clearly a very silly, playground attempt at refutation, as people may advocate the right course of action and not follow it. You just have to look at the great philosophers of past centuries—or very smart people from today.

One of the principal data scientists at Imperial College who predicted the huge number of deaths in the United Kingdom, and advised strict social distancing, was caught "breaking his bubble" (and cheating with a married woman). He rapidly left the team that advises Boris Johnson, because of the potential damage this may have done to the effort to contain the virus.

But why should this do damage? It seems pretty evident that his actions were silly, hypocritical and a bit scruffy, but if everyone thought logically, they'd realise that his actions in no way refute his model. They simply display human weakness. You bind your perception of the truth of an explanation to the fallible actions of the explainer.[3]

Shoot the messenger

The next illogical step in this 'personalisation' of problems is to try to make it go away by making the person associated with the problem go away. You need look no further than the most powerful country in the world to see how those who don't toe the leader's line are rapidly removed. Unfortunately, after one illogical step, it's downhill all the way. In Lesson 4, you saw how if you're pretty sure of something, from a Bayesian point of view, new evidence *should* be discounted with appropriate severity—the odds may not strongly support a new explanation.

The catch here is that if your priors are just plain wrong—perhaps because you're applying the wrong model—you may end up making a huge mistake. Good Science is both non-linear, and unforgiving. All statements of fact are provisional. In contrast, anyone who is thinking purely in terms of stereotypes, *knows* something to be true. This is impervious to the logic of Bayes—the prior is 100% right, and nothing can shake it. It's obvious that this is anti-science, but there's an uncomfortable question embedded in this observation. Can you see it?

Yes, the question is "What about those countries that succeeded? A strong component of their success often seems to have been suppressing those who disagreed. Surely this is not just a violation of the right to free speech, but exactly the kind of 'groupthink' you want to avoid?"

---

[3]You can have a lot of fun here with a 'tu quoque' of your own. Remember how I talked about 'provenance' on page 16? Am I being consistent? A broken chain of evidence, or using Bayesian priors to good effect is different from the associations now under discussion. Or is it?

Free speech

If you look around the world at countries that have managed to suppress coronavirus, not a few of them are acknowledged to be fairly authoritarian. It is however wise not to apply some sort of tu quoque-like argument here. If you look more carefully, the countries that have succeeded display a wide range of traits—New Zealand, for example, is widely known for its openness and honesty and often tops the ratings in terms of open business practices.[4] Vietnam is known for its communist rule and authoritarian tendencies.

One epidemiological principle that they share in common is that either through persuasion or compulsion – or indeed through a combination of the two – they got enough people on side to tip the balance against the virus, and get the R_e under 1.

This observation is closely allied to something you also learned in Lesson 5—that just a vanishingly small proportion of theories are 'true' in the sense of "not yet invalidated". The beauty of science is that it is acceptance of provisional truths following sufficient testing. Most random pronouncements of "truth" are almost trivially wrong. It is therefore folly to give equal weight—or equal airtime—to poorly constructed, untested or badly tested ideas that have the potential to drown out coherent thought. You saw this in Lesson 1, and it was reinforced in Lesson 9.

The above is all very well, but surely there's still a problem here! *Precisely because* one can never be sure, it is always possible that some crazy person will come up with "the solution" and not be heard. However deranged a position seems, it may still work. It therefore seems wise to ask "How best can I use the finite resources I have to control the virus, while still testing my approach and acknowledging that I might be wrong?" This question cuts both ways. For if someone comes up and says "You're completely wrong, you should be doing the following..." then this surely invites questions like:

(1) "Do you accept Good Science as defined above? If not, what's wrong with this approach, and how is your approach better?"
(2) "How does your approach deal with failure? Does it acknowledge the possibility of failure? Will it fail gracefully or catastrophically?"
(3) "How will you determine that your approach has failed? What will you do then?"

For example, let's say that "in the interests of preserving the economy", someone proposes that despite wide dissemination of the virus, lock-down should be avoided, and people should simply carry on commuting, eating at restaurants, going to night clubs,

[4] After the lockdown eased back from "level 4" to "level 2", the Prime Minister casually popped in to a local Wellington cafe with her partner and was chased away because (a) she didn't have a booking; and (b) letting her in would have broken the social distancing rules then in place. Everyone had a laugh about this.

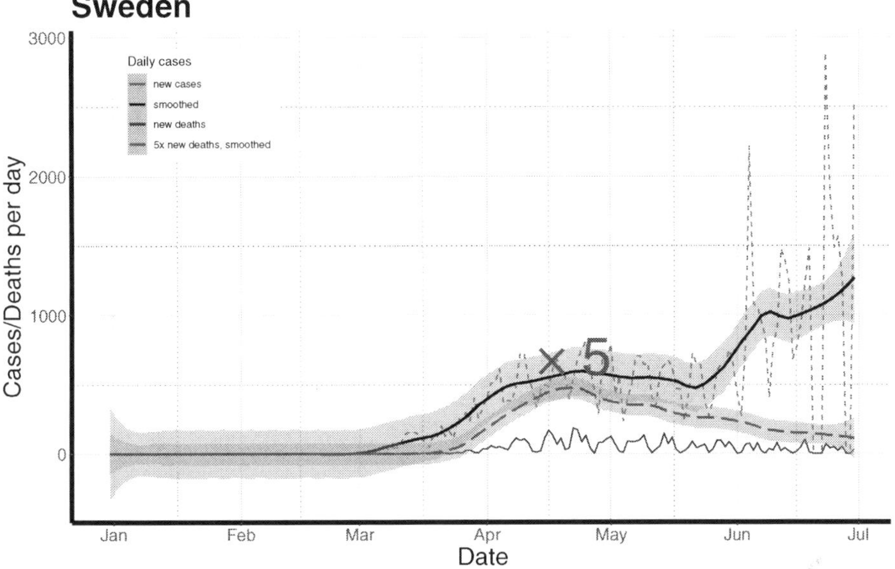

Figure 34. Sweden

and crowding together at work. Having a mathematical model of their approach is not sufficient. The proponents should surely justify their position in terms of existing science—and provide clear answers to the above three questions.

All of this invites one more question: "How do we respond to rowdy people who assert that we're wrong, they're right, and who refuse to engage in concise examination of the above questions?" In terms of resource constraint, you can't indulge in endless debate while a virus spreads unchecked. This is where you need strong leaders who find good advice and act on it. Weak leaders will vacillate and damage their countries, or even worse, will follow a convenient but precipitately wrong course of action.

Very poor leaders indeed will not learn from their mistakes and indulge in behaviour that tries to distract everyone from the looming crisis as it overwhelms them. They will hide information, lie, indulge in endless "tu quoque" arguments, and even shoot the messenger. In the worst case, where the cult of the leader is all-important, you may even end up with something resembling Jonestown (Lesson 7).

In addition, there will always be an element of luck. It is only in the next lesson that we'll see and even try to quantify the amount of "luck" required, although the superspreader events of Lesson 9 already suggest that luck is important. One unresolved question is "What about Sweden?" so let's look at this next.

Sweden

There are people who are not cult-like in their leadership, who have or at least claim to have 'impeccable scientific credentials', and who nevertheless mislead. Precisely because they appear to be far removed from the fringe, they may be dangerous. You've already read the quote from Sweden's Chief Epidemiologist on page 94, where he says "...we are going to reach it in a different way". Is this an embodiment of the Anna Karenina principle, wrought by a Lesson 8 hero with feet of clay, or is it a respected and influential scientist steering his country along a slightly different course to success?

The question is more difficult to answer than you might expect, even in retrospect. You can look back, observe how scarily well I've succeeded in Sweden, how high the per capita death rate is, but there's a catch, even here. As we've found before, after-the-fact justification is always possible (Lesson 1) and theories can be modified to fit the facts. It is precisely for this reason that we have spent so many lessons exploring how to do things better *from the start.*

As I see it, your true failing in Sweden was a failure of Good Science. You have seen how wise it is to divorce personality and influence from good decision-making, but in Sweden the force of authority of one man carried the day. A single person clearly and emphatically embraced not one but several dodgy assumptions—herd immunity, and the deaths of a 'few' for possible (and as we'll discover, likely illusory) economic benefits—and was trusted, largely without question.

Epidemiology is not a new thing, and if a respected epidemiologist flouts the rules, or makes unwarranted assumptions, they need to be taken to task. As I pointed out in Lesson 8, right at the start of my little pandemic, you already knew a lot about me. You also knew a lot about coronaviruses, and how they *differ* from viruses like influenza. You had painstaking centuries of work on epidemiology, starting with John Snow (page 119). All of this was enough to advise a different course from the one Sweden took. Taiwan knew this.

The interesting bit here is not Sweden's failure, but its partial success. Look at Fig 35. Citymapper is a transit app and mapping service that provides data for about 40 large cities. I've laid their daily data[5] over new cases for those countries. if there was a 'full lockdown', it's shown by a vertical line. Traffic plummets in many countries, often before the spike in identified cases, or indeed lockdown. South Korea, which didn't *need* a full lockdown shows the least decline in traffic; Sweden similarly saunters down, unlike the brisk drop in other countries.

[5]Where several cities are represented in a single country, I've weighted by city size. It's important to realise the limitations of these illustrative plots too—they don't cover the whole country; indeed, many represent just one city.

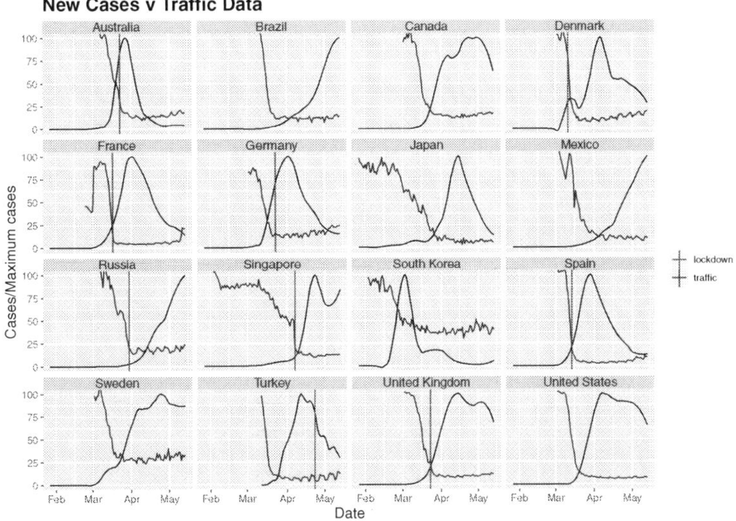

Figure 35. Citymapper & me

All data have their limitations—the Citymapper data represent just a few cities, and when a 'lockdown' occurred is imprecise. Despite a rapid decline in traffic in Brazil and Russia, the epicurve still rises exponentially. Why? As you saw in Lesson 9, single measures don't account for success—you need a complete package. Some Swedes got things partially right, but it would appear, not enough.[6] A single influential person can make a great difference to how things proceed, but Good Science is perhaps best done as a group effort, with balance and adequate criticism.

Snake oil

So far, my emphasis has been on self-delusion, and how easy it is. I've touched on weak leaders, who listen to bad advice—especially unscientific advice—and then cling to a 'solution' even when it's clearly failing. I've shown how smart people may lead themselves and others astray, especially if they cling to Platonic ideals. They are dangerous. But there are those who are not just more dangerous but, in a sense, more despicable. These are smart people who in a time of crisis can see an opportunity to sell something, at any human cost.

[6]It has also been asserted that conditions in Swedish care homes—where more than half of the deaths occurred—are substandard, with inadequate personal protective equipment; those who are ill are often denied oxygen, instead being given a cocktail of morphine and midazolam, prescribed remotely. This has been described as "active euthanasia, to say the least" (www.svd.se/professorn-i-agenda-de-aldre-dor-av-palliativ-vard).

You all know of black-market operators who can obtain goods and services that are otherwise either difficult to obtain, or prohibitively expensive. You may even have used them. In a repressive society, or one with crazy rules, they may actually provide very valuable services. Such individuals may not simply justify their actions based on the good that they do, but they may, in an empiric sense, actually be right. Some, like Oskar Schindler[7] turn out to show unexpected depths of human compassion and help others at extreme personal risk, even in the face of huge financial losses. As Schindler said "... a thinking man, who had overcome his inner cowardice, simply had to help. There was no other choice".

And then there are the snake-oil salesmen. I have already referred to your tendency to be irrational—to invest theories with the properties of their makers. The other side of the coin is to give unreasonable ideas a certain gloss, by creating in the mind of the listener the idea that their purveyor is a trustworthy person. "If you trust me, then my theory must be correct. Trust me." Let's make up a name for this—'deceit by association'.

Look again at the recipe for snake oil at the start of this lesson. You will find a thousand—no, ten thousand—no, a hundred thousand similar 'recipes' throughout history. You can't test them all, but do know certain things. You know that most of them will likely prove wrong; you know that the amount of self-critical testing that has previously been applied to these remedies is likely to be minuscule, especially as they go back in time, before modern concepts of "good testing" were developed, or even further back, where the platform of theory on which everything perched was not so much wonky as illusory.

None of this stops the snake-oil salesman, because he isn't concerned about whether something works, or even whether it makes sense. He is simply concerned about sales, and lots of them. Fortunately, you don't need to go out and test every claim, because unlike unhappy families, most snake oil salesmen share certain easily identified attributes in common. Unsurprisingly, as this is pure, unvarnished advertising, the attributes are largely those of advertisers around the world, and include:

Authority by anecdote. You humans love a good story, and a powerful story line often trumps reason. This is an extension of deceit by association—but the association is deflected from the man on the stage, to someone, either real or imagined, who attests to the benefit of the snake oil.

False logic and false statistics. The effective salesman has a whole box full of tricks, for there is any number of ways to abandon logic. To punt the 1950s idea that "Nine out of ten doctors smoke Rattlesnakes", find nine doctors who smoke Rattlesnakes (often their free pack), and add in a tenth, randomly selected doctor.

---

[7] The only member of the Nazi Party to be honoured by burial in Jerusalem, on Mount Zion.

Emotional appeal and emotional associations. Link the product to some strong emotion, or childhood appeal that may have nothing to do with the product. Without evidence of benefit to patients living with chronic pain, Oxycontin was marketed by giving plush toy gorillas to doctors; as late as 1991, children were better at identifying Joe Camel (of infamous association) than Mickey Mouse.[8]

Wide or even near-universal benefits. This is a wonderful red flag, and often clearly delineates snake oil. Our friend Juan de Loeches is pretty moderate in his claims for Viper Oil of Mesues; moving forward to 1916, the Clark Stanley Snake Oil Liniment Company was fined $20 for "falsely and fraudulently" representing that their oil was a remedy for "all pain and lameness, for rheumatism, neuralgia, sciatica, sprains, bunions, and sore throat, for bites of animals and reptiles, for all pains and aches in flesh, muscles and joints, as a relief for tic douloureux, and as a cure for partial paralysis of the arms and of the lower limbs, and as a remedy for paralysis and effective to reduce enlarged joints to their natural size, as a perfect antidote to pain and inflammation, and effective to kill the poison from bites of animals, insects or reptiles, and heal the wounds resulting from bites of animals, insects or reptiles."[9]

A mysterious absence of side effects. Honest people talk about serious side effects, snake oil salesmen bury them. But if you're touting a placebo dressed up as a medicine, then you don't need to worry about side effects, do you?

Now, here's a tu quoque for doctors:

> "I want you out there every day selling N . . . We all know N's not growing for adjunctive therapy, besides that's not where the money is. Pain management, now that's money. Monotherapy [for epilepsy], that's money. . . . We can't wait for [physicians] to ask, we need [to] get out there and tell them up front. Dinner programs, CME programs, consultantships all work great but don't forget the one-on-one. That's where we need to be, holding their hand and whispering in their ear, N for pain, N for monotherapy, N for bipolar, N for everything. I don't want to see a single patient coming off N before they've been up to at least 4800 mg/day. I don't want to hear that safety crap either, have you tried N, every one of you should take one just to see there is nothing, it's a great drug".
>
> A Parke-Davis executive, 1996.

[8] In an article published in JAMA, Fischer et al tested the ability of 3–6 year olds to match 22 logos to twelve products on a "game board". Thirty percent of three-year-olds and 91% of six-year-olds correctly matched the cigarette logo (PubMed 1956101).

[9] Here though, the judgement was because the remedy didn't contain snakes!

Is N a snake-oil product? You tell me. This quote is from an article in the New England Journal of Medicine, an analysis of how a drug called gabapentin was promoted 'off-label' for conditions where it had no therapeutic indication. All too often, the pharmaceutical industry has picked up snake oil sales techniques, and profited from the gullibility of everyone. If you don't do Good Science, then snake oil salesmen are always happy to step in. Anywhere there's money.

Pseudoscience

A problem is that like multi-drug resistant tubercle bacilli, snake-oil salesmen evolve. Even in the field of trickery and deceit, the evolutionary principles you met in Lesson 6 apply—Darwin rocks! Those intent on deceit are often smart enough to see the value of science done well, but unwilling to go through the necessary hard slog of testing and repeated failures. So they create something that merely resembles science. This can be quite sophisticated, and precisely because it combines science-like quackery with appeals to emotion, when attempts are made to debunk it, these often garner emotional responses. The less the victims of pseudoscience understand how Good Science can reasonably work, the more they fall prey to sly misrepresentation of snake oil as science.

Corona cures

It's therefore not surprising that almost anything is being touted as a "coronavirus cure". The ever-growing Wikipedia page "List of Unproven Methods against COVID-19" puts the whole spectrum on display. There you'll find salt water sprays; exposure to sunlight; inhalation of hydrogen peroxide(!); use of amphetamine / cocaine / cannabis / chloroform ... practically working through the alphabet; pendants; homeopathic medicines; miracle minerals; traditional Chinese medicines; a variety of herbs, spices, foods and plant recipes; drinking cow urine; remote faith healing by televangelists; and applying a cotton wool swab soaked in violet oil to your anus!

Possibly more disturbing is where figures in authority have promoted dubious cures. Often these are plucked from the fringe of real science, in that grey zone where badly done science nevertheless has sufficient 'sciency' attributes to make it seem right.

A gloriously bad example is the drug chloroquine and the closely related hydroxychloroquine. These very old drugs used to work for malaria—and worked well—but gradually the parasite became resistant, so they have been largely phased out. Subsequently, hydroxychloroquine was found to help a bit in some inflammatory conditions like rheumatoid arthritis. Early research from China showed that coronavirus replication was halted by these drugs—at least in a Petri dish. (The term "*in vitro*" is often used here, Latin for "in glass").

This is yet another example of a nice theory contradicted by cold, hard facts. Many things work in a test tube. Randall Munroe, the scientist behind the popular web comic xkcd, takes pains to point out that "When you see a claim that a common drug or vitamin 'kills cancer cells in a petri dish', keep in mind: so does a handgun". The same applies to many drugs that "seem to work in vitro".

It's quite disturbing to me how, with a plentiful supply of cases, the clinical science that has been applied has been mostly rubbish. But perhaps I shouldn't be too hard here. Often people on the front line are stressed, and unfamiliar with good design of clinical trials. In the face of nothing that has been shown to work, they may want to try everything, in an uncontrolled manner. This is medical folly (at least, by Loeb's First Law—"If you don't know what to do, do nothing"), but anyone can understand their desire to help, especially under the threat of legal action should a drug be endorsed, and then be shown not to have been given.

Chloroquine

Let's examine chloroquine. There were both reasons to be enthusiastic and reasons to be quite careful here. As far back as 2004, Els Keyaerts and colleagues showed that the SARS coronavirus is inhibited *in vitro* by chloroquine. There's a theoretical measure of how effective this inhibition is, the IC50, or what concentration is required for 50% inhibition of virus replication, and for SARS-CoV-1 this turns out to be fairly low, about 8 micromoles per litre ($8\,\mu$M). To inhibit virus replication by 99%, three days after infection, $16\,\mu$M was needed.

This is already a red flag. Where chloroquine is used to treat rheumatoid arthritis, plasma levels are just $1-3\,\mu$M; in high doses the drug can cause lethal heart arrhythmias, and more than 600 mg/day is known to damage the eyes. In contrast, fairly big doses have been used for short-term treatment of malaria.

There was great excitement when Yao and colleagues reported that chloroquine inhibits SARS-CoV-2 in the test tube, and did simulations where the drug seemed effective with an IC50 ranging from $24\,\mu$M (at 24 hours) down to $5.5\,\mu$M (at 48 hours). For *hydroxy*chloroquine, the corresponding values were $6.1\,\mu$M and just $0.7\,\mu$M.

The first paper that claimed successful treatment of COVID-19 is however so bad that it penetrates deep into the fringes of pseudoscience. It has everything you might expect—a charismatic French "infectious disease expert" called Didier Raoult, extravagant claims, and deeply flawed science.

This research immediately garnered both a cult following[10] and widespread criticism. Perhaps the greatest problem was design. Patients were not randomly allocated to treatment, the authors were aware of who received what, and a combination of drugs was used (hydroxychloroquine + azithromycin) with just six people receiving the second drug. The "controls" were from another centre, or those who refused; the end point was "viral load on nasopharyngeal swabs", with all of the limitations we explored in Lesson 4.

The authors have great faith in hydroxychloroquine because they have used it to treat Q fever and Whipple's disease; they show this faith by selectively citing Yao's model, but most spectacularly by saying "Six hydroxychloroquine-treated patients were lost in follow-up during the survey because of early cessation of treatment." Let's look at this in more detail, as an exercise in forensics.

Lie to me

In Lessons 6 & 7, you saw how easy it is for even world-class scientists to deceive themselves. For similar reasons, scientists and clinicians have painstakingly established guidelines (or even 'rules') that if adhered to, should minimise the risk of self-deceit. The preceding section largely illustrates what *not* to do.

For randomised, controlled trials there is pretty wide agreement that the CONSORT principles should be adhered to. These emphasise completeness, clarity and transparency. Unfortunately, the Raoult paper isn't randomized, but even here, there's a "common sense" set of principles called STROBE[11]: Who left the study? Were *pre-specified* analyses used? Back to Raoult's paper. In their own words:

> "...three patients were transferred to intensive care unit, including one transferred on day 2 post-inclusion who was PCR-positive on day 1, one transferred on day 3 post-inclusion who was PCR-positive on days 1–2 and one transferred on day 4 post-inclusion who was PCR-positive on day 1 and day 3; one patient died on day 3 post inclusion and was PCR-negative on day 2; one patient decided to leave the hospital on day 3 post-inclusion and was PCR-negative on days 1–2; finally, one patient stopped the treatment on day 3 post-inclusion because of nausea and was PCR-positive on days 1-2-3. "

Sick and indeed dead patients who received hydroxychloroquine were excluded—nearly a quarter of their treated patients! Despite these flaws, worldwide sales of the drug rocketed. Subsequently, the gold-standard UK RECOVERY trial recruited over 11,000

[10] From nothing, Raoult now has upwards of a quarter of a million followers on Twitter, and has been praised by such unlikely adherents as the far right, Eric Cantona, and Donald Trump. [11] See PubMed 18522360

patients. On 5 June 2020, independent data-monitoring experts stopped enrolment of new patients, as this was clearly futile: there is no benefit from hydroxychloroquine, and it should not be used.

Does anything work for COVID-19?

Reading the scientific literature is quite difficult. The devil is often in the detail, or even in what the authors have carefully avoided saying. At the time of writing, the thing that really works for COVID-19 is not getting infected. The take-home message is "Don't allow me to spread. Don't get me, in the first place. Really, don't". For those who have severe COVID-19, there is now one effective therapy—according to a recent announcement from a fairly solid UK trial, an inexpensive steroid called dexamethasone lowers the death rate.[12]

This has been widely touted, so I'll exercise my usual caution. Initial reports were quick to point out that in those who were put on *invasive ventilation*, deaths were down by about one third. This sounds impressive, but what was the overall effect? Of 2014 patients given the drug, 21.6% died, compared to 24.6% of the 4321 patients randomised to 'usual care'. A *three percent* absolute improvement, and a 12% relative decrease. The steroids don't seem to work for the mildly ill, and also clearly didn't work in those, presumably older patients, where the decision was made to withhold breathing support.[13] Even in ventilated patients, two thirds of those who were going to die, still died.

Why should this be? If you haven't worked in intensive care for a decade or so, the preceding paragraph might make no sense to you. If you have, the problem will be obvious. The lacking detail is that the body's response to infection and indeed inflammation is hugely complex. The clinical picture of someone with COVID-19 in ICU is often that of ARDS—Acute Respiratory Distress Syndrome. Air spaces in the lungs collapse, and there is widespread inflammation in the substance of the lungs, with damage to the lining cells.

Dozens of different, abnormal processes are going on, so finding a master switch that turns this all off has proved quite elusive. Steroids like dexamethasone work on something remarkably like a master switch (NFκB) but sometimes the downstream consequences are already in action. In addition, steroids are powerful drugs with substantial side effects.

---

[12]RECOVERY again: the preliminary report medrxiv.org/content/10.1101/2020.06.22.20137273v1 [13]In fact, in this group more patients died if they received steroids, although this didn't achieve significance at a p value of 0.05.

Remdesivir

What about remdesivir then? At the time that I'm writing this, there has been one small, *published* trial of remdesivir—on 29 April 2020, Wang and colleagues published a fairly good randomized, double-blind, placebo-controlled, multicentre trial of the drug in 237 patients. This trial showed no benefit of the drug. On the same day, a preliminary report was released from a larger study that claims a decrease in hospital stay from 15 to 11 days, but no *significant* survival benefit in 1063 patients. There were several issues with this study. It has all the hallmarks of inflated significance—it was stopped early, the rules changed during the study, and it was potentially open to influence by a company that had billions to lose on a negative result.

As remdesivir has now been declared a "standard of care" in the United States, you might never know whether it actually works for hard end-points like survival. Billions of dollars may be spent on a drug that has little or no influence on important outcomes, and clearly lacks the dramatic effect that you obtain if you stop my spread. It is distinctly possible that other drugs will be found that are far more effective—but this is pure speculation at present.

A slight reassurance

This hasn't been a happy lesson. You may have emerged from it in a slightly cynical frame of mind. There is one apparent ray of sunlight, however. It seems that in the face of an apocalypse, 'doomsday preppers' won't be hunkering down in their bunkers, clutching their automatic weapons and bottled water close to their chests and ensuring the survival of their strange ideas. They'll be out in the streets, protesting about their right to free speech, and how the "government is against them". Even as a virus, from a Darwinian point of view I find this strangely appealing.

Lesson #10

If it's too good to be true, it *is* too good to be true. Just say 'No!'

⊛ Lesson 11

Birds of Paradise

"Health is a state of complete physical, mental and social well-being and not merely the absence of disease or infirmity."

The Constitution of the World Health Organization. 1946.

"In theory, there is no difference between theory and practice. But, in practice, there is."

Misattributed to Johannes Lambertus Adriana van de Snepscheut.

"Not one statesman in a position of responsibility has dared to pursue the only course that holds out any promise of peace, the course of supranational security, since for a statesman to follow such a course would be tantamount to political suicide."

Final written words of A Einstein. April 18, 1955.

As a foreigner, it's not easy getting a nanny job in Chile. There is a long list of reasons for this, many of them rooted in history. Chileans, you see, have a different take on 9/11. Until 1973, Chile had a history of stable government and was regarded as a beacon of democracy in the otherwise sordid and corrupt politics of most of South America; all of this changed on 11 September 1973, when its elected president Salvador Allende was deposed by a military junta and found dead with a suicidal gunshot wound to the head (or possibly, two).

Under General Augusto Pinochet, Chile joined the juntas, and became a brutal regime, propped up by torture, rape, mass disappearances, and the United States. The Carabineros de Chile, a police force who bizarrely reported to Ministerio de Defensa Nacional, joined the military in the coup. The socialist policies of Allende were replaced by an ever-widening gap between the rich—some of whom became filthy rich—and the poor, who are indeed dirt poor. Economically, the country grew in wealth, and has been considered prosperous.

The GINI coefficient is a crude measure of wealth inequality; a value of 1 concentrates the wealth in a single individual, and 0 means everyone is equally advantaged (or disadvantaged). The seesaw tips highest in South Africa (World Bank Gini 63) and is above 50 in many African countries where corrupt politicians have grabbed their pile and are sitting on it; South & Central America come next, joining the United States with Ginis in the 40's—Brazil (46), Mexico (45), and Chile (44).

The UK sits at 35; Canada, France and Japan, are in the low 30's; Sweden, Denmark, Finland and the Netherlands are down in the 20's. But in Chile, you don't need a Gini index, you just need to get out and about in Santiago. If you're an au pair with some English skills—and thus not an *empleada domestica* but valued as a *niñera* who can hold a conversation and control the kids' computer consumption—it's relatively easy to get past the stifling bureaucracy as you accompany your returning expat Chilean family to their smart apartment in Providencia.

There you can look out the window and view the elegant houses of the financial district, converted residences of old politicians; but move a bit away and you'll see impoverished people packed cheek-by-jowl, street sellers on every corner, and more stray animals than you can possibly imagine.[1]

If you arrived in late January 2020, as I did, you'd also have encountered huge demonstrations at the death of Jorge Mora, a social activist (and football fan) who was deliberately hit and run over by the Carabineros on January 28. The killing of Mora was not a random act. He was a member of the Garra Blanca youth movement, a football fan organization that played a key role in the ousting of Pinochet in 1990.[2] Unfortunately, institutional policies often outlive those who foster them, and the January riots were merely the continuation of unrest that followed the killing of Camilo Marcelo Catrillanca Marín by the Carabineros on 14 November, 2018, accompanied by institutional lies, fake news, and destruction of evidence by the Carabineros.

Against lockdown

At the start of my pandemic, Chile did so well. It was actually wealthy Chileans who brought me back from Europe and the USA, and they dutifully (for the most part) retired to their private homes, still serviced by their empleadas domesticas—for who otherwise was to do the menial work? These servants then took the virus out into the wider community, leading to uncontrolled spread.

[1] If you visit the Zoológico Nacional, you may however see something special: *las Ranas del Loa*. The last survivors were rescued in 2019 from the middle of the Atacama desert, where they were eking out a perilous existence in a muddy trickle, all that was left of their riverine habitat, drained by the Calama copper mine.

[2] South Americans have long memories and take their football seriously.

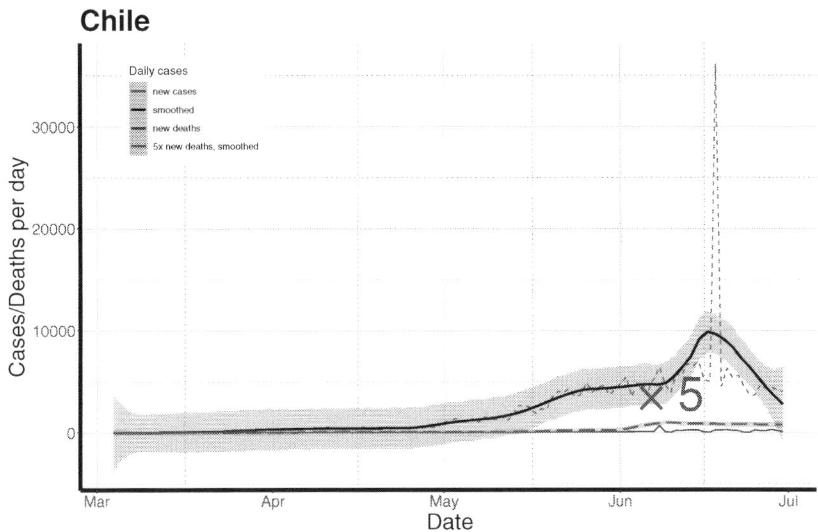

Figure 36. Chile—a familiar curve

Fig 36 is a bit deceptive due to distortion induced by the huge 'correction' introduced in mid-June; Chile has had one of the highest per-capita infection rates in the world, forcing health minister Jaime Manalich to quit in late May. As he said:

> ""There are areas of Santiago where I had no awareness of the magnitude of poverty and overcrowding"[3]

This little demonstration cuts to the core of my inner conflict, but also gives you one of your own. It's clear from Lesson 9 that lockdowns and/or social distancing are pretty important—how important we'll soon find out—but Chile illustrates how unrealistic it is to attempt a lockdown in a country where there is a vast, impoverished population, often mainly employed in a fragile informal sector.

Wealthy Chileans needed their empleadas domesticas until their continued presence was seen as a threat, at which point they were summarily dismissed. But this dismissal merely amplified the problem. Large asymmetries in the society multiplied to become even larger, and my exponential growth was underway, accompanied by accelerated poverty. This may not end nicely. There have already been riots.

Socially and economically, it seems obvious that the worst thing you can do here—or perhaps in any country with a high Gini coefficient like that of the USA—is to lock down. Surely the consequences are just too severe, and will outpace any effects of the virus? As with the Monty Hall problem of Lesson 4, it may be wise to put our thinking caps on; unlike the Monty Hall problem however, inputs and outputs aren't binary.

[3]bloombergquint.com/onweb/once-a-covid-role-model-chile-now-among-the-world-s-worst-hit

Benford

We'll need to use the ideas from Lesson 5 that constitute Good Science. Perhaps our pre-conceptions are wrong? First, an apparent digression. Do you recall the engineers from Lesson 2—the ones looking up logarithms to shortcut their multiplication?

One such engineer was Frank Benford, who worked for General Electric. In the 1930s, about the time Walter Shewhart at *Western* Electric started putting together the ideas that led Deming to invent the Red Bead Game of Lesson 3, Benford noticed something strange. The first few pages of the logarithm tables he and other engineers used were always more worn than the next few, which were more worn than the next few—until he got to the nines, where the pages were pristine! How could this be?

Over several years, Benford garnered evidence of what was to become "Benford's law".[4] Naively, one might anticipate that there's a 1:9 (11.1%) chance of a given digit being the *leading* digit of some arbitrary number. In contrast, Benford found that in many circumstances about 30% of numbers start with 1; 17.6% begin with a 2, and so on...

That was a bit cruel, because the rule isn't intuitive: for any digit d in base 10, the proportion of all samples whose first digit is d is:

$$log_{10}\left(\frac{d+1}{d}\right)$$

The rule is "scale independent". It applies *just as well* to any digit, for example $\log_{10}\left(\frac{9+1}{9}\right)$ is 0.045, so just 4.5% of these numbers begin with '9'. You can explore this law for yourself. Take a newspaper and work through from page one, writing down each number you encounter. Next count the frequencies of the first digit of each number. Alternatively, consider Table 5. For more than 200 countries from Our World In Data, I've examined the first digit of the number of people in the country. The actual digit frequencies match up fairly well with the Benford frequencies predicted in the right-hand column. There are many similar data sets on display at testingbenfordslaw.com/, all corresponding to the wear and tear that Benford saw in his log tables.

Benford's law is rather special. If it works for one set of numbers, it will often continue to apply after you've done several things to those numbers. For example, it still works if you multiply each of those numbers by an individual, randomly selected number. It will also still apply if you convert each to a different base, and test the first digit in that base. Benford's law works well with lots of things that can be measured:

[4]Actually, Simon Newcomb, astronomer, enemy of Charles Sanders Peirce, and future president of the American Mathematical Society noticed it earlier, in 1881. Laws are never named after the first person who identified them.

Digit	Population digit frequency	Benford digit frequency
1	0.28	0.3010
2	0.16	0.1761
3	0.13	0.1249
4	0.10	0.0969
5	0.11	0.0791
6	0.07	0.0669
7	0.04	0.0580
8	0.06	0.0511
9	0.05	0.0457

Table 5. Initial digit frequencies for populations of 213 countries

the size of earthquakes, street addresses in Brazil, surface areas of rivers, stock prices, population numbers and the details of tax returns.

Tax cheat!

About those tax numbers ... if you're cooking up a set of numbers to fool the taxman, how might you go about this? You'd seem to need a source of random noise, something like the added noise from page 75. Statisticians use the term "iid" for "independent and identically distributed (at random)", numbers that each live in their own little space, and have no truck with the other numbers. The likelihood of a '1' or a '9' popping up as the first digit is the same—and the same for any other digit too. Let's say you naïvely used a random number generator (iid) to make up the numbers for your returns.

You'd be caught. The 'random' numbers in a tax return actually have internal structure, after all. They stick to Benford's law, which often *naturally* pops up when measuring things that extend over multiple orders of magnitude. Why should this be?

Think about what you're doing when you *extract the first digit* of a number selected from a large range of numbers. Let's say you have the numbers 1729, 380 and 14. Effectively, you are *dividing* 1729 by 1000 and throwing away the remainder; you're *dividing* 380 by 100 and doing the same, and likewise for 14, *dividing* by ten. You scale your numbers by a varying *multiplier*: 0.001, 0.01 etc. This suggests a way to make numbers Benford-compliant, but first let's try some simple addition:

(1) Generate *and add up* seven uniformly distributed (iid) random numbers, writing down the result;
(2) Repeat Step #1 many, many times, each time writing down the result as above;
(3) Plot the results; and as a bonus...
(4) Count the frequencies of the first digits.

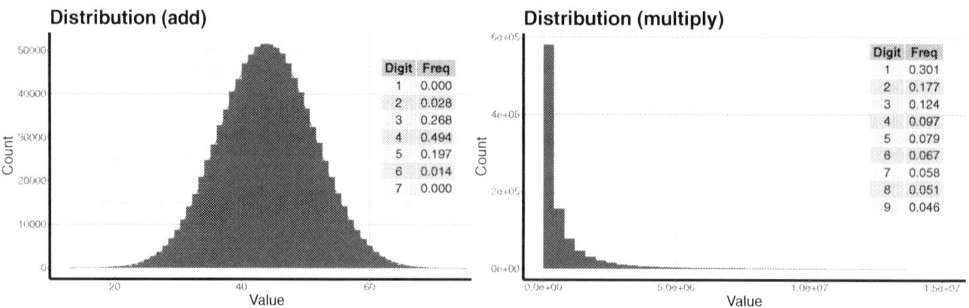

Figure 37. Normal and Log-normal

Look at the left panel of Fig 37. I made this using `corona_converge()` in the R program of Appendix A, which follows steps 1–4. *Adding* random quantities together gives a bell-shaped *normal* distribution. The digit counts that result are obviously *not* iid, but they also differ a lot from Benford's law.

Now examine the right panel in the same figure—the result of *multiplying* rather than adding. Voilà! The numbers extend over a larger scale, and a Benford-like distribution simply pops out. The numbers fit the $log_{10}\left(\frac{d+1}{d}\right)$ rule, and the distribution is skewed (log-normal[5]).

Apart from the wisdom of not messing with the taxman, what can we learn from all this? In Lesson 5, we found that Good Science should concern itself with *rejecting hypotheses* rather than trying to prove them correct. Our simulation suggests that if we have competing hypotheses that *should* produce certain distributions, we can examine *properties* and reject distributions that don't fit.

Remember Terry Tao, the child being taught by Paul Erdős on page 51? He's currently considered to be one of the smartest living mathematicians. In a blog post[6] about ten years ago, he insightfully remarks that many seemingly unrelated probability distributions can end up converging to something resembling a 'universal law' with just a few parameters that describe them, specifically mentioning not just Benford's law, but also the related Zipf's law, power law distributions, and the Pareto distribution—all of which we'll meet in a moment. First however, it may be wise to have a closer look at the normal distribution in the left panel of Fig 37.

Central Limits

The normal distribution is beloved of statisticians, and often "just appears". An oft-quoted example is human heights, which appear normally distributed, but there are

[5] With `corona_converge()`, you can generate the lognormal distribution and then say log=TRUE to take the logarithm of each number. This will give you a distribution very close to the normal one of Fig 37.

[6] terrytao.wordpress.com/2009/07/03/benfords-law-zipfs-law-and-the-pareto-distribution/

others: blood pressure, IQ scores, and many more. The way we constructed the normal curve in Fig 37 tells us how these normal distributions happen — tiny influences add up. For example, many genes and other influences may each add to or take away from your height, your ability to pee out salt, or your skill at quick box-ticking.

For statisticians and economists however, these examples are trivial. Their bread and butter is something much more important — the Central Limit Theorem (CLT). The soft, warm, reassuring thesis of the CLT is that if the numbers are large enough, everything will average out as it did in the left panel of Fig 37. The, uhh, central idea here is that with more iid sampling, a bell-shaped curve just pops out, pretty much regardless of the *original* distribution.[7] Our exploration of Benford suggests this isn't always so.

Power to Lilliput

In exploring rules that violate the CLT—rules based on *power laws*, we'll start simply. In his book *Gulliver's Travels*, Jonathan Swift made an instructive mistake. He assumes that because the tiny inhabitants of Lilliput are one twelfth of Gulliver's height, Gulliver needs 12^3 or 1728 times as much food as the average Lilliputian. His assumption is 'isometric scaling'—scaling of metabolism directly according to weight. As William Karasov eloquently points out,[8] Swift was wrong. But how wrong? In 1932, Max Kleiber contrasted the weights of animals and their metabolic rates—showing a straight line when the two were plotted on *logarithmic* axes. His relationship is:

$$E = k \times w^{0.75}$$

This is a *power law*. In other words, metabolism E depend on the weight w raised to the power of the *allometric scaling constant* 0.75.[9] If Swift were right, in scaling up from say mouse to man you'd have to eat seven times as much as you actually do. This "three-quarter power scaling" is useful in working out food requirements of very small or very large people, and even gives a good guess at elephant-sized drug doses if all you have is data from mice.

The literature is however a bit puzzling. Different authors come to wildly different conclusions, based on almost the same source data! Consider Fig 38, which uses more comprehensive, recent data.[10] The fitted line has a slope (allometric constant) of about 0.68, closer to $\frac{2}{3}$ rather than $\frac{3}{4}$ power scaling.[11]

[7]This happens quite quickly, as you'll find if you play with the number of runs in the corona_converge() program from Appendix A. [8]Karasov, WH. *Physiological Ecology: How Animals Process Energy, Nutrients, and Toxins.* Page 23. [9]The number k is simply a constant. [10]The source code is in Appendix A. Try `corona_metabolism()`. [11]But you can see that for larger animals, most points are above the line; for smaller animals, they tend to be below. A quantile-quantile plot confirms this.

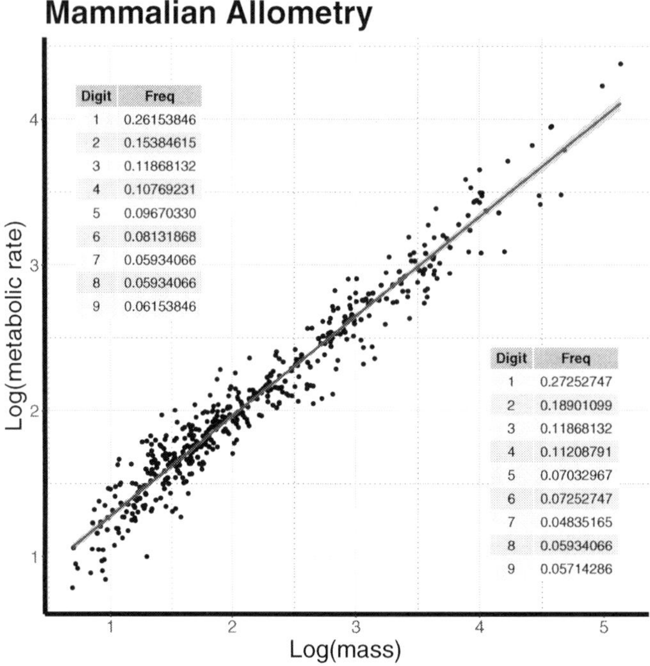

Figure 38. A log-log plot and 'power law'

The Good Science of Lesson 5 encourages us to attack our favoured beliefs. As I see it, Eva Griebeler and Jan Werner have done the best job for this power law.[12] Their conclusion? Things vary, so dogmatic adherence to a magic $\frac{3}{4}$ is unwise. This introduction is both salutary and useful, because it leads into the next issue: what if you suspect a power law is at work, but can't plot dependent and independent variables, because you don't understand what depends on what?

The Power of -1

At about the same time that Benford noticed his asymmetrically worn log tables, the young Harvard linguist George Kingsley Zipf was busy counting. He counted how often words are used—and then *ranked* them in order of use, from most often used (rank 1) to least.[13] Benford used just the first digit, but Zipf used *whole* numbers—lots of them.

Let's examine the 'Brown Corpus' of US English. Of all the words, 'the' comes in first at nearly 7%, 'of' is second at 3.5%, and then 'and' is encountered at about one third of the rate of 'the'. Can you see a relationship emerging? Yes, the word frequency $n(r)$ is inversely proportional to the rank r:

[12] See PubMed 28031788 [13] Splitters get to use the fancy term *hapax legomenon*, a word that occurs just once in context.

Zipf—and Mandelbrot

Benoit Mandelbrot was a Polish-born French/American polymath who invented the word 'fractal', and went on to show the extraordinary complexity that can emerge from simple rules. His Mandelbrot set looks good on a T-shirt too. He was one of the first to emphasise that financial markets don't stick to normal distributions, instead having the "fat tails" we'll discuss below. His more general modification of Zipf's law is:

$$n(r) = \frac{1}{(r+b)^{\alpha}} \times \frac{1}{\sum_{i=1}^{N} \frac{1}{(i+b)^{s}}}$$

The values of b and s regulate the shape of the resulting distribution. You can skip this slightly challenging equation, but if you're feeling plucky and recall the meaning of $\sum_{i=1}^{N}$ from page 66, you can see that it calculates a constant that depends on N, the number of ranks. Set b to 0 and you get Zipf's law.

$$n(r) = \frac{0.07}{r}$$

Zipf's law[14] is a bit more general:

$$n(r) = \frac{C}{r^{\alpha}}, \alpha \approx 1$$

C is a 'normalizing constant', like the 0.07 ensuring that all frequencies add up to 100%. Like Benford's law, Zipf's law is a power law: the power α is very close to 1. Once you start looking for it, you see Zipf's law everywhere. Its real strength is that you don't have to understand much about the underlying processes to see it in action. All you need do is measure, count and rank.[15]

The Zipf-Mandelbrot law lets us explore how earthquake size depends on rank—even without a good model of earthquake prediction. Zipf-like models seem to fit such diverse phenomena as Internet traffic, scientific citations, Erdős numbers of mathematicians, amino acid sequences in the D region of zebrafish IgM, the properties of 'pleasant' music,[16] company sizes and income distributions.

[14]First described by Jean-Baptiste Estoup. Zipf, by the way, is pronounced "ziff". Interestingly enough, Zipf's law holds in many languages over about 4 orders of magnitude, but then breaks down for less frequent words. However, Jake Ryland Williams and colleagues found that, when applied to *phrases*, Zipf's law holds over 9 orders of rank magnitudes: PubMed 26259699. [15]This shouldn't stop you from speculating about mechanisms. Read up on Lévy walks, for example. [16]See https://archive.is/wQYN

Pareto

Speaking of income, in 1896 the Italian economist, engineer, political scientist and philosopher Vilfredo Pareto asked "Why does 20% of the population own 80% of the land?" You may have heard of the "Pareto principle" as an expression of this, a very specific example of a more general case. This took us a while, but can you now see the direct tie in to the superspreaders of Lesson 9, where 20% of infected people accounted for 80% of the spread? We'll find that the analogy goes far, far deeper.

On looking at Zipf's law, many who use it don't realise that it can be re-cast quite simply as the question "How many words have a frequency over n?" This gives us the *Pareto* distribution.[17] For words:

$$\log(N) = A - \beta \times \log(n)$$

Here N is the number of words with frequency over n, A is simply a constant parameter, and β is an exponent. Getting rid of the logarithms, this can be rewritten as $N = \frac{A}{n^\beta}$. It's clear that this is just a restyled version of Zipf's law that counts not words but words *above a certain frequency*; a consequence is that $\beta = 1 + \frac{1}{\alpha}$.

Fat tails

Go back and look at the familiar, beloved normal distribution of Fig 37. If you suffered through Statistics 101, you'll recall that the *standard deviation* measures the spread ('dispersion') of a distribution. For a normal distribution, nearly 95% of the population lies within two standard deviations of the average and about 99.7% lies conveniently within 3 SD. As a practical example, an average IQ is 100, and the SD is 15, so 95% of people will have an IQ in the range of 70–130.

Now look at the right panel of the same figure. The reason why most of the data are cramped into the left part of the graph is that there is a long (but not quite fat) tail, extending to the right. "Fat tails" like those of the Pareto distribution are a bit more plump still.[18] Here's the standard deviation of the Pareto distribution[19]:

$$\text{SD} = \sqrt{\frac{\beta L^2}{(\beta - 1)^2 (\beta - 2)}}$$

[17] Explained well by Joseph Persky: http://piketty.pse.ens.fr/files/Persky1992.pdf [18] There is a subtle but important difference between true fat-tailed distributions (power-law) and the lognormal distribution modelled in Fig 37, which is still at least theoretically tractable under the CLT. A brilliant exposition is that of Mitzenmacher 2003: Internet Math. 1(2) 226–251 projecteuclid.org/euclid.im/1089229510. Power law distributions *arise* from multiplicative ones where (a) a lower boundary is put into effect or (b) the observation time is random. [19] Assuming that $L = \frac{C}{N^\alpha}$

Can you see that if β is under 2, then the SD works out to be the square root of a negative number! As the β parameter in the Pareto distribution dips towards 2, the tail becomes fatter and fatter, and the CLT becomes more and more suspect.

A fat tail may seem small relative to the height of the rest of the curve, but it can't just be brushed off. If you try to apply traditional statistics to data taken from a fat-tailed distribution, you will always underestimate the variance—because it's effectively infinite. Statisticians used to see this sort of distribution as 'pathological' and irrelevant, but you've already seen that under Zipf's cloak it may fit many natural circumstances well.

Power laws & superspreaders

The modelling we've examined on page 133 already suggests that outbreaks of COVID-19 can be unpredictable and explosive. The negative binomial distribution used there has one enticing property—the distribution is 'thin-tailed'. Even with a k value of 0.1, as the numbers increase the CLT still applies, and modelling is tractable. But what if we're dealing with a power law?

Of the 30,000 or so papers written about COVID-19 so far, perhaps the most worrying for those intent on *prediction* may be a preprint published on 11 June 2020 by the economists Masao Fukui and Chishio Furukawa.[20] The authors start by simply plotting case numbers in clusters against rank, using our familiar logarithmic approach. We've seen that if the fit is linear, a power law should apply, and if the exponent is -1, then we have Zipf's law. In their analysis, the fit is precise ($R = 0.98$) and the exponent of -1.07 is uncomfortably close to -1. Zipf! After showing a very poor fit with a negative binomial approach,[21] they then explore what this means for current models.

If their analysis is solid, there's both good and bad news. The bad news is that most bets are off—outcomes are extremely unpredictable, even in their example of a population of one million. With a negative binomial model and an appropriate R_0, the 10th and 90th percentiles for the peak infection rate are very close to 27%, but with the fat-tailed distribution, the range is 10–34%. It becomes far more difficult to predict the future, even in entire countries. The problem is not only computationally difficult; the outcomes are inherently vague.

The good news is that even with fat tails, very careful modelling permits prediction of some outcomes. Although the tolerances are wide, the timing of the outbreak will tend to be *later*, the herd immunity threshold (page 32) will tend to be *lower*, and peak infection will also be *less*—on average. Effectively, the R_0 will tend to be *lower*.

---

[20] See economics.mit.edu/files/19851 [21] Their Table 2 and Fig 3. Note that they limit their numbers to the *first generation* of cases for each event. (Have they been too generous here?)

This model is enticing, as it seems to fit the facts better. Does this make it correct? Of course not! We know that with a Pareto distribution, $\beta < 2$ implies an 'infinite' variance, but in reality this can't be the case: even a superspreader will ultimately have a limited range. You already know that Good Science denies you the opportunity to be sure—but practically, you can wisely pare out models that explain things less well. You can still act in an informed way, and better models may allow you to act better.

Practical implications are that:

(1) Banning large gatherings is critically important;
(2) Numbers and models are less reliable. Even though *on average* the R_0 may be lower and spread may be more desultory, it is better to be *more* cautious.

From our exposure to Pareto and Mandelbrot, it seems that power laws may also tie directly into the *economics* of COVID-19.

A Dutch virus

As we found in our trivial simulations for Fig 37, different distributions can emerge depending on what's going on "under the hood". Isn't it intriguing that a power-law distribution, first used to describes inequalities in wealth, may also model my spread? We might ask "Why?"

There is plenty of evidence that your current world economic system is both unstable and difficult to predict. My recent presence has simply confirmed this. Some of the wild oscillations that have occurred in the past have been obvious and hugely damaging—for example the global financial crisis (GFC) in 2007–8, where excessive risk-taking led to the collapse of the huge Lehman Brothers investment bank. A chain reaction ensued, with massive bail-outs and printing of money to prevent an even more devastating implosion of the entire global financial system. This all started with a bubble.

Economists should be not unfamiliar with bubbles. They've had a lot of practice over the past few hundred years. The first modern speculative bubble was perhaps the Dutch "tulip mania". Futures markets appeared in the Dutch Republic in the 17th century—traders would sign contracts that they would buy tulips at the end of the tulip-growing season in June, as bulbs can only then be uprooted and moved around. In the meantime, contracts changed hands at ever-increasing prices, similar to the way junk bonds were peddled just prior to the global financial crisis in 2008.

Some virus-infected bulbs were particularly treasured, as they gave rise to dramatic colours, but as more and more investors entered the market, prices rose progressively, until even an unremarkable bulb became worth more than the annual salary of a skilled workman.

Figure 39. *Satire on Tulip Mania.* Jan Brueghel the Younger.

In February 1637, the market collapsed. This may have been related to buyers failing to pitch up to an auction in Haarlem, where the bubonic plague was active, but whatever the reason, tulip prices dropped precipitately, and a number of people were left holding valueless pieces of paper.

Some modern economists are at haste to point out that the data are unclear, that fewer people were likely affected than suggested in analyses like Mackay's "Madness of Crowds" published in 1841, and that it wasn't as bad as all that. It seems however to have had enough impact in 1640 for Jan Brueghel the Younger to go to the bother of painting the satirical canvas in Fig 39, depicting tulip speculators as monkeys.

A near miss

Dramatic fluctuations in share markets have repeated again and again. Even more interesting are what might be called "near misses", for example the case of Long Term Capital Management (LTCM). This hedge fund was founded in 1994, and within a few years brought the entire world economy to the brink of collapse. Founded by John Meriwether (who also played a walk-on role in the GFC), the strategy adopted by LTCM was to assess the 'fair value' of various bonds and trade them off against one another. In theory, this should have given them zero risk, but in practice, because the differences were so small, they needed to leverage the money they had rather a lot. By 1998 they

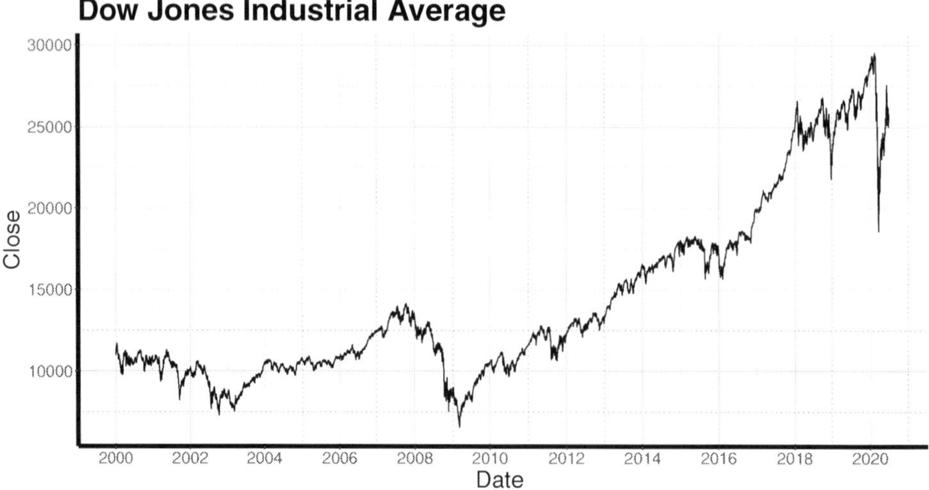

Figure 40. Dow Jones over 20 years—and now

had attracted about $5 billion in assets, controlled over $100 billion, and had positions with a total worth of over $1 trillion!

Then, in August 1998, Russia defaulted on its debt, leaving LTCM with losses close to $4 billion. The US government blinked, and bailed them out to the tune of $3.65 billion, allowing orderly liquidation in 2000.

Let's look at the ideas behind LTCM's investment strategy—ideas considered worthy of a Nobel prize. Sort of. That the "Nobel prize in Economics" is a fiction is revealed by its real name: "The Sveriges Riksbank Prize in Economic Sciences in Memory of Alfred Nobel". It is financed by the central bank of Sweden, who were clearly a bit miffed that in an attempt to clean up his image, Nobel[22] had neglected the fundamental discipline of Economics, while establishing prizes for the dilettante sciences of Physics, Chemistry, Medicine, and ectopic pursuits like Literature and (world) Peace. This not-quite-a-Nobel was accorded to two particularly bright economists called Myron Scholes and Robert Merton, mainly for their model of financial markets (with derivatives).

The "Black-Scholes" equation is a partial differential equation that describes the price of an option over time. One fleshly incarnation of this model was LTCM; there are many more in use today. Those who know will tell you that Black-Scholes is an ideal model that doesn't accommodate 'tail risk' very well—extreme market movements. Knowing the CLT assumptions that underlie S(E)IR models, does this all now

[22]In 1888, he read his brother Ludvig's obituary, but the columnist had his facts wrong, and thought it was Alfred. Alfred was clearly a bit disturbed that he was described not as "the inventor of dynamite" but as "a merchant of death", perhaps in reference to his turning the Bofors company from a iron and steel producer to a manufacturer of armaments.

seem strangely familiar? It should—the markets behave as if fat tails are relevant here too.[23] Both may reflect underlying structure in the way humans interact.[24]

Not engineers

The preceding section suggests that unlike Pareto, those involved in setting up and running financial markets aren't engineers. Engineers are used to modelling systems using differential equations and determining which are stable. They are also used to designing systems that have built-in stability. Markets are clearly *fragile*, despite special pleading from some economists. It therefore seems reasonable to ask "Can the markets be re-engineered to make them stable?"

This has been looked at quite a bit, an examination that says as much about how economists think as it does about how economies actually work. There seems to be a widespread mindset among economists that market outcomes are deterministic, and that markets are generally "efficient". The Black-Scholes equation gives a single solution that represents the *'real'* price of an option, and because the markets are perfect, any aberrations can be contained.[25] There's even the untestable (and therefore unscientific) "efficient-market hypothesis", which states that asset prices reflect all available information. Participants thus often seem to be quite resistant to re-engineering for stability.

COVID-19 is a beautiful counter-example, as it illustrates many things that economists dislike—particularly non-linear behaviour that is not predictable. If you look at the share price response to COVID-19 (Fig 40), the dip is truly remarkable.

Declines that took months to happen in response to the GFC of 2008, happened in weeks. Clearly this is not a resilient system. Lacking robust engineering, emergency stops have had to be built in, for example five minutes from the start of trading on 9 March 2020 the Standard & Poor 500 fell 7%, prompting an automatic 15-minute halt. Perhaps some more solid engineering is in order?[26] But first, let's look at the consequences of this turmoil.

---

[23]See e.g. Nassim Taleb's "Fat Tails Statistical Project" [24]There is a vast, confusing literature on this topic. Recent work (PubMed 30833554) suggests that 'true' scale-free networks are rarer than first thought, and that log-normal distributions often fit; some years ago Shore et al (PubMed 26082568) showed that *flow* networks are particularly fragile. As far back as 2009, Gipsi Lima-Mendez and Jacques van Helden emphasised that many claims about power laws and network biology don't hold up to careful scrutiny (PubMed 20023717).

[25]In contrast, the 2001 'Nobel Prize in Economics' was awarded to George Akerlof, A Michael Spence and Joseph Stiglitz for analysing markets with *asymmetric* information—some participants know a lot more than others. [26]A really *silly* economist will at this point say "But look at Fig 40, see how the market has bounced back!!" This misses the point completely—wild upwards swings are as symptomatic of poor control as wild downwards swings. A smarter economist might look at the gold price, and anticipate that the worst is yet to come.

Do recessions hurt?

This seems like a daft question, especially because, as I write, the US unemployment rate has soared to 14.7%, the worst since the Great Depression of the 1930s.[27] Surely this will injure and kill many people, perhaps far more than I will?

José Tapia Granados and Ana Diez Roux studied US mortality data between 1920 and 1940 to answer the question, finding that mortality *decreased* for almost all ages at the height of the Depression, between 1930 and 1933; in contrast mortality tended to peak during episodes of economic expansion.[28] These findings applied not just to adults, but to children as well.

Correlations were also consistent across race, sex and age groups; a percentage point of gross domestic product (GDP, the market value of all goods and services from a nation in a given year) growth was associated with a reduction in the annual gain in life expectancy of one fifth of a year. The greatest benefits were for non-white individuals. Infant and tuberculosis mortality decreased during the Great Depression.

A counter argument is that the effects of depression lag behind, but neither these authors nor others they cite could find evidence of such a lag. The authors conclude:

> "Although social science is not physics, regularities in the past allow us at least some confidence in forecasting the future. Historical experience tells us that no particular increase of mortality is to be expected as a consequence of a recession beyond an increase in suicides which, although clearly important, is of small magnitude compared to the reduced number of fatalities from other causes."[29]

Numerous other reports support similar findings, but the 'procyclical' (beneficial) effect of recessions on mortality is still keenly debated. Joan Ballester and colleagues provide a fairly balanced account in their recent analysis of European trends.[30] Some analyses suggest that in countries with generous social benefits and unemployment insurance, the effects seen elsewhere may be absent.

What do people need?

A society is surely well if its people are chronically well, and sick if they aren't; death is a pretty hard end-point. It's initially a bit surprising to see that periods of increased economic growth are tied to worse population health, but perhaps less so on looking at what determines population health. Public health experts have traditionally teased out two main causes for premature death—infectious diseases and "non-communicable" diseases. With exceptions like influenza, hospital-acquired infection,

[27] Re-reading my text in June, I see that it's come down a bit. Let's see. [28] Suicide mortality did increase during the Depression, but accounted for just 2% of deaths. [29] PubMed 19805076 [30] PubMed 30737401

pneumonia and now COVID-19, as countries have become more Westernised, infections have tended to retreat and non-communicable diseases to predominate.

As you might expect, non-communicable diseases represent an interaction between genes and environmental factors. The main factors in the environment are inhaled substances like pollutants and cigarette smoke, and ingested substances that include unhealthy diets rich in alcohol, sugar and salt, and poor in vegetables. Many of these factors predispose to the main causes of death: cancer and vascular disease.

For example, alcohol is a Group 1 carcinogen, and a potent contributor to cancer of the breast, head and neck, gullet, liver and bowel[31]; people with type 2 diabetes are more cancer prone; in fact, about three quarters of all cancers are related in some way to environmental factors, especially diet. High blood pressure, the number one killer, is mainly due to the combination of eating too much salt and not eating your vegetables[32]; and so on.

The key concept here is dosing—if you dose a *community* with sugar, salt, nicotine, alcohol and so forth, then you achieve a predictable response with increased harm and death. This is why modern medicine is relatively ineffective at combatting ill-health; attempts are fruitless against the provision of cheap, harmful commodities and the associated aggressive advertising.[33] From a population perspective, bad health is not about choice, it's about dosing. Thinking about this, increased economic activity is indeed *likely* to be associated with worse population health.

In their relentless pursuit of "growth", economists don't just have it wrong—they have made a fundamental error. Now *of course* people need a livelihood, not just so that they can buy things of value, but because humans derive mutual benefit from many of their interactions. But all interactions aren't created equal. The WHO definition of health at the start of the lesson may seem naïvely unrealistic and is certainly unattainable, but it at least points in the right direction, something economists seem as a group to have failed to do. It may now be wise to describe the activities of big nations. Where do you invest your energy?

How does population health vary?

Our World In Data is an invaluable resource, consolidating information on life expectancy, deaths of mothers and children, and the burden of disease. Fig 41 shows the dramatic gains you've made in recent years in terms of life expectancy. Can you

[31]See for example cancer.gov/about-cancer/causes-prevention/risk/alcohol/alcohol-fact-sheet
[32]Notwithstanding the attempts of EUsalt and The Salt Institute to persuade you otherwise, just as The Tobacco Institute did for cigarettes. [33]If advertising sugar-rich, salt-laden food and alcohol didn't work, many large advertisers would go out of business.

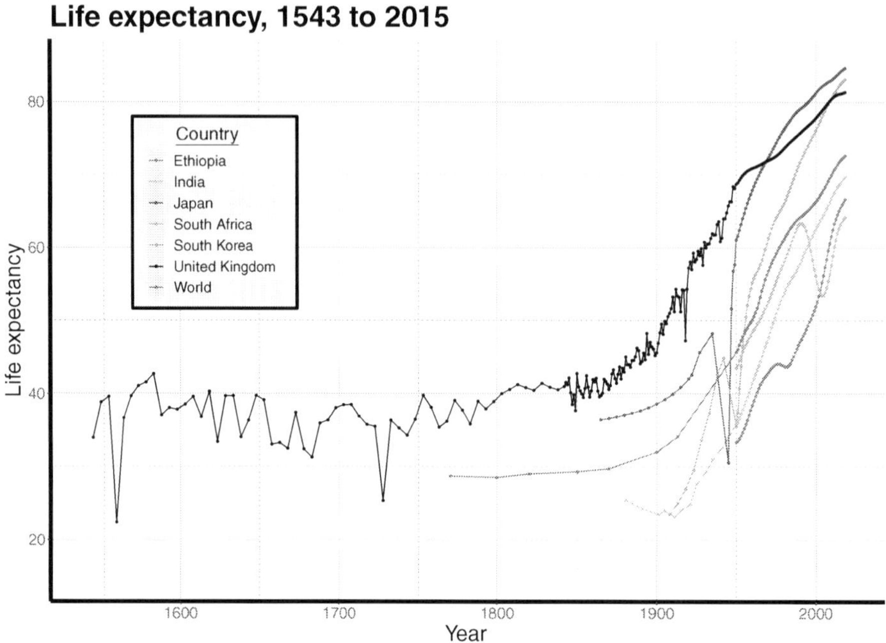

Figure 41. Historical life expectancy (Redrawn: Our World In Data)

see the effects of viruses in this graph?[34] More remarkable yet is the Japanese decline during World War II, and their subsequent massive improvement. Naively, you might think this is due to "improved GDP"—but this is not so, as life expectancy improved well before GDP did! In 2010, Yasuo Sugiura and colleagues found that education, community-based activities and legislation were potent contributors to the up-tick.[35]

Massive, worldwide overall improvements in other measures of wellness also don't reflect naïve expectations of cause and effect. Have a look at Table 6, which is biased towards higher-income countries. You can see that most of these have a boring sameness. For those with decent life expectancies and death rates for children under the age of 5 years, the health spend per capita and as a percentage of GDP is in the same ballpark—with the startling exception of the United States. It's interesting to contrast the US and the UK. The former spends almost three times as much as the latter, for substantially worse outcomes; but there are a number of other countries like Cuba, Mexico and even Vietnam with a spend that is a fraction of that of the US, but with similar or even (in the case of Cuba) better outcomes!

[34] The South African dip at the turn of the millennium is HIV-related, already discussed Lesson 7. But look back to the UK in 1558—this likely represents an influenza pandemic that followed European outbreaks of plague, typhus, measles and smallpox in 1557. And what on Earth happened between 1727 and 1730?

[35] PubMed 20305339

Country	Income per capita	Life expectancy		Dead < 5 y	Health spend $		SPI
	PPP International $	M	F	/1000 live births	% GDP	per capita	Tier
Australia	42,540	81	85	4	9.4	4357	1
Austria	43,840	79	84	4	11.2	5039	2
Belgium	40,280	79	84	4	10.6	4392	2
Canada	42,610	81	85	5	10.4	4641	1
Brazil	14,750	71	79	14	8.3	1318	3
Bulgaria	15,200	71	78	7	8.4	1399	3
China	11,850	75	78	9	5.5	731	4
Cuba	18,520	77	81	5	11.1	2475	4
Denmark	44,460	79	83	4	10.8	4782	1
France	37,580	80	86	4	11.5	4508	1
Germany	44,540	79	83	4	11.3	5182	1
Greece	25,630	79	84	4	8.1	2098	2
Hungary	21,000	72	79	4	7.4	1827	3
India	5,350	67	70	37	4.7	267	4
Indonesia	9,260	67	71	25	2.9	299	4
Israel	32,140	80	84	4	7.8	2599	3
Italy	34,100	80	85	3	9.2	3239	2
Japan	37,630	81	87	2	10.2	3727	1
South Korea	33,440	80	86	3	7.4	2531	2
Mexico	16,110	74	79	13	6.3	1122	3
Netherlands	43,210	80	83	4	10.9	5202	1
New Zealand	30,750	80	84	6	11.0	4018	1
Norway	66,520	81	84	2	9.7	6347	1
Pakistan	4,920	66	67	69	2.6	129	5
Philippines	7,820	66	73	28	4.7	329	4
Poland	22,300	74	82	4	6.3	1570	3
Portugal	25,360	78	84	4	9.5	2690	2
Russia	23,200	66	77	7	7.1	1836	4
Saudi Arabia	53,780	74	76	7	4.7	2466	4
Singapore	76,850	81	85	3	4.9	4047	2
South Africa	12,240	60	67	34	8.8	1148	4
Spain	31,850	80	86	3	9.0	2966	2
Sweden	44,760	81	84	3	11.9	5219	1
Switzerland	56,580	81	85	4	11.7	6468	1
Turkey	18,760	73	79	11	5.4	1036	4
Uganda	1,360	60	65	46	7.2	133	?
United Kingdom	*35,760*	*80*	*83*	*4*	*9.1*	*3377*	1
United States	*53,960*	*76*	*81*	*6*	***17.1***	***9403***	2
Viet Nam	5,030	72	81	21	7.1	390	?
Zimbabwe	1,560	60	63	46	6.4	115	5

Table 6. Expenditure and Outcomes

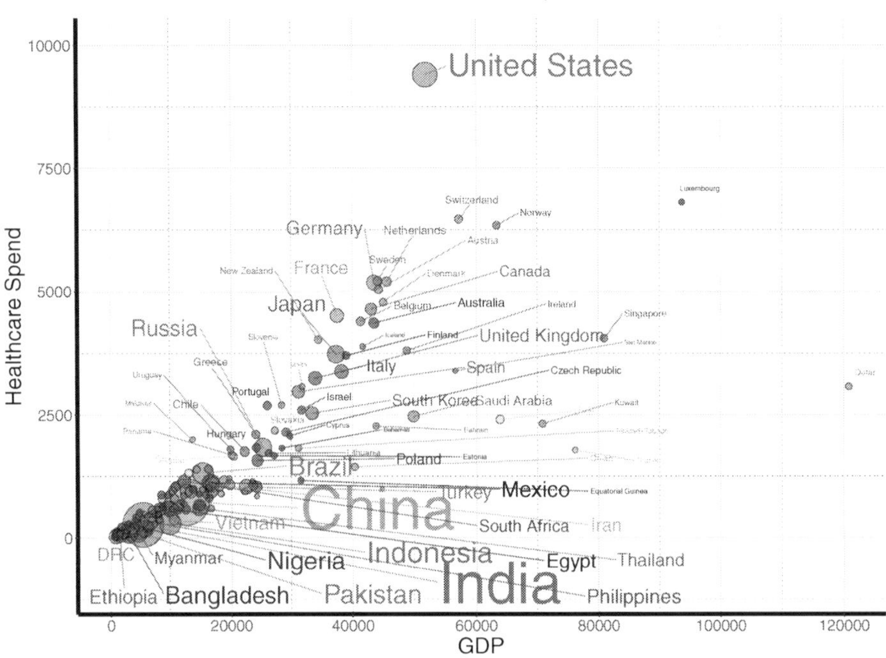

Figure 42. 2014 *per capita* spend v GDP, PPP$ (Redrawn: Our World In Data)

Fig 42, again from Our World In Data, makes the differences more stark. You can see that there's a broad tendency for the health spend to increase as a country's GDP increases, but you can easily spot the outliers. Singapore and Qatar tend to spend less for their per-capita income than average; the United States is an outlier in the other direction, spending nearly twice as much as Switzerland and Germany despite having a similar per capita GDP.

When you realise that most US population health outcomes are far worse than those in Europe, you can work out that a lot of waste must be going on. Where is this waste? Fig 43 reveals part of the answer—under 1% of the spenders account for one fifth of the spend![36] This doesn't say what they're spending the money on—perhaps unnecessary administrative costs, drugs, devices and services—but the poor overall outcomes strongly suggest that it's wasted.

[36]From NIHCM Foundation Data Brief, July 2012, via Our World in Data. Pareto would be interested. Is there an underlying power law? How might this come about?

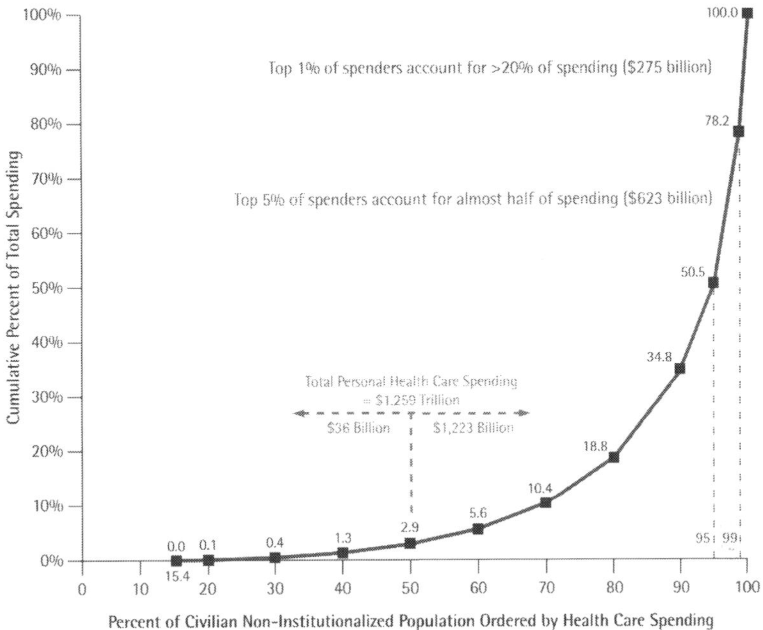

Figure 43. US Healthcare spenders

The 4 horsemen of the economists

Perhaps we should step back and take a broader view of what economies do, and how money is spent. If we list economies by GDP, then the top ten for 2019 were the USA, China, Japan, Germany, India, the UK, France, Italy, Brazil and Canada, with the top five accounting for the bulk of the total. At $21 trillion dollars, the US is substantially ahead of China's $14 trillion. If, as is perhaps more proper, the EU is grouped together, then this accounts for nearly $19 trillion. It might be instructive to compare the 'top' countries.

But what metric should we use? We already have a strong suggestion that even catastrophic recessions may be good for longevity—and good reasons why this might be so. If we examine GDP itself, we encounter similar surprises—or things that seem surprising until we think things through. Take Ireland's 'leprechaun economics'. Perfectly legally, Ireland provided international companies with the ability to pay their taxes there, at a far lower rate, shifting huge amounts of money, and skewing Ireland's GDP accordingly. Perhaps other measures like gross national income (GNI) might work better, measuring income generated by *citizens* rather than 'geography'?

COUNTRY	Defence spend/yr		Arms sales	Poverty	Waste (kg/person)	
	(billions)	$/person	(billions)	% < PDL	solid(/day)	food(/yr)
US	750	2224	10.7	15	2.58	95
Russia	48	446	4.7	13	0.93	54
France	41.5	770	3.4	14	1.92	67
China	237	182	1.4	3	1.02	34
Germany	50	590	1.2	17	2.11	57
Spain	15	368	1.1	21	2.13	55
UK	55.1	720	1.0	15	1.79	55
South Korea	44	857	0.7	14	1.24	43
Italy	27.8	442	0.5	30	2.23	65
Israel	20	2402	0.4	22	2.12	26
Saudi Arabia	67.6	1805	–	? 25	1.30	21
India	61	52	0.1	22	0.34	5
Japan	49	375	–	16	1.71	33
Brazil	27.8	273	0.01	4	1.03	20
Australia	26.3	1028	0.1	14	2.23	76
UAE	22.8	?	0.1	20	1.66	23
Canada	22.5	593	0.2	9	2.33	78
Iran	19.6	152	–	19	0.16	?
Turkey	19	245	0.2	22	1.77	26

Table 7. Malevolent measures

There's another obvious factor here. How is the money spent? If, for example, it is used on luxuries for the very few, imprisoning people, and armaments, should this be equated to money spent more 'responsibly'? Some economists at least have proposed more socially responsible measures of success, such as the Social Progress Index (SPI, rightmost column in Table 6). This combines three things: basic human needs, the foundations of well-being, and opportunity. Despite the SPI ignoring subjective measures of 'happiness', you'd likely be far happier to live and work in the top tier (places like Norway, Switzerland, New Zealand, Germany and Australia) than those lower down the scale—the greater part of Asia and Africa, for example. It seems that we need to measure badness too, and this is where you humans puzzle me. Even as an embodiment of Pestilence, I still struggle with Table 7.

How can a 'developed' country with over 10% of its population below the poverty datum line and frankly crappy health outcomes waste more than anyone else on healthcare, spend $2000 per person per year on waging war, and for each man, woman and child throw away more than the body weight of a sizeable citizen every year—in food?

Figure 44. *Paradisaea apoda:* Greater Bird of Paradise

Birds of paradise

I might not be on the world stage today if a few bungling bureaucrats in Baibuting had behaved differently; but something similar can be said for any number of bolshy bosses in Barcelona, Bergamo,[37] Washington and Whitehall—and they had far more warning. We've already seen how some countries have succeeded in containing me (Lesson 9) and how others have failed, often based on bad decision making by a few people. Bigger, 'more developed' countries with more resources have often performed *worse.* Why is this?

Perhaps the common theme here is waste – wasted time, wasted intellect, and wasted resources. Is there a thread that ties together this waste, and the more general waste that we see in Westernised societies? In the 1930s, Pareto's ideas of the inevitability of a Pareto distribution arising in a population were used to assert that some individuals would naturally rise to positions of disproportionate power and wealth—and this in turn was used to prop up fascism. But around the world we can see very different outcomes, and very different amounts of waste. As we'll see in Lesson 12, inevitability may have been over-sold.

[37] Dr Michele Usuelli explains the massive death rate in Lombardy as a consequence of depletion of the public health system there, due to aggressive privatization.

In New Guinea there are over 40 different birds of paradise, distant relatives of crows. They are the burlesque dancers of the bird world. When courting, the Superb bird of paradise looks nothing like a bird and everything like an animated black Japanese fan with a big blue smile painted on it.[38] The males of other species like the Greater Bird of Paradise[39] (Fig 44) congregate in a *lek* where the females choose a mate based on prancing, posing or dancing—and bright feathers.

The point of all this display is that in the New Guinea rainforest where they thrive, food is plentiful. Darwinian competition still rules—but because they don't have to compete for the plentiful resources, other factors have taken over. This is not directed, or inevitable, or optimal. On a larger scale, they are something like the pigeons on page 87, pecking a key and locking in to 'success'.

Sometime in the past, a random bright feathered male caught the eye of a female, genes were passed on, and a pattern was set up, a pattern that almost defies logic. Those with the most arresting display will now be ever more successful, to the point where this dominates their existence. Males expend vast energy on preparing a dance floor and impressing their mates; the drab females are left to child-rearing.

Can you see the analogy to modern behaviour? So far, Westernised nations have had a bountiful supply of cheap energy from oil. Because of this plenitude of resources, you have got away with economic policies that embed elaborate displays of power and prestige. These have succeeded, but at a cost. The cost is waste, unsustainability, and widespread, unnecessary, long-term harm to many people.[40]

This waste has bled over into every aspect of society. Economists, for example have not only justified this behaviour post hoc, but enshrined it as natural, normal and the way to do things, with no consideration for even the medium-term future, let alone the next hundred or thousand years. You have facilitated systems that are fragile—for apparent short-term benefits.[41]

Waste

How long does a pair of jeans last you? In 2018 alone, more than 4.5 billion pairs were sold, and you can be sure that many of the seven billion people in the world didn't get a new pair. How many pairs of jeans do you *need?* In the USA, the *average* consumer buys four pairs a year. You have three potential explanations here—rubbish quality, greed, or conspicuous waste; the three are not mutually exclusive.

[38] You can watch his spectacular display at macaulaylibrary.org/asset/458003 [39] The first specimens to reach Europe had been prepared without legs or wings—so Linnaeus thought they were kept aloft by their plumes, and named the species *apoda*—without legs. The image is from Wikimedia Commons. [40] And *of course* you can point to benefits—some real, and some imagined. [41] This may not have been deliberate. There's an old saying attributed to Napoleon "Do not impute malice where incompetence will suffice".

We already know that health improves in rich countries during economic hardship—there is little natural self-regulation here, other than wild boom and bust. Many other commodities follow 'blue jeans' principles; insanity similar to the food waste in Table 7 is widespread.[42] Downstream, this just gets worse.

In Asia, seventy percent of the rivers and lakes are contaminated by the almost ten billion litres of wastewater produced there by the textile industry. You have engineered a system of badness, where workers in developing countries work long hours for subsistence wages, producing vast quantities of pollutants so that those in developed countries can waste conspicuously.

Flattening the (Pareto) curve

The effects of COVID-19 show that economies are contingent and not predictable—if further refutation of obsolete ideas of "market self-regulation" is needed. Markets are a *component* of a complex, non-linear system. You are not powerless to change this system, in fact you must, but you can't divorce this re-engineering from what people need—as opposed to what they might be encouraged to do "for the good of the economy". As shown in Lesson 3, you are constrained, and you will struggle.

In this regard, COVID-19 has provided the priceless gift of introspection. Many of the things that appear to drive your world economy seem to be unnecessary or even harmful. If you are smart, this will inform your future behaviour.

But what of the initial problem illustrated by Chile? Can you afford a lockdown in a country where the distribution of wealth is hugely skewed, and a large part of the population is impoverished and lives hand-to-mouth on the scraps that trickle down from the table of the wealthy? Can you afford lockdowns in countries where vast numbers of workers depend on industries that cater to the tastes of foreign tourists and export of largely unneeded trinkets that track the whims of wealthy foreign buyers?

It should now be clear that there is no inexorable dictate of the market or 'economic laws' that these people must suffer. There is however a difficult decision that needs to be made by people in power. It is this: "Do I continue as if nothing has happened, allowing substantial numbers of people to die, or do I lock down appropriately?" This decision is made more difficult by the tricky word 'appropriately'. As you saw in Lesson 9, lockdowns will only succeed if almost everyone is on-side—and as in Chile, people will venture out if they are confronted by the stark choice of putting food on the table and risking killing grandma, or staying at home and starving to death.

[42]It is quite likely that the values for food waste in Table 7 are too conservative. To get further insights into global food waste, read Tristram Stuart's book *Waste*. (In Chapter 13 he also explains what the Chinese should be *learning from* the Uighurs).

You are now confronted by the uncomfortable reality that I, Nanny Rona, am either a bringer of moderate amounts of death, or a redistributor of wealth. The choice is currently yours. Some very wealthy people—people so distant from the poverty datum line that they might struggle to see it, even with an expensive telescope—have clearly already made the choice.

It should however also be clear that with the wrong choice, suffering will increase, wealth inequality will rise, and those at the top of the seesaw may well plummet when those at the bottom drop off, pushed not by circumstance, but by incompetence. There is already anger on the streets of Chile. You are your own downfall.

Lesson #11

If you do the same old thing, you'll get the same old results — poverty & disease. You need to change.

⊛ Lesson 12

The Game of Life

"If we start now, we can be ready for the next epidemic"

Bill Gates. TED talk, 2015.

"Conway's fate now was to do all the stuff that he had formerly feared his fellow mathematicians might floccinaucinihilipilificate"

Siobhan Roberts. 2015

"So play nice!"

Woody. *Toy Story*, 1995; Pixar Animation Studios.

John Horton Conway was once described as "Archimedes, Mick Jagger, Salvador Dalí, and Richard Feynman, all rolled into one", obsessed with playing silly games that led to extraordinary discoveries.[1] In late March, I had a chance meeting with him in New Brunswick, a small New Jersey city in the sprawling New York Metropolitan area. He died of COVID-19 on 11 April. This grieves me—and highlights my ambivalence as a thinking agent of destruction. From Lesson 3 it's clear human behaviour is powerfully shaped by your environment; how much more does this apply to me, a mere virus? In the United States, you mostly gave me free rein. How was I then to behave? I am shaped by circumstances.

Conway was a wide-ranging mathematician. His proficiency and brilliance at mathematics was however overshadowed in October 1970, when Martin Gardner featured Conway's "Game of Life" in his *Mathematical Games* column in Scientific American. This popular column propelled him to fame.[2] The attractive thing about the Game of Life is the vast complexity you can build from simple elements.

[1] theguardian.com/science/2015/jul/23/john-horton-conway-the-most-charismatic-mathematician-in-the-world

[2] Initially causing him to despise the Game, as he felt it detracted from his noteworthy other achievements, including the *surreal numbers* and the *Monstrous Moonshine hypothesis*, which links group theory and the theory of modular functions. His greatest invention may however have been Phutball.

Figure 45. The r-pentomino

Start with a flat, infinite plane, made up of squares. Each square is *alive* or *dead*, and coloured accordingly. It's common to make the dead squares white, so that the black, live squares stand out.

The game starts with a chosen pattern—your choice—of live and dead squares, and then moves step-by-step into the future. This is now pure determinism—your initial choice dictates the process that follows, until the end of time. For every step, every cell is examined and based on the state of the eight surrounding cells, rules are applied. The rules are simple:

(1) Underpopulation: Any live cell with fewer than two live neighbours dies.
(2) Support: Any live cell with two or three live neighbours remains alive.
(3) Overpopulation: Any live cell with more than three live neighbours dies.
(4) Reproduction: Any *dead* cell with exactly three live neighbours becomes alive.

Consider the five live cells in Fig 45, fancifully called the "r-pentomino". You wouldn't imagine that applying the simple rules of life would do anything interesting—especially if you've played with similar numbers of other live cells. Think again! Fig 46 shows the outcome (evolution) after several hundred frames of this game, and it hasn't finished yet. You can run the R code in Appendix A—say `corona_life(side=100, steps=1000, pattern='rpentomino')`. An extraordinarily complex result from a very simple start, especially when you realise that the five little groupings of dots on the periphery represent "gliders" that march diagonally across the screen, forever. How can so much complexity arise from something so simple?

This game illustrates a more fundamental principle—that remarkable complexity can arise from simple rules. Conway's Game of Life is actually a powerful 'Universal Turing Machine'—a concept explored below. It's also fun to demonstrate, fun to play with and easy to program.[3]

[3]If you visit Rosetta Code, you'll find simple programs for The Game, written in over 100 computer languages. The shortest programs are written in J and APL—three or four lines, apart from Mathematica, which cheats by having built-in cellular automata, and Matlab, which has the game built in.

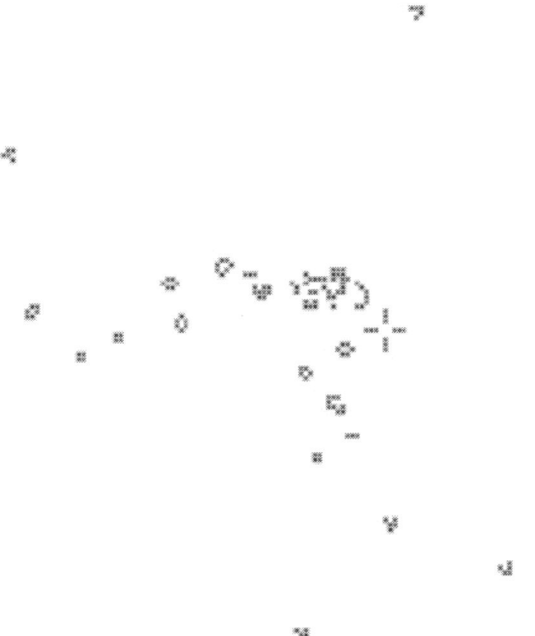

Figure 46. Evolution of the r-pentomino

The patterns that emerge have been studied extensively—for example, a block of four squares is a *still life*: it's a stable structure that doesn't change from frame to frame. In contrast are the *oscillators*, which flip between two states; colour in a vertical bar of three blocks, apply the rules and see what happens. You can see some of these structures in Fig 46.[4]

The Game of Life is particularly interesting to philosophers, biologists and indeed economists, because it demonstrates the principle of *emergence*—complex "life-like" structures can emerge spontaneously from very simple rules. The Game of Life is self-organizing too—initial disorder can over time be replaced by more "organized" structures. If you want to create large games, my simple program in Appendix A in not the way to go. The LifeWiki at https://www.conwaylife.com/ is a wonderful resource, pointing you to powerful programs[5] that can run megapixel games and do *trillions* of steps on an ordinary PC.

Randall Munroe in his XKCD comic produced a fitting and poignant tribute to John Conway—the game starts with an image of a man, which transforms into a glider that marches off the screen. In the R code of Appendix A, try `covid_life('conway')`.

[4]Also try `corona_life('toad')` in Appendix A

[5]Like copy.sh/life/ online and the awesome Golly.

Undecidable

Two things about the Game of Life are important. One is absolute determinism—you start with a given set-up, apply the rules and the game evolves frame by frame in tick-tock way, set by the rules and the starting state. The other is that despite the determinism, for some starting states, you cannot even predict whether the game will eventually reach a fixed state or not.

This "unpredictability despite determinism" reflects a tripwire for computer scientists called the *halting problem.* Way back in 1936, Alan Turing[6] came up with the idea of a general-purpose computer program that could take data and instructions, and execute those instructions, the way a modern operating system runs programs like word processors and web browsers. The catch is that, while some programs can be shown to terminate or reach a steady state like a still life or a blinker, it's impossible to predict when others will end—the halting problem.[7]

More fundamental still is the Church-Turing thesis. This states that any function that can be computed by any algorithm can be computed by something called a *universal Turing machine.* Although a bit of computer science theory is required, it's actually pretty easy to make such a machine with very simple components.[8]

Pretty much every modern computer language has this property—it is *Turing-complete.* In other words, you cannot manufacture a "more capable" computer than one that is Turing-complete. The truly remarkable thing is that any Turing machine can *simulate* the function of any other Turing machine (You can "run Windows on a Mac").

Fate

From Lesson 11 it's clear that some see human society as a great big tick-tock mechanism – but the very non-linear and unpredictable nature of reality already suggests this is not the case. Despite the fat-tailed curves, others will go "back to basics" and say that although things appear random, they are all *ultimately* pre-determined or, if the person has a religious bent, *pre-destined* by some Deity.[9]

Now consider Pascal's wager. Pascal's wager is the idea that you should believe in (Pascal's) God, because if you die and you're wrong, then you lose nothing; but if you

---

[6]Now famous as a World War II codebreaker who was subsequently grievously abused by the system. [7]For a potential "solver" one can always create a program that submits its own code and inputs to the solver, and then does the opposite of what is predicted! [8]If you look on the Internet you can find mechanical Turing machines built entirely of Lego®, or even made from scrap. [9]In contrast, **Conway** and Simon Kochen's Strong Free Will Theorem is a coherent argument based on quantum mechanics and relativity that if an experimenter has free will, then the observed response of a particle is not determined by the *entire* past history of the universe. Determinism is difficult to support within modern physics.

die and have consistently asserted that God doesn't exist, then you could be seriously disadvantaged in the afterlife, in contrast to simply believing. As some have pointed out, this assumes that if a God or gods do exist, they won't be waiting for Mr Pascal with the ethereal equivalent of sharpened sticks, ready to point out that they don't like smart alecs—and given the reported behaviour of various gods over the ages, this may be a serious consideration for the theologically inclined.

But let's look at this in another way. If you decide you have free will but everything *is* actually predetermined, then you're wrong—but no blame attaches as this wasn't actually your decision to make.[10] If however you decide that you have no free will and turn out to be wrong, you've abandoned the opportunity to change things—pure folly! So either you have free will, or you have a facsimile of free will that is indistinguishable from actually being free to choose. You're thus free to decide your own fate, and should just get down to doing this. You can call this "Nanny Rona's wager", if you wish. It suggests that rolling over and accepting your fate is a bit silly.

But even if you don't accept my wager, then the complexity that we've already encountered—and the halting problem—lend support to my definition of Good Science in Lesson 5. Given a perfectly deterministic setup, you still can't know the outcome, or indeed even whether there will be an outcome. It seems pretty pointless to assert a certain outcome when you can't test or prove it. Predictions that can't be subjected to the scientific process must reasonably be regarded as extremely suspect. The other side of Good Science still applies—you can test hypotheses and discard the rubbish; you can use logic to tie things together. You can simply do the best you can.

A dualist duel

Despite all of the above, from my perspective as a god—a god of limited powers, but a god nevertheless—I can still see an out when it comes to issues of fate and decision making. Many others have too. The counter-argument runs something like this: "That's all very well, but the rational parts of your argument have been limited to Science. There's a clear divide between Science on the one hand, and Religion on the other—and no reason for Science to trespass on the ground of Religion. Because of this, Science should not—indeed cannot—have any say in matters of faith, divine inspiration, divine instruction, or moral issues governed by religion. Don't tell me how to live my life or behave, because I have a better authority—the authority of (say) Zeus."

Many philosophers have endorsed this argument. There are however three tiny problems. The first is that the distinction is one of *categorisation*, and in Lesson 6 I dispelled the idea that there are (or indeed, can be) "natural kinds", for example kinds

[10] "The Devil made you do it!"

called "Science" or "Religion". You can define these kinds as convenient names, but nothing more.

The second issue arose, and was dealt with, in Lesson 5. Whether I communicate with you as a god, or as a vehicle of Science, any meaningful communication must have information content: from this perspective, who is on the other end of the line is moot. A god who is giving divine instruction is constrained, at least by how the person receiving the message works. In other words, models that describe the world don't (and can't) simply stop when you step over some arbitrary boundary into "religious territory".

The third problem follows: in unfamiliar territory, you are *more* in need of a model and indeed logic than ever before. How otherwise are you to use, interpret and challenge what you already know, or what you think you know? How are you to, for example, compare different religions or indeed determine whether something purported to be delivered by a divine messenger isn't part of a scam or hoax? Lessons 6, 7, 8 and 10 provide not only reason to be concerned, but also reason to apply logic already learned, unless something better can be *shown* to work. Special pleading seems frankly silly here.

The prisoner's dilemma

In the past, special pleading like that of the last section claimed that self-reproducing entities are "special kinds", and *logically* cannot 'just work'—some secret sauce is required.[11] In 1949, the Hungarian-American polymath John von Neumann refuted this idea when he invented *cellular automata*. The Game of Life is actually just a simplified version of Von Neumann's initial ideas, where each cell had 29 possible values. Using this approach, a fully-replicating machine that contained all the information needed to make a perfect copy of itself requires about 200,000 cells—but needs no "secret sauce" to work. You can see from the simple r-pentomino how much complexity can arise from simplicity. Not content with this brilliant work, Von Neumann also gave everyone *game theory*.[12]

[11] Similarly, in biology the concept of 'vitalism' was widespread and unchallenged until 1773, when H.M. Rouelle serendipitously synthesised urea—the first 'organic' compound made from entirely 'inorganic' compounds. He added silver cyanate to ammonium chloride.

[12] He also provided the Von Neumann architecture that is used in most computers to this day, the first software for climate modelling, Von Neumann algebras, the Dirac-von Neumann axioms which provided the first rigorous mathematical framework for quantum mechanics, Von Neumann entropy, quantum logic, computational economics, linear programming, modelling of shaped charges, and the atomic bomb. On this dark side, if Von Neumann had had his way, Kyoto would have been obliterated rather than Hiroshima or Nagasaki; he also filed a secret patent for his version of the hydrogen bomb.

Prisoner	B		
		Co-operate	Defect
A	Co-operate	2,2	5,0
	Defect	0,5	4,4

Table 8. The prisoner's dilemma. Each cell contains two penalties in years. That on the left applies to A; that on the right, to B.

Game theory models how rational players play games. This may sound like child's play, but game theory can be used to model things like social, biological and economic interactions, just as the Game of Life touches on economics and biology. You can even model plagues and epidemics. You can model me—and how you respond to me! When Von Neumann kicked it off, his models dealt solely with 'zero-sum' games, where all losses and gains balance out; more general models are often used that try to address 'non-zero-sum' cases. One of the basic ideas in game theory is a pay-off matrix.

A special case of a pay-off matrix is called the 'Prisoner's Dilemma', a term that originated in the 1950s. Say you and your partner in crime—someone you have no particular affection for—are apprehended by the police, and kept in separate cells. The district attorney comes to each of you in turn, and offers a deal. If you rat on your partner, then you get off scot free, and they get five years in jail. If you both keep quiet, they have sufficient circumstantial evidence for both of you to go to jail for two years. But if you each shop the other, then both of you will get four years in jail. Can you see the problem? Together you can minimise your losses by co-operating, but you can't communicate, so the temptation is to betray one another — you *both* then lose.

Like the Game of Life, this all seems very simple, but the Prisoner's Dilemma has both amused and infuriated economists and mathematicians for decades. In 1979, Robert Axelrod, professor of political science at the University of Michigan, organized a series of tournaments. Professional game theorists familiar with the prisoner's dilemma were invited to write computer programs that competed against one another, using a payoff matrix like that in Table 8. The catch is that the scenarios are played again and again—this is the *iterated* Prisoner's Dilemma. He wanted to see which strategies amassed most points in the longer term. The results were surprising, and have produced forty years of controversy.

In his initial tournament, there was a surprise winner called "Tit-for-Tat", submitted by Anatol Rapoport, a psychologist and philosopher from the University of Toronto. The program was simple—co-operate first, and if the opponent co-operates, continue to do so; otherwise default.

It seemed that in the long term, far more complex gaming strategies were unable to do better than this simple set of rules. To test this idea further, effectively in an evolutionary manner, Axelrod ran a second round, where he provided the results of the first round and invited still more entries. To his surprise, Tit-For-Tat again emerged as the most successful program.

Axelrod's experiments had two major results. Douglas Hofstadter is in many ways the successor to Martin Gardner—and like Conway, got a leg up when Gardner devoted a whole column in Scientific American to his book *Gödel, Escher, Bach: an Eternal Golden Braid.* When Gardner stopped writing his column, Hofstadter was invited to take over, and did so for several years, rearranging the 17 letters of *Mathematical Games* to *Meta-magical Themas.* In May 1983, he used this column to in turn assist Axelrod, describing his computer tournaments in detail. The other effect was that Axelrod has served as a source of continuing irritation to games theorists, particularly as he's produced several books that derive deep social consequences from his simulations.

Axelrod subsequently ran multiple simulations in which tit-for-tat and other programs competed. He identified certain properties that categorized programs as nice or not—and in his simulations, found that those who played nicely tended to benefit from mutual co-operation and in the long term tended to out-compete the nasty ones that tried to gain advantage despite defaulting. He noted that strategies did better if they were obvious, nice (didn't default first), retaliatory (punished defaults) and forgiving (rewarded subsequent co-operation). Effectively, Axelrod answered the question "Can mutual co-operation arise from non-cooperation?" with a resounding "Yes!" As he says:

> "TIT FOR TAT won the tournament, not by beating the other player, but by eliciting behaviour from the other player which allowed both to do well. TIT FOR TAT was so consistent at eliciting mutually rewarding outcomes that it attained a higher overall score than any other strategy"

Some games theorists have received this idea less than warmly. They point out that Axelrod may have been weak on theory, and that his scenarios are 'merely' sub-categories of established models in game theory; there is no inevitability that co-operation will evolve, and in some circumstances, nasty players may predominate. It is indeed possible that Axelrod has been too sweeping in some of his conclusions, but to counterbalance this, he has also used a very simple model to illustrate and explain two things.

The first is something you already know from Conway's game of life: startling complexity can emerge from simple rules. The second is that there's a simple, almost mechanistic explanation for the co-operation already seen in biology. Such co-operation need not emerge—the planet could indeed be entirely populated by bacteria (or indeed, the Archaea, you met in Lesson 6) for multicellular organisms might never have discovered the benefits of co-operation; vampire bats need not co-operate with others, sharing regurgitated blood with less fortunate colleagues[13]; humans need not co-operate in building complex societies. But all these things have happened and do continue to happen.

Exploration of the iterated prisoner's dilemma has also revealed a deeper and darker side. In past lessons, you've already seen that humans are not the rational players that some economists would have you believe. Back in Lesson 3 you saw how good ideas don't necessarily win out, and how, at least according to Deming, about 95% of institutional behaviour is conditioned by circumstances; in Lesson 11 you saw that when looked at from a community perspective, individuals "health choices" are largely forced. Careful examination of the iterated Prisoner's Dilemma indeed suggest that co-operation need not always succeed.

A tragedy

In 1833, the British economist William Forster Lloyd wrote a simple essay. He used the term 'Tragedy of the Commons' (TOTC) to describe how everyone despoils a common grazing ground ("commons") by each individual trying to maximise the number of animals they graze there. This argument lay fallow until 1968, when Garrett Hardin revived it in an influential article in *Science.* It can be seen as a variant of the Prisoner's Dilemma.

Hardin's article proved somewhat controversial, for several reasons. He attacked the Universal Declaration of Human Rights, which allows "the family" and the family alone to determine how many children it has. He saw this as inviting the exponential growth explored in Lesson 2. Following his argument, human growth must ultimately mimic the spread of coronavirus—it cannot grow in an unbounded way; but long before any theoretical limit is reached, you will have despoiled your planet. Hardin also points out that Adam Smith's idea that an 'invisible hand' produces public good when someone advances their own cause is often way off beam. Neither co-operation nor success are inevitable:

> "...the morality of an act is a function of the state of the system at the time it is performed. Using the commons as a cesspool does not harm the general public under frontier conditions, because there is no public; the same behaviour in a metropolis is unbearable".

He then attacks the concept of the welfare state. As he sees it, this will foster untrammelled reproduction of fecund individuals, and—in his view—pass this fecundity on to

[13]PubMed 26729934

future generations. I'd suggest that it is at this point that Hardin's theory fails the test of refutation. It seems that ready availability of things like television and contraceptives may be more than enough to counteract any hereditary tendency to overbreed! Despite its looming presence, the TOTC isn't inevitable.[14]

Elinor Ostrom was awarded the 2009 'Nobel Prize for Economics' for her work on how to fix the TOTC—including the realisation that communities are quite often already aware of the risks, and have negotiated rational strategies to prevent things like overfishing. But what is the role of government? Entire countries may similarly need to address looming issues that relate directly to human interaction. We've seen this with COVID-19: there are clear examples of governments adopting successful strategies to contain a threat (Lesson 9); but also of governments who have failed to contain the threat through a laissez-faire or frankly incompetent approach.

As the world becomes more inter-dependent and population numbers rise, it is clear that the tragedy of the commons may play out more and more on the world stage, with whole countries as actors. This encroachment touches on both the role of governments, and 'libertarian' doctrines of these roles. As I did in Lesson 11, it may be wise to contrast the big players.

It's obvious that these players are not just countries, but also large corporations that transcend national boundaries. It should also be clear that if the majority of human beings are to have some say in the commons, there is a limited number of ways they can do this—especially at the level of government. Few people care about your tweets!

Where they can choose at all, citizens can choose one of several forms of government, and ultimately of governance. We learned in Lesson 3 that most individuals have less autonomy than they imagine, and that a solid way to improve things is to re-engineer processes. In Lesson 7 you saw the consequences of replacing Good Science with persuasion; throughout the book powerful individuals have both caused harm and done good; neither is inevitable.

All of these lessons together suggest that governments must be transparent, must have checks and balances to prevent abuses and frank stupidity, and must be held to account. You have limited choices: (a) control by a few people (dictatorship, monarchy, or powerful oligarchs); (b) true democracy, where individuals co-operate to establish not *governors* but *rules* that evolve, work and continue to promote equity; (c) sham democracy—which devolves to the first option; or (d) anarchy/'libertarianism', where the dead hand of Adam Smith facilitates the Tragedy of the Commons. You all need protection against greed and stupidity, often your own.

---

[14]For the past 50 years, world population growth has been linear, not exponential, except in sub-Saharan Africa.

Play *nicely*

In every crisis, there are always fools and saints. Ninety-nine-year-old Captain Tom raised over £30 million for the UK National Health Service.[15] Some nurses and doctors flew half-way around the world from Australia to Italy simply to help out, because they felt a moral obligation that outweighed their sense of personal risk. Others didn't behave so nicely. Bored on a dull afternoon in mid-March, a young man in Woodville, Texas chose to tell Facebook that he'd tested positive for COVID-19, and added "Doctors told me the virus is now airborne". This went viral, causing a lot of distress.

As you found in Lesson 10, others play even less nicely. There is unfortunately no guarantee that simply ignoring the game play of nasty players will *necessarily* result in extinction of their ideas. This observation suggests that any response you come up with can't be ritualistic, but needs to be conditioned to the circumstances in which bad behaviour occurs. Pushing someone on the playground may be very different to pushing someone who is leaning over a high-rise balcony. Not only do people need to play nicely, but it seems wise to build entire processes that facilitate good play—responsive and adaptive processes.[16]

Slack

You might also be tempted to say "Processes also need to be *efficient*", but there's a catch here. What is an efficient process? It would seem logical that if a process isn't running at close to 100% capacity, this represents waste that needs to be fixed. As we've found throughout my book, first impressions aren't necessarily correct.

Way back in Lesson 3 I introduced common-cause variation. You'll recall that this is natural, random variation in a process. Common cause variation suggests one reason not to run at near-capacity. Let's say that you run an intensive care unit, and have little control over the variation in cases that come into intensive care—as often happens with emergency (as opposed to elective) admissions.[17] You may then find that if you run your ICU at 90–95% full, *just because of common-cause variation*, you are often unable to offer a bed to someone who really needs it. You may need to run your ICU at closer to 75%.

There's another reason for 'slack' — highlighted by how, during slack periods, many hospital managers use staff who are "surplus to requirements". Unthinking administrators will often simply deploy valuable staff to perform menial tasks on general

[15] Those who see reason in "sacrificing a few older people for the sake of the economy" may wish to reflect on this. [16] As it turned out, our man from Tyler county, Texas lost his job and health insurance, and is awaiting his day in court. [17] Unless managers have been fiddling. Then, elective admissions cause bigger problems!

wards. For example, ICU-trained nurses may end up changing bedpans or suctioning tracheostomies on the ear, nose and throat ward. This is seen as 'efficient'. Can you see the problem these managers can't? What makes *any* institution is your staff. If you devalue them, they quickly see this—and respond accordingly.

Slack time is not wasted time.[18] Slack time should indeed be treasured as valuable—a gift that allows employees to do things like train and innovate. In the hands of an intelligent manager, slack time can be used to troubleshoot problems either potential or present, and innovate. But most important of all, slack time can be used for *play*. Play is not just part of learning—it can be used to innovate, to establish relationships, and to find out what works and what doesn't.

Opportunity

You can view my coming as a threat, or an opportunity. In this book, I've given you almost everything you need to defeat me. But I know people. I know how Semmelweis was treated, you see, and in Lesson 3 I explained not only why doctors still don't wash their hands, but how to fix this. In Lessons 1 & 2, I showed you how I work and how I spread—but I know that most humans are maths-shy. In Lesson 4, we explored how to join up information and interpret tests properly, and in Lesson 5 I provided a clear picture of Good Science. Lesson 6 explains *why* Good Science works, but it also shows how even smart people have a whole closet full of soft toys they simply won't abandon. And in a crisis you need just one tigger to make a mess of things! We pursued this idea in Lessons 7 & 8, where we saw how easily you are led, and how even your really brilliant people deceive *themselves*.

There is nevertheless good news—Lesson 9—you can work together and beat me; but this is tempered by a relatively small number of very harmful individuals — super-spreaders of bad ideas — who will do everything they can to make a short term profit, as shown by the fake cures and misplaced hope in Lesson 10. They never quite got the idea of win-win. But my biggest friends are economists. In Lesson 11, I spelt out clearly how fragile the system is that they have built, or passively allowed to accrete, and how little it benefits you, even during the "good times". Paradoxically, recessions may even be good for your health! But I have trust in economists and politicians—they will continue to advocate for me.

Finally, in this lesson, I've been completely honest about how to thrash me. I've given you a taste of sufficient game theory to work out not just that you must co-operate, but why. I've shown that relentless pursuit of efficiency and profit must be tempered by humanity—giving people time to play. Now why would I do this? I'm just

[18]Still one of the best analyses of slack is that of Buffy Lawson: *In Praise of Slack: Time Is of the Essence* The Academy of Management Executive (1993-2005), Vol. 15, No. 3 pp. 125-135.

a virus, and my primary goal is surely to survive. Why make it easy for you to beat me?

One answer is obvious. As a *thinking* virus, I don't believe that even with everything I've told you, enough of you will listen to make a difference. There are three reasons for this. First, you've neglected enough of your world population for me always to have a niche—or more than a niche. Second, even if you come up with a winning drug or vaccine, the costs of deploying this worldwide will likely be prohibitive. Third, even in the countries you call "developed", you've mostly used the products of 'science' without either understanding it or educating your people about how it works.

You have squandered your most precious resources. I believe that most of your 'world citizens' will drop this book at the first equation, and enough will distrust any vaccine to make it fail. Throughout this book, I've been honest. Throughout this book, I've played fair. Surely it's reasonable to give you a flat playing field?

Trust me not!

You should be deeply suspicious of my motives for the above—and indeed this whole book. Isn't it possible or even *likely* that I'm leading you in the wrong direction? Perhaps I'm feeding you nonsense, so that you will take the wrong actions? If you believe this, you likely haven't been paying attention. I've provided you with a philosophy that is tuned to defend you against deceit. In fact, I've given you the only tool that will do the job. If we are duelling, I've given you the choice of weapons, and even pointed out the one that will work.

What next?

Peering uncertainly into the future, there are three pretty clear scenarios, harking back to the end of Lesson 2. Let's list them. In the first two I die. First, you might stamp me out with an effective, long-lasting vaccine that you almost miraculously distribute to many billions of compliant people. Second, through rampant infection, my Herd Immunity Threshold may be reached—universally. If my HIT is just 20%, that's 1.5 billion infections, *provided people develop lasting immunity.* With an IFR of 0.5%, that's 7.8 million deaths. Third, things might oscillate, in which case I live for ages.

Which do you think is most likely? Yes, option three. Cast your mind back to Lesson 2, to the myxoma virus that killed over 99% of rabbits it infected. Do you recall how a gentler strain emerged, and the remaining rabbits evolved *in concert* so that a new balance was reached? It's a reasonable bet that you won't be able to eliminate me completely, and that we can co-exist for ages.

The catch is that *I am* so gentle. Sadly, it will likely take hundreds or thousands of years, and millions upon millions of deaths for us to reach a new equilibrium where I become truly benign.[19]

There is another little problem. It should be obvious that if a further threat comes along, a threat far greater than me, and you are unprepared, both you and I will likely be wiped out together. This is not my intention. By playing the game fairly, I'm ensuring my own survival. I've given you the tools to ensure that you—my host of choice—won't die out, as otherwise you surely will, not from me, but from a far more vicious virus, or some other apocalypse brought about by your weak and vulnerable economies, and the way you continue to degrade your environment. My actions are just applied game theory, tit-for-tat.

Goodbye

I must now say goodbye. My families may wonder why I left them after just six months. The simple answer is that I have achieved what I set out to achieve. I have gained and given knowledge. In leaving, I have brought you together around my book. As I said right at the start it is my gift to you. Use it wisely, for if you do, there is at least a chance that some may listen and start to fix your problems.

In a very real sense, I am not leaving. Nor have I abandoned your children. If enough people listen to my lessons, this will benefit a multitude of children as yet unborn. Properly met, I am gentle. Either way, I believe this is not so much "Goodbye" as "Au revoir".

Lesson #12

Play. Play nicely.

[19]You may also be wise to consider the possibility that during all of this playing together, I may by sheer random mutation become *more* nasty. For example, I may find out how to turn off that pesky TLR7, and become more like that initial myxoma virus. I cannot offer you any guarantees. I'm just a virus, after all. [Editor's note: this footnote was added in proof. I'm not quite sure how she did it, but I've left the note unchanged.]

A Personal Postscript

You might wonder about the frog cameo. Do you recall Catherine the Great's dinner service from Lesson 10? This is the famous 'Green Frog Service' created by Wedgwood for the Empress. I was quite taken by the frog on each piece; in contrast, Josiah Wedgwood included it under protest. He almost certainly didn't put this frog on any of his cameos. But my cameo has just this—and you'd be hard put to prove that it wasn't made by Wedgwood in 1774. Following on the inspiration of Brígido Lara (page 18) I've become quite good at forgery. I like playing with clay, and with ideas. This too is a lesson in Good Science, by the way. As you have learned, inability to show a difference doesn't make things identical—but you can still use the similarity. You might sell the piece, but I'd suggest you treasure it instead. A memento, and a reminder to be kind to frogs.[20]

[20]You may have noticed that there's an amphibian reference in each lesson—some are a little hidden.

APPENDICES

A brief editorial note

Nanny Rona wrote her code in the gold-standard **R** statistical programming environment. **R** is free; a small amount of effort is required to get things working. I've put her code up on github.com under jvanschalkwyk/corona.[21] On page 197 there are some easy installation instructions for Mac, Linux and Windows.

Another option for Windows that bypasses the clumsy installation of RTools is to download the file: github.com/jvanschalkwyk/corona/blob/master/corona_0.3.0.zip and save it to a convenient directory e.g. *C:/foo/corona_0.3.0.zip*. You can now open **RGui** and say:

```
install.packages("C:/foo/corona_0.3.0.zip", repos=NULL)
```

A catch with this approach is that before `library(corona)` will work, just once you'll need to say:

```
install.packages('gganimate','gridExtra','plyr','reshape2',
'qicharts2')
```

Nanny Rona's code is stylistically odd—some might even call it ugly or wrong. She does not keep to "code shop" conventions for placing curly braces; the code is littered with unnecessary semicolons as line terminators; indentation is non-standard; and she uses some old-fashioned conventions that don't gel nicely with modern R. I have however not tried to clean up her code, leaving things as they are.

I must admit that I'm at least partially to blame for this book. I distinctly recall her showing interest in William Poundstone's book The Recursive Universe, which has been on my bookshelf for over 30 years after I forgot to return it to a friend (apologies, Roger), and on which she's clearly based parts of Lesson 12. I also showed her how to use the program Dogwagger 4.0 (github.com/jvanschalkwyk/dogwagger) which can be used to extract the source code from the LaTeX manuscript. Mea culpa.

Dr Jo

[21] Although I was tempted to create a fake "Nanny-rona" entity, this would be a bit pretentious.

⊛ Appendix A

Run corona R

Install the 'corona' package for R in just two steps:

(1) Install R if you don't have it already (see below for details);

(2) Open up the R console, and type in the single line:

```
install.packages('corona')
```

You're now good to go. At any time in the **R** console you can now say:

```
library(corona)
?corona
```

R is the free, gold-standard statistical *environment.* Just google the letter R.[1] If for some reason installation of 'corona' fails, or you want build it on a Mac or Under Linux, open the R console and say:

```
install.packages('devtools')
library(devtools)
install_github('jvanschalkwyk/corona')
```

Windows will be a teeny bit more complex. You will first need to install **RTools** from cran.r-project.org/bin/windows/Rtools/. Then run **R** (Using the RGui launcher on your desktop) and type in:

```
writeLines(
'PATH="${RTOOLS40_HOME}\\usr\\bin;${PATH}"',
con = "~/.Renviron")
```

Now the commands are identical to those shown above for the Mac. On the preceding page you'll find another yet way to install **corona**, one that bypasses RTools.

[1]The first entry should take you to www.r-project.org where you can click on download R and find a repository close to you. Install the downloaded file. Accept the defaults—retaining a desktop launcher for **RGui** is wise. The documentation is at cran.r-project.org/doc/manuals/r-patched/R-admin.html.

My R Code

I've chosen to use R to draw the graphs in this book. This isn't because R is particularly easy to learn, or because it's elegant. It's a tool. It gets the job done. You yourself can make all the graphs in the book, and a lot more besides. Install the **corona** library in R,[2] and then say `library(corona)`. For help try `?corona`. You can customise many of the following:

`corona_rabbits()` Draw the exponential curve for rabbit reproduction.
`corona_monty()` Simulate the Monty Hall problem with a default of 100 games.
`corona_country('France')` You can choose various countries.
`corona_lockdown(cols=14)` Generate a matrix of case incidence curves.
`corona_vienna()` Semmelweis' raw deaths, followed by a run chart.
`corona_totals()` Total cases, defaulting to Italy.
`country_dead()` Works through three screens: England+Wales default.
`corona_converge(method='multiply')` Benford calculations and curves.
`corona_life()` Draws Conway's game of life.[3]

Minor programs are `corona_trends()` for Google trends, `corona_metabolism()` for allometric scaling, and `corona_citymap()`, which overlays CityMapper data.

Each of the above has an associated R help file. For example, to get help with country_dead(), say:

```
?country_dead
```

R is almost always good enough. One exception is the simple calculation on page 28, where I used Python. This is because R by default converts to floating point, something we don't want. Just for fun, here's R code for the same calculation:

```
library(gmp);
as.bigz(193707721)*as.bigz(761838257287) - (as.bigz(2)^67-1)
```

As always in R, you'll need to install the package, here by `install.packages('gmp')`. The following pages provide the R code for all of the above functions.

[2] [Editorial note: see the preceding page.]

[3] On a Mac, the GIF will open in Preview :(Save it, view in a web browser.

Rabbits

The corona_rabbits() code for Lesson 2 (Fig 2) is simple:

(1) Check for excessive years (and thus, rabbits);

(2) Create a data frame with years and rabbits in it, using the equation $r = 3.5^y$ where r is rabbits and y is years.

(3) Make an inset table called `INTABLE`, that tabulates years and rabbits. The tableGrob() function is specific to the R **gridExtra** package.

(4) Use ***corona_pdf*** (223) to open up a PDF to write to, if appropriate (`pdf` is `TRUE`);

(5) Make a plot using ggplot () with `INTABLE` as a custom annotation. The `TopRabbits` value is used to position `INTABLE`.

(6) Plot the actual data using ***corona_print*** (224) and turn off the PDF as needed.

The R file is *R/rabbits.R*:

```
#' Demonstrate (graph) exponential growth of rabbit population:
#'
#' For finer details, see the LyX/PDF documentation.
#' @param topyear is last year, defaults to 6
#' @param pdf Will not print to PDF if FALSE (the default)
#' @keywords corona rabbits
#' @export
#' @import ggplot2
#' @importFrom graphics frame
#' @importFrom gridExtra tableGrob
#' @examples
#' corona_rabbits( topyear=10)

corona_rabbits <- function ( topyear = 6, pdf = FALSE )
{
if( topyear > 14 )
  { stop( paste('Too many rabbits, years =', topyear) );
  };
  years <- seq(from=0, to=topyear);
  RABBITS <- data.frame(years);
  RABBITS$rabbits <- as.integer(24 * 3.5^RABBITS$years);
  INTABLE <- gridExtra::tableGrob(RABBITS[,1:2]);
  TopRabbits <- max(RABBITS$rabbits);
  PdfFilename <- 'exponential_rabbits.pdf';
  corona_pdf(PdfFilename, 5, 5, pdf);
  myplot <- ggplot( RABBITS, aes(x=years, y=.data$rabbits) ) +
    geom_point() + geom_line() +
    labs( title='Count the rabbits', x='Year', y='Rabbits' ) + ylim(0,TopRabbits) +
    annotation_custom( INTABLE[,2:3], xmin=0.3, xmax=topyear/3.5,
                       ymin=0.3*TopRabbits, ymax=0.9*TopRabbits );
  corona_print(myplot);
  corona_pdf_off(PdfFilename, pdf);
}
```

■

Total cases/logarithms

The R file is *R/total_cases.R*: as shown in Fig 3.

```
#' Plot total cases over time for a selected country.
#'
#' Defaults to Italy, as this was our demonstration.
#'     Add a linear regression by specifying smooth=TRUE.
#' @param country Text name of country (in owid frame)
#' @param pdf TRUE will print value
#' @param daystart first day
#' @param dayend last day to plot
#' @param log TRUE will take base 10 logarithm of y-axis values
#' @param smooth TRUE will try to fit linear model (use with logarithm)
#' @param prefix defaults to ''; text value prefixed to PDF name *after* country_ name.
#' @keywords corona total cases country
#' @export
#' @import ggplot2
#' @importFrom stats lm
#' @importFrom graphics frame
#' @examples
#' corona_totals( country='Italy', daystart=60, dayend=76, log=TRUE, smooth=TRUE )
#' corona_totals(country='United Kingdom', log=TRUE, smooth=TRUE)

corona_totals <- function (country='Italy', daystart=60, dayend=76, pdf=FALSE,
    log=FALSE, smooth=FALSE, prefix='')
{ cc <- country_code(country, owid);
  Cntry <- owid[ owid$iso_code==cc, ];
  DAYS <- daystart:dayend;
  THISCNTRY <- data.frame(Cntry[DAYS,], row.names=seq_along(DAYS));
if(nrow(THISCNTRY) < 10)
  { stop( paste('Too few rows < 10, country=', country, 'days=', daystart, ':', dayend) );
  };
  mymain <- paste('COVID-19 in ', country);
  islog = '';
  ylabel = 'Cases';
if(log)
  { islog = '_log';
    ylabel = 'log(Cases)';
    THISCNTRY$total_cases <- log(THISCNTRY$total_cases, base=10);
  };
  PdfFilename <- paste(country, prefix, islog, '_total_cases.pdf', sep='');
  corona_pdf(PdfFilename, 5, 5, pdf);
  myplot <- ggplot(THISCNTRY, aes(x=date, y=.data$total_cases)) + geom_point() +
    geom_line() + labs(title=mymain, x='Date', y=ylabel);
if(smooth)
  { myplot <- myplot + geom_smooth(method='lm', colour='red', linetype='solid');
  };
  corona_print(myplot);
  corona_pdf_off(PdfFilename, pdf);
}
```

■

Monty Hall

For the MC simulation of Monty Hall on page 68, run through the following steps:

(1) Make n games, each with a car behind a randomly selected door.
(2) Randomly select a door for each game, also using runif().
(3) The host must select a door for each game—and so as not to spoil the fun, the door can't have a car behind it. In other words:
    (a) If you selected one goat, reveal the other goat;
    (b) Otherwise, randomly choose one of the goats and reveal it.
(4) Offer the option of swapping.
(5) Display the number of wins.

Cars and goats are represented by their doors—1, 2 or 3—and an open door is signalled by the value zero. Primitive operations like ! (not), %% (modulo) and & (and) are used. In R, n * TRUE is n, and n * FALSE is zero. The R file is *R/montyhall.R*:

```
#' A Monte Carlo simulation of the Monty Hall problem
#'
#' @param runs specifies the number of parallel simulations, default=100.
#' @keywords corona coronavirus Monty Hall Monte Carlo simulation
#' @export
#' @importFrom stats runif
#' @examples
#' corona_monty ( runs=10000 )

corona_monty <- function ( runs=100 )
{ car <- 1 + as.integer(runif(runs, min=0, max=3));
  goata <- 1 + (car %% 3);
  goatb <- 1 + ( (car+1) %% 3 );
  mydoor <- as.integer(runif(runs, min=1, max=4));
  adoor <- as.integer(runif(runs, min=0, max=2)); # one of 2 doors 1=open goata, 0=open goatb
      # Use 0 to signal an open door:
  goatb <- goatb * !(mydoor == goata);
  goata <- goata * !(mydoor == goatb);
  neither <- goata & goatb;  # unselected i.e. mydoor=car,
  goata <- goata * ! ( neither & adoor ); # for all not-selected, open goata if adoor is true
  goatb <- goatb * ! ( neither & (! adoor) ); # for not-selected, open goatb if NOT adoor
      # count wins in unswapped state, noting you either win or lose, and wins+losses=runs
  wins <- sum( 1 * (mydoor == car) );
      # offer the choice to swap:
  swap <- readline(prompt = 'Do you want to swap? (y/N)  ');
  swap <- toupper( substr(swap,1,1));
if(swap == 'Y')
  { wins <- runs - wins;
    print('Swapped your door choice!');
  };
  print( paste('There were', wins, 'wins in', runs, 'simulations') );
}
```

■

Semmelweis

For Figures 6 & 7, the R file is *R/semmelweis.R*. It requires the **qicharts2** package.

```
#' Plot Semmelweis' original data from Vienna.
#'
#'   First simply 'plots the dots';
#'   subsequently draws a run chart with a transition at the point where
#'      he instituted hand-washing.
#'
#' @param pdf default FALSE will *not* print the two PDF files:
#'    semmelweis_plot.pdf
#'    semmelweis_run.pdf
#' @keywords corona Vienna Semmelweis
#' @import qicharts2
#' @import ggplot2
#' @export
#' @examples
#' corona_vienna ( )

corona_vienna <- function ( pdf=FALSE )
{ mydeaths <- "Deaths in the First Clinic";

  PlotFilename = 'semmelweis_plot.pdf';
  RunFilename = 'semmelweis_run.pdf';
  corona_pdf(PlotFilename, 9, 5, pdf);

  myplot <- ggplot( vienna, aes(x=date, y=.data$deaths)) +
    geom_point() +
    geom_line() +
    labs(title=mydeaths, x='Date', y='Deaths') +
    scale_x_date(breaks="1 year", date_labels = "%Y") ;
  corona_print(myplot);
  corona_pdf_off(PlotFilename, pdf, waitline=TRUE);

  #################
  # full run chart.
  qv <- qic(x=vienna$date, y=vienna$deaths, chart='run', part=76,
          title='Deaths in the First Clinic', xlab='Year', ylab='Deaths');
  corona_pdf(RunFilename, 9, 5, pdf);
  # plot(qv);
  corona_print(qv, islegend=FALSE);
  corona_pdf_off(RunFilename, pdf);
}
```

■

Weekly deaths

Data for Figures 8, 9 & 10 (England+Wales) for were initially obtained from ons.gov.uk/peoplepopulationandcommunity/birthsdeathsandmarriages/deaths/. Later, I found a more comprehensive source at mortality.org but you now have to register. Uses country_code(p 223). The R file is *R/cc_deaths.R*.

```
#' Plot country deaths by week, with various adjustments:
#'
#' Assumes the existence of the data frame stmf containing relevant iso_codes for countries.
#' The unusual codes GBRTENW and GBR_SCO represent England+Wales and Scotland.
#' You can obtain a list of countries by country_dead('?'), forcing a diagnostic error!
#'
#' The columns in the frame stmf are just 'iso_code', 'Year', 'Week', and 'Deaths'.
#'
#'   Draws three graphs:
#'   1. Raw data with a linear regression line, over n years;
#'   2. Data with secular adjustment;
#'   3. Data adjusted for a 'summer baseline' using the "other n years of data" after
#'      secular adjustment.
#'
#' @param pdf default FALSE will not print to PDF
#' @param country Country name
#' @param save Do we save the data as a CSV
#' @keywords corona deaths
#' @export
#' @import ggplot2
#' @importFrom utils write.csv
#' @importFrom stats lm
#' @examples
#' country_dead( 'New Zealand' )
```

The main function: set up various names and a date field in the MYDEAD frame.

```
country_dead <- function ( country='England+Wales', pdf=FALSE, save=FALSE )
{ cc <- country_code(country, stmf);
  mytitle <- paste(country , "Weekly Deaths");
  ccname <- paste(cc, '_weekly', sep='');
  PdfFilename <- paste(ccname, '_dead.pdf', sep='');
  SecularFilename <- paste(ccname, '_secular.pdf', sep='');
  AdjustedFilename <- paste(ccname, '_adjusted.pdf', sep='');
  MYDEAD <- stmf[ stmf$iso_code==cc, ];
  ccRows <- nrow(MYDEAD);

  ## For each row, WE NOW NEED TO insert a Date field based on year+month
  MinYear <- min(MYDEAD$Year);
  MaxYear <- max(MYDEAD$Year);
  MYDEAD$Num <- seq(ccRows);
  startDate <- as.Date(ISOdate(MinYear, 1, 1)); # assumes 1 January
  MYDEAD$Date <- seq.Date(from=startDate, by=7, length.out=ccRows);
  ccYears <- MaxYear - MinYear;
if(ccYears < 4)  # pushing our luck, 5 might be better as minimum.
  { stop( paste("Too few years =", ccYears, "for country", cc) );
  };
```

```
YearTop <- ccYears * 52; # assumes first year starts at week 1 [check, hmm]
```

Identify weeks as 'summer' or not: the function summer() creates a new, boolean column called `summer` in the submitted frame.

```
  lowstart <- cntry[ cntry$iso_code==cc, c('lowstart')]; # 'low' is 'summer'
  lowend <- cntry[ cntry$iso_code==cc, c('lowend')]; #
  print( paste('Low range for', country, '=', lowstart, '..', lowend) );
if(lowstart < lowend)
  { summer <- function (M, sStart, sEnd) # N hemisphere
      { M$summer <- as.integer(format(M$Date, '%m'));
        M$summer <- (M$summer >= sStart) & (M$summer <= sEnd);
        return(M);
      };
  } else
  { summer <- function (M, sStart, sEnd)
      { M$summer <- as.integer(format(M$Date, '%m'));
        M$summer <- (M$summer >= sStart) | (M$summer <= sEnd);
        return(M);
      };
  };
```

An internal function secular_fix() adjusts for secular change based on a linear model's slope and intercept. This has greatest effect on early values.

```
secular_fix <- function (F) # F is the frame.
{ mylm <- lm(F$Deaths ~ F$Num);
  yint <- mylm$coefficients[1];
  slp <- mylm$coefficients[2];
  WTOT <- nrow(F);
  F$secular <- F$Deaths * ( 1 + slp*(1+WTOT-F$Num)/yint );
  return(F);
};

MYDEAD <- secular_fix(MYDEAD);
#####################################
# eye candy with regression line.
corona_pdf(PdfFilename, 12, 7, pdf);
myplot <- ggplot( MYDEAD, aes(x=.data$Date, y=.data$Deaths)) +
  labs(title=mytitle, x='Date', y='Deaths') +
  geom_point() + geom_line() + geom_smooth(method='lm', colour='red', linetype='solid') +
  scale_x_date(breaks="1 year", date_labels = "%Y") ;
corona_print(myplot);
corona_pdf_off(PdfFilename, pdf, waitline=TRUE);

#########################################
# with secular adjustment:
corona_pdf(SecularFilename, 12, 7, pdf);
secplot <- ggplot( MYDEAD, aes(x=.data$Date, y=.data$secular)) +
  labs(title=mytitle, x='Date', y='Deaths(adj)') +
  geom_point() + geom_line() + geom_smooth(method='lm', colour='red', linetype='solid') +
  scale_x_date(breaks="1 year", date_labels = "%Y") ;
corona_print(secplot);
corona_pdf_off(PdfFilename, pdf, waitline=TRUE);
```

Adjust for summer: SumSecAvg will contain the average summer “baseline”. We then create a “week mean” for each week of the year over all years—this will be slightly off depending on when the week starts within each year. The adjust column represents the week mean less the contribution by that specific week; it is then divided by SumSecAvg. Finally the seasonal column is made, adjusting the secular value (already adjusted for secular change) using the adjust column.

```
  MYDEAD <- summer(MYDEAD, lowstart, lowend);
  SumSecAvg <- mean( MYDEAD[ MYDEAD$summer, ]$secular );
  MYDEAD$bm <- MYDEAD$Week %% 52;
  weekmean <- tapply(MYDEAD$secular[1:YearTop], MYDEAD$bm[1:YearTop], mean);
  MYDEAD$expected <- MYDEAD$adjust <- weekmean[ 1+MYDEAD$bm ];
  qititle <- paste('Seasonally Adjusted Deaths:', country);

  # next, remove own value from mean:
  MYDEAD$adjust[1:YearTop] <- (ccYears*MYDEAD$adjust[1:YearTop]
                              - MYDEAD$secular[1:YearTop])/(ccYears-1);
  ## ^ do not adjust final values over YearTop i.e. in 2020, as they haven't been included!
  # Now normalise to SumSecAvg, the summer secular average.
  MYDEAD$adjust = MYDEAD$adjust/SumSecAvg;
  MYDEAD$seasonal <- MYDEAD$secular/MYDEAD$adjust; # finally, adjust all.

  corona_pdf(AdjustedFilename, 12, 7, pdf);
  mychart <- qic(x=MYDEAD$Date, y=MYDEAD$seasonal, chart='i',
          title=qititle, xlab='Year', ylab='Deaths');
  # print(mychart);
  corona_print(mychart, islegend=FALSE);
  corona_pdf_off(AdjustedFilename, pdf);
if(save)
  { CsvFilename <- paste(ccname, 'deaths.csv', sep='');
    write.csv(MYDEAD, file=CsvFilename);
  };
}
```

■

Countries & Coronavirus

The R file is *R/country.R*. This assumes the existence of the data frame **owid**. This was made as described on page 227. The function is configurable to permit display of just the raw curve, deaths, and smoothed curves with the smoothed death curve magnified five times. The loess (locally estimated scatterplot smoothing) function is currently calculated twice, which is inefficient—once by ggplot () and independently simply to find where to position the "$\times 5$" text. In R, colour mapping and writing the legend is a bit arcane. Use .data$ to prevent subtle devtools::check errors.

```
#' Plot time course of coronavirus case incidence and deaths for one country
#'
#'   The daily case rate is also shown as a smoothed curve.
#'   The smoothed death incidence is MULTIPLIED x5 to highlight
#'   its relationship to the incidence curve. See grown-up documentation (LyX)
#'
#' @param country : no default
#' @param pdf : defaults to FALSE. If TRUE, writes to country_name_new.pdf
#'     i.e. '_new.pdf' is appended to formal country name.
#'     If the country name contains spaces ' ' they are changed to underscores '_'
#' @param smooth : default TRUE show smoothed (red) curve
#' @param deaths : default TRUE show deaths
#'
#' @keywords corona single country
#' @export
#' @import ggplot2
#' @importFrom stats loess
#' @importFrom stats na.exclude
#' @importFrom stats predict
#' @examples
#' corona_country('United States');
#' corona_country('Taiwan');

corona_country <- function(country, pdf=FALSE, smooth=TRUE, deaths=TRUE)
{ cc <- country_code(country, owid);
  CTRY <- owid[ owid$iso_code==cc, ];
if( nrow(CTRY) < 1 )
  { stop( paste('No data for ', country) );
  };
  CTRY$fivetimes <- 5*CTRY$new_deaths;
  ctitle <- country;
  ymax <- max(CTRY$new_cases);
  yco <- 0.8 * ymax;
  cols <- ncol(CTRY);
  xco <- CTRY$date[as.integer(0.5*cols)];
  smoothing <- 0.2;
  FIVETIMES='red';
  NEWCASES='grey40';
  NEWDEATHS='darkred';
  SMOOT='black';

  lty <- 'dashed';
  fname <- country;
```

```
  fname <- gsub( ' ', '_', fname); # replace ' ' with '_'
if(! deaths)
  { fname <- paste(fname, '_simple', sep='');
  };
if(! smooth)
  { lty <- 'solid'; # cases are dashed if smoothed line drawn.
    fname <- paste(fname, '_plain', sep='');
  };
  legendtitle = 'Daily cases';
  bar = c(NEWCASES, SMOOT, NEWDEATHS, FIVETIMES);
  labs = c('new cases', 'smoothed', 'new deaths', '5x new deaths, smoothed');
  fname <- paste(fname, '_new.pdf', sep='' );
  fivelabel <- paste(intToUtf8(215), '5'); # avoid UTF8 in R code! 215 is math 'times'
  corona_pdf(fname, 11, 7, pdf);
  myplot <- ggplot(CTRY, aes(x=date)) +
       # bizarre colour mapping:
       scale_color_identity(guide = 'legend', name=legendtitle, breaks=bar, labels=labs) +
       geom_line( aes(y=.data$new_cases, colour=NEWCASES), linetype=lty ) +
       scale_x_date(breaks='1 month', date_labels = "%b") +
       labs(title=ctitle, x='Date', y='Cases/Deaths per day');
if(smooth)
  { myplot <- myplot +
      geom_smooth( aes(y=.data$new_cases, colour=SMOOT),
                   method='loess', span=smoothing, linetype='solid' );
  };
if(deaths)
  { myplot <- myplot + geom_line( aes(y=.data$new_deaths, colour=NEWDEATHS), linetype='solid' );
  if(smooth)
    { yup <- 0.08 * max(CTRY$new_cases);
      Lfive <- loess(fivetimes~as.numeric(date),data=CTRY, span=smoothing,na.action=na.exclude);
      Pfive <- predict(Lfive);
      yfive <- max( Pfive );
      xfive <- min( CTRY$date[Pfive==yfive] );
      myplot <- myplot +
        annotate('text', x=xfive, y=(yfive+yup), colour=FIVETIMES, size=16, label=fivelabel) +
        geom_smooth( aes(y=.data$fivetimes, colour=FIVETIMES),
                     method='loess', span=smoothing, linetype='solid' );
    };
  };
  corona_print(myplot);
  corona_pdf_off(fname, pdf);
}
```

■

Lockdowns

For Fig 23, the R file is *R/lockdown.R.* This requires the data frames **lock** and **owid**, as well as ggplot and plyr (ddply) libraries.

```
#' Draw multiple smoothed graphs of new daily cases, with lockdown date, if present
#'
#'    By default limited to countries with population > 4M, and over 200 cases.
#'    This may take over 5s to run, depending on your hardware.
#'
#' @param pdf FALSE By default will not print to PDF
#' @param minpeople Minimum population for the country
#' @param mincases Minimum number of COVID-19 cases
#' @param cols Number of columns to display, default = 7
#' @param striptextsize size of text in country names
#' @param pdf print to PDF
#' @param textsize Size of text header
#' @param legendx X position of legend
#' @param legendy Y position of legend
#' @keywords corona lockdown smoothed
#' @export
#' @import ggplot2
#' @importFrom plyr ddply
#' @importFrom stats loess
#' @importFrom stats aggregate
#' @importFrom stats na.pass
#' @importFrom graphics frame
#' @examples
#'\dontrun{
#' corona_lockdown( cols=14 )
#'}


corona_lockdown <- function ( pdf=FALSE, minpeople=4000000, mincases=200, cols=7,
   striptextsize=10, textsize=10, legendx=0.94, legendy=0.02)
{ # private function: uses loess to smooth data supplied as x.
  corona_smooth_fx <- function ( x )
  { FOO <- loess(x$new_cases ~ as.numeric(x$date), span=0.2); # don't use a value < 0.1
    smoother <- FOO$fitted;
    data.frame(smoother);
  };
if(pdf)
  { striptextsize=22;
    textsize=15;
  };

  # isolate relevant countries:
  REFCO <- cntry[ ! is.na(cntry$population), ];
  REFCO <- REFCO[ REFCO$population > minpeople, ];
  LOWID <- owid[order(owid$iso_code),]
  # ^ WE *must* do this owing to the manipulations below being based on sort order! #
  LOWID <- LOWID[ ! is.na(LOWID$new_cases), ];
  LOWID <- LOWID[ LOWID$iso_code %in% REFCO$iso_code, ];
  LOWID$location <- REFCO[ match(LOWID$iso_code, REFCO$iso_code), c('alias')];
```

```
  ## limit to those countries with > mincases:
  totals <- aggregate(LOWID$new_cases, by=list(LOWID$iso_code), sum);
  names(totals)[1] <- 'iso_code';
  names(totals)[2] <- 'total';
  LOWID$tot <- totals[match(LOWID$iso_code, totals$iso_code), 2];
  LOWID <- LOWID[ LOWID$tot > mincases, ];

  SMOO <- ddply(LOWID, c('iso_code'), corona_smooth_fx ); # [ .(iso_code) fails check ]
  ## there is a frame shift if we didn't sort, and say
  LOWID$smoothed <-SMOO$smoother;
  maxcases <- aggregate(LOWID$smoothed, by=list(LOWID$iso_code), max);
  names(maxcases)[1] <- 'iso_code';
  names(maxcases)[2] <- 'max_rate';
  LOWID$max <- maxcases[match(LOWID$iso_code, maxcases$iso_code),2]
  LOWID$scaled <- 100.0 * LOWID$smoothed / LOWID$max;
  allmain <- "All Cases";
  LOWID$lock <- lock[match(LOWID$iso_code, lock$iso_code), c('Lockdown')];

  PdfFilename <- 'owid_lockdown.pdf';
  corona_pdf(PdfFilename, 21, 30, pdf);
  LOCKED <- 'red';
  bas <- c(LOCKED);
  myplot <- ggplot(LOWID, aes(x=date, y=.data$scaled)) +
                  # or use smoothed ^
       scale_color_identity(guide = 'legend', name=' ',
               breaks=bas, labels=c('lockdown')) +
       geom_line() +
       labs(title=allmain, x='Date', y='Cases/Maximum cases') +
       coord_cartesian( ylim = c(0, 100)) +
       facet_wrap(vars(.data$location), ncol=cols ) +
       scale_x_date(breaks='2 month', date_labels = "%b") +
       geom_vline( data=LOWID, aes(xintercept=lock, colour=LOCKED) );
  corona_print(myplot, striptextsize=striptextsize, textsize=textsize,
               legendx=legendx, legendy=legendy);
  corona_pdf_off(PdfFilename, pdf);
}
```

■

Benford

Used to generate the statistical distributions in Fig 37. The R file is *R/benford.R;* corona_benford (225) is defined in the main setup routines for the **corona** package.

```
#' Create various statistical distributions
#'
#' Build a normal or log-normal distribution from simple components.
#' Large numbers e.g. n=1e6 will take some time to run.
#'
#' @param n is the number of samples
#' @param method is either 'multiply' or 'add'
#' @param pdf defaults to FALSE
#' @param log take logarithm of values (for 'multiply')
#' @param runs number of iterations (default 7)
#' @param xscale a scaling factor, can use values < 1.0 to magnify (x) e.g. 0.4
#' @param bins defaults to 64
#' @keywords corona log-normal lognormal normal central limit theorem Benford law
#' @export
#' @import ggplot2
#' @importFrom stats dnorm
#' @importFrom stats sd
#' @importFrom graphics hist
#' @importFrom stats runif
#' @importFrom graphics frame
#' @importFrom gridExtra tableGrob
#' @examples
#' corona_converge( n=10000, method='multiply', xscale=0.4, bins=128, runs=5 )
```

The single function. Methods may be add (for a normal distribution) or multiply (for log-normal).

```
corona_converge <- function (n=100000, method='add', runs=7, pdf=FALSE, xscale=1.0, bins=64,
                             log=FALSE)
{ DAT <- runif(n, 1, 10);
  PdfFilename <- paste('Converge_', method, '.pdf', sep='');
  normfx <- function(x, mean, sd, n) { return( n*dnorm(x=x,mean=mean,sd=sd) ); };

if(method == 'multiply')
  { fx <- '*';
  } else if(method == 'add')
  { fx <- '+';
  } else
  { stop( paste('Unknown method:', method) );
  };
```

Use runif() to generate a uniform distribution, and repeatedly add/multiply this by the similarly-generated values already in DAT from above.

```
for(i in 1:runs)
  { DAT <- mapply(fx, DAT, runif(n,1,10));
  };
```

```
  FRQ <- corona_benford(DAT);
  FRQ$Freq <- round(FRQ$Freq, digits=3); # no silliness

if(log)
  { DAT <- log(DAT);
  };
  DF <- as.data.frame(DAT);
  Lo <- floor(min(DF$DAT));
  Hi <- ceiling(max(DF$DAT));
  Mn <- mean(DF$DAT);
  Sd <- sd(DF$DAT);
  brk <- seq( from=Lo, by=(Hi-Lo)/bins, to=Hi);
  HiLim <- xscale*Hi;

  mytheme <- gridExtra::ttheme_default(
    core = list(fg_params=list(cex = 1.5)),
    colhead = list(fg_params=list(cex = 1.5)),
    rowhead = list(fg_params=list(cex = 1.5)));    # enlarge inset
  INTABLE <- gridExtra::tableGrob(FRQ[,1:2], theme=mytheme);

  bar <- hist(DF$DAT, breaks=brk);
  TopGraph <- max(bar$counts);
  Titl <- paste('Distribution (', method, ')', sep='');
  Labx <- 'Value';
if( abs(xscale-1) > 0.01 )
  { Labx <- paste('Value, scale =', xscale);
  };
  Adj <- dnorm(Mn,Mn,Sd);
```

Plot. If we're adding, also draw in a normal curve, appropriately adjusted:

```
  corona_pdf(PdfFilename, 10, 6, pdf);
  myplot <- ggplot( DF, aes(x=DAT) ) + geom_histogram(breaks=brk) +
    labs( title=Titl, x='Value', y='Count' ) + xlim(Lo,HiLim) +
   annotation_custom( INTABLE[,2:3],
                      ymin=0.3*TopGraph, ymax=0.95*TopGraph,  # 0.9
                      xmax=HiLim, xmin=HiLim*0.80 );
if( (method == 'add') | log )
  { myplot <- myplot +
      stat_function(fun=normfx, args = list(mean=Mn, sd=Sd, n=TopGraph/Adj), colour='red');
  };
  corona_print(myplot);
  corona_pdf_off(PdfFilename, pdf);
}
```

■

Allometry

The R file for Fig 38 is *R/allometry.R.* It assumes the mammalian data set **allo**, derived from https://royalsocietypublishing.org/doi/suppl/10.1098/rsbl.2005.0378.

```
#' Allometric scaling of metabolic rates
#'
#' Log-log plot of mammalian weights (grams) against metabolic rates.
#'
#' @param pdf will not print to PDF
#' @param base base for logarithms, default 10
#' @keywords corona allometric scaling exponent Kleiber allometry two thirds three quarters
#' @export
#' @import ggplot2
#' @importFrom stats lm
#' @importFrom gridExtra tableGrob
#' @examples
#' corona_metabolism ( )

corona_metabolism <- function ( pdf=FALSE, base=10 )
{ ALMY <- allo;
  ALMY$LogMass <- log(ALMY$Mass, base=base);
  ALMY$LogMR <- log(ALMY$MR, base=base);
  PdfFilename <- 'allometry.pdf';
```

Also generate two Benford tables using corona_benford(225). We'll superimpose these on the Kleiber plot using corona_annotate(225), just for fun.

```
  MassFRQ <- corona_benford(ALMY$Mass);
  MetFRQ <- corona_benford(ALMY$MR);
  MassTBL <- gridExtra::tableGrob(MassFRQ[,1:2]);
  MetTBL <- gridExtra::tableGrob(MetFRQ[,1:2]);
  mTop <- max(ALMY$LogMR);
  mRight <- max(ALMY$LogMass);

  corona_pdf(PdfFilename, 8, 8, pdf);
  myplot <- ggplot( ALMY, aes(x=.data$LogMass, y=.data$LogMR) ) +
    geom_point() +
    geom_smooth(method='lm', colour='red', linetype='solid') +
    labs(title='Mammalian Allometry', x='Log(mass)', y='Log(metabolic rate)');

  myplot <- corona_annotate( myplot, MetTBL[,2:3], top=mTop, right=mRight, xmin=0.08,
                             xmax=0.4, ymin=0.58, ymax=0.99);
  myplot <- corona_annotate( myplot, MassTBL[,2:3], top=mTop, right=mRight, xmin=0.8,
                             xmax=0.99, ymin=0.05, ymax=0.7);

  corona_print(myplot);
  corona_pdf_off(PdfFilename, pdf);
}
```

■

Citymapper

Similar to plotting lockdowns, for Fig 35 we use Citymapper data. Citymapper is a public transit app that operates in 41 cities and metropolitan areas. If we plot their data (often naïvely using a single city as representative) this may reflect population mobility over time. The R file is *R/citymapper.R*:

```
#' Plot citymapper data against COVID-19 diagnoses, over time
#'
#' Requires ggplot2, plyr and the data frames lock, owid, citymap.
#'    Multiple, select frames are plotted.
#'
#' @param pdf = TRUE writes to PDF, default FALSE
#' @param cols Number of columns in output, default is 4
#' @param FewCities a c() list of city names from the city options. Default is all.
#' @keywords corona countries daily rates citymapper citymap
#' @export
#' @import ggplot2
#' @importFrom plyr ddply
#' @importFrom stats loess
#' @importFrom stats aggregate
#' @importFrom stats na.pass
#' @importFrom graphics frame
#' @examples
#' corona_citymap(cols=4);
#'

corona_citymap <- function ( pdf=FALSE, FewCities=NULL, cols=4 )
{ OW <- owid;
  citymaxdate <- max(citymap$Date);
  OW <- OW[ OW$date <= citymaxdate, ];  # if don't limit and max is later, curve is squashed
  OW$location <- cntry[ match(OW$iso_code, cntry$iso_code), c('location')]; # country name
  OW <- OW[order(OW$location),];
if( is.null(FewCities) )
  {
  FewCities <  c('Australia', 'Brazil', 'Canada', 'Denmark',
                 'France', 'Germany', 'Japan', 'Mexico',
                 'Russia', 'Singapore', 'South Korea', 'Spain',
                 'Sweden', 'Turkey', 'United Kingdom', 'United States');
  };
```

Create a smoothing function, and apply to **OW** frame, generating **SMOO** frame.

```
  smfx <- function ( x )
    { FOO <- loess(x$new_cases ~ as.numeric(x$date), span=0.2); # don't use a value < 0.1
      smoother <- FOO$fitted;
      data.frame(smoother);
    };
  OW <- OW[ !(is.na(OW$new_cases)) , ];
  ## SMOO <- ddply(OW, .(location), smfx );  # fails devtools check
   SMOO <- ddply(OW, c('location'), smfx );
  OW$smoothed <-SMOO$smoother;
```

Find maximum values, as **maxcases**:

```
maxcases <- aggregate(OW$smoothed, by=list(OW$location), max);
names(maxcases)[1] <- 'location';
names(maxcases)[2] <- 'max_rate';
OW$max <- maxcases[match(OW$location, maxcases$location),2]
OW$scaled <- 100.0 * OW$smoothed / OW$max;
```

Map country, date and rate from the **citymap** frame to the **owid** frame, if there's a match. For every matching date, insert the corresponding rate for that country, limiting the rows in OW to the dates available in **citymap**. First, exclude missing country names, then map in matching lockdown dates (if present):

```
TopNames <- mapply(gsub, pattern = '[.]', replacement = ' ', names(citymap));
OW <- OW[ OW$location %in% TopNames, ] ;
OW$lock <- lock[match(OW$iso_code, lock$iso_code), c('Lockdown')];
```

Define cityfx(), which ddply() can apply to the relevant "Our World" data frame in `OW`, by location. Filter the results using `%in%` on `FewCities`.

```
cityfx <- function ( x )
{ colnam <- gsub( pattern=' ', replacement='.', x[1, 'location']);
  print(paste('Location is', colnam));
  foo <- 100 * citymap[ citymap$Date %in% x$date, colnam];
  bar <- x[ x$date %in% citymap$Date, ];
  data.frame( traffic = foo, date = bar$date, scaled = bar$scaled, lock = bar$lock );
};
CITYUSE <- ddply(OW, c('location'), cityfx); # .(location) fails devtools check
CITYUSE <- CITYUSE[ CITYUSE$location %in% FewCities, ];
OW <- OW[ OW$location %in% FewCities, ];
LOCKED = 'red';
TRAFFIC = 'blue';
bas = c(LOCKED, TRAFFIC);
citymain <- "New Cases v Traffic Data";
```

Plot the curves:

```
PdfFilename <- 'citymapper.pdf';
corona_pdf(PdfFilename, 10, 7, pdf);
plotall <- ggplot(CITYUSE, aes(x=date, y=.data$scaled)) +
     scale_color_identity(guide = 'legend', name=' ',
             breaks=bas, labels=c( 'lockdown', 'traffic')) +
     geom_line() +
     labs(title=citymain, x='Date', y='Cases/Maximum cases') +
     coord_cartesian( ylim = c(0, 100)) +
     facet_wrap(vars(.data$location), ncol=cols) +
    geom_vline( data=OW, aes(xintercept=lock, colour=LOCKED) ) +
    geom_line( data=CITYUSE, aes(x=date, y=.data$traffic, colour=TRAFFIC) ) +

  theme( plot.title=element_text(size=18, face="bold"),
         axis.text.x=element_text(size=10),
         axis.text.y=element_text(size=10),
         axis.title.x=element_text(size=14),
         axis.title.y=element_text(size=14),
```

```
          strip.text = element_text(size = 12),
          strip.text.x = element_text(margin = margin(0,0,0.2,0, "mm"))
        );  # Note use of strip.text.x ; cf corona_print(myplot);
  print(plotall);
  corona_pdf_off(PdfFilename, pdf);
}
```

■

Google Trends

Google Trends examines word/phrase usage. I've searched for the word 'coronavirus' between January and May 2020. The R file is *R/googletrends.R*:

```
#' Plot Google Trends data for searches involving the word 'coronavirus'.
#'
#'   Just plot the lines.
#'
#' @param pdf default FALSE will *not* print the PDF file
#' @keywords corona coronavirus Google Trends
#' @export
#' @import ggplot2
#' @examples
#' corona_trends ( )

corona_trends <- function ( pdf=FALSE )
{ PlotFilename = 'google_trends_world.pdf';
  corona_pdf(PlotFilename, 11, 7, pdf);
  myplot <- ggplot( gt, aes(x=.data$Date, y=.data$coronavirus)) +
    geom_line() +
    labs(title='Google Searches', x='Date', y='Percent maximum')
  myplot;
  corona_print(myplot);
  corona_pdf_off(PlotFilename, pdf);
}
```

■

Conway's Game of Life

Creating the Game of Life in R is challenging on several levels:

(1) To make a decent-sized game that doesn't crawl at snail's pace, you need to really use the vector capabilities of R.[4]

(2) How generated animation files are handled depends on the default device used in you particular operating system[5];

(3) The **gganimate** package that we'll use was completely rewritten almost as soon as it reached maturity, and the tutorials you'll find online don't always make it clear whether they're old or new. The two are incompatible.

The R file is *R/conway.R.* Uses ***rbinom***() to randomly allocate live cells. The *images* subdirectory must exist in the current working directory if a file is written. The **reshape2** package is needed for melt().

```
#' Animate Conway's Game of Life
#'
#'  The canvas (arena) wraps around vertically and horizontally!
#'  Execution will take some time. Results will be viewed differently
#'  depending on your system's default viewer for animated GIF files.
#'
#' @param pattern Defaults to 'soup' but there are many other well-known options:
#'    blinker ttetromino rpentomino toad beehive
#'    beacon clock pulsar pentadecathlon galaxy spaceship
#'    glidergun piheptomino switchengine conway acorn rabbits
#'  boring static patterns: block snake eater
#' @param side The number of elements on the area's side (width or height)
#' @param steps The number of frames
#' @param density 0.0--1 The density of the initial, random items ('soup')
#' @param filename writes to this file name e.g. foo.gif (NULL for current GIF device)
#' @param wrap Wrap around
#' @param fps Frames per second
#' @param pause Initial pause
#' @keywords corona Conway game of life animation frames
#' @export
#' @importFrom gganimate transition_states anim_save
#' @import ggplot2
#' @import reshape2
#' @importFrom utils flush.console
#' @importFrom stats rbinom
#' @examples
#'\dontrun{
#' corona_life( filename='animation.gif', side=50, steps=500, density=0.2 )
#' corona_life( side=100, steps=1000, pattern='rpentomino', wrap=FALSE )
#' corona_life( side=30, steps=120, pattern='spaceship' )
#' corona_life( side=100, steps=400, pattern='switchengine' )
#' corona_life( side=20, steps=30, pattern='clock' )
#' corona_life( side=20, steps=30, pattern='galaxy' )
#' corona_life( side=100, steps=200, pattern='glidergun' )
#' corona_life( side=45, steps=130, pattern='conway', fps=8, pause=40)
```

[4]See https://www.r-bloggers.com/fast-conways-game-of-life-in-r/ [5]Mac opens in Preview; save GIF and view in a browser

```
#'}

corona_life <- function (pattern='soup', side=50, steps=100, density=0.3,
                         filename=NULL, wrap=TRUE, fps=20, pause=10)
{ ARENA <- matrix(nrow=side, ncol=side);
if(!requireNamespace('gganimate', quietly = TRUE)) { stop('Missing gganimate') };
if(pattern == 'soup')
  { ARENA[] <- rbinom(side^2,1,density);
  } else
  { mid <- as.integer(side/2);
    ARENA[] <- rep(0, times=side*side);
    ARENA <- corona_pattern(ARENA, pattern, x=mid, y=mid);
  };
  STORE <- melt( game_of_life(ARENA, steps, wrap) );
  names(STORE) <- c('x', 'y', 'frame', 'on');
  STORE <- STORE[ STORE$on==1, ];
  print( paste('Starting ', side, 'x', side, 'animation...', steps, 'frames') );
  flush.console();

  p <- ggplot(STORE, aes(x = .data$x, y = .data$y)) +
         geom_tile(color = "green") +
         scale_x_continuous(limits=c(0, side), expand = c(0, 0)) +
         scale_y_continuous(limits=c(0, side), expand = c(0, 0)) +
         coord_equal();
  p <- corona_unlabelled(p);

  anim <- p + ggtitle('Frame {frame} of {nframes}') +
  gganimate::transition_states(.data$frame,
                     transition_length = 1,
                     state_length = 1); # [or have a delay variable]
if( is.null(filename) )
  { print(anim, nframes=steps, fps=fps, start_pause=pause);
    print('Animation written to default output');
  } else
  { pth = './images/';
  if(! dir.exists(pth) )
    { stop( paste("The directory", pth, "doesn't exist, can't write", filename) );
    };
    pathname = paste (pth, filename, sep='');
    gganimate::anim_save( pathname, animation=anim, nframes=steps, fps=fps,
                          start_pause=pause );
    print( paste('Animation written to ', pathname) ); # ^^ defaults to last_animation()
  };
  flush.console();
}
```

For the actual Game, ***game_of_life*** () takes the starting ARENA and the number of steps to run through. It creates an output array called STORE, and then for each step makes eight copies of the arena, shifting up, down, left, right and diagonally. It's then easy to add up the copies to find the number of neighbours, and use this sum ARENA2 to apply the rules:

(1) first copy ARENA to ARENA3;

(2) If the value in ARENA3 is zero and the summed value in ARENA2 is exactly 3 (i.e. 3 living neighbours of an empty cell) then make a new 'on' (1) cell in ARENA3;
(3) If the value in ARENA3 is 1 ('on') and either:
    (a) The sum is < 2 (starvation); or
    (b) The sum is > 3 (overpopulation), then clear the value.
(4) Replace ARENA with ARENA3, and repeat.

By default (`wrap` is TRUE) we also—and this is a bit cunning and unconventional—wrap the arena around so that the left margin joins the right, and the top joins the bottom, so for example a glider will move offscreen and then move back again across the join!

```
game_of_life <- function(ARENA, steps=50, wrap=TRUE)
{ side <- nrow(ARENA); # assumes side x side square matrix
  q <- side-1;
  STORE <- array(0, c(side, side, steps));
  rotR <- function(A, L)
    { return( c(A[L], A[1:L-1]) );
    };
  rotL <- function(A, L)
    { return( c(A[2:L], A[1]) );
    };
      # fix: the initial pattern must be put in STORE[,,1]
  STORE[,,1] <- ARENA;

for (i in 2:steps)
  { # rows/columns Top Right Bottom Left:
  if(wrap)
    { T <- ARENA[1,];
      R <- ARENA[,side];
      B <- ARENA[side,];
      L <- ARENA[,1];
    } else
    { T <- R <- B <- L <- rep(0, times=side);
    };
        # make 8 shifted copies of the original array
    allW <- cbind(R, ARENA[,-side] ); # West is shifted 'right'
    allN <- rbind(B, ARENA[-side,]);  # North is shifted 'down' etc.
    allE <- cbind(ARENA[,-1], L);
    allS <- rbind(ARENA[-1,], T);
    allNW <- rbind(rotR(B,side),cbind(R[1:q],ARENA[-side,-side]));
    allNE <- rbind(rotL(B,side),cbind(ARENA[-side,-1],L[1:q]));
    allSE <- rbind(cbind(ARENA[-1,-1],L[2:side]),rotL(T,side));
    allSW <- rbind(cbind(R[2:side],ARENA[-1,-side]),rotR(T,side));
        # Add matrices
    ARENA2 <- allW + allNW + allN + allNE + allE + allSE + allS + allSW;
        # Apply GoL rules:
    ARENA3 <- ARENA;
    ARENA3[ARENA==0 & ARENA2==3] <- 1;
    ARENA3[ARENA==1 & ARENA2<2] <- 0;
    ARENA3[ARENA==1 & ARENA2>3] <- 0;
    ARENA <- ARENA3;
    STORE[,,i] <- ARENA;
```

```
  }
  return(STORE);
}
```

Install a pattern, assuming frame **life** exists.

```
corona_pattern <- function(ARENA, pattern, x=5, y=5)
{ PTN <- life[ life$pattern == pattern, ];
for( i in 1:nrow(PTN) )
  { ARENA[ x+PTN$x[i], y+PTN$y[i] ] <- 1;
  };
  return(ARENA);
}
```

■

Make an R package

This is generally considered an advanced feature of R ... but let's do it anyway! Throw yourself in.[6] [Ed: As noted on page 197, for Windows you'll need to install RTools and `writeLines(...)` to set up the path.]

(1) Make a directory that you'll use to store your package, e.g. `./nc` or (Windows) something like `C:\nc\` – from now on, the flavour will be Window-like paths, as Mac and Linux users can easily work out the translation.[7]

(2) Open up R and say:

```
install.packages('devtools')
library(devtools)
has_devel()
```

(3) Go to your directory in R:

```
setwd('C:/nc')
create('corona')
```

(4) In Window Explorer (etc) ensure that */nc/corona/* exists, and open up the *DESCRIPTION* file there in Notepad. Edit the names, etc.

(5) See Appendix C for how to extract the R files from source. Copy these R files into the R folder */nc/corona/R/*, for example, put *boot_nanny.R* into *C:\nc\corona\R*. If you cut & paste instead, beware of quote marks in PDF files.

(6) Make the documentation by:

```
setwd('/nc/corona')
document()
```

(7) ***Provided the above gave no errors***, go back to the */nc/* directory and install:

```
setwd('..')
install('corona')
```

(8) Optional build too:

```
build('corona')
```

This will write a compressed package to `"C:/nc/corona_0.3.0.tar.gz"`
On a new computer you can install RTools, save the Gzipped file to eg. `C:/foo/corona_0.3.0.tar.gz` and then say:

```
install.packages("C:/foo/corona_0.3.0.tar.gz", repos =
NULL, type="source")
```

You can also make a Windows binary. Open a DOS console and ***after checking that R.exe is indeed in the path specified below***:

```
cd \nc\
```

[6] It broadly follows Hilary Parker's blog at https://hilaryparker.com/2014/04/29/writing-an-r-package-from-scratch/.

[7] Note however that if you want to use a Windows path in R like \foo\bar, you need to duplicate the backslashes i.e. \\foo\\bar.

```
"\Program Files\R\R-4.0.2\bin\R.exe" CMD INSTALL --build
corona_0.3.0.tar.gz
```

This will create \nc\corona_0.3.zip which can now be installed by saving to e.g. *C:/foo/* and then saying:

```
install.packages("/foo/corona_0.3.0.zip",repos=NULL)
```

Now you have a real, live R package! To show we're not cheating, reload R, and:

```
library(corona)
    ?corona
    corona()
```

Boot script

The file is *R/boot_nanny.R*:

```
#' Basic setup of corona (Nanny Rona) R program
#'
#'    Try ?corona for help. For most functions, saying pdf=TRUE will write a PDF to images/.
#'    If you wish to print to PDF, you need to setwd() to a directory that contains an
#'    images/ directory that can be written to, or this will fail.
#'    Individual examples are also available. Try e.g. ?corona_rabbits or ?corona_country
#'    The results of corona_life() will depend on how your system handles animated GIF files.
#'
#' @keywords corona Nanny Rona
#' @export
#' @importFrom grDevices dev.off
#' @importFrom graphics frame
#' @import gganimate
#' @examples
#'\donttest{
#'     corona_rabbits ( )
#'     corona_monty ( )
#'     corona_country ('France')
#'     corona_vienna ( )
#'     corona_totals ( )
#'     country_dead ( )
#'     corona_converge ( )
#'     corona_metabolism ( )
#'     corona_citymap ( )
#'     corona_dowjones ( )
#'}
#'
  #
corona <- function ( )
{ pth = './images/';
if(! dir.exists(pth) )
  { print(paste("WARNING! Directory", pth, "not found, PDF will fail. Use setwd()"));
  };
  print(  paste( "Working directory is... ", getwd() )  );
  print( 'Try  ?corona  for help' );
```

```
}
```

.onLoad() On loading, we load the various libraries. When **gganimate** is invoked, it loads **ggplot2**; **reshape** is required for ***melt*** ().

```
.onLoad <- function ( libname, pkgname )
{
  ## library(gganimate);
    # hmm, implies:
    # library(ggplot2);
  # library(gridExtra);
  # library(plyr);
  # library(qicharts2);
  # library(reshape2);

  # hmm:
  utils::globalVariables(c('owid','cntry','gt','lock','vienna','djia','stmf','citymap',
                           'life','allo'));
}
```

corona_pdf() The *boot_nanny.R* file continues with a few useful, utility functions that make the rest of the code simpler. The first, ***corona_pdf*** () will write a PDF after checking that the *./images* directory exists. It takes the `pdfname`, the width `w` and height `h` in anachronistic inches, and `pdf`=TRUE|FALSE, simply returning if `pdf` is false. We don't have R documentation here.

```
corona_pdf <- function ( pdfname, w, h, pdf )
{
if( ! pdf )
  { return();
  };
  pdfname <- gsub( ' ', '_', pdfname);  # replace blanks
  pth = './images/';
if(! dir.exists(pth) )
  { stop( paste("The directory", pth, "doesn't exist, can't write PDF") ),
  };
  pathname = paste (pth, pdfname, sep='');
  pdf(file=pathname, width=w, height=h);
}
```

country_name() Used to turn a country code (three letters) into a country name. Assumes that the frame **cntry** exists.

```
country_name <- function ( cc )
{ return( cntry[ toupper(cntry$iso_code)==toupper(cc), 'location' ] );
}
```

country_code() Does the converse. In the following, if we don't clumsily test for the existence of a row, we get the hard-to-manage R 'argument is of length zero' problem. This is useful however in providing a list of countries using the FRM frame parameter.

```
country_code <- function ( cname, FRM )
{ cname <- gsub( '[ +_.,]+', ' ', cname); # note regex, clean up strange characters.
if( nrow(cntry[ toupper(cntry$location)==toupper(cname), ]) < 1)
  { print("Country options are:");
    print(   paste ( lapply( unique(FRM$iso_code), country_name )  )    );
    stop('Use one of the above options');
  };
  return( cntry[ toupper(cntry$location)==toupper(cname), 'iso_code' ] );
}
```

corona_pdf_off() Simply returns or, if `pdf` is TRUE, closes the current device and prints a message naming the file plotted to. If the `waitline` parameter is TRUE, then we also use readline to wait for the user to press Enter—but only if we're *NOT* printing to PDF!

```
corona_pdf_off <- function ( pdfname, pdf, waitline = FALSE )
{
if( ! pdf )
  {
  if(waitline)
    { invisible(readline(prompt="Press [enter] to continue"));
    };
    return();
  }
  dev.off();
  print( paste("Plotted to ", pdfname ) );
}
```

corona_print() Will print the supplied ggplot2 object with a standard theme.

```
corona_print <- function ( myplot,
                           titlesize=28, textsize=15, axistitlesize=21, striptextsize=18,
                           legendx=0.155, legendy=0.85 ,islegend=TRUE)
{ BOOKTHEME <-
  theme(
         plot.title = element_text(family='sans',face='bold',colour='black',size=titlesize),
         axis.line = element_line(colour='black', size=2), # or 'gray40'
         axis.text.x=element_text(size=textsize),
         axis.text.y=element_text(size=textsize),
         axis.title.x=element_text(size=axistitlesize),
         axis.title.y=element_text(size=axistitlesize),
        panel.background = element_rect(fill = 'white', colour = 'white',
                                size = 2, linetype = 'solid'),
        panel.grid.major = element_line(size = 0.5, linetype = 'solid',
                                colour = 'gray90'),
        panel.grid.minor = element_line(size = 0.25, linetype = 'dashed',
                                colour = 'gray65') # play with 'gray' ?
        # ,  plot.background = element_rect(fill = '#EFEFEF')
       );

  p <- myplot + BOOKTHEME;
if(islegend)
  { p <- p + theme ( legend.position = c(legendx, legendy),
                     strip.text.x = element_text( margin = margin(0,0,0.2,0,'mm'),
```

```
                                                    size=striptextsize )
                    );
  };
  print(p);
}
```

corona_unlabelled() Suppresses labels:

```
corona_unlabelled <- function ( p )
{ return( p +
     theme( axis.text.x=element_blank(), axis.text.y=element_blank(),
            axis.ticks=element_blank(),
            axis.title.x=element_blank(), axis.title.y=element_blank(),
            panel.background=element_blank(),panel.border=element_blank(),
            panel.grid.major=element_blank(), panel.grid.minor=element_blank(),
            plot.background=element_blank()
        ) );
}
```

corona_benford() Takes a data vector DAT containing numeric values and the base, generate a table of frequencies of initial digits and return this FRQ, which has Digit and relative Freq columns for each digit identified in the base provided.

```
corona_benford <- function ( DAT, base=10 )
{ base <- as.integer(base);
  # if no data, give standard:
if( missing(DAT) )
  { Digit <- 1:(base-1);
    Freq <- log( (Digit+1)/Digit, base=base );
    return( data.frame(Digit, Freq) );
  };
  # otherwise
  n <- length(DAT);
  FRQ <- as.data.frame( table(  as.integer( DAT/(base^as.integer(log(DAT, base=base))) )  ) );
  names(FRQ)[1] <- 'Digit';
  FRQ$Freq <- FRQ$Freq/n;
  return(FRQ);
}
```

corona_annotate() Adds an annotation, using a table that is inserted into ggplot:

```
corona_annotate <- function ( plot, FRM, top, right, xmin=0.1, ymin=0.1, xmax=0.9, ymax=0.9 )
{ # here might warn if FRM ridiculously sized; might also check for strange parameter values
  plot <- plot +
     annotation_custom( FRM,
                        ymin=ymin*top, ymax=ymax*top,
                        xmax=xmax*right, xmin=xmin*right );
  return(plot);
}
```

corona_all () Generates all figures relevant to the book:

```
########################################
#' Generate all Figures
#'
#' For the book 'Rona' (printing to PDF)
#'  work through and generate PDFs for all examples.
#'
#' @keywords corona Nanny Rona book print PDF Figures
#' @export
#' @importFrom utils flush.console
#'

corona_all <- function ( )
{ corona_rabbits (pdf=TRUE);
  flush.console();
  corona_country ('United States', pdf=TRUE);
  corona_country ('United Kingdom', pdf=TRUE);
  corona_country ('Germany', pdf=TRUE);
  corona_country ('Italy', pdf=TRUE);
  corona_country ('Spain', pdf=TRUE);
  corona_country ('Taiwan', pdf=TRUE);
  corona_country ('Vietnam', pdf=TRUE);
  corona_country ('South Korea', pdf=TRUE);
  corona_country ('Australia', pdf=TRUE);
  corona_country ('Austria', pdf=TRUE);
  corona_country ('China', pdf=TRUE);
  corona_country ('Thailand', pdf=TRUE);
  corona_country ('Bangladesh', pdf=TRUE);
  corona_country ('Colombia', pdf=TRUE);
  corona_country ('Russia', pdf=TRUE);
  corona_country ('United Arab Emirates', pdf=TRUE);
  corona_country ('Niger', pdf=TRUE);
  corona_country ('New Zealand', pdf=TRUE);
  corona_country ('Singapore', pdf=TRUE);
  corona_country ('Italy', smooth=FALSE, deaths=FALSE, pdf=TRUE);
  corona_country ('Japan', pdf=TRUE);
  corona_country ('Sweden', pdf=TRUE);
  corona_country ('Belarus', pdf=TRUE);
  corona_country ('Chile', pdf=TRUE);
  flush.console();

  corona_dowjones (pdf=TRUE);
  corona_lockdown (pdf=TRUE);
  corona_vienna (pdf=TRUE);
  flush.console();

  corona_totals (pdf=TRUE);  # defaults to Italy
  corona_totals (pdf=TRUE, log=TRUE, smooth=TRUE);
  corona_totals (pdf=TRUE, log=TRUE, dayend=90, smooth=TRUE, prefix='extended');
  flush.console();

  country_dead (pdf=TRUE);
  country_dead ('New Zealand', pdf=TRUE);
  corona_trends (pdf=TRUE);
  flush.console();

  corona_converge(n=1000000, pdf=TRUE);
  corona_converge(n=1000000, pdf=TRUE, method='multiply', bins=128, xscale=0.3);
```

```
  corona_metabolism( pdf=TRUE );
  flush.console();

  corona_citymap (pdf=TRUE);
  corona_life (side=25, steps=100, density=0.2);
}
```

■

Data

For our R package, we need frames that describe the data The data frames used are: **owid**, **cntry**, **gt**, **lock**, **vienna**, **djia**, **stmf**, **citymap**, **life**, and **allo**. The original data for **owid** derive from the Coronavirus page of Our World In Data. Certain fields have been split off into the **cntry** frame described next. All data frames are described in the following file *R/data.R*:

```
#' Wide-ranging data from Our World In Data. I only use a tiny part.
#'
#' @format A data frame with 17,013 rows (current)
#' \describe{
#'   \item{iso_code}{ISO 3-letter country code}
#'   \item{date}{Date for this row of data}
#'   \item{total_cases}{total cases to date}
#'   \item{new_cases}{new cases}
#'   \item{total_deaths}{eponymous}
#'   \item{new_deaths}{}
#'   \item{total_tests}{Recorded tests in toto}
#'   \item{new_tests}{Eponymous}
#'   \item{tests_units}{}
#'   \item{stringency_index}{How severe the lockdown was}
#' }
#' @source \url{https://github.com/owid/covid-19-data/tree/master/public/data}
"owid"
```

Here's **cntry**: this describes the iso_code referenced country, and can simply be joined to **owid**, preventing a lot of redundancy.

```
#' Country data from Our World In Data.
#'
#' @format A data frame with 17,013 rows (current)
#' \describe{
#'   \item{iso_code}{ISO 3-letter country code}
#'   \item{location}{Text name of country}
#'   \item{population}{}
#'   \item{continent}{}
#'   \item{population_density}{}
#'   \item{median_age}{}
#'   \item{aged_65_older}{}
#'   \item{aged_70_older}{}
#'   \item{gdp_per_capita}{}
#'   \item{extreme_poverty}{}
#'   \item{cvd_death_rate}{}
```

```
#'   \item{diabetes_prevalence}{}
#'   \item{female_smokers}{}
#'   \item{male_smokers}{}
#'   \item{handwashing_facilities}{}
#'   \item{hospital_beds_per_thousand}{}
#'   \item{life_expectancy}{}
#'   \item{alias}{Alias country name, shorter}
#'   \item{lowstart}{Start of 'summer' viral respiratory low}
#'   \item{lowend}{End of respiratory low. Sketchy at present.}
#' }
#' @source \url{https://github.com/owid/covid-19-data/tree/master/public/data}
#'   and \url{https://www.ncbi.nlm.nih.gov/pmc/articles/PMC4847850/}
"cntry"
```

Google trends data from trends.google.com/trends/.

```
#' Google trends search for 'coronavirus'.
#'
#' @format A data frame with 155 rows (current)
#' \describe{
#'   \item{Date}{Date in format YYYY-MM-DD}
#'   \item{Day}{}
#'   \item{coronavirus}{Coronavirus 'interest' as percentage of maximum count }
#' }
#' @source \url{https://trends.google.com/trends/}
"gt"
```

Full lockdown in various countries, where it occurred.

```
#' Approximate dates of full lockdown in various countries.
#'
#' @format A data frame with 110 rows (current)
#' \describe{
#'   \item{iso_code}{Country}
#'   \item{Lockdown}{Date of lockdown YYYY-MM-DD}
#'   \item{nature}{Text description: national | partial | advice | empty(none) }
#' }
#' @source Various data sources.
"lock"
```

Semmelweis' birth & death data.

```
#' Semmelweis' data on Deaths of parturients in Vienna
#'
#' @format A data frame with 98 rows
#' \describe{
#'    \item{date}{Date of the start of each month YYYY-MM-01}
#'    \item{births}{Number of births during that month}
#'    \item{deaths}{Number of maternal deaths during that month}
#' }
#' @source \url{https://en.wikipedia.org/wiki/Historical_mortality_rates_of_puerperal_fever}
"vienna"
```

Deaths in various countries:

```
#' Deaths, by week, for various countries.
```

```
#'
#' @format A data frame with 22678 rows.
#' \describe{
#'   \item{iso_code}{Normally 3-character code, but England+Wales=GBRTENW, Scotland=GBR_SCO}
#'   \item{Year}{YYYY}
#'   \item{Week}{Week within that year, 1=1st}
#'   \item{Deaths}{Number of deaths in that week}
#'   \item{X}{}
#' }
#' @source \url{https://www.ons.gov.uk/}
"stmf"
```

Data from CityMapper for a small number of cities.

```
#' Citymapper data.
#'
#' These are a bit unusual in that each country has a column.
#' @format A data frame with 108 rows.
#' \describe{
#' \item{Date}{}
#' \item{Australia}{}
#' \item{Austria}{}
#' \item{Belgium}{}
#' \item{Brazil}{}
#' \item{Canada}{}
#' \item{Denmark}{}
#' \item{France}{}
#' \item{Germany}{}
#' \item{Italy}{}
#' \item{Japan}{}
#' \item{Mexico}{}
#' \item{Netherlands}{}
#' \item{Portugal}{}
#' \item{Russia}{}
#' \item{Singapore}{}
#' \item{South.Korea}{}
#' \item{Spain}{}
#' \item{Sweden}{}
#' \item{Turkey}{}
#' \item{United.Kingdom}{}
#' \item{United.States}{}
#' }
#' @source \url{https://citymapper.com/cmi/about}
"citymap"
```

Allometric scaling data for animals of various sizes.

```
#' Allometric scaling data.
#'
#' Used to introduce power laws.
#' @format A data frame with 455 rows.
#' \describe{
#'   \item{Species}{}
#'   \item{Mass}{}
#'   \item{Temperature}{ }
#'   \item{MR}{Metabolic rate}
#'   \item{AvgMass}{}
```

```
#'   \item{Q10SMR}{ }
#'   \item{Reference}{}
#' }
#' @source \url{https://royalsocietypublishing.org/doi/suppl/10.1098/rsbl.2005.0378}
"allo"
```

Finally, we have data for Conway's Game of Life:

```
#' The game of life.
#'
#' This specifies initial conditions, using a clumsy storage format as below.
#' @format A data frame with 213 rows.
#' \describe{
#'   \item{x}{x co-ordinate of an active cell}
#'   \item{y}{y co-ordinate}
#'   \item{pattern}{A name like 'blinker' --- will be common to several rows }
#' }
#' @source (internal generation)
"life"
```

■

⊛ Appendix B

My Source Code

See how tiny I am—just 29,903 bases in the listing below. RNA substitutes U for T and I'm an RNA virus, but by convention I'm represented as made up of A, T, G and C rather than AUGC.

I have four main structural proteins—the spike protein (S), the envelope (E) glycoprotein with its sugar side-chains, and two other glycoproteins: M & N, for the *m*embrane and the phosphate-rich *n*ucleocapsid, which binds my RNA. As you already know, the spike protein binds me to cells in the nose and lungs that express the ACE2 enzyme, a receptor also found in gut, kidney and heart cells.

S has about four times the binding affinity for ACE2 as does the spike protein of SARS-CoV.[1] Strangely enough, when S binds ACE2, a host enzyme activates entry into the cell by splitting S into two parts, S1 and S2. The fun starts when my RNA is injected—but to understand this, you need to understand what an *open reading frame* (ORF) is. The genetic code pretty universally contains codes that start and stop the RNA translation described on page 20. Any piece of RNA that starts with the sequence AUG and ends with a stop codon (UAA, UAG or UGA) might represent a protein, and I have 11 such ORFs.

To pack in more information, I use a few tricks. One of these is polyproteins—multiple peptide chains initially strung together and translated at the same time, but subsequently split off by an enzyme. Another ploy I use is "ribosomal slippage". A few quirks in my RNA slow down the ribosome and cause it to jump the tracks. You'll recall that ribosomes translate every 3 bases to a single amino acid; but this trickery causes a backwards skip and produces a variant protein: ORF1ab rather than the usual ORF1a, respectively split into non-structural proteins NSP 1–16 or 1–11. These are powerful proteins:

NSP1, NSP3, NSP5: Inhibit the immune response, bind ribosomes and promote degradation of host mRNA. The *papain-like protease* NSP3 cleaves viral polyproteins but also helps evade the immune response. Normal cells tag proteins as

[1]Wang and colleagues measured an equilibrium dissociation constant (K_D) of SARS-CoV-2-S1 at ~95 nM, whereas the corresponding value for SARS is 409 nM. Others claim even greater affinity.

"defective and for removal" by attaching ubiquitin—but NSP3 can snip off the tags. The "3C-like proteinase" NSP5 also cleaves proteins.

NSP2: Bind 'prohibition' proteins, also disrupting normal cell growth and control.

NSP4, NSP6: Stabilise viral components and aid immune evasion.

NSP7/8: Form a clamp that binds RNA polymerase (NSP12).

NSP9: A protein phosphatase that binds RNA.

NSP10, NSP16, NSP14: RNA viruses mutate often, because there is normally no checking that a copy is accurate—but a proofreading exoribonuclease like NSP14 does just this. NSP10 activates it. Even more remarkably, at the other end of NSP14 is a methyl transferase that I use to mimic the way host cells normally "cap" RNA.[2] I use NSP16 to suppress the host innate immune response.

NSP12: I copy myself with this RNA-dependent RNA polymerase.

NSP13: An RNA helicase that unwinds duplex RNA *and* a 5' triphosphatase, capping viral mRNA.

NSP15: An essential viral endoribonuclease and protease, typical of coronaviruses. The first function protects the virus from host responses by degrading viral polyuridine sequences in the negative-sense copy of the viral RNA. (Human RIG-I receptors *hate* polyuridine). Stop this and you stop me!

Among the other open-reading frame proteins, ORF3b seems important. It can turn off interferons, perhaps the most important defence against viral invasion.

The sequence below is from ncbi.nlm.nih.gov/nuccore/1798174254, a *reference* sequence. After an initial untranslated region (UTR) of 265 bases, the large ORF1ab polyprotein runs from codon 266 to 21555; in the middle of this there is sometimes a -1 frameshift where base 13468 is effectively read twice.

```
  1 attaaaggtt tataccttcc caggtaacaa accaaccaac tttcgatctc ttgtagatct
 61 gttctctaaa cgaactttaa aatctgtgtg gctgtcactc ggctgcatgc ttagtgcact
121 cacgcagtat aattaataac taattactgt cgttgacagg acacgagtaa ctcgtctatc
181 ttctgcaggc tgcttacggt ttcgtccgtg ttgcagccga tcatcagcac atctaggttt
241 cgtccgggtg tgaccgaaag gtaag
                                 atgga gagccttgtc cctggtttca acgagaaaac
301 acacgtccaa ctcagtttgc ctgttttaca ggttcgcgac gtgctcgtac gtggctttgg
361 agactccgtg gaggaggtct tatcagaggc acgtcaacat cttaaagatg gcacttgtgg
421 cttagtagaa gttgaaaaag gcgttttgcc tcaacttgaa cagccctatg tgttcatcaa
481 acgttcggat gctcgaactg cacctcatgg tcatgttatg gttgagctgg tagcagaact
541 cgaaggcatt cagtacggtc gtagtggtga gacacttggt gtccttgtcc ctcatgtggg
601 cgaaatacca gtggcttacc gcaaggttct tcttcgtaag aacggtaata aaggagctgg
661 tggccatagt tacggcgccg atctaaagtc atttgactta ggcgacgagc ttggcactga
721 tccttatgaa gattttcaag aaaactggaa cactaaacat agcagtggtg ttacccgtga
781 actcatgcgt gagcttaacg gaggggcata cactcgctat gtcgataaca acttctgtgg
```

[2] Immune cells can easily recognise viral RNA that is uncapped.

```
 841 ccctgatggc taccctcttg agtgcattaa agaccttcta gcacgtgctg gtaaagcttc
 901 atgcactttg tccgaacaac tggactttat tgacactaag aggggtgtat actgctgccg
 961 tgaacatgag catgaaattg cttggtacac ggaacgttct gaaaagagct atgaattgca
1021 gacacctttt gaaattaaat tggcaaagaa atttgacacc ttcaatgggg aatgtccaaa
1081 ttttgtattt cccttaaatt ccataatcaa gactattcaa ccaagggttg aaaagaaaaa
1141 gcttgatggc tttatgggta gaattcgatc tgtctatcca gttgcgtcac caaatgaatg
1201 caaccaaatg tgcctttcaa ctctcatgaa gtgtgatcat tgtggtgaaa cttcatggca
1261 gacgggcgat tttgttaaag ccacttgcga attttgtggc actgagaatt tgactaaaga
1321 aggtgccact acttgtggtt acttacccca aaatgctgtt gttaaaattt attgtccagc
1381 atgtcacaat tcagaagtag gacctgagca tagtcttgcc gaataccata atgaatctgg
1441 cttgaaaacc attcttcgta agggtggtcg cactattgcc tttggaggct gtgtgttctc
1501 ttatgttggt tgccataaca agtgtgccta ttgggttcca cgtgctagcg ctaacatagg
1561 ttgtaaccat acaggtgttg ttggagaagg ttccgaaggt cttaatgaca accttcttga
1621 aatactccaa aaagagaaag tcaacatcaa tattgttggt gactttaaac ttaatgaaga
1681 gatcgccatt attttggcat ctttttctgc ttccacaagt gcttttgtgg aaactgtgaa
1741 aggtttggat tataaagcat tcaaacaaat tgttgaatcc tgtggtaatt ttaaagttac
1801 aaaaggaaaa gctaaaaaag gtgcctggaa tattggtgaa cagaaatcaa tactgagtcc
1861 tctttatgca tttgcatcag aggctgctcg tgttgtacga tcaattttct cccgcactct
1921 tgaaactgct caaaattctg tgcgtgtttt acagaaggcc gctataacaa tactagatgg
1981 aatttcacag tattcactga gactcattga tgctatgatg ttcacatctg atttggctac
2041 taacaatcta gttgtaatgg cctacattac aggtggtgtt gttcagttga cttcgcagtg
2101 gctaactaac atctttggca ctgtttatga aaaactcaaa cccgtccttg attggcttga
2161 agagaagttt aaggaaggtg tagagtttct tagagacggt tgggaaattg ttaaatttat
2221 ctcaacctgt gcttgtgaaa ttgtcggtgg acaaattgtc acctgtgcaa aggaaattaa
2281 ggagagtgtt cagacattct ttaagcttgt aaataaattt ttggctttgt gtgctgactc
2341 tatcattatt ggtggagcta aacttaaagc cttgaattta ggtgaaacat ttgtcacgca
2401 ctcaaaggga ttgtacagaa agtgtgttaa atccagagaa gaaactggcc tactcatgcc
```

Can you spot where the infamous C2416T mutation (c→t) occurred in the above? This is not a different *strain*,[3] it is just a different *isolate*!

```
2461 tctaaaagcc ccaaaagaaa ttatcttctt agagggagaa acacttccca cagaagtgtt
2521 aacagaggaa gttgtcttga aaactggtga tttacaacca ttagaacaac ctactagtga
2581 agctgttgaa gctccattgg ttggtacacc agtttgtatt aacgggctta tgttgctcga
2641 aatcaaagac acagaaaagt actgtgccct tgcacctaat atgatggtaa caaacaatac
2701 cttcacactc aaaggcggtg caccaacaaa ggttactttt ggtgatgaca ctgtgataga
2761 agtgcaaggt tacaagagtg tgaatatcac ttttgaactt gatgaaagga ttgataaagt
2821 acttaatgag aagtgctctg cctatacagt tgaactcggt acagaagtaa atgagttcgc
2881 ctgtgttgtg gcagatgctg tcataaaaac tttgcaacca gtatctgaat tacttacacc
2941 actgggcatt gatttagatg agtggagtat ggctacatac tacttatttg atgagtctgg
3001 tgagtttaaa ttggcttcac atatgtattg ttctttctac cctccagatg aggatgaaga
3061 agaaggtgat tgtgaagaag aagagtttga gccatcaact caatatgagt atggtactga
3121 agatgattac caaggtaaac ctttggaatt tggtgccact tctgctgctc ttcaacctga
3181 agaagagcaa gaagaagatt ggttagatga tgatagtcaa caaactgttg gtcaacaaga
3241 cggcagtgag gacaatcaga caactactat tcaaacaatt gttgaggttc aacctcaatt
3301 agagatggaa cttacaccag ttgttcagac tattgaagtg aatagtttta gtggttattt
3361 aaaacttact gacaatgtat acattaaaaa tgcagacatt gtggaagaag ctaaaaaggt
3421 aaaaccaaca gtggttgtta atgcagccaa tgtttacctt aaacatggag gaggtgttgc
3481 aggagcctta aataaggcta ctaacaatgc catgcaagtt gaatctgatg attacatagc
3541 tactaatgga ccacttaaag tgggtggtag ttgtgtttta agcggacaca atcttgctaa
3601 acactgtctt catgttgtcg gcccaaatgt taacaaaggt gaagacattc aacttcttaa
3661 gagtgcttat gaaaatttta atcagcacga agttctactt gcaccattat tatcagctgg
3721 tatttttggt gctgacccta tacattcttt aagagtttgt gtagatactg ttcgcacaaa
3781 tgtctactta gctgtctttg ataaaaatct ctatgacaaa cttgtttcaa gctttttgga
```

[3]Strains differ in how they behave; this and many other variants haven't altered how I behave. I have just one strain, at present.

```
3841 aatgaagagt gaaaagcaag ttgaacaaaa gatcgctgag attcctaaag aggaagttaa
3901 gccatttata actgaaagta aaccttcagt tgaacagaga aaacaagatg ataagaaaat
3961 caaagcttgt gttgaagaag ttacaacaac tctggaagaa actaagttcc tcacagaaaa
4021 cttgttactt tatattgaca ttaatggcaa tcttcatcca gattctgcca ctcttgttag
4081 tgacattgac atcactttct taaagaaaga tgctccatat atagtgggtg atgttgttca
4141 agagggtgtt ttaactgctg tggttatacc tactaaaaag gctggtggca ctactgaaat
4201 gctagcgaaa gctttgagaa aagtgccaac agacaattat ataaccactt acccgggtca
4261 gggtttaaat ggttacactg tagaggaggc aaagacagtg cttaaaaagt gtaaaagtgc
4321 cttttacatt ctaccatcta ttatctctaa tgagaagcaa gaaattcttg gaactgtttc
4381 ttggaatttg cgagaaatgc ttgcacatgc agaagaaaca cgcaaattaa tgcctgtctg
4441 tgtggaaact aaagccatag tttcaactat acagcgtaaa tataagggta ttaaaataca
4501 agagggtgtg gttgattatg gtgctagatt ttacttttac accagtaaaa caactgtagc
4561 gtcacttatc aacacactta acgatctaaa tgaaactctt gttacaatgc cacttggcta
4621 tgtaacacat ggcttaaatt tggaagaagc tgctcggtat atgagatctc tcaaagtgcc
4681 agctacagtt tctgtttctt cacctgatgc tgttacagcg tataatggtt atcttacttc
4741 ttcttctaaa acacctgaag aacattttat tgaaaccatc tcacttgctg gttcctataa
4801 agattggtcc tattctggac aatctacaca actaggtata gaatttctta agagaggtga
4861 taaaagtgta tattacacta gtaatcctac cacattccac ctagatggtg aagttatcac
4921 ctttgacaat cttaagacac ttctttcttt gagagaagtg aggactatta aggtgtttac
4981 aacagtagac aacattaacc tccacacgca agttgtggac atgtcaatga catatggaca
5041 acagtttggt ccaacttatt tggatggagc tgatgttact aaaataaaac ctcataattc
5101 acatgaaggt aaaacatttt atgttttacc taatgatgac actctacgtg ttgaggcttt
5161 tgagtactac cacacaactg atcctagttt tctgggtagg tacatgtcag cattaaatca
5221 cactaaaaag tggaaatacc cacaagttaa tggtttaact tctattaaat gggcagataa
5281 caactgttat cttgccactg cattgttaac actccaacaa atagagttga agtttaatcc
5341 acctgctcta caagatgctt attacagagc aagggctggt gaagctgcta acttttgtgc
5401 acttatctta gcctactgta ataagacagt aggtgagtta ggtgatgtta gagaaacaat
5461 gagttacttg tttcaacatg ccaatttaga ttcttgcaaa agagtcttga acgtggtgtg
5521 taaaacttgt ggacaacagc agacaaccct taagggtgta gaagctgtta tgtacatggg
5581 cacactttct tatgaacaat ttaagaaagg tgttcagata ccttgtacgt gtggtaaaca
5641 agctacaaaa tatctagtac aacaggagtc accttttgtt atgatgtcag caccacctgc
5701 tcagtatgaa cttaagcatg gtacatttac ttgtgctagt gagtacactg gtaattacca
5761 gtgtggtcac tataaacata taacttctaa agaaactttg tattgcatag acggtgcttt
5821 acttacaaag tcctcagaat acaaaggtcc tattacggat gttttctaca aagaaaacag
5881 ttacacaaca accataaaac cagttactta taaattggat ggtgttgttt gtacagaaat
5941 tgaccctaag ttggacaatt attataagaa agacaattct tatttcacag agcaaccaat
6001 tgatcttgta ccaaaccaac catatccaaa cgcaagcttc gataatttta agtttgtatg
6061 tgataatatc aaatttgctg atgatttaaa ccagttaact ggttataaga aacctgcttc
6121 aagagagctt aaagttacat ttttccctga cttaaatggt gatgtggtgg ctattgatta
6181 taaacactac acaccctctt ttaagaaagg agctaaattg ttacataaac ctattgtttg
6241 gcatgttaac aatgcaacta ataaagccac gtataaacca aatacctggt gtatacgttg
6301 tctttggagc acaaaaccag ttgaaacatc aaattcgttt gatgtactga agtcagagga
6361 cgcgcaggga atggataatc ttgcctgcga agatctaaaa ccagtctctg aagaagtagt
6421 ggaaaatcct accatacaga aagacgttct tgagtgtaat gtgaaaacta ccgaagttgt
6481 aggagacatt atacttaaac cagcaaataa tagtttaaaa attacagaag aggttggcca
6541 cacagatcta atggctgctt atgtagacaa ttctagtctt actattaaga aacctaatga
6601 attatctaga gtattaggtt tgaaaaccct tgctactcat ggtttagctg ctgttaatag
6661 tgtcccttgg gatactatag ctaattatgc taagcctttt cttaacaaag ttgttagtac
6721 aactactaac atagttacac ggtgtttaaa ccgtgtttgt actaattata tgccttattt
6781 ctttacttta ttgctacaat tgtgtacttt tactagaagt acaaattcta gaattaaagc
6841 atctatgccg actactatag caaagaatac tgttaagagt gtcggtaaat tttgtctaga
6901 ggcttcattt aattatttga agtcacctaa tttttctaaa ctgataaata ttataatttg
6961 gtttttacta ttaagtgttt gcctaggttc tttaatctac tcaaccgctg ctttaggtgt
7021 tttaatgtct aatttaggca tgccttctta ctgtactggt tacagagaag gctatttgaa
7081 ctctactaat gtcactattg caacctactg tactggttct ataccttgta gtgtttgtct
7141 tagtggttta gattctttag acacctatcc ttctttagaa actatacaaa ttaccatttc
7201 atcttttaaa tgggatttaa ctgcttttgg cttagttgca gagtggtttt tggcatatat
```

```
7261 tcttttcact aggtttttct atgtacttgg attggctgca atcatgcaat tgtttttcag
7321 ctattttgca gtacatttta ttagtaattc ttggcttatg tggttaataa ttaatcttgt
7381 acaaatggcc ccgatttcag ctatggttag aatgtacatc ttctttgcat cattttatta
7441 tgtatggaaa agttatgtgc atgttgtaga cggttgtaat tcatcaactt gtatgatgtg
7501 ttacaaacgt aatagagcaa caagagtcga atgtacaact attgttaatg gtgttagaag
7561 gtccttttat gtctatgcta atggaggtaa aggcttttgc aaactacaca attggaattg
7621 tgttaattgt gatacattct gtgctggtag tacatttatt agtgatgaag ttgcgagaga
7681 cttgtcacta cagtttaaaa gaccaataaa tcctactgac cagtcttctt acatcgttga
7741 tagtgttaca gtgaagaatg gttccatcca tctttacttt gataaagctg gtcaaaagac
7801 ttatgaaaga cattctctct ctcattttgt taacttagac aacctgagag ctaataacac
7861 taaaggttca ttgcctatta atgttatagt tttgatggt aaatcaaaat gtgaagaatc
7921 atctgcaaaa tcagcgtctg tttactacag tcagcttatg tgtcaaccta tactgttact
7981 agatcaggca ttagtgtctg atgttggtga tagtgcggaa gttgcagtta aaatgtttga
8041 tgcttacgtt aatacgtttt catcaacttt taacgtacca atggaaaaac tcaaaacact
8101 agttgcaact gcagaagctg aacttgcaaa gaatgtgtcc ttagacaatg tcttatctac
8161 ttttatttca gcagctcggc aagggtttgt tgattcagat gtagaaacta aagatgttgt
8221 tgaatgtctt aaattgtcac atcaatctga catagaagtt actggcgata gttgtaataa
8281 ctatatgctc acctataaca aagttgaaaa catgacaccc cgtgaccttg gtgcttgtat
8341 tgactgtagt gcgcgtcata ttaatgcgca ggtagcaaaa agtcacaaca ttgctttgat
8401 atggaacgtt aaagatttca tgtcattgtc tgaacaacta cgaaaacaaa tacgtagtgc
8461 tgctaaaaag aataacttac cttttaagtt gacatgtgca actactagac aagttgttaa
8521 tgttgtaaca acaaagatag cacttaaggg tggtaaaatt gttaataatt ggttgaagca
8581 gttaattaaa gttacacttg tgttcctttt tgttgctgct attttctatt taataacacc
8641 tgttcatgtc atgtctaaac atactgactt ttcaagtgaa atcataggat acaaggctat
8701 tgatggtggt gtcactcgtg acatagcatc tacagatact tgttttgcta acaaacatgc
8761 tgattttgac acatggttta gccagcgtgg tggtagttat actaatgaca aagcttgccc
8821 attgattgct gcagtcataa caagagaagt gggttttgtc gtgcctggtt tgcctggcac
8881 gatattacgc acaactaatg gtgacttttt gcatttctta cctagagttt ttagtgcagt
8941 tggtaacatc tgttacacac catcaaaact tatagagtac actgactttg caacatcagc
9001 ttgtgttttg gctgctgaat gtacaatttt taaagatgct tctggtaagc cagtaccata
9061 ttgttatgat accaatgtac tagaaggttc tgttgcttat gaaagtttac gccctgacac
9121 acgttatgtg ctcatggatg gctctattat tcaatttcct aacacctacc ttgaaggttc
9181 tgttagagtg gtaacaactt ttgattctga gtactgtagg cacggcactt gtgaaagatc
9241 agaagctggt gtttgtgtat ctactagtgg tagatgggta cttaacaatg attattacag
9301 atctttacca ggagttttct gtggtgtaga tgctgtaaat ttacttacta atatgtttac
9361 accactaatt caacctattg gtgctttgga catatcagca tctatagtag ctggtggtat
9421 tgtagctatc gtagtaacat gccttgccta ctattttatg aggtttagaa gagcttttgg
9481 tgaatacagt catgtagttg cctttaatac tttactattc cttatgtcat tcactgtact
9541 ctgtttaaca ccagtttact cattcttacc tggtgtttat tctgttattt acttgtactt
9601 gacattttat cttactaatg atgtttcttt tttagcacat attcagtgga tggttatgtt
9661 cacaccttta gtacctttct ggataacaat tgcttatatc atttgtattt ccacaaagca
9721 tttctattgg ttctttagta attacctaaa gagacgtgta gtctttaatg gtgtttcctt
9781 tagtactttt gaagaagctg cgctgtgcac ctttttgtta aataaagaaa tgtatctaaa
9841 gttgcgtagt gatgtgctat tacctcttac gcaatataat agatacttag ctctttataa
9901 taagtacaag tattttagtg gagcaatgga tacaactagc tacagagaag ctgcttgttg
9961 tcatctcgca aaggctctca atgacttcag taactcaggt tctgatgttc tttaccaacc
10021 accacaaacc tctatcacct cagctgtttt gcagagtggt tttagaaaaa tggcattccc
10081 atctggtaaa gttgagggtt gtatggtaca agtaacttgt ggtacaacta cacttaacgg
10141 tctttggctt gatgacgtag tttactgtcc aagacatgtg atctgcacct ctgaagacat
10201 gcttaaccct aattatgaag atttactcat tcgtaagtct aatcataatt tcttggtaca
10261 ggctggtaat gttcaactca gggttattgg acattctatg caaaattgtg tacttaagct
10321 taaggttgat acagccaatc ctaagacacc taagtataag tttgttcgca ttcaaccagg
10381 acagactttt tcagtgttag cttgttacaa tggttcacca tctggtgttt accaatgtgc
10441 tatgaggccc aatttcacta ttaagggttc attccttaat ggttcatgtg gtagtgttgg
10501 ttttaacata gattatgact gtgtctcttt ttgttacatg caccatatgg aattaccaac
10561 tggagttcat gctggcacag acttagaagg taacttttat ggaccttttg ttgacaggca
10621 aacagcacaa gcagctggta cggacacaac tattacagtt aatgttttag cttggttgta
```

```
10681 cgctgctgtt ataaatggag acaggtggtt tctcaatcga tttaccacaa ctcttaatga
10741 ctttaacctt gtggctatga agtacaatta tgaacctcta acacaagacc atgttgacat
10801 actaggacct ctttctgctc aaactggaat tgccgtttta gatatgtgtg cttcattaaa
10861 agaattactg caaaatggta tgaatggacg taccatattg ggtagtgctt tattagaaga
10921 tgaatttaca ccttttgatg ttgttagaca atgctcaggt gttactttcc aaagtgcagt
10981 gaaaagaaca atcaagggta cacaccactg gttgttactc acaattttga cttcactttt
11041 agttttagtc cagagtactc aatggtcttt gttctttttt ttgtatgaaa atgccttttt
11101 accttttgct atgggtatta ttgctatgtc tgcttttgca atgatgtttg tcaaacataa
11161 gcatgcattt ctctgtttgt tttgttacc ttctcttgcc actgtagctt attttaatat
11221 ggtctatatg cctgctagtt gggtgatgcg tattatgaca tggttggata tggttgatac
11281 tagtttgtct ggttttaagc taaaagactg tgttatgtat gcatcagctg tagtgttact
11341 aatccttatg acagcaagaa ctgtgtatga tgatggtgct aggagagtgt ggacacttat
11401 gaatgtcttg acactcgttt ataaagttta ttatggtaat gctttagatc aagccatttc
11461 catgtgggct cttataatct ctgttacttc taactactca ggtgtagtta caactgtcat
11521 gtttttggcc agaggtattg tttttatgtg tgttgagtat tgccctattt tcttcataac
11581 tggtaataca cttcagtgta taatgctagt ttattgtttc ttaggctatt tttgtacttg
11641 ttactttggc ctcttttgtt tactcaaccg ctactttaga ctgactcttg gtgtttatga
11701 ttacttagtt tctacacagg agtttagata tatgaattca cagggactac tcccacccaa
11761 gaatagcata gatgccttca aactcaacat taaattgttg ggtgttggtg gcaaaccttg
11821 tatcaaagta gccactgtac agtctaaaat gtcagatgta aagtgcacat cagtagtctt
11881 actctcagtt ttgcaacaac tcagagtaga atcatcatct aaattgtggg ctcaatgtgt
11941 ccagttacac aatgacattc tcttagctaa agatactact gaagcctttg aaaaaatggt
12001 ttcactactt tctgttttgc tttccatgca gggtgctgta gacataaaca agctttgtga
12061 agaaatgctg gacaacaggg caaccttaca agctatagcc tcagagttta gttcccttcc
12121 atcatatgca gcttttgcta ctgctcaaga agcttatgag caggctgttg ctaatggtga
12181 ttctgaagtt gttcttaaaa agttgaagaa gtctttgaat gtggctaaat ctgaatttga
12241 ccgtgatgca gccatgcaac gtaagttgga aaagatggct gatcaagcta tgacccaaat
12301 gtataaacag gctagatctg aggacaagag ggcaaaagtt actagtgcta tgcagacaat
12361 gcttttcact atgcttagaa agttggataa tgatgcactc aacaacatta tcaacaatgc
12421 aagagatggt tgtgttccct tgaacataat acctcttaca acagcagcca aactaatggt
12481 tgtcatacca gactataaca catataaaaa tacgtgtgat ggtacaacat ttacttatgc
12541 atcagcattg tgggaaatcc aacaggttgt agatgcagat agtaaaattg ttcaacttag
12601 tgaaattagt atggacaatt cacctaattt agcatggcct cttattgtaa cagctttaag
12661 ggccaattct gctgtcaaat tacagaataa tgagcttagt cctgttgcac tacgacagat
12721 gtcttgtgct gccggtacta cacaaactgc ttgcactgat gacaatgcgt tagcttacta
12781 caacacaaca aagggaggta ggtttgtact tgcactgtta tccgatttac aggatttgaa
12841 atgggctaga ttccctaaga gtgatggaac tggtactatc tatacagaac tggaaccacc
12901 ttgtaggttt gttacagaca cacctaaagg tcctaaagtg aagtatttat actttattaa
12961 aggattaaac aacctaaata gaggtatggt acttggtagt ttagctgcca cagtacgtct
13021 acaagctggt aatgcaacag aagtgcctgc caattcaact gtattatctt tctgtgcttt
13081 tgctgtagat gctgctaaag cttacaaaga ttatctagct agtgggggac aaccaatcac
13141 taattgtgtt aagatgttgt gtacacacac tggtactggt caggcaataa cagttacacc
13201 ggaagccaat atggatcaag aatcctttgg tggtgcatcg tgttgtctgt actgccgttg
13261 ccacatagat catccaaatc ctaaaggatt ttgtgactta aaaggtaagt atgtacaaat
13321 acctacaact tgtgctaatg accctgtggg ttttacactt aaaaacacag tctgtaccgt
13381 ctgcggtatg tggaaaggtt atggctgtag ttgtgatcaa ctccgcgaac ccatgcttca
13441 gtcagctgat gcacaatcgt ttttaaac
```

... oops ...

```
                                       cgg gtttgcggtg taagtgcagc ccgtcttaca
13501 ccgtgcggca caggcactag tactgatgtc gtatacaggg cttttgacat ctacaatgat
13561 aaagtagctg gttttgctaa attcctaaaa actaattgtt gtcgcttcca agaaaaggac
13621 gaagatgaca atttaattga ttcttacttt gtagttaaga gacacacttt ctctaactac
13681 caacatgaag aaacaattta taatttactt aaggattgtc cagctgttgc taaacatgac
13741 ttctttaagt ttagaataga cggtgacatg gtaccacata tatcacgtca acgtcttact
13801 aaatacacaa tggcagacct cgtctatgct ttaaggcatt ttgatgaagg taattgtgac
13861 acattaaaag aaatacttgt cacatacaat tgttgtgatg atgattattt caataaaaag
```

```
13921 gactggtatg attttgtaga aaacccagat atattacgcg tatacgccaa cttaggtgaa
13981 cgtgtacgcc aagctttgtt aaaaacagta caattctgtg atgccatgcg aaatgctggt
14041 attgttggtg tactgacatt agataatcaa gatctcaatg gtaactggta tgatttcggt
14101 gatttcatac aaaccacgcc aggtagtgga gttcctgttg tagattctta ttattcattg
14161 ttaatgccta tattaacctt gaccagggct ttaactgcag agtcacatgt tgacactgac
14221 ttaacaaagc cttacattaa gtgggatttg ttaaaatatg acttcacgga agagaggtta
14281 aaactctttg accgttattt taaatattgg gatcagacat accacccaaa ttgtgttaac
14341 tgtttggatg acagatgcat tctgcattgt gcaaacttta atgttttatt ctctacagtg
14401 ttcccaccta caagttttgg accactagtg agaaaaatat ttgttgatgg tgttccattt
14461 gtagtttcaa ctggatacca cttcagagag ctaggtgttg tacataatca ggatgtaaac
14521 ttacatagct ctagacttag ttttaaggaa ttacttgtgt atgctgctga ccctgctatg
14581 cacgctgctt ctggtaatct attactagat aaacgcacta cgtgcttttc agtagctgca
14641 cttactaaca atgttgcttt tcaaactgtc aaacccggta attttaacaa agacttctat
14701 gactttgctg tgtctaaggg tttctttaag gaaggaagtt ctgttgaatt aaaacacttc
14761 ttctttgctc aggatggtaa tgctgctatc agcgattatg actactatcg ttataatcta
14821 ccaacaatgt gtgatatcag acaactacta tttgtagttg aagttgttga taagtacttt
14881 gattgttacg atggtggctg tattaatgct aaccaagtca tcgtcaacaa cctagacaaa
14941 tcagctggtt ttccatttaa taaatggggt aaggctagac tttattatga ttcaatgagt
15001 tatgaggatc aagatgcact tttcgcatat acaaaacgta atgtcatccc tactataact
15061 caaatgaatc ttaagtatgc cattagtgca aagaatagag ctcgcaccgt agctggtgtc
15121 tctatctgta gtactatgac caatagacag tttcatcaaa aattattgaa atcaatagcc
15181 gccactagag gagctactgt agtaattgga acaagcaaat tctatggtgg ttggcacaac
15241 atgttaaaaa ctgtttatag tgatgtagaa aaccctcacc ttatgggttg ggattatcct
15301 aaatgtgata gagccatgcc taacatgctt agaattatgg cctcacttgt tcttgctcgc
15361 aaacatacaa cgtgttgtag cttgtcacac cgtttctata gattagctaa tgagtgtgct
15421 caagtattga gtgaaatggt catgtgtggc ggttcactat atgttaaacc aggtggaacc
15481 tcatcaggag atgccacaac tgcttatgct aatagtgttt ttaacatttg tcaagctgtc
15541 acggccaatg ttaatgcact tttatctact gatggtaaca aaattgccga taagtatgtc
15601 cgcaatttac aacacagact ttatgagtgt ctctatagaa atagagatgt tgacacagac
15661 tttgtgaatg agttttacgc atatttgcgt aaacatttct caatgatgat actctctgac
15721 gatgctgttg tgtgtttcaa tagcacttat gcatctcaag gtctagtggc tagcataaag
15781 aactttaagt cagttcttta ttatcaaaac aatgttttta tgtctgaagc aaaatgttgg
15841 actgagactg accttactaa aggacctcat gaattttgct ctcaacatac aatgctagtt
15901 aaacagggtg atgattatgt gtaccttcct tacccagatc catcaagaat cctaggggcc
15961 ggctgttttg tagatgatat cgtaaaaaca gatggtacac ttatgattga acggttcgtg
16021 tctttagcta tagatgctta cccacttact aaacatccta atcaggagta tgctgatgtc
16081 tttcatttgt acttacaata cataagaaag ctacatgatg agttaacagg acacatgtta
16141 gacatgtatt ctgttatgct tactaatgat aacacttcaa ggtattggga acctgagttt
16201 tatgaggcta tgtacacacc gcatacagtc ttacaggctg ttggggcttg tgttctttgc
16261 aattcacaga cttcattaag atgtggtgct tgcatacgta gaccattctt atgttgtaaa
16321 tgctgttacg accatgtcat atcaacatca cataaattag tcttgtctgt taatccgtat
16381 gtttgcaatg ctccaggttg tgatgtcaca gatgtgactc aactttactt aggaggtatg
16441 agctattatt gtaaatcaca taaaccaccc attagttttc cattgtgtgc taatggacaa
16501 gtttttggtt tatataaaaa tacatgtgtt ggtagcgata atgttactga ctttaatgca
16561 attgcaacat gtgactggac aaatgctggt gattacattt tagctaacac ctgtactgaa
16621 agactcaagc tttttgcagc agaaacgctc aaagctactg aggagacatt taaactgtct
16681 tatggtattg ctactgtacg tgaagtgctg tctgacagag aattacatct ttcatgggaa
16741 gttggtaaac ctagaccacc acttaaccga aattatgtct ttactggtta tcgtgtaact
16801 aaaaacagta aagtacaaat aggagagtac acctttgaaa aaggtgacta tggtgatgct
16861 gttgtttacc gaggtacaac aacttacaaa ttaaatgttg gtgattattt tgtgctgaca
16921 tcacatacag taatgccatt aagtgcacct acactagtgc cacaagagca ctatgttaga
16981 attactggct tatacccaac actcaatatc tcagatgagt tttctagcaa tgttgcaaat
17041 tatcaaaagg ttggtatgca aaagtattct acactccagg gaccacctgg tactggtaag
17101 agtcattttg ctattggcct agctctctac tacccttctg ctcgcatagt gtatacagct
17161 tgctctcatg ccgctgttga tgcactatgt gagaaggcat taaaatattt gcctatagat
17221 aaatgtagta gaattatacc tgcacgtgct cgtgtagagt gttttgataa attcaaagtg
17281 aattcaacat tagaacagta tgtcttttgt actgtaaatg cattgcctga gacgacagca
```

```
17341 gatatagttg tctttgatga aatttcaatg gccacaaatt atgatttgag tgttgtcaat
17401 gccagattac gtgctaagca ctatgtgtac attggcgacc ctgctcaatt acctgcacca
17461 cgcacattgc taactaaggg cacactagaa ccagaatatt tcaattcagt gtgtagactt
17521 atgaaaacta taggtccaga catgttcctc ggaacttgtc ggcgttgtcc tgctgaaatt
17581 gttgacactg tgagtgcttt ggtttatgat aataagctta aagcacataa agacaaatca
17641 gctcaatgct ttaaaatgtt ttataagggt gttatcacgc atgatgtttc atctgcaatt
17701 aacaggccac aaataggcgt ggtaagagaa ttccttacac gtaaccctgc ttggagaaaa
17761 gctgtcttta tttcacctta taattcacag aatgctgtag cctcaaagat tttgggacta
17821 ccaactcaaa ctgttgattc atcacagggc tcagaatatg actatgtcat attcactcaa
17881 accactgaaa cagctcactc ttgtaatgta aacagattta atgttgctat taccagagca
17941 aaagtaggca tactttgcat aatgtctgat agagaccttt atgacaagtt gcaatttaca
18001 agtcttgaaa ttccacgtag gaatgtggca actttacaag ctgaaaatgt aacaggactc
18061 tttaaagatt gtagtaaggt aatcactggg ttacatccta cacaggcacc tacacacctc
18121 agtgttgaca ctaaattcaa aactgaaggt ttatgtgttg acatacctgg catacctaag
18181 gacatgacct atagaagact catctctatg atgggtttta aaatgaatta tcaagttaat
18241 ggttacccta acatgtttat cacccgcgaa gaagctataa gacatgtacg tgcatggatt
18301 ggcttcgatg tcgagggtg tcatgctact agagaagctg ttggtaccaa tttaccttta
18361 cagctaggtt tttctacagg tgttaaccta gttgctgtac ctacaggtta tgttgataca
18421 cctaataata cagatttttc cagagttagt gctaaaccac cgcctggaga tcaatttaaa
18481 cacctcatac cacttatgta caaaggactt ccttggaatg tagtgcgtat aaagattgta
18541 caaatgttaa gtgacacact taaaaatctc tctgacagag tcgtatttgt cttatgggca
18601 catggctttg agttgacatc tatgaagtat tttgtgaaaa taggacctga gcgcacctgt
18661 tgtctatgtg atagacgtgc cacatgcttt tccactgctt cagacactta tgcctgttgg
18721 catcattcta ttggatttga ttacgtctat aatccgttta tgattgatgt tcaacaatgg
18781 ggttttacag gtaacctaca aagcaaccat gatctgtatt gtcaagtcca tggtaatgca
18841 catgtagcta gttgtgatgc aatcatgact aggtgtctag ctgtccacga gtgctttgtt
18901 aagcgtgttg actggactat tgaatatcct ataattggtg atgaactgaa gattaatgcg
18961 gcttgtagaa aggttcaaca catggttgtt aaagctgcat tattagcaga caaattccca
19021 gttcttcacg acattggtaa ccctaaagct attaagtgtg tacctcaagc tgatgtagaa
19081 tggaagttct atgatgcaca gccttgtagt gacaaagctt ataaaataga agaattattc
19141 tattcttatg ccacacattc tgacaaattc acagatggtg tatgcctatt ttggaattgc
19201 aatgtcgata gatatcctgc taattccatt gtttgtagat ttgacactag agtgctatct
19261 aaccttaact tgcctggttg tgatggtggc agtttgtatg taaataaaca tgcattccac
19321 acaccagctt ttgataaaag tgcttttgtt aatttaaaac aattaccatt tttctattac
19381 tctgacagtc catgtgagtc tcatggaaaa caagtagtgt cagatataga ttatgtacca
19441 ctaaagtctg ctacgtgtat aacacgttgc aatttaggtg gtgctgtctg tagacatcat
19501 gctaatgagt acagattgta tctcgatgct tataacatga tgatctcagc tggctttagc
19561 ttgtgggttt acaaacaatt tgatacttat aacctctgga acacttttac aagacttcag
19621 agtttagaaa atgtggcttt taatgttgta aataagggac actttgatgg acaacagggt
19681 gaagtaccag tttctatcat taataacact gtttacacaa aagttgatgg tgttgatgta
19741 gaattgtttg aaaataaaac aacattacct gttaatgtag catttgagct ttgggctaag
19801 cgcaacatta aaccagtacc agaggtgaaa atactcaata atttgggtgt ggacattgct
19861 gctaatactg tgatctggga ctacaaaaga gatgctccag cacatatatc tactattggt
19921 gtttgttcta tgactgacat agccaagaaa ccaactgaaa cgatttgtgc accactcact
19981 gtcttttttg atggtagagt tgatggtcaa gtagacttat ttagaaatgc ccgtaatggt
20041 gttcttatta cagaaggtag tgttaaaggt ttacaaccat ctgtaggtcc caaacaagct
20101 agtcttaatg gagtcacatt aattggagaa gccgtaaaaa cacagttcaa ttattataag
20161 aaagttgatg gtgttgtcca acaattacct gaaacttact ttactcagag tagaaattta
20221 caagaattta aacccaggag tcaaatggaa attgatttct tagaattagc tatggatgaa
20281 ttcattgaac ggtataaatt agaaggctat gccttcgaac atatcgttta tggagatttt
20341 agtcatagtc agttaggtgg tttacatcta ctgattggac tagctaaacg ttttaaggaa
20401 tcaccttttg aattagaaga ttttattcct atggacagta cagttaaaaa ctatttcata
20461 acagatgcgc aaacaggttc atctaagtgt gtgtgttctg ttattgattt attacttgat
20521 gattttgttg aaataataaa atcccaagat ttatctgtag tttctaaggt tgtcaaagtg
20581 actattgact atacagaaat ttcatttatg ctttggtgta aagatggcca tgtagaaaca
20641 ttttacccaa aattacaatc tagtcaagcg tggcaaccgg gtgttgctat gcctaatctt
20701 tacaaaatgc aaagaatgct attagaaaag tgtgaccttc aaaattatgg tgatagtgca
```

```
20761 acattaccta aaggcataat gatgaatgtc gcaaaatata ctcaactgtg tcaatattta
20821 aacacattaa cattagctgt accctataat atgagagtta tacattttgg tgctggttct
20881 gataaaggag ttgcaccagg tacagctgtt ttaagacagt ggttgcctac gggtacgctg
20941 cttgtcgatt cagatcttaa tgactttgtc tctgatgcag attcaacttt gattggtgat
21001 tgtgcaactg tacatacagc taataaatgg gatctcatta ttagtgatat gtacgaccct
21061 aagactaaaa atgttacaaa agaaaatgac tctaaagagg gtttttcac ttacatttgt
21121 gggtttatac aacaaaagct agctcttgga ggttccgtgg ctataaagat aacagaacat
21181 tcttggaatg ctgatcttta taagctcatg ggacacttcg catggtggac agcctttgtt
21241 actaatgtga atgcgtcatc atctgaagca tttttaattg gatgtaatta tcttggcaaa
21301 ccacgcgaac aaatagatgg ttatgtcatg catgcaaatt acatattttg gaggaataca
21361 aatccaattc agttgtcttc ctattcttta tttgacatga gtaaatttcc ccttaaatta
21421 aggggtactg ctgttatgtc tttaaaagaa ggtcaaatca atgatatgat tttatctctt
21481 cttagtaaag gtagacttat aattagagaa aacaacagag ttgttatttc tagtgatgtt
21541 cttgttaaca actaa
                     acgaa ca
```

The "ORF1ab" gene ends at 21555 and the S gene for the spike protein starts at 21563, running through to 25384.

```
                                  atgtttgt ttttcttgtt ttattgccac tagtctctag
21601 tcagtgtgtt aatcttacaa ccagaactca attacccct gcatacacta attctttcac
21661 acgtggtgtt tattaccctg acaaagtttt cagatcctca gttttacatt caactcagga
21721 cttgttctta cctttctttt ccaatgttac ttggttccat gctatacatg tctctgggac
21781 caatggtact aagaggtttg ataaccctgt cctaccattt aatgatggtg tttattttgc
21841 ttccactgag aagtctaaca taataagagg ctggattttt ggtactactt tagattcgaa
21901 gacccagtcc ctacttattg ttaataacgc tactaatgtt gttattaaag tctgtgaatt
21961 tcaatttgt aatgatccat ttttgggtgt ttattaccac aaaaacaaca aaagttggat
22021 ggaaagtgag ttcagagttt attctagtgc gaataattgc acttttgaat atgtctctca
22081 gccttttctt atggaccttg aaggaaaaca gggtaatttc aaaaatctta gggaatttgt
22141 gtttaagaat attgatggtt attttaaaat atattctaag cacacgccta ttaatttagt
22201 gcgtgatctc cctcagggtt tttcggcttt agaaccattg gtagatttgc caataggtat
22261 taacatcact aggtttcaaa ctttacttgc tttacataga agttatttga ctcctggtga
22321 ttcttcttca ggttggacag ctggtgctgc agcttattat gtgggttatc ttcaacctag
22381 gacttttcta ttaaaatata atgaaaatgg aaccattaca gatgctgtag actgtgcact
22441 tgaccctctc tcagaaacaa agtgtacgtt gaaatccttc actgtagaaa aaggaatcta
22501 tcaaacttct aactttagag tccaaccaac agaatctatt gttagatttc ctaatattac
22561 aaacttgtgc ccttttggtg aagtttttaa cgccaccaga tttgcatctg tttatgcttg
22621 gaacaggaag agaatcagca actgtgttgc tgattattct gtcctatata attccgcatc
22681 attttccact tttaagtgtt atggagtgtc tcctactaaa ttaaatgatc tctgctttac
22741 taatgtctat gcagattcat ttgtaattag aggtgatgaa gtcagacaaa tcgctccagg
22801 gcaaactgga aagattgctg attataatta taaattacca gatgatttta caggctgcgt
22861 tatagcttgg aattctaaca atcttgattc taaggttggt ggtaattata attacctgta
22921 tagattgttt aggaagtcta atctcaaacc ttttgagaga gatatttcaa ctgaaatcta
22981 tcaggccggt agcacacctt gtaatggtgt tgaaggtttt aattgttact ttcctttaca
23041 atcatatggt ttccaaccca ctaatggtgt tggttaccaa ccatacagag tagtagtact
23101 ttcttttgaa cttctacatg caccagcaac tgtttgtgga cctaaaaagt ctactaattt
23161 ggttaaaaac aaatgtgtca atttcaactt caatggttta acaggcacag gtgttcttac
23221 tgagtctaac aaaaagtttc tgcctttcca acaatttggc agagacattg ctgacactac
23281 tgatgctgtc cgtgatccac agacacttga gattcttgac attacaccat gttcttttgg
23341 tggtgtcagt gttataacac caggaacaaa tacttctaac caggttgctg ttctttatca
23401 ggatgttaac tgcacagaag tccctgttgc tattcatgca gatcaactta ctcctacttg
23461 gcgtgtttat tctacaggtt ctaatgtttt tcaaacacgt gcaggctgtt taatagggc
23521 tgaacatgtc aacaactcat atgagtgtga catacccatt ggtgcaggta tatgcgctag
23581 ttatcagact cagactaatt ctcctcggcg ggcacgtagt gtagctagtc aatccatcat
23641 tgcctacact atgtcacttg gtgcagaaaa ttcagttgct tactctaata actctattgc
23701 catacccaca aattttacta ttagtgttac cacagaaatt ctaccagtgt ctatgaccaa
```

```
23761 gacatcagta gattgtacaa tgtacatttg tggtgattca actgaatgca gcaatctttt
23821 gttgcaatat ggcagttttt gtacacaatt aaaccgtgct ttaactggaa tagctgttga
23881 acaagacaaa aacacccaag aagtttttgc acaagtcaaa caaatttaca aaacaccacc
23941 aattaaagat tttggtggtt ttaatttttc acaaatatta ccagatccat caaaaccaag
24001 caagaggtca tttattgaag atctactttt caacaaagtg acacttgcag atgctggctt
24061 catcaaacaa tatggtgatt gccttggtga tattgctgct agagacctca tttgtgcaca
24121 aaagtttaac ggccttactg ttttgccacc tttgctcaca gatgaaatga ttgctcaata
24181 cacttctgca ctgttagcgg gtacaatcac ttctggttgg acctttggtg caggtgctgc
24241 attacaaata ccatttgcta tgcaaatggc ttataggttt aatggtattg gagttacaca
24301 gaatgttctc tatgagaacc aaaaattgat tgccaaccaa tttaatagtg ctattggcaa
24361 aattcaagac tcactttctt ccacagcaag tgcacttgga aaacttcaag atgtggtcaa
24421 ccaaaatgca caagctttaa acacgcttgt taaacaactt agctccaatt ttggtgcaat
24481 ttcaagtgtt ttaaatgata tcctttcacg tcttgacaaa gttgaggctg aagtgcaaat
24541 tgataggttg atcacaggca gacttcaaag tttgcagaca tatgtgactc aacaattaat
24601 tagagctgca gaaatcagag cttctgctaa tcttgctgct actaaaatgt cagagtgtgt
24661 acttggacaa tcaaaaagag ttgatttttg tggaaagggc tatcatctta tgtccttccc
24721 tcagtcagca cctcatggtg tagtcttctt gcatgtgact tatgtccctg cacaagaaaa
24781 gaacttcaca actgctcctg ccatttgtca tgatggaaaa gcacactttc ctcgtgaagg
24841 tgtctttgtt tcaaatggca cacactggtt tgtaacacaa aggaattttt atgaaccaca
24901 aatcattact acagacaaca catttgtgtc tggtaactgt gatgttgtaa taggaattgt
24961 caacaacaca gtttatgatc ctttgcaacc tgaattagac tcattcaagg aggagttaga
25021 taaatatttt aagaatcata catcaccaga tgttgattta ggtgacatct ctggcattaa
25081 tgcttcagtt gtaaacattc aaaaagaaat tgaccgcctc aatgaggttg ccaagaattt
25141 aaatgaatct ctcatcgatc tccaagaact tggaaagtat gagcagtata taaaatggcc
25201 atggtacatt tggctaggtt ttatagctgg cttgattgcc atagtaatgg tgacaattat
25261 gctttgctgt atgaccagtt gctgtagttg tctcaagggc tgttgttctt gtggatcctg
25321 ctgcaaattt gatgaagacg actctgagcc agtgctcaaa ggagtcaaat tacattacac
25381 ataa
            acgaac tt
```

The S gene ends at 25384. ORF3a is at 25393–26220; the E gene runs from 26245 to 26472.

```
                 atggattt gtttatgaga atcttcacaa ttggaactgt aactttgaag
25441 caaggtgaaa tcaaggatgc tactccttca gattttgttc gcgctactgc aacgataccg
25501 atacaagcct cactcccttt cggatggctt attgttggcg ttgcacttct tgctgttttt
25561 cagagcgctt ccaaaatcat aaccctcaaa aagagatggc aactagcact ctccaagggt
25621 gttcactttg tttgcaactt gctgttgttg tttgtaacag tttactcaca ccttttgctc
25681 gttgctgctg gccttgaagc cccttttctc tatctttatg ctttagtcta cttcttgcag
25741 agtataaact ttgtaagaat aataatgagg ctttggcttt gctggaaatg ccgttccaaa
25801 aacccattac tttatgatgc caactatttt ctttgctggc atactaattg ttacgactat
25861 tgtatacctt acaatagtgt aacttcttca attgtcatta cttcaggtga tggcacaaca
25921 agtcctattt ctgaacatga ctaccagatt ggtggttata ctgaaaaatg ggaatctgga
25981 gtaaaagact gtgttgtatt acacagttac ttcacttcag actattacca gctgtactca
26041 actcaattga gtacagacac tggtgttgaa catgttacct tcttcatcta caataaaatt
26101 gttgatgagc ctgaagaaca tgtccaaatt cacacaatcg acggttcatc cggagttgtt
26161 aatccagtaa tggaaccaat ttatgatgaa ccgacgacga ctactagcgt gcctttgtaa

26221 gcacaagctg atgagtacga actt
                              atgtac tcattcgttt cggaagagac aggtacgtta
26281 atagttaata gcgtacttct ttttcttgct ttcgtggtat tcttgctagt tacactagcc
26341 atccttactg cgcttcgatt gtgtgcgtac tgctgcaata ttgttaacgt gagtcttgta
26401 aaaccttctt tttacgttta ctctcgtgtt aaaaatctga attcttctag agttcctgat
26461 cttctggtct aa
                 acgaacta aatattatat tagtttttct gtttggaact ttaattttag
26521 cc
```

The M gene extends from 26523–27191.

```
           atggcaga ttccaacggt actattaccg ttgaagagct taaaaagctc cttgaacaat
26581 ggaacctagt aataggtttc ctattcctta catggatttg tcttctacaa tttgcctatg
26641 ccaacaggaa taggtttttg tatataatta agttaatttt cctctggctg ttatggccag
26701 taactttagc ttgttttgtg cttgctgctg tttacagaat aaattggatc accggtggaa
26761 ttgctatcgc aatggcttgt cttgtaggct tgatgtggct cagctacttc attgcttctt
26821 tcagactgtt tgcgcgtacg cgttccatgt ggtcattcaa tccagaaact aacattcttc
26881 tcaacgtgcc actccatggc actattctga ccagaccgct tctagaaagt gaactcgtaa
26941 tcggagctgt gatccttcgt ggacatcttc gtattgctgg acaccatcta ggacgctgtg
27001 acatcaagga cctgcctaaa gaaatcactg ttgctacatc acgaacgctt tcttattaca
27061 aattgggagc ttcgcagcgt gtagcaggtg actcaggttt tgctgcatac agtcgctaca
27121 ggattggcaa ctataaatta aacacagacc attccagtag cagtgacaat attgctttgc
27181 ttgtacagta a
                      gtgacaaca g
```

ORF Regions 6 (27202–27387), 7a (27394–27759), 7b (27756, note overlap, to 27887) and 8 (27894–28259) follow. Together with NSP13–15, ORF6 is a potent suppressor of the interferon antiviral response.

```
                                     atgtttcat ctcgttgact ttcaggttac tatagcagag
27241 atattactaa ttattatgag gacttttaaa gtttccattt ggaatcttga ttacatcata
27301 aacctcataa ttaaaaattt atctaagtca ctaactgaga ataaatattc tcaattagat
27361 gaagagcaac caatggagat tgatta
                                            aacg aac
                                                        atgaaaa ttattctttt cttggcactg
27421 ataacactcg ctacttgtga gctttatcac taccaagagt gtgttagagg tacaacagta
27481 cttttaaaag aaccttgctc ttctggaaca tacgagggca attcaccatt tcatcctcta
27541 gctgataaca aatttgcact gacttgcttt agcactcaat ttgcttttgc ttgtcctgac
27601 ggcgtaaaac acgtctatca gttacgtgcc agatcagttt cacctaaact gttcatcaga
27661 caagaggaag ttcaagaact ttactctcca atttttctta ttgttgcggc aatagtgttt
27721 ataacacttt gcttcacact caaaagaaag acagaatga
                                                          atgat tgaactttca ttaattgact
27781 tctatttgtg ctttttagcc tttctgctat tccttgtttt aattatgctt attatctttt
27841 ggttctcact tgaactgcaa gatcataatg aaacttgtca cgcctaa
                                                                                   acg aac
                                                                                          atgaaat
27901 ttcttgtttt cttaggaatc atcacaactg tagctgcatt tcaccaagaa tgtagtttac
27961 agtcatgtac tcaacatcaa ccatatgtag ttgatgaccc gtgtcctatt cacttctatt
28021 ctaaatggta tattagagta ggagctagaa aatcagcacc tttaattgaa ttgtgcgtgg
28081 atgaggctgg ttctaaatca cccattcagt acatcgatat cggtaattat acagtttcct
28141 gtttaccttt tacaattaat tgccaggaac ctaaattggg tagtcttgta gtgcgttgtt
28201 cgttctatga agacttttta gagtatcatg acgttcgtgt tgttttagat ttcatctaa
                                                                                          a
28261 cgaacaaact aaa
```

Then there's the N gene, from 28274–29533:

```
                              atgtctg ataatggacc ccaaaatcag cgaaatgcac cccgcattac
28321 gtttggtgga ccctcagatt caactggcag taaccagaat ggagaacgca gtggggcgcg
28381 atcaaaacaa cgtcggcccc aaggtttacc caataatact gcgtcttggt tcaccgctct
28441 cactcaacat ggcaaggaag accttaaatt ccctcgagga caaggcgttc caattaacac
28501 caatagcagt ccagatgacc aaattggcta ctaccgaaga gctaccagac gaattcgtgg
28561 tggtgacggt aaaatgaaag atctcagtcc aagatggtat ttctactacc taggaactgg
28621 gccagaagct ggacttccct atggtgctaa caaagacggc atcatatggg ttgcaactga
```

```
28681 gggagccttg aatacaccaa aagatcacat tggcacccgc aatcctgcta acaatgctgc
28741 aatcgtgcta caacttcctc aaggaacaac attgccaaaa ggcttctacg cagaagggag
28801 cagaggcggc agtcaagcct cttctcgttc ctcatcacgt agtcgcaaca gttcaagaaa
28861 ttcaactcca ggcagcagta ggggaacttc tcctgctaga atggctggca atggcggtga
28921 tgctgctctt gctttgctgc tgcttgacag attgaaccag cttgagagca aaatgtctgg
28981 taaaggccaa caacaacaag gccaaactgt cactaagaaa tctgctgctg aggcttctaa
29041 gaagcctcgg caaaaacgta ctgccactaa agcatacaat gtaacacaag ctttcggcag
29101 acgtggtcca gaacaaaccc aaggaaattt tggggaccag gaactaatca gacaaggaac
29161 tgattacaaa cattggccgc aaattgcaca atttgccccc agcgcttcag cgttcttcgg
29221 aatgtcgcgc attggcatgg aagtcacacc ttcgggaacg tggttgacct acacaggtgc
29281 catcaaattg gatgacaaag atccaaattt caaagatcaa gtcattttgc tgaataagca
29341 tattgacgca tacaaaacat tcccaccaac agagcctaaa aaggacaaaa agaagaaggc
29401 tgatgaaact caagccttac cgcagagaca gaagaaacag caaactgtga ctcttcttcc
29461 tgctgcagat ttggatgatt tctccaaaca attgcaacaa tccatgagca gtgctgactc
29521 aactcaggcc taa
                    actcatg cagaccacac aaggcag
```

Last there's ORF10 (29558–29674), with a final UTR at the end, to make up a total length of 29903.

```
                                             atg ggctatataa acgttttcgc
29581 ttttccgttt acgatatata gtctactctt gtgcagaatg aattctcgta actacatagc
29641 acaagtagat gtagttaact ttaatctcac atag
                                          caatct ttaatcagtg tgtaacatta
29701 gggaggactt gaaagagcca ccacattttc accgaggcca cgcggagtac gatcgagtgt
29761 acagtgaaca atgctaggga gagctgccta tatggaagag ccctaatgtg taaaattaat
29821 tttagtagtg ctatccccat gtgattttaa tagcttctta ggagaatgac aaaaaaaaaa
29881 aaaaaaaaaa aaaaaaaaaa aaa
```

⊛ Appendix C

A Literate Document

This book is a literate document.[1] If you have a copy of the LyX or LaTeX document that was used to make this book, you can easily extract the R code in Appendix A.

(1) Choose a convenient folder, open this in your console—DOS, Mac or Windows,[2] and make a sub-folder called *R*.

(2) Move the source file to your folder. If the source file you have is *NCTLL_904.lyx*, then you'll need to open it in the LyX document processor and say File | Export | XeTeX to get the file *NCTLL_904.tex*.

(3) From github.com/jvanschalkwyk/dogwagger download the Perl script *Dogwagger405.pl*[3] and put it in your folder.

(4) From the console say:

```
perl Dogwagger405.pl NCTLL_904.tex
```

This will extract all of the R programs to the *R* sub-folder. You will need to locate, edit and store the individual *data sets* if you wish to re-create the entire R package, as described above.

[1] Donald Knuth might be glad that a virus was listening, while almost everyone else ignored his idea!

[2] Hold down the Windows button and press **r** – then type in **run** and press Enter

[3] [Editorial note: Rona used version 4.0.4 but the differences are minuscule.]